Praise for *T*

"With a gorgeously picturesque setting, an utterly charming cast, and a hilarious protagonist, *The Summer Job* is my perfect summer read! Sure to be one of the sweetest, funniest, and sexiest books of the year. As soon as I finished it, I wanted to read it again. Do not miss this one!"
—Emily Henry, author of *People We Meet on Vacation*

"This novel is what happens when you combine *Sweetbitter* with *The Princess Switch*, place it in the Scottish Highlands, and throw in a whole lot of wine."
—*Entertainment Weekly*

"A rom-com-esque adventure in which a girl steals her best friend's identity to spend the season at a luxury Scottish Highland resort. Lol, same."
—*Cosmopolitan*

"Funny, romantic, hilariously chaotic, and full to the brim with Scottish charm."
—*Parade*

"If you're a fan of *Outlander* but want an adventure in the Scottish Highlands with a little more Wi-Fi, this is the read for you."
—Shondaland.com

"Dent hits a home run."
—*Library Journal* (starred review)

"Escapist fun with surprising emotional depth; fans of Emily Henry and Katie Fforde should add this to their summer-read list."
—*Booklist*

"This book is fun with a capital F. It made me want to go to Scotland, drink wine, and kiss hot chefs, IMMEDIATELY. Dent has such a fresh voice, and so many of us will identify with Birdy Finch. If you've ever felt you're getting left behind in life, or don't have everything worked out quite yet, this is the book for you."   —Sophie Cousens, author of *Just Haven't Met You Yet*

"What a welcome escape . . . It's witty and funny and it packs an emotional punch, too. . . . Loved it, I'm in the queue for more Lizzy Dent."
—Josie Silver, author of *One Day in December*

"Funny and heartwarming, *The Summer Job* is a delightful summer escape. . . . The Scottish setting is pure magic, and fans of Emily Henry or Sophie Kinsella will fall for debut novelist Lizzy Dent."   —*Shelf Awareness*

Praise for *The Setup*

One of *PopSugar*'s "Best New Books of 2022"
One of Motherly's "Buzziest Books of 2022 So Far"
One of Love to Know's "19 Must-Read Books of 2022"

"I fell in love with Lizzy Dent's writing with *The Summer Job* and have been waiting with bated breath to see what she does next. This book is everything I wanted and then some. With Dent's usual humor, wit, and warmth, and a spectacularly charming cast of weirdos, *The Setup* is exactly the kind of summer read I'm constantly on the hunt for. I love astrology-obsessed hot-mess Mara, I love the crumbling little Broadgate lido she's out to save, and I love, love, love Lizzy Dent."

—Emily Henry, author of
People We Meet on Vacation and *Book Lovers*

"An adorable rom-com packed full of nostalgia and Dent's trademark wit."
—Sophie Cousens, author of *Just Haven't Met You Yet*

"Witty . . . filled with love and lighthearted humor."   —*PopSugar*

"[A] sweet and funny tale of a woman who has been barely scraping by as she opens herself up to new friends and new experiences. For fans of Abbi Waxman and Emily Henry."   —*Booklist*

"Grab your SPF and your carry-on because we have the ultimate beach read for your summer getaway. *The Setup* is a laugh-out-loud story. . . . You can't imagine the twists and turns [it] takes."   —Love to Know

ALSO BY LIZZY DENT

The Setup
The Summer Job

The Sweetest Revenge

LIZZY DENT

G. P. Putnam's Sons · New York

PUTNAM
— EST. 1838 —

G. P. Putnam's Sons
Publishers Since 1838
An imprint of Penguin Random House LLC
penguinrandomhouse.com

Library of Congress Cataloging-in-Publication Data
has been applied for.

ISBN 9780593545478 (trade paperback)
ISBN 9780593545485 (ebook)

Printed in the United States of America

1st Printing

Book design by Elke Sigal

For Nicki Sunderland xx

One

"**W**e need to talk."

Nothing good ever comes after that sentence. *Nothing.* All I can think is: *Whatever happens, do not let him talk to you about anything until you're on that fucking train.*

"*You* need to get ready," I say lightly, nodding toward the dry-cleaning bag slung over his bed. "I picked up your suit, and there's a coffee waiting for you. Or a whisky. Whichever you need."

I can see the seriousness in his dark brown eyes as he remains fixed on me. He lifts his hand to his face and rubs his freshly shaved chin. "Okay, but *then* we need to talk."

For now it's enough to know we're still going to get the train, but I'm anxious. Work? Incurable disease? *Us?* My phone buzzes again, and I leap to the bed to free it from its charger.

"Amy. You better be on top of Bradley fucking Cooper," shouts Ruth, my cousin and the bride-to-be. The phone is then handed to my mother, who continues the dressing-down. "Everyone's waiting for you, Amy."

"And *I'm* the one who is supposed to keep everyone waiting!" shouts Ruth in the background. "*I'm the fucking bride!*"

"I'm so sorry, Mom, Chris just got home, he had a meeting—"

"I'm not sure a meeting is more important than your cousin's wedding."

"I'm not going to miss it!" I shout, impatient now. "I'm standing here in the damn dress. The train leaves in forty-five minutes."

"This guy can't drive you both in his fancy car?" she says. I had already made the grave error of mentioning his new car. In my concern they might not like Chris, I'd oversold him and turned him into a rich asshole.

"The Uber has been ordered," I reply.

I hang up the phone and quickly order an Uber.

Moments later, Chris, who seems to be moving at a glacial pace, emerges from the bathroom in a pale blue linen suit and cream shirt. No tie. I melt like butter at the sight of him. He always looks so put together. So clean somehow. But I say playfully, "We're going to Long Island, not the Bahamas." My massive family will all be in off-the-rack suits and ties and Chris is going to stand out like a walking *GQ* cover.

"I thought it was going to match you. But I'm afraid Tom Ford doesn't do that shade of virgin blue," he says teasingly as I fiddle with the top of the bridesmaid dress, trying to squeeze a little cleavage out of the modest neckline. "Although it has improved with *you* in it." He smiles flirtatiously at me. Chris always knows how to weaken me. A single raised eyebrow can have my pants off in a whip. I glance down at the dress. Ruth hadn't done a terrible job with the design—but it did come off a little polygamist Mormon for my taste.

"Only polyester taffeta can deliver this kind of shine," I say, grinning at him. But I'm anxious. He seems to sense this and pulls me close, delivering a heavy kiss on my lips, crushing the skirt of my dress. I want to collapse into him. "Mind the gown," I say instead, pushing him back.

"I do really need to talk to you," he says in that crisp, upbeat business tone I was used to hearing in the boardroom at work. Sexy. Strong. Capable.

"I love you," I reply, "but this is the first time you're going to meet my family, and they're going to be at their most insane, so let's talk later."

Chris is an only child, and he grew up in Providence, and although I've never been there, nor have I met his parents, I can just imagine his quiet picket-fenced cul-de-sac, with a boat in the driveway and an organized recycling area. And his parents: slim, refined, and classy—but also slightly terrifying (because what did they *really* think?). My family, on the other hand, is like walking into a room full of kindergartners on a sugar high, but with six-foot men and beer. Within thirty seconds of arrival, my brother, Floyd, will give Chris an excruciating nickname, one that pierces the very heart of who Chris is. It will exemplify a truly extraordinary ability to read people, and in some ways is a superpower, but all I will hear is my brother calling my boyfriend the Little Stinger because he's only five nine and a WASP.

"Amy, we need to talk *now*," he replies, and then after a beat of staring at me in a way that makes me stiffen with unease, he adds, "We're not going ahead with the series, Amy."

"What do you mean, we're not going ahead with the series?"

I shift to autopilot, picking up my overnight bag and moving toward the front door. I push it open and walk down the stairs, then out onto his stoop and the tree-lined street.

"The Uber is here," I call to hurry him along, my eyes on his brand-new silver Audi, which could get us there in half the time and hassle. He's moving so slowly. Or am I running? I feel like I'm running. I feel like I'm running away from what he's telling me, as though if I stay a few feet ahead, the information will not catch up with me.

"The content board met, and that was the decision," he says as we slide into the back seat of the car.

"I see," I reply, the gravity of this situation too overwhelming to fully accept or even acknowledge. I swallow a scream. It can't be. It's a mistake. It's a temporary setback.

I have been working on *The Darkening Web* for as long as I've been at Wolf Studios. It's a crime series set between Palo Alto and Pebble Beach in Northern California, in the creepy underbelly of Silicon Valley. Pitched as *Big Little Lies* meets *Ozark*, with a *Black Mirror* twist, it's four years of my blood, sweat, and tears.

In TV development, having a show fall down before being greenlit is all part of the game. It's happened a dozen times in my career, but this one, this one that I adored, was meant to fly. This was *my* moment. I had the most incredible showrunner poised to sign on. A brilliant young writer had drafted a pilot script described by the VP of development as a game-changer. All it needed was the green-light team to say yes, and we would be moving to pitch and, hopefully, pilot.

This was the meeting that had been important enough to stay for. The meeting that I missed my cousin's rehearsal dinner for. The meeting where, Chris promised, he would finally get the green light for my show.

As we pull up to Atlantic Terminal, Chris is still trying to get me to talk about it.

"I can't," I repeat for the hundredth time, pulling away from his pitying arm, which he's trying to drape around my shoulders. "I wish you'd waited to tell me."

"I just want you to understand why I voted—"

"*You* voted?" I say, jumping out of the car, tugging him toward the building. "*You* voted to green-light it. Because it's brilliant and because *you* said *you* would."

"I didn't vote for it," he says, frowning.

"Sorry, did I mishear?" I say, spinning around to face him.

"Amy—I'm your boss. That's a reality," he says, dropping his canvas weekender to the sidewalk. He puts his hands on my shoulders, squeezing me lightly. "Today we become official. I'm meeting your family, and people at work are starting to figure it out."

"What does this have to do with *The Darkening Web*?" I ask, although I suspect I know the answer.

"I can't be seen to be favoring my girlfriend," he says, and I cringe.

"Your girlfriend? I was a development executive first," I say, "a pretty fucking good one too."

"You understand, though?" he asks, shaking out his hand so his stupid, expensive vintage watch slides down his wrist. Then he checks the time and looks at me with a great deal of discomfort. "I was worried about the blowback. It's highly unprofessional, what we're doing. I can't be fucking you and then elevating your work. It looks terrible."

I raise my hands to my face. "Oh my God," I say finally. "Oh my God. Four years of my work. Four years!"

"We talked about this," he says impatiently. "I explained to you that it would be problematic. I gave you options."

"You gave me the option to let *you* pitch it as *yours*. I thought you were joking!"

Chris shrugs at this. "It made the most sense. That way, no one thinks I've made a decision with my dick. And your project can be viewed without bias."

"But it's mine!" I say, stamping my heeled foot as I say it.

"Of course it is, to everyone else. It would have only been the network heads who would have thought otherwise."

I cannot make sense of what he is saying to me. I just keep shaking my head in disbelief.

"I thought you'd want to keep exploring whatever this is becoming," he says, frantically motioning between the two of us. "I can't green-light a potentially fifty-million-per-season show for my girlfriend. Can you not see this? I thought you would get it."

I can't speak. *I thought you would get it.* I feel sucker punched. My thoughts are scattered like confetti in a hurricane.

"You must have known there was going to be a conflict," he says. "I'm your boss. I do your annual review. I can't grade you at your day job when you've just given me a blow job." Chris half laughs at this. I feel like I'm going to throw up.

"Sorry, that was supposed to be a joke," he says now,

rubbing his face with both hands and then resting one hand back on my shoulder.

"Ugh," I say, shrugging him off. I hold my hand to my stomach, the layers of taffeta skirting crunching under my fingers. "I can't believe you." I feel my lip start to quiver and turn swiftly away from him, marching into the building.

"Amy!" he says in a tone one might use for a toddler as he follows behind.

I close my eyes and stop short as a cascade of visceral memories floods my brain. Kisses in elevators. Cocktails in hotel bars. His hand inching up my bare thigh at the Independent Screen Awards dinner. Him on his knees, face buried between my legs behind the changing room's curtain at Saks. Making love on the beach on Fire Island, me staring up at the stars. The words. The promises. My stomach lurches, and I open my eyes to see Chris looking into the distance, a deep crevasse between his eyebrows. He looks different suddenly.

"Let's just go, Amy," he is saying, leading me down the stairs toward the platform so I have to follow him now. "You're becoming overly emotional," he says over his shoulder.

I narrow my eyes, scoffing in disgust, as I'm elbowed in the ribs by a rushing commuter. "Don't say that. God, I knew you were cutthroat, but I never saw the knife at my own throat."

"Oh, come on," he says, turning back as he takes his place on the platform edge, and I spot a brief eye roll. "I chose *us*. I thought you'd be pleased."

"You chose yourself," I retort, setting down my bag. "You were worried *you* would look bad. Chris, you've just killed my whole dream. The dream of everyone who worked on it, because you didn't want to admit that you fell in love . . ." I pause to consider this word anew. *Is he even in love with me?* ". . . that you were *involved* with a junior person on your staff."

"No, I chose *us*. I'm coming to this wedding with you, aren't I?"

The train pulls into the station, and the wind picks up my skirt, which puffs up like a pastel lampshade. I pick up my bag, remaining dignified. "Let's just go," I say.

Chris hesitates. It's subtle, but I see it and pounce.

"You don't want to come?"

"It's fine," he replies. "I said I would."

"You don't want to come." My voice is tight now.

"Amy, no one wants to come to a family wedding where the only person they know is a bridesmaid. I'm coming for *you*."

I feel a deep sense of dread in the pit of my stomach. This is *wrong*. I don't want someone dragging themselves to somewhere they don't want to be out of obligation. I want Chris to *want* to come because he *wants* to know my family. Because being invited excites him. Maybe even makes him nervous. Because it's an *honor* to be asked. I think about how he was dragging his feet to get ready. How I had to arrange the dry cleaning. How he insisted we catch the very last possible train because, despite my asking him three months ago, he still booked in a morning of meetings today. Including, unconscionably, the meeting that canceled my show.

I narrow my eyes, staring at Chris hard while I compute this new reality.

I suddenly don't want him anywhere near my family.

"You know what? Fuck you," I say. "Don't fucking come."

"I'm coming," he says, heading toward the train door.

"I'm uninviting you," I say.

"You're overreacting to a work issue and convoluting the two," he says, holding the train door open as the train whistles. "Which is exactly why I had to block your show."

People say the line between love and hate is thin, but I am truly stunned to find how thin it is. It's thin like rice paper, apparently. I glare at him as everything around us blurs. In TV we call this pulling focus, but in real life it's more like a momentary madness. Everything is silent except for the sound of the blood boiling in my veins. *Block my show?*

He's saying something to me now, but I can't hear it. It's like he's speaking in slow motion. *Block my fucking show?*

"Amy!" I feel his hands on my shoulders, shaking me. I spin around to see the train as it pulls away, and we are standing there on an empty platform, bags at our feet, my cousin's wedding slowly becoming a thing I was not just going to be late for but going to actually miss.

"Fuck!" I shout. "I have to call another bloody Uber. All the way to the venue now. What's the use of a fucking convertible that never leaves your driveway?"

My head is spinning and my throat is dry, but I am fixed on the most important task now—getting to the wedding.

"I explained that I don't like driving it on freeways," Chris replies evenly, hands thrust into his stupid linen pants. He lets out a deep sigh. "Amy, I can't deal with this."

My breath catches in my throat.

"I thought you loved me. I thought this was going somewhere," he says.

I exhale through my nose slowly, trying to calm myself.

"I *do* love you," I say, my voice faltering. "I'm trying to take you to meet my family."

"But you'd rather have your show than have me," he says.

"It's *my* show. Why can't I have both?" I hear the whimpering in my voice now.

"You don't get it," he says, picking up his overnight bag. He smiles grimly at me. Pityingly, even. Before turning and heading back up the stairs.

"I'm calling an Uber," I shout after him. "Wait!"

"I think we both need to cool off. Let's talk when you're back," he replies over his shoulder as he walks away. "I'm going home."

It takes me a moment to figure out that he doesn't want me to follow him. I stand there stunned as the air is squeezed out of me, wondering if this is *my* fault. What the hell just happened?

A few hours later, I'm sitting at the Dirty Dog's Lounge, five minutes' walk from the train station, with a small circle of people crowded around me. It was meant to be one quick drink. A straightener, as I pulled my shit together. But I'm into my eighth bourbon, and now I have my own entourage; they came for the wild dress and stayed for the feminist raging.

"And then he says, *You don't love me!*" I am slurring, pulling Jim from Queens by the collar as I use him as my stand-in Chris for more dramatic effect. "And I said, *I'm taking you to meet my family, you stupid asshole.* And then he said, *You'd rather have your show than me.*"

"That's Gaslighting 101," says a woman, raising her glass

toward me to accentuate the point. "A gaslighter. Just like my ex-husband."

"More toxic than this fucking mai tai," says another. "By the way, honey, you've got a false eyelash stuck to your cheek."

"You need to call your mom, Cinderella," says the bartender, pulling the bourbon out of my reach.

"So, I'm *right* to be angry," I say to the animated groans and angry gesticulations of my audience. I *am* right to be angry. He *was* gaslighting me.

"You know what?" I stand, knocking over my stool in the process. "I'm going to go and tell him what an absolute prick he is. I'm going to walk to his stupid apartment and I'm going to knock on his stupid door and I'm going to tell him."

My phone rings for the hundredth time, and, under the influence of adrenaline and bourbon, and the encouragement of my gaggle of daytime drunks, I throw the phone into a pint of beer, and everyone cheers. "You guys love drama," I say, feeling momentarily sober as I stare at the tiny bubbles escaping my submerged iPhone 13.

I take another shot, and before I know it, I'm stumbling toward his apartment in Prospect Park, drinking the dregs of the bourbon I swiped from the bar, the long skirts of my bridesmaid dress floating in my wake. I wave at the folks who stare, and occasionally shout "Asshole!" to the sky. I am crazed.

As I turn onto Chris's street, my mood darkens further.

I pass his brand-new silver Audi TT convertible and kick the hubcap, injuring my toe in the process, before heading up the short flight of stairs to his front door. I ring, I knock, I shout, I ring, and I shout some more.

Someone from a neighboring apartment yells for me to "shut the hell up!" but it only serves to rile me further. *Where the fuck is he?*

"Where are you, you gaslighting son of a bitch?" I scream.

I turn back to the street and plunk down on the stairs, glaring out at the symbol of my hate: that stupid car. Who the hell is too scared to drive on an expressway? I mean, I am, but I don't own a car specifically designed to speed on expressways with the top down.

Suddenly, possessed, I stand and lift the several layers of my skirt and walk toward his car. I slide my shoes off and climb up on the hood to the roof of the car. Then I pull my underwear down and feel a cathartic release as I pee onto the canvas roof of his Audi TT.

A moment later, my stockinged foot slips on a runaway trail of pee, and I cascade backward onto the roof of the car, my skirt rising in a blue poof of cheap fabric as the canvas top buckles underneath me. And then I cackle. I cackle and I cackle, and at some point the cackling turns to sobbing.

I lie there in a pile of polyester, the sky a darkening blue, the clouds turning a slight pink, and I think about Ruth's wedding. They would be heading to the tent for dinner, an empty seat at the head table where my sorry ass should be. I think about my mom and how deeply I have let her down. I think about my show, and the four years' work that came to an end because I decided it was worth it to explore an office affair with my boss. And I think about Chris, and my heart squeezes. Despite everything, I am grieving, because no matter how much I hate him right now, I also love him.

How quickly a day can turn from giddy excitement, full of hope and possibility, to this: a fugitive bridesmaid, lying in a pool of her own pee, on the collapsed roof of her boss/boyfriend's car, probably expelled from her family for life.

"The only way is up," I whisper quietly to the heavens, deciding I'd better escape the scene of the crime. I groan as I realize I've hurt my butt in the fall.

And then I hear it. "Oh my God, did you get it?"

"All of it," says another voice. "Holy shit, that's hilarious. Look at that fall."

My heart picks up, and I try to crane my neck to see. Who is that?

"Is that Amy Duffy?" says the first voice.

No.

"Holy shit, that ballbuster from Wolf?" says the second voice. That *ballbuster?*

No.

No!

"Hello? Who's there?" I ask, panicking, craning my neck in all directions. "This is not what it looks like. Also, why am I a ballbuster?"

"Shit," one of the voices says, "let's go." And then the sound of steps hurrying off down the street.

I pull my head up, struggling to see, stuck in the huge dent I've made in the Audi's soft top. But I can just spot the back of them. Two men, one clutching an iPhone, and the end of my life as I know it.

Two

Two Years Later

I am straightening my hair—a Monday enthusiasm for looking professional that usually wanes by Wednesday. When I finish I down my morning coffee and turn my attention to the long mirror in my hall and ready myself to leave.

"You, Amy Duffy, are not just one bad day in July. You are not a hashtag. You are not a trending topic. You are thirty-two years of awesomeness," I say, a mantra I've preached every morning for the past two years, since I left New York.

It was impossible to stay after "the incident." The video was filmed—we think—by a disgruntled freelance editor whom I'd had to fire from a project earlier that year at Chris's instruction. The editor sent it to some intern on the Wolf Studios social media team, who shared it in a company Slack channel, and by Tuesday, everyone at my office had seen it. By Wednesday, so had my cousin Ruth, my mom, and my entire extended family. I'm not sure what it was that made it go quite so viral—the bridesmaid dress, the defacing of a fancy asshole's car, my serene expression as I relieved myself, the slapstick slip, or the insane cackling—but people loved to share it, and within four short days, my humiliation was complete.

And I mean *humiliation*. The kind that continues to replay in your mind and causes a fresh surge of sickness and shame over and over and over again. An inescapable, continuous loop of agonizing humiliation that can only be erased by acquiring a drug addiction, or a plane ticket to London. The person I was— Amy Duffy, the tough television executive with that rare blend of both creative flair and an instinct you couldn't teach (Chris's words, not mine)—she was gone. In her place was a haunted, nervous slip of my former self, who spent two years trying to erase the past by never sitting still, unless I was watching TV or at the pub.

It turns my stomach when I think about it. The call from my hysterical mother. The handwritten letter of shame from Cousin Ruth. Penned, apparently, on her honeymoon, with streaks of what might have been tears causing the ink to run through the words *You had to make it all about you, didn't you?* My peers at work finding out I'd been sneaking around with our boss. And Chris. Chris apparently denied the relationship publicly while he broke up with me privately over text.

I think it's best if we go our separate ways.

And so, I left. You *could* say that I ran away, but is it really running away if it's the only path to take? Who was going to take me seriously at work? The New York TV business had a lot of sharks in a very small pond. One false move and you go from great white to hapless baby fur seal practically begging to be swallowed whole. I was finished.

I left New York to start afresh in London just two weeks after that fateful Friday. It was the right decision and I have never looked back. And I'm *never* going back.

I shake my hair over my shoulders so I can see the sweetheart neckline of my bodysuit and smooth down my high-waisted trousers. I have this wavy caramel hair that hangs to the middle of my back. It is the single best asset I have, and I am constantly complimented on it. But it is literally the only thing I like about myself. I have never liked my eyes, which are catalog brown and surrounded by more laugh lines than I feel I've reasonably earned. I'm short. And curvy, but not in an even way. That is to say, I have no butt, and boobs that cannot be minimized no matter what the lady at Victoria's Secret claims. I will never be described as chic, or willowy, or elegant. I cannot wear "anything" and look amazing. I require structured, well-made clothing, and a bra stiff enough to scaffold the Empire State Building.

On my way to work, I read the news about last night's episode of the reality dating series and British cultural behemoth *Fantasy Island*. Jake Jones—writer, thirty-two, and my draw in the office *Fantasy Island* sweepstakes—walked off the show in spectacular fashion. He drank four beers, spent an hour in the booty booth alone with his head in his hands, and then leapt off a thirty-foot cliff and tried to swim to freedom.

He was pulled out of the water by a local fisherman just as the camera crews caught up with him. The show's host was practically salivating at the press potential of it all, thrusting a microphone into Jake's face, demanding to know how he was feeling. Jake took one tortured look at the camera and then he was off over the side of the boat again.

And so today he is in all the tabloids as well as every possible showbiz column. WRITE-OFF! FANTASY FLOP! scream the headlines. WRITER IN HIS OWN DRAMATIC PLOT TWIST! There were even cheap op-eds in the tabloids, and inevitably a piece by some hack about how Jake Jones's outrageous behavior is yet another "clear example of the entitlement shown by millennial, lefty-woke liberals."

"That's right, British press, a writer wanting to escape a reality dating show is why we should stop funding the arts," I mutter, rolling my eyes. I felt for poor Jake Jones, the current laughingstock of the nation, even if—unlike me—he had signed up for it. And I was disappointed. I'd been looking forward to several weeks of staring at his pretty face on the TV.

When I get to CTV's reception in the heart of London's Soho, it's the first thing Gabby, our security guard, gossips with me about.

"Did you see it?"

"Yes," I say. "What else would I be doing on a warm summer night? Going out? *Socializing?*"

Gabby laughs, and I glide in through the barriers, taking the elevator to my floor: the marketing and creative department of CTV.

Our team is responsible for all the bits on TV that are *not* the show. This means I write and produce the channel promotions, the trailers, and the end-credit voice-overs that say, "Next up, it's *Legally Mine*, the husband-and-wife legal team defending love one high-profile divorce at a time."

It was a big change, from premium TV series development to making trailers. It's like leaving a pop career to sell the band T-shirts. Don't get me wrong, selling band T-shirts is a cool job, but it wasn't what I'd been drawn to TV to do. My dream, in the before times, was to develop the next *Breaking Bad*. But I liked it here. It was just what I needed.

I push through the glass doors into our big open-plan office, skirting a camera crew sorting kit on the floor. I dodge a sponsorship intern carrying a large peanut M&M'S character and duck under the production team, who are stringing up bunting for the launch of a newly acquired cartoon.

"Hi, Amy," says Penny, my boss's PA and our office *Fantasy Island* fanatic. "You're out of the sweepstakes."

"I know," I say, grimacing. "Poor guy. Jake Jones was a disaster. At least I came in third in the Eurovision Song Contest."

In this office, people bet on TV like most people bet on sports. We have a sweepstakes for almost everything: talent shows, dating shows—even a baking competition.

"I can't wait for his exit interview," Penny says breathlessly, flicking her shiny dark hair back across her shoulders. "Goddamn, he was fine."

"If your type is broody writer," I say.

"My type is available," she replies as she glides off toward Creative Director Danny's office with a take-out coffee.

I stop by the editing suites on the way to my desk, peering in through the windows to check on my trailer for *The Comeback*

Special, a high-camp series that takes singers out of obscurity and gives them a second shot at fame. It wasn't original, but it was still a bit of a cult classic and pulled in a decent audience. It was being color-graded by our resident editor Micky.

"Hi, Micky," I say, pushing open the door.

"How 'bout this, Amy?" he says, sitting back in his chair so I can see the monitors. "Too warm?"

"I think we want super-sparkly bright for this one," I reply. "Think Katy Perry music video. Delicious and garish as hell."

"You got it," he says.

"And, Micky," I say, pulling a sympathetic face, "the executive producer wants to see the cut before we deliver."

"Crap," he says without looking back at me.

It is a universal truth that having senior management interested in your work makes everything less joyful.

"Hey, chick," says a warmly familiar voice behind me. *Maggie.* My heart lifts when I see her.

"You didn't call me back yesterday," I grumble after we hug.

"Oh shit, yes, that's right," she says, her hands on her hips, grinning. "I'm sorry I didn't get off the Thames River cruise with the head of talent from Pixar to call you back."

"Get the fuck out!" I gasp, slapping her on the arm. Maggie's dream is Pixar. As the art director here at CTV, she is absolutely primed to take her next big step—she just needs an in. "How the *hell* did you manage that?"

"The hustle, baby," she says, grinning. "Oh, Amy, you should come out with us more! I told you that BAFTA lunch would evolve into a drunken career opportunity. You used to be *such* a good networker. Like a human LinkedIn."

I recoil at the description. But she is right. I *had been* a human LinkedIn, and now I don't network at all, online or in person. In fact, I've stayed well away from social media, or pretty much social anything since "the incident." Whereas Maggie Barnes is a social animal, as long as that social situation will get her somewhere she wants. She is pure power. She has a razor-sharp dark bob that swings about like vertical blinds as she moves. Maggie towers over me at five foot ten and is the most extroverted introvert I've ever known; she has a layer of openhearted boisterousness that draws people to her, but very few people get past that first layer. I'm not even sure I have. Not *completely*.

I met Maggie in New York three years ago. She came to work at Wolf as a graphic designer, and we immediately bonded over our fierce ambition. Like everything with Maggie, her move to New York was calculated. "A one-year stint in New York to gather experience and fast-track my career," she'd told me. I took great pleasure in showing her around the city, late-night live TV tickets, comedy in the Village, cocktails, shared Ubers home to our respective apartments in Williamsburg. She was the one who spotted the spark between me and Chris, even before I really did, and warned me of those age-old clichés: "When you screw someone at work, your work gets screwed." Or "Don't dip your pen in the company ink."

How right she was.

I was devastated when she said she'd had enough of New York and wanted to go home. But in the end, it was perfect she was here in London. She got me a job freelancing at CTV, which quickly became permanent, and we've been inseparable ever since.

"I promise I'll come to the next thing," I lie. And my God, it comes so easily these days.

"It was honestly *so* much fun, though I've had two hours' sleep and I'm feeling it. I had to buy some pants at Marks and Spencer this morning. Why does everyone in this damn industry drink and do drugs like they're still at university?" she says, pulling an elegant lip gloss out of her back pocket, which she slides across her lips. "Oh, and I saw Benny and Claire emerge from the Soho Hotel this morning."

"Well, they won't be the first stars of a show to be secretly fucking," I reply.

"You'd know," she says, smirking, looping her arm in mine and guiding us to our desks.

"I know *so many* stories," I reply, laughing.

"You do." She laughs too.

"I miss it," I say, shrugging.

Maggie sighs.

"What?"

"You *know* you can get back to it," she says with an encouraging sidelong glance. I feel my body tense in response. "Anytime. You just dust off that CV."

"I am. I *will*," I shoot back, more sharply than I mean to.

"And if the rumors about the merger are true . . . ," she begins in a singsongy voice.

"I might need to anyway," I say, sighing. "Yes, yes. I *know*."

She boots up her machine without sitting and we have just a moment's silence before I'm overwhelmed with feelings of both guilt and inadequacy. I am *not* the woman Maggie met in New York, and while she understands why I left, she does not understand why I have not moved on. Sometimes I'm terrified that the shell that remains is not deserving enough of her friendship. That my lack of ambition and bite will eventually frustrate Maggie just a little too much, and the whole friendship will dissolve, another casualty of that awful day.

"So," I begin, ready to change the subject, "did *you* watch *Fantasy Island* last night?"

"I was out, so no. But I heard about the dramatic sea escape," she says, spinning around to face me, her entire demeanor softening.

"What makes these people do it to themselves? It's like watching a car crash in real time. But, like, dude! You actually signed up for this."

"Money?" says Maggie.

"Fame," I counter. "It's only a hundred thousand pounds if you win."

"'*It's only a hundred thousand pounds*,'" Maggie says mockingly.

"No amount of money is worth public humiliation," I say, folding my arms. "Imagine being him this morning reading that all over social media. Makes me feel sick."

"Your situation was entirely different," she says.

"Not really," I reply, "it's all humiliation."

"Not if you *want* it," she replies. "Anyway, he won't be out yet, will he?" Maggie slings her vintage Chloe saddle bag over the back of her chair and sits at her desk, which has been right next to mine since we bullied our boss, Danny, into moving us together. "Won't he be in some holding place, with lots of producers shielding him from the worst of it? He was only evicted last night."

"In *Big Brother* you're thrown into a hotel the night you're out, and apart from a fifteen-minute call from a psychologist two weeks later, you're pretty much on your own when you check out at eleven a.m. the next day."

"Really?"

"Yes, I met one of the executive producers at a development workshop and I grilled him."

"You're *such* a TV nerd," Maggie says while pressing the tops of her eye sockets with her thumbs, trying to massage her headache away.

"Proudly," I reply with a shrug.

"Sometimes I think we're all piranhas," she says with a sigh, meaning everyone who works in television. "I don't know. In my darkest hours, I just want to move to the coast and become a painter."

I laugh. It's impossible to imagine Maggie outside the energy of London and the world of TV. "How long have we got until our production meeting?"

"Half an hour," Maggie replies.

"Amy," says Penny, tapping on my computer, moving so smoothly she's like a cat in cashmere. "Danny wants an update on the *Comeback Special* campaign. Can you add it to the production meeting agenda?"

"You bet," I say. "Not going to be able to sneak this one through quietly, am I?"

"It's our Saturday night summertime flagship show," she says, as if I wasn't painfully aware.

"And we'll *all* be watching," says Maggie, saluting in jest.

"Danny can't hear you," Penny whispers. "You don't have to pretend, Maggie."

"Well then, I will be out living my best thirty-something life. *Amy* will be at home watching."

"With a very good bottle of red wine," I say, "a claret, a vibrator, and perhaps some very stinky cheese."

"We need to get you out more," Maggie mutters, laughing. "I've failed in your social rehabilitation."

"But my night in is *so* good," I say breathlessly, trying to joke.

Maggie sighs, folding her arms. "I worry about you."

"I'm getting there, Maggie. I really am. I have a feeling that this year is going to be my year," I say. And, in truth, the words do feel a little more real, the more I pretend I mean them.

Three

~~~

"Same again?" says the cashier that evening as I'm checking out.

I look down at my basket. Sauvignon Blanc and a ready meal of salmon and mashed potatoes. It's a dine-in-for-one offer of a half bottle of wine and a single microwave meal. I don't want to make it sound too grim—this was a premium ready meal, packaged in biodegradable cardboard, with LINE-CAUGHT WILD ATLANTIC SALMON emblazoned across the top. I have taste. I have *standards*. The wine is crisp and delicious, the salmon is organic, and together they make the perfect midweek meal. I love it, and I love coming to the Notting Hill grocer on my way home.

However, when this scruffy-haired cashier—Glenn—with his long white nose and several angry pimples across his cheeks says the words *same again*, I cringe. He is right. It *is* the same again. It was the same last Wednesday, and the Tuesday before. And if it wasn't the salmon ready meal it was the vegetarian lasagna or a *tom kha gai* or the mushroom risotto.

I feel mortified. I need to mix it up and go to different stores, like some kind of addict.

"No," I say, tilting my chin up slightly. "Not exactly the *same again*. This is a different wine. I usually get the Chablis."

His lips purse in an amused smirk. The kind of look that says, *Whatever you tell yourself, lady*, and it fills me with incandescent rage. I've been both *seen* and *ridiculed*. By a pimply teenager, no less. I walk away from the counter, feeling my cheeks flame as I head to the fresh vegetable section, sliding the ready meal back onto the shelf en route. I could always cook. I loved to cook. I was good at cooking. In the times before Chris, my dinner parties were legendary. Fuck Glenn. I bet he lives on Domino's.

I tilt my chin and pick up a single potato, dropping it into my basket, my eyes not leaving his. And then I step sideways and do the same with an onion. Some garlic. Then a bunch of celery. A couple of turnips. Italian flat-leaf parsley. I swap aisles and continue. A can of borlotti beans. A can of crushed tomatoes. Some chipotle paste. A box of cumin. Some tinned tuna. A stinky blue cheese. Tampons. Baby wipes. I am not thinking about what I'm doing, but I'll be damned if this judgmental little shit is going to shame me about my life choices.

I scan the contents of my basket and grimace. What the hell am I going to make with all this? I look up and see him cover his mouth to laugh, before I toss in a jar of pickled fish, some Italian breadsticks, and dried apricots. I am a mess.

I've filled my basket with nearly a hundred pounds' worth of food to prove a point to a teenager, who, in the time it took me to round the final aisle and head to the register, appears to have gone on a break.

"Is this really where we are, Amy?" I ask myself, staring

into the mirror that hangs on the ceiling above the conveyor belt. "Revenge groceries? Don't you want more?" It comes out rather more loudly than I intend.

"If you're still deciding?" says a voice. I turn to see a tall, horsey woman with that particular brand of infuriating English politeness. The kind of person who is willing to wait a lifetime in frustrated misery rather than ask me explicitly just to *please move*.

"Go ahead," I say, waving her through.

I do want more than this. And I *deserve* more than this.

My mother would certainly tell me that. My mother has told me that since the day I was born. *You deserve the whole world, Amy*, she would tell me.

I dump the basket behind a wall of two-for-one energy drinks and walk briskly out the door, vowing never to return.

Moments later, as if summoned by some transatlantic maternal force, my phone vibrates, and it's my mom.

"Hi," I say, my mind instantly transported to the kitchen of my parents' place, an ache for home washing over me. Mom would have just finished lunch. Dad, who is not quite retired yet, would be bothering her at home before heading back to the garage.

"I'm sorry to call you so late, Amy darling," she says.

"It's not late, Mom," I say, hit with the waves of guilt I feel whenever we speak. Of all the casualties from "the incident," the impact on my relationship with my family has been the hardest. I am estranged and I hate the estrangement. But I'm too ashamed to see them and feel the weight of their pity. Once upon a time I was the pride of my family with my big job in Manhattan, working in television. And now I feel like the family embarrassment, even if my mom insists that everyone has moved on and it is time to come home. I haven't seen them in two years, and I'm running out of excuses.

"Right, well, I won't hold you up. Your father has a prostate exam at three p.m., and you'd think he's getting a dirty massage the way he's carrying on," she says.

"Finger up the ass!" I hear Dad shout in the background.

"I'm just checking in, really," she says, then puts her hand over the receiver and shushes my dad. I can picture him, almost certainly motioning toward *her* ass with a finger. I can't help but laugh at the image of the two of them. That's my family. That was me. Rough and loud and ready for anything.

"Mom, you're not just checking in," I reply.

"Well, of course, I was wondering about your nana's—"

"I don't have an answer for you yet," I say quickly, feeling my heart squeeze. I push my feelings aside and hitch my canvas backpack up higher on my shoulders, readying myself to walk home.

"It's only that you can't leave it until the last moment, Amy," she says.

"Mom, I'll try to come," I say quickly, leaning as hard as I can into the *try to.*

"Everyone wants to see you," she says firmly.

"Everyone hates me," I reply petulantly.

"You think if they forgive Uncle Ray for running off with his proctologist, they can't forgive you?" I picture my cousin Ruth's look of anger and disappointment. I picture my brother,

Floyd, shaking his head when he sees my face. And I picture my dad. My dad, whose baby girl was the apple of his eye, casting those same eyes aside when I walk back into the house.

"I don't know," I reply as a huge red double-decker bus hisses to a stop beside me, the doors open, and a flood of commuters pushes past and rushes into into the residential streets that run off the main road.

"What can I do to convince you?" she says, her voice tight and pleading.

"Mom," I moan. "Please. I love you."

"Oh, Amy," she says now with a sigh, and I stiffen. I loathe this tone even more than I loathe her pleading. The pitying. Sometimes the pain of letting Mom down is worse than almost anything. Even the shame of "the incident" can start to pale next to the resigned sigh my mom has just made down the phone.

"I understand you'll miss some things now that you live in London, but so far you've missed everything," she says.

"I'll try to come for Nana's eightieth," I say again. "Mom, I am about to walk into a restaurant for dinner."

"Okay, darling," she says, pulling herself together, adopting a brighter tone. "I'll send you the money for the flight, if that's the issue. Anything you need."

"I don't need the money, Mom," I say gently, wishing for a hug. For me. But also for *her*. "I have to go. There are people waiting for me."

I grimace at the lie as I slide my phone into my back pocket and stare down at my feet. There is no gang of friends waiting to stand and embrace me as I jostle my way into a busy restaurant for dinner. There is no lively chatter over pitchers of beer or shared plates of tapas. There is only my empty apartment. There is not even a microwave meal to eat alone while watching an ancient episode of *L.A. Law*.

Shame washes over me. My nana's birthday is the first weekend in August, just under nine weeks away, and I really, truly want to go, but when I close my eyes and imagine walking into a hand-decorated room in the front of Nana's house, with too many balloons and not enough beer, I feel a shudder of anxiety. All I see is at least thirty pairs of judging eyes on me.

I look across at the organic grocer and see my nemesis, Glenn, back behind the counter, and I narrow my eyes. I have lost so much. Even the ability to buy myself a bottle of wine. Maggie is right. Hell, my mother is right. I *need* to start making some changes. I *need* to move on.

Four

~~~~~~~~~

My apartment has been my savior these last two years. I live on the cutest street. Every terraced house is a different color—sunflower yellow, lilac, powder gray, coral, flushed spring green—and the sidewalk is flanked by a row of cherry trees, which, in late April, are powder pink against the azure-blue sky. In May, the petals fall in the breeze like snowflakes. Now, in early June, the boughs hang heavy with green leaves, casting a dappled light onto the pavement and through the front windows.

When I arrived here from New York, I threw myself into the fantasy of living in London. Something cute, above a pub maybe. A place of my own.

"Good fucking luck with that," Maggie had said. "Lucky if you can find a house with a private power socket these days."

But I was *determined*. And my determination paid off. After looking at what felt like every damp, dingy basement flat in London, finally, a one-bedroom of my own I could afford. The downside was living with a nosy landlady in the ground-floor apartment. But the upsides were numerous: reasonable rent, roof-terrace access, and a leafy garden. The landlord never used these spaces, and the last tenant in flat B was a hermit. So, it was practically all mine.

Until it suddenly wasn't.

"Hello?" I say to the two men unloading a dismantled bed frame and leaning it against the door, while a third is pressing hard on the buzzer with my name next to it. "Can I help you?"

"Delivery for 14C?"

"Oh, I'm in 14C," I say, looking at the bed frame. "But I didn't order a bed. At least not a double." I laugh cheekily, but the removal guy is aggressively displeased.

"You have to sign this," he says, thrusting a digital device under my nose.

"Can you wait just one moment?" I ask, finger in the air.

He looks at his watch and grunts.

I push through the small lobby area and to the staircase, where I can see brown boxes and suitcases haphazardly piled and leading upward. I bound up the stairs to find that the boxes lead to 14B, which has been vacant for a week.

"Hello?" I call out. "Amy here, from upstairs!?"

"Yes," a deep male voice replies. Just a *yes*. Not a *hello*.

"There's a delivery here for you. A bed?"

"Right," replies the voice. "Thanks." The *thanks* is added as an afterthought. Tacked on, like he caught himself being rude and should know better. But still, he does not emerge.

"They're literally outside now. You need to sign for it."

"On my way," I hear, followed by the loud bang of something being dropped and an accompanying irritated sigh.

I glance at his belongings. A small side table piled high with

The Sweetest Revenge   33

plain IKEA dishes, an old plastic electric kettle with its cord neatly wound up. A single fold-up chair. A rattan lamp. A large red barbecue. What looks like one of those Bakelite briefcase record players from, like, 1982. Four novelty wine openers. A chaotic and incoherent pile of things that reminds me of the haphazard boxes I threw together when I left New York. No order. No clear personality type. Pure chaos. A creative person, I guess.

I can hear the buzzer to my apartment going, so I head upstairs, and before the delivery guy can protest I shout, "He's on his way, *right now*," into the receiver. Then I head back out into the hall and lean over the banister just in time to catch the back of my neighbor's dark, tousled hair and broad shoulders, his casual blue-and-white-striped tee and gray linen trousers as he heads down the stairs.

He's quite stylish. That kind of effortless Mediterranean stylish that Chris aspired to but could never achieve because he was too high-maintenance. *Intriguing.*

Inside my apartment the buzzing of the front door ends, and I toss my bag over the hook and hang my trench on the back of the door. But, a few moments later and just as I'm about to collapse on the sofa, the buzzer goes again.

"Hello?" I say into the receiver.

"Hi, delivery for, umm . . . number 14C."

"You mean 14B, I think," I say wearily. "Give me a sec."

I bound down the stairs and knock again on his open door, but this time the new tenant, with his dark floppy hair and his slightly flushed complexion, appears almost immediately.

"Yes?" he says gruffly, eyes not meeting mine.

I feel a judder of recognition this time, like a defibrillator to the brain.

"I don't know how many deliveries you've got coming today, but there's another one downstairs," I say to the very attractive man in front of me. "You're 14*B*. I'm 14C."

He sighs. "Oh shit."

I know him! I fucking know him!

I squint at his face, his moody gaze, long bushy lashes framing hazel eyes. Where have I seen that brooding look before? My mind works like frenzied fingers through index cards. Back home? Work? No. The gym? No. Liberty makeup counter? No. *Crimewatch*? No.

"Holy shit! You're Jake Jones from *Fantasy Island*."

It comes out as an accusation. It *is* Jake. My horse in the office *Fantasy Island* sweepstakes! Jake Jones, *writer*. I immediately recall the image that came up on the TV screen—topless Jake, arms crossed—and compare the image with the man in front of me. In the flesh, or rather in *clothing*, he's different. Softer.

And he's also . . . just moved in?

He startles at my comment. "I'm Amy," I say lightly, but though his eyes flicker up toward my face, they will not meet mine.

"Hi," he says, playing with a rubber band on his wrist impatiently. I hear the buzzing coming from my apartment again.

"The delivery," I remind him.

Jake's eyes finally lift to mine—they hold, and I feel an immediate fizzing at the base of my spine that unsteadies me. I take a step backward. We hold each other's gaze for a beat.

I look away, mumble something about getting back, and rush two stairs at a time to my apartment and slam my door behind me. I'm completely out of breath. Not from the dozen stairs I just ran up, but from the surprising tug of desire that his look awoke inside me.

I glance around for my phone to text Maggie.

Um, that guy Jake Jones, the one who swam off the set?
Jake from Fantasy Island is . . . my new neighbor?
Call me?

And then, for the laughs:

I think I'm dating again.

Calm down, Amy, I think over and over. *You've been cool around major celebrities; you can certainly be cool around minor ones.* But it isn't his celebrity that has unsettled me; it's those eyes. And his shoulders. Almost without thinking about it, I'm in my bedroom brushing my hair and touching up my face.

Twenty minutes later, my buzzer goes again. This time when I get to his apartment, I simply shout, "Another delivery, Jake!"

"Sorry," he calls out, and I run back upstairs, peering over the banister like a giddy schoolgirl as he passes below me on the way to the door.

Fifteen minutes later, I'm down there once more.

"I think that's the last one," he responds, somewhat apologetically.

But ten minutes after that, there is another.

"Groceries this time," I holler. I wait for him to emerge, my heart picking up as he does. "I was hoping to go to bed soon." I don't mean this in irritation; frankly, I'm enjoying having a reason to keep coming back down.

He pulls out a phone with a cracked screen and checks the time: 8:35 p.m. Early. Makes me look like a bit of a loser.

"I have work early tomorrow. I work in *television*," I try.

"I think that's it," he says, ignoring my attempt at a connection. "At least for today."

The *for today* is an apology ahead of tomorrow, because I think Jake has a lot of things arriving to the wrong address.

"It said on the show you're a writer?"

"No," he says, with almost disgust. The tip of his bare foot kicks against the edge of the doorframe.

"Oh," I reply, confused. And then, to fill the air, I blurt out, "Well, you did great."

A sharp sigh. "No. I didn't." His green-brown eyes meet mine fleetingly, a deep line forming between his brows. He's searching my face for something—to see if I'm joking maybe? After all, he didn't do great. It was a dumb thing to say.

"Okay," I concede, "you didn't do *great* exactly. What I mean to say is, you were really entertaining."

There, I thought. That's what all these people were in there for, right? To be *remembered*. To be *launched*. I smile broadly at him, but he doesn't respond. Instead, he says, "Huh," while the color seems to drain from his face. And, before I can backpedal once more, he pushes open the door to his apartment and disappears inside with a hollow bang, and the little metal *B* sways and falls off onto the floor.

I stand for a moment in stunned silence, but before I can take myself back upstairs and contemplate what his arrival at 14 Parkview Place will mean for me, the main character of my universe, his door opens and he's standing there again, broad shoulders slumped forward.

"I forgot the groceries," he says, his eyes meeting mine, and I feel that zing again.

"Uh-huh," I say, pointing up the stairs as my buzzer goes again. "He's still there."

"Sorry about the mistake on the address. I was in a hurry when I organized everything." His voice is gruff, and I notice for the first time the dark rings under his eyes.

"It's fine, *really*," I reply with a smile, but I can feel my pulse quickening with the interaction, and I want it to continue.

But Jake Jones says, "I need . . . to be left *alone*."

"Yes," I reply, a little irritated, as we both hear an impatient knock coming from downstairs. Then I see it in his face. The *regret*. The shame. He wants quiet and he wants to be left alone because he is embarrassed. My heart immediately goes out to him, and I let out a sympathetic sigh, which he stiffens at.

"I get it," I reply quickly. "You have my word."

"Thank you," he says. And then he heads downstairs, and I'm left with the feeling that someone turned off the sun and told me it was bedtime and it's really unfair because *I'm not tired, Mommy*.

I head back upstairs and pace the flat, cursing the fact I

have no wine or food. It would feel somehow absurd to order it now and wait for my buzzer to go.

It was the look on his face when I mentioned his performance on the show. That wasn't the sulky disappointment of a reality TV contestant who thought he had blown his only chance.

It was a different kind of embarrassment. The kind you feel in a naked dream, after you wake up in a cold sweat. An *I didn't do this! This isn't me! I didn't want to be here!* kind of embarrassment.

A desperate, hopeless shame that comes with making a dreadful and very public mistake that can be recalled and replayed forever by anyone with cell-phone coverage. I knew more than a little of how that felt. I knew that look.

I glance across at the buzzer, willing it to buzz again. But the building has fallen silent.

"Poor bastard," I say aloud. "Poor, attractive bastard."

Five

$\sim$

I didn't think you could get a hangover from scrolling on your phone until the early hours. Like a proper dead-body, aching-head, *did I black out?* feeling when you wake up. Disorientation. Confusion. Even a dash of shame at your lack of sense and restraint. And yet, that's exactly what I experience this morning after googling Jake Jones until well after 2 a.m., heading down rabbit hole after rabbit hole. Eventually I fell asleep on the sofa in my clothes, ironically knocking over a nonalcoholic beer in the process. *Not good, Amy Duffy.*

I scramble to find my phone, ignoring the message from my mother that came in at 1 a.m. I'll read it later.

Here are some of the things I have found out about Jake Jones.

1. He is Welsh.
2. He is around thirty-two years old. I ascertain this from his slightly dormant LinkedIn, where he is listed as having done a bachelor of arts.

3. He is, frustratingly, not a big social media user. His Facebook is private.
4. His *Fantasy Island* profile says he likes "chilling out and reading."
5. He is a screenwriter. I know this because I found his agent. She is based in North Wales, and on her site she has him listed as a screenwriter, a catalog model, and a film extra.

I frown as I recall this. It just isn't a good way to represent him if he's serious about writing. But it *is* a good way to represent him if he wants to get on a reality show.

All in all, I didn't find much. And so I'm utterly intrigued by him.

Coffee. Shower. Work, I tell myself as I look at my glassy red eyes in the mirror and am startled by my buzzer once again.

"Oh, good God," I mutter, fishing around for a Post-it note in my kitchen drawer and a red pen. Then I pick up the receiver. "If I buzz you in, can you just leave it in the hallway?" I say to the delivery kid, who shrugs and does as I ask.

On the way out, I stick a note to the front buzzer.

JAKE JONES APARTMENT 14B with a red arrow pointing to his buzzer. And for good measure, I stick black tape over my own.

"Jake Jones from *Fantasy Island* has moved into your building?" Maggie says in the voice message I receive when I come out of the underground station in Soho. "I need a full debrief."

I text her. Audio Suite. I have a mixing session this morning.

The reply is appropriately fast, given the magnitude of the gossip:

See you in fifteen.

I hurry into the building, stopping for just a second to peek in on the set for *The Comeback Special* inside Studio 1 on the ground floor.

Rehearsals will start next week, and while I am aware it is hardly *X Factor* or *American Idol*, it is *live television*, and I am excited. As I peer around the door, a bulky first assistant director walks toward me with his hands raised.

"You're not supposed to be in here!" he says gruffly.

"Oh, but I'm doing the launch campaign—" I begin.

"I don't care if you're the Queen of England, sweetheart, I need my team to finish."

"You have a *king* now!" I shout as I pull the door shut.

I stand there for a moment, irritated. Two years ago, I would have been one of the most important people on set. Now I can't even get in to watch the lights being rigged. And it's starting to piss me off.

I stare at the little glass window on the door, toying with the idea of pushing it open and insisting I be allowed inside, when my boss, Creative Director Danny Cummings, comes flying out of it.

"Amy?" he says, looking surprised.

Danny looks a bit like Prince Harry. He's got the same *very* posh accent, the same preppy dress sense, the same ginger hair, but his is thick and curly. He was divorced last summer at thirty-eight—but where his marriage failed, his career kept humming along. He's won a bunch of marketing awards, which sit among his vintage *Star Wars* toys on the shelves of his office. He hired me and has spent the last two years confused as to why I wanted the job when I could have been off making "*real bloody tele.*"

"Everything okay?" he asks me, his bushy orange brows squished together in concern.

"Fine, I just wanted to see the set," I say, rolling my eyes. "No lowly promotion producers allowed."

"Don't feel too lowly. I got kicked out too," he says, shaking his head.

I'm about to head to the audio suite, but Danny pauses like he has something to say.

"Is everything okay, Danny?"

"Everything is a jolly-big unknown, Amy," he says, sighing, running his hands through his hair. "But the big guy wants all the directors upstairs for a meeting right away."

"Changes?" I frown, pretending that I haven't heard the rumors. Even though everyone has.

"Yes," he says, eyeing me as though he wants to divulge but can't. "Anyway, back to our jobs while we still have them, eh?"

I gasp.

"I'm mostly kidding," he says quickly. Then he drops his voice to a near whisper. "*But you should think about your future.* Amy, you know they're talking about a new development studio."

"At CTV?" I say, the little hairs standing up on my arms. *Development studio?* "Really?"

Danny runs his fingers across his lips to zip them up. Then

he hastily unzips them again. "Not sure what they'll do with two creative directors," he mutters glumly before shrugging and sauntering off toward the elevator, leaving me standing by the studio alone.

Down the hall, our voice-over artist has finished recording, and I'm joining Moe to add sound effects and music and mix the final trailer.

"Happy Tuesday," says Moe, the loveliest sound engineer in the business, as he hits the playback and my trailer starts on the big screen above the mixing desk. "Shall we just crack on and get this over with?"

"Please," I say, glancing at my watch. "Maggie's going to pop in."

"Oooh, is there gossip?" he says, sliding the volume up as I nod excitedly. I take a seat in the spare swivel chair and sit back to watch the trailer. It looks good.

"It's back! The smash hit of last summer," the voice-over begins, deep and dramatic.

"*Smash hit* is a stretch," whispers Moe, and I scowl at him good-naturedly.

"They found fame with a massive breakthrough song," the voice continues, crisp through the speakers. "And we're bringing them back. CTV's singing competition like no other. Can these one-hit wonders stage the ultimate comeback?"

"Another Amy Duffy delight," says Moe as the noise subsides. "You make great trailers."

"Yep," I agree. "Living the dream." This doesn't come out quite as enthusiastic as I would have liked it to, and Moe jumps on it straightaway.

"What?" he says.

"Oh nothing," I reply. Moe doesn't really know about my past job in New York, except to say I worked at a production company.

"You don't like making trailers?" he asks, eyes round and genuine.

"No, it's super fun," I say. "Who wouldn't like this job? I basically watch a lot of TV and pull out all the best bits for a living. It's heaven."

"But it's the CTV catalog." Moe smirks.

"It's still great."

"You *like* watching *Legally Mine*? *Digging Ancient Brittany*?" Moe says, eyebrow raised. "I know you don't take home early screeners of *Frying for England*."

"Come on, Moe, who wouldn't love a cooking competition around deep-frying?" I say with a wry smile. "You forget, I'm *American*."

"Hey, did you watch *Fantasy Island*?" Moe says, turning the volume down to a level we can keep an ear on.

"I actually didn't," I say, realizing that in my googling frenzy, I'd entirely missed the episode last night. "But, related. The guy who walked off, or rather swam off, *Jake Jones*, has moved into my building!"

"The guy who jumped into the sea?"

"Yep," I say, eyes wide.

"Yikes, *really*?" Moe says with a mocking chuckle. "The writer?"

"The *screen*writer!" I say dramatically.

"Who's a screenwriter?" Maggie says, slipping into the

studio and settling in on the couch at the back. I spin around in my chair and beam at her.

"*Jake Jones*. He writes for the *screen*," I say breathlessly. "He's agented and everything. I looked it up last night. I'd be fascinated to know if he's any good."

"Any good at what?" she says, raising an eyebrow.

"Maggie!" I chortle, quickly bringing a finger up to my mouth. Anything said under the audio suite's sound-absorption panels is not for broadcast. Unless Moe is accidently recording, which happened once before.

"As if you're interested in his *writing*," she says, smirking.

"I am!" I say overexcitedly. "It's *so* weird to think of a writer on a dating show."

"Are you hoping he's truly looking for love?" Maggie says, examining her perfect nails in fresh vibrant blue polish. I feel my cheeks flame, and Maggie spots it, shaking her head at me as she laughs.

"No, I just find it odd is all!" I say, swinging around in the chair, trying not to look too giddy. "From a purely psychological perspective. I know it's a bit cliché, but writers are generally quiet, insecure creatures."

"Or insanely self-aggrandizing because they also act?" Maggie shoots back.

"Ben Affleck," Moe says, nodding.

"Would we still call Ben Affleck a screenwriter?" I ask.

"That's how he started," says Moe.

"Like Sylvester Stallone," agrees Maggie, nodding.

"You guys, I'm trying to be *serious*," I say.

"He could have been one of their casting wild cards," Moe

suggests. "You know, they don't find them through an agent; they just scout on the street. He was probably standing on Brighton Pier looking beefy." Moe pretends to flex his muscles, pointing at the small curves that appear in his lean limbs.

"Beefy?" I reply, laughing.

"Was he beefy?" Maggie asks, shooting me a sly grin.

"I . . ." I pause for a moment and then realize I cannot lie to my friend. "Yes."

Maggie and Moe both cackle now, and I pretend to be annoyed, rolling my eyes at their childishness.

"In all seriousness—"

"In all seriousness, a hot guy with a couple of mild red flags has moved in and you want to find out more," Maggie says teasingly. "You're doing your due diligence. I get it. Did you speak to him?"

"Yes. I think he moved in in a hurry because he had all this stuff delivered and they kept buzzing my apartment," I say quietly. "But, guys, he was just really . . . You know when someone can't look you in the eye?"

"Ashamed," she says.

"Exactly," I reply, giving her a *knowing* look. "Like he didn't mean to go on the show. Like it was a mistake."

And then I slump down on the sofa next to Maggie and sigh.

"And . . . I would just love to read some of his work."

"I see." Maggie raises both eyebrows at me, and I jut out my bottom lip. She already knows what's coming.

"To see if he's any good, or a failed screenwriter for a reason."

"Dunk," says Moe, making the gesture with his hand.

"Okay, sorry, that was mean," I concede, letting out a big sigh.

"Ladies. I'm very sorry to break up the party, but we have to finish this," says Moe, motioning to the frame of *The Comeback Special* frozen on the big screen. I nod furiously at Moe as Maggie picks up her bag and readies herself to leave.

"And so . . . ," I say in my best singsongy voice.

"Here it comes," says Maggie.

"Do you reckon you could call his agent and get some samples for me? I can't do it, obviously, because we're neighbors now," I say quickly.

"Sure," she says with a shrug, pushing on the door of the suite. And then she shoots me a wicked grin. "I'll look into your future boyfriend for you."

"Not my future boyfriend," I say.

"Okay, Amy Duffy," she says, "but you forget, I've seen that hot-guy-who-works-in-TV look before."

Six

~~~~~~

There is a certain camera angle, used most often in dystopian science fiction, but you can find it almost anywhere, when the filmmaker wants to give the audience a sense of ill ease. The camera is tilted off-center, and when the shot sits at this angle, instinctively you feel off-center yourself. It's like the televisual version of vertigo, and I'm feeling exactly that when I get in today.

I don't know exactly what's happening, but Danny never calls a meeting unless there's something big to announce, and arriving to a calendar invite with the title COMPULSORY ATTEN-DANCE all in capitals, I am concerned. The message reads:

> Please join us outside Danny's office for an update
> from our CEO, Jeff Wilson.

Employees are not stupid. We don't get an email like this and flitter around pretending our day is normal. We whisper. We worry. We panic. When Maggie arrives, we catch each other's eyes and she lets out a breath, her lips pursed, while I pull my mouth back into a toothy grimace.

"All the rumors are true, yeah?" I say.

"It's the merger all right," says Maggie.

Danny waves us all into the open-plan office area at the back of the building, where the windows overlook a permanent rotation of smokers. I gaze across at them as Danny drones on about quarterly reports and then segues awkwardly to making sure we clean out the fridge, as food will be thrown out—without delay—by the cleaning staff every Friday evening. He seems to be buying time, which is making the whole situation even more ominous. I watch as designers fidget; production managers subtly check their emails; and Penny, whose desk is in everyone's eyeline, begins topping up her makeup as if she knows exactly what's coming. Because of course she does.

"I saw Jake Jones last night," I whisper to Maggie, who, like me, has lost interest in whatever Danny is saying, and, like me, is waiting for the main event.

"You did?"

"Yes, I heard a noise in the hall and peeked out to see him trying to maneuver his barbecue up to my terrace," I say, frowning.

"The shared terrace," Maggie sternly reminds me. "That good time wasn't going to last forever."

"I know. I know. It's just that it was my little safe space," I say, and Maggie raises a single eyebrow in response.

"I spoke to the agent," Maggie says. "She's going to send over a sample of his work."

I cringe slightly. "Consider this reading of a script a dipping of my toe back into *development* again."

"I'd be thrilled if I didn't think you weren't simply casting a potential fuck," she says sharply. As I stiffen, though, she grins. "It's my job to keep you real, *Duffy*."

"Oh please," I say, tapping her playfully on the shoulder. "I'm not casting a fuck."

"Well, it's about time you did," she says just as playfully back to me.

The glass doors fly open and in walks Jeff, the president of CTV. I whip my head around to Maggie and we both stand a little straighter. Murmurs roll out across the crowd of about seventy employees from the entertainment division.

"Here we go," says Maggie, smoothing her hair, poker face engaged.

"Hi, everyone," says Jeff, brushing his hair back, slipping off his jacket, and rolling up his sleeves. It *is* warm in here, but I've been in corporate life long enough to know that this is a metaphor for him "getting his hands dirty."

"Right, team, I guess the best thing here is to cut straight to the point. As you know, we've struggled with our streaming service. For UK-only subscribers we sit at around last place—miles behind the BBC and Netflix. It's not good enough, but it does reflect the very acquisitions-focused strategy that CTV have pursued for the last decade. The fact is, to be competitive today, we need to be developing and piloting our own IP."

"I hate that we call stories *intellectual property*. I hate it," I whisper.

"Shh," says Maggie.

"So, you may have already heard the rumors, but we have accepted terms on a deal with Screen Global for a merger, which will include a sharing of content assets. As a US company, Screen Global were excited by our heritage UK and European programming, and obviously, we are excited by their back catalog, but more importantly their contemporary slate. So, that's the first news.

"The second part of the deal is significant investment in new programming. What does that mean? It means a brand-new development department charged with coming up with new content ideas for production by us, for our market. CTV Studios will launch without delay, with a huge investment from Screen Global and a remit for wide-ranging entertainment and scripted formats. We will begin recruiting right away," he says, nodding at Helen from HR, who nods in return, "and will look to bring in a big industry name to spearhead this critical new venture."

I feel like I just downed two cans of Red Bull. My eyes widen. A new development department? Danny was right. What kind of gift from the gods is this? A chance to stay here in the safe, loving arms of CTV and move back into making TV.

I let out a soft moan of delight, and Maggie swings her head around to grin at me.

"We're really going to start to commission original scripted series? Like, no more 1980s reruns?" someone at the front calls out, and laughter rounds the room.

"We are," Jeff says, nodding.

Maggie shoots her hand up, and to my surprise Jeff nods at her. "Yes, Maggie?"

"Will there be redundancies?"

Jeff chuckles, I think at Maggie's hubris, and I look over at Danny, who is nervously running his hands through his hair again.

"Of course there will be some changes in the coming weeks and months. As you know, Screen Global has its own offices here in London, and it makes little sense to operate them completely separately."

There are more murmurs and some groans, as the crowd voices its unrest in unison.

"But these things take time," Jeff says, motioning with his hands to tell people to calm down. "For now, our focus is on creating the development team—and kick-starting that. I have put together a brief, and everyone is welcome to pitch an idea. Or two. I'd be so pleased to recruit from CTV's own creative team. Danny says there's plenty of untapped talent in here."

Danny shoots me a look now, and I turn fire-engine red. But this is exciting.

"Briefs are on their way," chimes in Danny, glancing across at me. "We're looking for something food- or culture-based, comedy. And a drama. Crime. Police procedural or anything London-based, really. No Sherlock," he quips to laughs from a few in the room.

A ripple of pleasure rages through me. *Crime.* God, I love crime. And if it leans toward the macabre, so much the better.

"What a turn-on," I whisper.

"Are you back?" Maggie says.

"It's . . . very . . . *yes.* I'm interested," I reply, almost drooling.

"Today is not about getting into the granular," says Jeff, shutting Danny down on the details. Danny folds his arms and

I'm sure I see a slight eye roll. "I hope you can see the amazing possibilities ahead. I hope this merger will secure us as a nimble, agile media operator well into the future.

"As always, my office is open and you're very welcome to find some time with Janet to talk if you want to."

And with that, he's gone with a wave and a nod to Danny.

"I know this feels like big news, everyone. And it is!" Danny says, returning to the front. "Lots to take in. Creative team, let's meet for our production update as usual, please, and the rest of you, we'll catch up over the next weeks. I think for those on the team who love television, for those who want to really expand, and grow and learn"—Danny shoots another look over at me—"this is your chance to step up."

And all I can think as I let out my breath, slowly and with purpose, is that after two long, painful years, *I'm ready*.

Seven

〜〜

It's the most glorious early summer evening as I head home, feeling a creeping excitement waiting for Danny's email with the development brief. I climb onto the bus, and as it rolls down the busy stretch of sprawling department stores on Bond Street, I feel the sun hit my face in intervals as it peers over the tops of the hundreds-of-years-old buildings.

It has been a week of excited chatter at work, and I have felt myself sucked into the anticipation completely. Moe, Penny, and Maggie are all gunning for me to apply, and I have let slip, on far too many occasions to be karmically good, that I want this job.

It's the perfect time to get a FaceTime from my brother, when for once, I'm feeling optimistic.

"Hi, Floyd! Hi, girls!" I say down the video call, as my brother and his twins, Rose and Mathilda, are scooched up on the couch to chat.

"Hi, Auntie Amy," they reply in unison.

"Did you get the birthday present from me?" I say too loudly, and I startle some passengers sitting nearby.

"It arrived!" Floyd says, and one of the girls scoots off to bring said bear into the shot and then pushes it so close to the camera that all I can see is brown fuzz. "They loved the movie," says Floyd, pushing the bear away from the camera. "She can't see if you squash it up there, Rose," he says, amused.

"Good. Yes, I have even more of an appreciation for Paddington, living here," I say in a loud whisper. "I'm sorry! I'm on the bus!"

"It's fine. Mom told me to call you and ask if we're going to see you in August," Floyd asks, half listening, half telling the twins to be quiet. It's always mayhem when they're on the phone. "The girls think you *live* in the phone now."

"I'm gonna try, Floyd," I say. "I promise."

"Fine," he says, sighing. "I can tell her I asked. Don't forget to call us on Sunday morning. The girls want to sing you something they learned in choir."

"I will!" I say, blowing a kiss down the phone as the girls start fighting over who gets to hang up.

I laugh to myself, and then almost immediately my phone *dings* in my hand.

"Finally!" I mutter as I glance down at the screen. !!Development Brief!! reads the subject line from Danny. I feel a delicious wave of déjà vu. What excitement we used to feel back in the day when the big bosses would pull us into the boardroom with fresh information from Netflix or NBC. "NBC want a *Stranger Things*," or "Netflix are looking for the next *Game of Thrones*!" Chris and I would do our best not to encourage the growing attraction as we chewed on stale sandwiches and avoided too much distracting eye contact, working right through the night on a new slate of my ideas.

I smiled at the memory of us inviting unsuspecting writers into our development den as we used their presence as a toy. A pretend obstacle to our inevitable affair. There is nothing sexier or more alluring than a forbidden kind of romance. It was intoxicating. But it was also toxic. If only I'd understood I was playing with fire. I was playing with my career. My life.

I breathe slowly as I stare out the window at the city, bouncing with every pothole, and for the first time in so long, I start to open up that small part inside me that just wants to create awesome shit. This is it. *This* is my way back in.

I pour a large glass of wine, grab my laptop, and decide to avoid the terrace, just in case Jake is there with his big red barbecue. But it is too delicious an evening to be inside, so I take my laptop to the backyard.

It's a gloriously overgrown secret garden with an arch made of willow and climbing ivy. The back of the building is covered in wisteria, in full purple bloom, and the modest lawn ends by a stone-and-brick wall, also being eaten alive by ivy, and an endless row of knotweed. It's a glorious mess.

Behind the arch, just out of view, there is a little marble table and a single wrought iron chair with the most elaborate lacing. I take a seat, arranging my wine and my computer, and begin to digest the brief. I click open the email, download the file, and take a huge sip of my wine.

BRIEF 1: URBAN CRIME/POLICE DRAMA

BRIEF 2: ENSEMBLE COMEDY/DRAMEDY/CITY LIFE

My stomach tingles with excitement as I settle in to read.

"Pitch date: August 6th." Hmm. August 6 is the day before my grandmother's eightieth. Good timing, I suppose, if I actually end up going. The thought makes me immediately anxious. I read on, pushing the thought away for another day.

"Female-centric crime/spy drama, set in London. In a sea of crime dramas, how do we create a British series with a unique twist?" I read in a whisper, glancing at my wine and realizing with irritation I'm going to have to go back inside and get the bottle, when I hear the banging of metal and an occasional grunt from around the other side of the arch.

I stand, and after knocking back what's left in my glass, I peer around with a nervous sense of anticipation.

And then I see him. *Jake.* Jake Jones with only a threadbare, sweat-dampened white tank on doing push-ups on the grass patch by the back door.

I marvel at him, arm and shoulder muscles straining, back and ass tight, and then, when I'm about to duck behind the safety of the arch, he spots me.

"Oh. Hi!" he says as he pulls up to seated and rubs the sweat off his forehead with his arm. His cheeks are flushed with heat. "Shit, I didn't think anyone would be in the garden."

"Yeah, I'm working," I say, staring at anything but him. The back door. The chipped cladding below my window. The red-breasted robin that lands on the grass a mere foot from his hand. *I can work anywhere,* I think. *This is really the only decent place to exercise. Unless he goes to the park. Why isn't he at the park?*

"Sure," he says, his eyes on the robin too, before it takes flight and he turns his gaze to me.

"If you wanted to work out out here, I could go to the terrace?" I say quickly.

"It's okay, you were here first," he says, standing up. His shorts cling to his thighs, and he wipes his forehead again with the back of his hand.

"You know what? I need more wine. And it's too hot to work out here. You stay." I say this more sharply than I mean to. I'm eager to get back to the briefs and am discomfited by the effect the sight of his sweat-damp chest is having on my heart rate.

Jake doesn't protest, but I can feel his eyes on me as I disappear behind the arch. I glance down at my jogger bottoms and old T-shirt and wish—just one time—I looked fresh in his presence.

I close my laptop and take a moment to calm myself. The strangeness of sharing a private space with a man is going to take some getting used to.

I glance up at the sky, where the wispy strips of cloud are starting to turn a shade of pale gold. The sun warms my cheeks and then I am transported back to the sandy shores of Watch Hill, on Fire Island. I recall Chris's arms around my waist as the ferry chugged into the station and we hauled our bags, filled with picnic food and a bright umbrella for a day at the beach. We had been together only six weeks, but it was that time when everything sparkles. Everything you do together feels like playacting, a game of distraction—because all either of you really wants to do is to go to bed and fuck.

When I was lying on the sand, my skin wet and salty, he poured premade margaritas out of a flask into two paper cups and told me he was falling in love with me.

"It's like a sickness," he'd said, his finger tracing the edges of my bikini and down to the indent of my stomach. "It's consuming."

I'd felt like someone fired off a hundred sparklers inside me. I knew what he meant. Some days I could barely breathe thinking about him.

A bird calls nearby and I shake myself out of my reverie, tamping down the flicker of anger that memories of Chris can still bring, anger and sadness. There have been a few dates over the past two years, but it's been some time since I've been in the same proximity to a man—a very attractive man—in this kind of domestic setting.

As I pass Jake, I avert my eyes, and he does the same, examining the wisteria as I slip in through the back door.

While I'm up in my room, I peer through the window and watch Jake as he does his jumping jacks, and then his sit-ups, and then some kind of stretching routine whereby his head is twisted upward and he catches me staring at him through the window. I duck back out of the way.

My phone buzzes in my pocket and I see a message has come in from Maggie.

> Okay, I called the Agent, and apparently, she's had a lot of bogus requests for his work since he was on the show.

(Not surprising), so she really grilled me. Anyway, she
sent me some samples which I emailed to you. BTW he's
film not TV. In case you were wondering . . .

I message back quickly.

Me: Brilliant. Thanks. I'm just curious
Maggie: You're not "just" curious
Me: It's a background check. That's all 😊

Maggie texts me back a middle finger emoji and I laugh.

I open my email immediately, and there is the attachment,
a script titled *The Wild Years*. I feel a shiver of anticipation. Will
it be terrible? Will it be good? Will it be fiercely commercial,
some kind of *Fast & Furious* knockoff? Or navel-gazing, über-
serious? I stare down at Jake. I don't know the guy well, but it
won't be either of those.

I look back at the briefs, and then at the open script.

The briefs can wait.

Eight

~~~~~~~~

Oh, it's good. It's really, really good.

I put my phone down and lie back on the sofa, wiping the tears from my face as I let the full experience of *The Wild Years* wash over me. A coming-of-age story of two kids in Blackpool, Northern England: their run-ins with police and their parents, and their eventual runaway. It was heartbreaking and funny and uplifting and beautiful.

Who could have imagined? Jake Jones, a beautiful writer turned reality TV car crash. Had it all gotten too difficult to break through? *Did* he actually need money? Reading this story has left me with so many questions about my handsome neighbor and, admittedly, even a little more swoony for him. There is nothing sexier than a gift like this.

The next morning I pull myself off the sofa, yawn, stretch, and try to wake up with a cup of coffee. I was up until just after 2 a.m. finishing the screenplay, mainly because I had to keep stopping and googling photos of Jake to try to make sense of how this hunk o' junk, as he was being called on PopSlut's gossip pages, was actually a deeply beautiful writer.

I could see, however, why it was never made. I knew enough about film to know that the independent section of the market was increasingly struggling for money, and with cinemas closing down and nothing but Marvel, DC, and Tom Cruise getting the big money, sweet little indie films like this needed either someone with a *name* and impeccable connections to champion them, or a shitload of luck.

I look in the mirror as I get ready for work, pulling my hair back into a high ponytail and tucking my white T-shirt into my high-waisted jeans. Then I slip on my trainers, still not used to their casual comfort at work. In New York it was all high heels and blazers.

"You, Amy Duffy, are not just one bad day in July. You are not a hashtag. You are not a trending topic. You are thirty-two years of awesomeness," I say to myself, quickly nodding from side to side to indicate that I probably only believe it seventy-seven percent this morning, but that will do.

At work, I'm excited to dish with Maggie about how incredible the script is. But she's completely engrossed in her emails, and before I can utter a word she starts speaking, eyes still on her screen.

"They've hired the new person already," she says, glancing across at me. "Apparently, they're coming in today. But, look, it says 'interim head of development.' *Interim*."

"Interim? Interesting," I reply, eager to know more. "So, it could be an internal hire?"

"Could be, but unlikely. Who would it be?"

I nod in agreement. There really isn't anyone with the experience on our team.

"It's only been a week; they must have been working on it for a while," continues Maggie, and then she looks over at me and shrugs. "We'll find out soon enough, I guess."

Danny's email about the introduction comes just moments later, instructing us all to come to the area outside his office at 3 p.m.

"Shit. Certainly not wasting any time, are they?" I say as I open the folder containing the final version of the *Comeback Special* trailer. I click on it and hit play.

But rather than my usual sense of quiet pride at my weeks of work coming to fruition, I feel my stomach drop as I watch it. Memories of Jake's screenplay push their way into my thoughts as each brightly colored campy costume floats across the screen to the beat of some long-forgotten earworm from 1978, the voice-over booming out my fucking earnest script. I need to get into development again. I'm done with this shit.

"It looks great," says Maggie over my shoulder. "Excellent motion graphics."

I give her a look. Maggie made the graphics. Maggie makes all my graphics.

"What's wrong? You're not happy?"

"I'm not *not* happy," I say. "It just all seems so ridiculous suddenly."

"Oh, come on, that's what you love about it," she says, elbowing me in the shoulder.

"It needs irony," I say. "It's too *Glee*."

"You used to love *Glee*," Maggie says.

"Maybe you need more actual glee in your life to appreciate *Glee*," I mutter. "I have to go downstairs now and show it to the EP."

"She'll love it," Maggie says simply.

When I enter the studio, the lights are being tested at the same time as the audio, which means trying to have a conversation with Danny and the executive producer, Zadie, in what feels like a multicolored seizure.

"Don't fret about the distractions," Danny says, leaning over and hitting the space bar on my machine to start the trailer. I frown, but Danny's and Zadie's faces are fixed on my screen.

"It's perfect," says Zadie, standing up when it's finished. I blink several times, but before I can ask if she even heard it, she says wearily, "A perfect trailer for a perfect final season."

"Final season?" I say, snapping my laptop shut, wondering now if the trailer is "perfect" or if she just doesn't care because the series is being axed. But before I get an answer she's off in a waft of too much vanilla with background notes of Marlboro Red, leaning over a monitor on the stage floor, pointing at the screen with purpose. Zadie is probably the only *real* executive producer in this building, and it shows. She's great.

"Final season," says Danny with both eyebrows raised. "At least, those are the noises we're getting from the seventh floor. Zadie will be fine." He adds the part about Zadie perhaps because I look so surprised.

"Looks like the new guy is already making his opinions known." He looks at me for a moment as if he wants to say more, but doesn't.

"Speaking of. Danny, I want to move into the new development team," I say, looking down at my finger as I say it.

"Good. Good for you," says Danny, nodding, and I snap my head up, beaming at him.

"Any tips?" I ask. "Any inside knowledge you can share?"

"Write a really good pitch," he replies cheerily. "That's my tip."

I frown. "Danny, please?"

Danny slides his vibrating phone out of his pocket, answering. "He's here? I'll see you in fifteen," he says brightly to whoever is on the other end of the line. Then he hangs up and says less brightly to me, "The new interim head is here. I'll see you in a bit, Amy. And don't worry, this is all good. It's all positive." I'm not sure if he's talking to me or himself.

As I head back up in the elevator, an anxious excitement pulls gently at me, willing me to give in to its call. I want to be on this team. I want a job in development. It's intoxicating to feel this way again.

You, Amy Duffy, don't just want this job a little. You want this job more than you've wanted anything before.

When the new head of development starts, I'm going to hustle like I've never hustled before. I'm going to go for it.

At 3 p.m., we all gather around outside Danny's office, and I unwrap the bagel I brought for lunch and take a huge bite out of it. Someone pushes open a window, and someone else complains they must keep it shut for the air-conditioning to work. The breeze that comes in is indeed blisteringly hot.

"Maggie," I whisper, "can you please do me a favor and help me design my pitch when I've finished it?"

Maggie fake groans. "Fine," she says. "For you. And only because I'm excited to see you going for this, Amy." She gives me a side squeeze.

"Thank you, m'lady," I say, grinning gratefully and doing a wee curtsy.

"Don't," she says.

I turn my head at the sound of Danny's door opening and watch as he guides someone ahead of him and out into the crowded office. The usual murmurs ripple around the room.

"Oh shit," says Maggie, suddenly clutching my arm. "Shit, shit, shit."

"What?" I say, craning my head to see what she's seeing, but my view is obscured by my editor, Moe, who is standing just in front of me. Maggie has the advantage of being five foot ten and seeing over everyone else.

"Oh, Amy," Maggie says now, looking across at me, her face pinched in concern.

"What is it?" I reply hastily.

I lean forward and tap Moe out of the way, and he steps aside. And then I gasp. I gasp and I feel the whole of my insides squeezing and the room start to spin. I take a step forward, looking more closely, but just as I do, the person turns their head forward, a huge smile across their face, and looks directly at me.

"Hi, everyone," says Danny. "I'd like to introduce you to Chris Ellis."

Nine

I drop to the floor and gasp for breath.

"*Fuck, fuck, fuck, fuck,*" I repeat over and over and over again under my breath.

Then I do the only thing that makes sense in that moment. I crawl along the carpet, between the legs of my colleagues, toward the exit. I have to get out of here. *Now.*

"This is just a quick introduction. Chris Ellis was most recently the head of development at Wolf Studios in New York," Danny announces to the room. "But before that, he worked at Shine, NBC, and Turner Broadcasting in Atlanta."

I can't listen. I block it out the best I can as I make my way behind desks and around chairs, looking up to my colleagues and begging them with a finger to my lips to pretend I'm not there. My heart is pounding and I feel disorientated as I crawl over bags and shoes, clambering over the black plastic bottoms of the IKEA desk chairs with their octopus feet. It's crowded and difficult to find a route out with the least amount of interruption. And then I hear it. Chris's deep voice, like runny honey on buttered bread.

"Most recently, four Emmys for my work on . . ."

"Oh, for the love of God," I mutter. *Argh*. This cannot be happening.

"Amy." I hear Maggie's strangled whisper and turn to see her on hands and knees following me along the carpet, giving anyone who protests the Maggie Barnes look of death. She's like Moses parting the sea. "Amy! Wait!"

I turn my head, my neck craning over my shoulder. "Nope," I whisper, my voice like gravel. "No fucking way am I staying."

"Is everything okay over there?" Danny asks as the crowd above me reluctantly parts to let me through, their heads dropping to watch the commotion.

Maggie stands up. "Sorry, just dropped a contact lens," she says, buying me a moment to escape. "As you were, everyone!"

When I emerge from the semicircle of people, I keep myself crouched and run to my desk with the single aim of getting the fuck out of there as quickly as possible.

Maggie catches up and grabs me by the arm.

"Don't fucking run," she says.

"It's Chris," I say in an angry whisper. "It's *Chris*."

"It's not that surprising, is it?"

"Of course its fucking surprising," I say. "Surprising, shocking, awful, terrible, catastrophic, apocalyptic."

"Okay, it's a plot twist," she concedes, looking back over her shoulder at the crowd, who have burst into laughter at something Chris is saying. Maggie groans.

"Stupid, charismatic, still-fucking-handsome bastard," I growl angrily.

I pull my backpack on and clutch my stomach, my voice twisting with actual physical pain. "I'm going to throw up."

"No, you're not," says Maggie. "You're going to stay. And you're going to look him in the eye, and you're going to be fucking brave."

"I'm not brave," I snap, unfairly directing two years of pent-up rage at myself toward her. "I'm just not brave, Maggie. We established that some time ago."

"Amy. *Please*," she begs. "Please don't run. Not again."

My heart is pounding, and I don't have time for Maggie's lectures. I take in a deep breath and I shake my head. "I'm going. I'll call you later. *Don't* follow me."

I push past her and rush to head out the back to the elevators, hitting the down button repeatedly and praying that Chris stays on the other side of the glass door. From here, I can see his back. His hair is the same, closely cropped, and his sandstone linen suit jacket and dark blue chinos make him look like he's cosplaying as an Oxford graduate. My heart kicks up further as I see him waving again to the group. My colleagues. *Fuck*. They're finishing up.

I smash the down button again and glance across at the stairs. I rush toward the door, but just as I do, Chris emerges with Danny, and with nowhere to hide I have no option but to acknowledge them both.

I feel like someone has squeezed all the air out of me as they approach. Chris looks divine, as he always did. I notice his hair is a cut a little closer on the sides and slightly longer on top, and I can see stubble—something very un-Chris. It's good on him. Devastating, in fact. I wonder if he's just touched down from New York and come right in, and if this is the latest tweak to his look. Or has he just returned from, like, Greece? And if so, with whom? There are so many questions suddenly. And my blood boils.

"Amy," Danny says, looking quizzically at me as he watches me step back and press the down button again. I'm clearly agitated, so I fold my hands together and force a smile, my foot tapping fast on the carpet.

"I have an edit," I say, looking across at Chris briefly. I am praying he doesn't say anything to me. Praying, ridiculously, that he doesn't recognize me with my hair a few inches longer. I look down at my sneakers and feel wave after wave of shame.

"Did you miss the introduction, Amy? This is Chris Ellis," he says, smiling brightly. "But I think you two might have crossed paths before. I was going to ask you earlier, but Jeff swore me to secrecy until the contract was penned."

He chuckles at this, and the two men exchange warm grins. I recognize that early, welcoming chemistry before they surely will become rivals if Chris has anything to do with it.

"Hi, Chris," I say quickly, my voice sharp, a mix of anxiety and anger. My eyes beg him for some goodwill here. I'm clinging to the hope he has some tiny shred of compassion for me after what happened. *Please.*

Chris gallantly takes the cue. "Nice to see you again," he says, a very subtle knowing smile on his face. I recognize that look. *It's our secret*, it tells me. I've had that look from him so many times before. My eyes dart to the stairs again.

"Amy makes excellent trailers," says Danny as people from the office pour through the doors behind them, heading back to their various desks or toward the kitchen area. I don't dare lock eyes with anyone.

"Trailers?" Chris replies, his brow furrowing, and I feel my cheeks redden.

"But she's expressed interest in pitching for a role on your new development team," Danny is saying now, and I feel my throat begin to tighten. "Which is probably where you belong, isn't it, Amy? Under Chris."

Danny has no idea what he's just innocently said, but Chris cannot hold back a snort, and I wilt completely inside.

"Um," I say quickly. "I really, really have to go to an edit. Nice to see you again, Chris."

And with that, I hear the elevator *ding* behind me, watch Danny gesture toward it, and shake my head, pushing open the door to the stairs.

The trip home is a blur of wiped-away tears, rising beats of near panic, and a hasty visit to my local grocer, where I pick up a bottle of wine and then another (just in case), a bag of salt-and-vinegar potato chips, and a blow-up paddling pool from the seasonal shelf of summery plastic crap. I glare at Glenn as he scans my goods. *Say fucking something*, I dare him with my eyes. His never leave mine, but his expression is entirely blank. I press my card to the reader, and as I'm heading out the door he says, "Have an exciting evening."

I swing my head around and open my mouth to talk, but an elderly lady asks me gently to please move and I decide against it.

. . .

The first glass of wine goes down quickly, but my mind is scrambled as I sit on the Astroturf floor of the roof terrace blowing up my paddling pool. It's surprisingly tough to blow up a cheap plastic paddling pool, and I alternate between blowing and drinking when I need a break. My head is dizzy with the lack of oxygen, the wine, and the blunt trauma to my heart.

Fucking hell. What does this mean? Do I have to leave London now? I certainly have to leave CTV. But then, he's only the *interim* head. What does that mean? Does that mean he will be gone in a few months? Do I just have to get through a few months? Or is *interim* more like a year?

I blow again, harder now, and have to stop to gasp for air. I'm sweating in my jeans on this unshaded roof, and so I stand and peel them off, knocking back my second glass of wine in less than fifteen minutes.

How long will it take for everyone to find out about that fucking video? I'll need to admit we know each other; Danny knows. Maggie knows. It's not worth trying to keep that a secret. But the relationship. The *video*. Will Moe and Penny find it now? How about Danny? My stomach tightens, and I let out an almighty scream into the air above.

I feel the sting of tears in my eyes, but I push them away, feeling vaguely satisfied as the pool stiffens into a perfect ring. I stare at it. *Okay, Amy, you've inflated a fucking toddler paddling pool. Now you have to fill the fucking thing. Didn't think about that, did you?*

I head down to my apartment, keys still in the door. I snatch them out and fill a jug with lukewarm water and head up the stairs, tipping the contents into the pool. It barely makes a difference, and the slight angle of the roof makes the water run to one side.

"Fucking cunting cunts," I murmur, taking another sip of my wine as I walk up and back another three times until there is a centimeter of water and I've had enough. I head down one last time, change into a red one-piece swimsuit I bought off a costume director who worked on the kitsch-as-fuck nineties classic *Baywatch*. I look like I'm cosplaying as I slide my mirrored aviator Ray-Bans back on. I grab my phone out of my bag, quickly skim/read several messages of comfort and encouragement from Maggie among her many missed calls, and then wander back upstairs, tripping on the top step as I go.

I'm becoming drunk, *quickly*.

Good.

It's my job, I think, wailing to myself as I hear the door to the roof slam behind me.

It's my fucking town, I think as I stare out across the rooftops of London, swigging back another chug of wine, wiping away a tear that has forced its way out and down my cheek.

It's my fucking roof terrace, I think as I see Jake's big red barbecue in the corner and some new outdoor furniture, which, while obviously a wonderful addition, is also a symbol of yet another man encroaching on my life and space and happiness.

I take an awkward seat in the pool, feeling a little more pleased as the water rises a few millimeters, and just as I do, the terrace door opens and Jake is standing there, concern scrawled all over his face.

"I heard a door slam," he says, "I just wanted to—"

"What?" I say.

Jake looks at me, and then at the wine next to me, and then smirks. "You're okay, then?"

"I'm a *lifeguard*," I say. "A lifeguard of my own tiny terrace pool." I splash at the minuscule amount of water with my fingers.

"Looks like the tide is out," he says as his eyes move from my face down to the rainbow-striped paddling pool, and then, I notice, down the length of my bare legs, which are dangling over the edge.

"Come on out here, Jake Jones," I say, swallowing a burp. My stomach churns with anxiety and thirteen and a half percent Australian Chardonnay. "You can come and join me on my terrace."

"Well, thanks, I was actually going to—"

"I am *drunk*," I announce flatly. Then I take a huge swig directly out of the bottle to make the point that I am *really* drunk. I probably also look slightly unhinged. I put the bottle down on the turf next to me, and it teeters but doesn't fall. My body slips sideways against the wet plastic as I lean over the rubber rim of the pool.

"I tried to fill it all the way. You really need a hose, and there isn't a spout on the roof," I say. "I'm just so hot. I miss the ocean."

"I understand," he replies, slowly pulling his eyes away from my legs.

"Would you like to join me for a drink so I can tell you about how terrible my day has been?" I wave at the rest of the terrace, indicating he should find somewhere to sit.

Jake doesn't answer. His mouth pulls down at the sides, and he looks back over his shoulder like maybe he should get help. I lift the bottle of wine again, but then when I hold it up to look at the level, I notice there is really only a single glass left. Sheesh, on an empty stomach too. It's no wonder I'm so drunk.

"Oh, maybe not," I say. "I appear to have drunk away all of my feelings and all of my wine."

"I have a beer in my fridge," he says.

"Oh, a whole one beer. Party time," I reply, and it comes out rather more sarcastic than I mean it to. He frowns, shielding his eyes as he looks up toward the hot sun.

"I've . . . um . . . been trying to avoid any more embarrassing incidents," he says, looking a bit sheepishly at his shoes. "I know you saw the show."

"Well, good news, Jake," I say, squinting slightly so I see one Jake instead of two. "You're old news now. Yesterday's gossip. No more Jake the Jerk." Again, this comes out rather more cruelly than I mean it to, but I'm starting to feel my head spinning.

"I was going to cook up some sausages," he replies after a beat, the crease returning between his brows as he eyes the bottle that has now slipped out of my hand and fallen onto the Astroturf. I scoop it up quickly.

"Nothing spilled!" I yelp. "Nothing has spilled, because nothing is left." I put my hand to my forehead. "Oh God. I think I'm really drunk."

"Didn't your mum ever tell you not to drink in the sun?" he asks.

"Yes. And you'll go blind if you watch too much television.

And don't swim until thirty minutes after lunch, which is bullshit, by the way."

"I think the not drinking in the sun is a good tip," he says again. "I'll get you some water."

"I can't actually get up anyway," I say, removing my sunglasses and rubbing my eyes.

Jake returns after some time with a large glass of ice-cold water, a bundle of fatty pink sausages, some bread, and a bottle of ketchup. He hands the glass to me and says, "You should drink this." He then disappears and comes back, yanking on the end of a hose. "Top-up?" he asks, pointing the hose into the pool next to me.

"How did you—?"

"It's from the garden. I fixed it to the faucet in the kitchen," he replies.

"Not just a pretty face?" I say, and I see his eyes roll slightly.

"A top-up please," I say, moving my leg and bracing myself as the cold water starts to flow.

Jake is looking away, across the garden, because there is no denying, even in my state, that the act of a man hosing you, or next to you, while you're in a swimsuit is . . . quite erotic. The stream of water moves slightly as he glances at the barbecue, hitting my thigh. It takes me a moment to adjust my position, but the splash back has soaked my chest, face, and hair.

"Let me know when you've had enough," Jake says, and I have to swallow to stop myself from giggling. He finally glances down and quickly runs inside to turn the hose off, realizing, I suspect, how weirdly intimate this is.

"Why are you being nice?" I ask when he returns, the cold

water ushering in a moment of clarity. "I thought you wanted to be left alone."

Jake shrugs and then heads over to fire up the barbecue. "I just got you some water," he says, ripping open the packet of sausages and cracking back the tab of the can of beer. I reach over and tear open my bag of chips and force down a few mouthfuls, my stomach still unsettled. The vinegary flavoring stings my mouth and adds to the feeling of queasiness.

"Why was your day so bad?" he asks.

My day. The brief distraction of the last fifteen minutes falls instantly away and my head drops. I run my finger across the LIFEGUARD logo on my swimsuit, and everything continues to sharpen. My day. My terrible day.

My eyes feel heavy and I look at Jake and I am about to ask him if he's ever done anything so stupid, so deeply humiliating, that if anyone saw it, his life would feel over. But no, I know Jake knows *that* feeling. So instead I ask, "Have you ever been so close to something . . . No, close to everything you've ever wanted and had it snatched away? By someone you really love?"

Jake stiffens, puts down the sausages he's about to grill, and appears to think very carefully about his reply. "No," he replies quietly. "Not *exactly* that."

"Right," I say, "because I have. And let me tell you, it's fucking brutal."

And just as Jake is about to reply, I throw up. Large, potato-chip-chunk-filled streams of acidic wine. All over myself and in the pool.

Ten

I wake up on a sofa I don't recognize in an apartment I do not know. A feeling I'm familiar with from my roaring twenties, but at thirty-two it feels more than a little undignified. I'm in a T-shirt and a pair of boxer shorts, neither of which is my own. Slowly, like a figure emerging from the mist, a picture of unimaginable horror emerges.

Last night I threw up. And then . . . *Oh my God.*

I want the sofa to envelop me. I want to disappear in between the cushions and curl myself up among the cold metal springs.

I recall Jake handing me the hose, helping me to wash myself down as I . . . cried? Was I crying? I try to picture his face—was he angry? Did he judge me?

Then he somehow helped me down to my flat, but we realized that I'd managed to drunkenly lock my keys inside. I have flashes of him trying to get hold of our landlady, Agnes, while I sat in my wet swimsuit, his towel around me. She wasn't home, and in the end, with no other options, he offered me his couch.

I recall him handing me his freshly laundered soft cotton T-shirt and a pair of boxer shorts that were still in the package, and then closing the door to his bathroom so I could wash the wine and chunks of potato chips out of my hair. I recall him putting a sheet and a pillow on his sofa, and a soft pale gray cashmere blanket, which he told me was a present from his mother one Christmas years ago. I remember him explaining to me his mother gives everyone cashmere for Christmas. At least, she used to. I remember him saying that. That she *used* to. Did his mother die? He said something about missing her.

I remember him checking in on me, but I cannot remember if it was a dream that he came to the side of the sofa and took away the wet towel I'd left on the floor next to me. I remember telling him my mom said you should never go to sleep with wet hair, and that he laughed and suggested one time wouldn't kill me.

And then I remember what I said before he closed his living room door.

"You're a beautiful writer, Jake Jones," I said. "*The Wild Years* was beautiful."

And now I'm awake in his apartment, presumably still locked out of mine, and he is asleep somewhere close by.

And then I remember the reason all this came to pass.

Chris. I feel my empty stomach churn.

My head pounds as I pull myself up, noticing the glass of water and the two acetaminophen that have been left on an up-turned milk crate Jake is using for a coffee table. The whole room is in a state of his having just moved in. There's a large record collection, boxed but opened, and his Bakelite record player is plugged in but sitting on the floor. In the corner of the room is a little desk with a good office chair and an Apple laptop, closed. A cup with several pens, a closed notebook, and some paperwork that I can see is emblazoned with the *Fantasy Island* logo.

I thirstily down the water and both pills.

Then I notice my keys sitting on the floor next to my phone and my wet swimsuit in a plastic bag, and I cringe with embarrassment. What time is it? Has he already spoken to Agnes, then, and gotten my keys for me?

I pick up my keys and my phone and I creep to the front door, turning the knob as quietly as I can. I push the door open and slip out into the hallway, pulling the door gently shut behind me. Then I head back upstairs to my apartment and start the coffee maker.

I pace around my apartment while I wait for the coffee to percolate, pausing briefly to look into the hallway mirror.

"You are Amy Duffy. You're a fucking nightmare, and you're never going to escape your past," I say to my reflection. My still slightly damp hair needs conditioner and a brush. There are huge bags under my eyes, but the best part is the slight red sunburn that has appeared in a perfect mirrored aviator cutout on my face.

I look . . . dreadful.

And then I pick up my phone, with its twelve percent battery, and I call the only person who can help make sense of all this—Maggie.

"Amy," she says breathlessly. "I called and I called."

"Sorry, I self-medicated in the sun and I made myself a bit sick."

"Heatstroke," she says.

"Maybe. I didn't think you could get heatstroke in London," I say. "I thought I'd be wearing petticoats and fortune hunting." I laugh, but my laugh is hollow, and Maggie hears it.

"Oh, sweetheart," she says, the compassion in her voice forcing out my tears.

"What am I going to do?" I ask her, sniffing. "I was so excited, Maggie. *Finally.* I held that brief in my hand and I was ready to go for it. I was going to pitch an idea and try to get a job . . ."

"You should *still* pitch, Amy," she says.

"Why? So I can work with Chris again?"

"He's not necessarily going to stay. He's the interim head, remember," Maggie says. "But regardless of that. You should still go for that job because it's the career you deserve. The best revenge is success, honey. Show him what you're made of."

"I pissed on his car," I remind her.

"Fuck the damn video," Maggie says. "It's been two years."

"You can still find it online," I say.

"Not really. It's actually quite hard to. It was the first thing I looked for when I got home last night. It was of momentary interest to work and people who knew you in New York, but it's not like you were the public face of outdoor urinating or anything."

"There was a hashtag," I say woefully.

"Let me put this in television terms, so you understand it.

You, Amy Duffy, are a walk-on part in most people's lives. There are almost eight billion people on this damn planet. They do not want or need to know your backstory. And if they do, it's a funny story over a pint. You didn't kill anyone. You didn't hurt anyone. You made a bit of a dick of yourself, but who hasn't?"

You probably never have, I think, imagining Maggie's perfect hair bobbing from side to side as she lectures me. Maggie, with her impeccable social media accounts and scrupulous work ethic. I hear Maggie tut. She's given me this speech in a number of ways over the last two years, but this is definitely the version where she is losing all her patience.

"I feel like I should be offended," I say.

"Fuck me, what the hell else are you going to do? You can't run again, Amy."

"I can't?" I say, glancing over at the small globe that sits perched on my bookshelf. *What about New Zealand?* I find myself thinking.

"He's not going to tell anyone about the video, is he? It undermines him as much as it does you," she says now. "The only thing you need to navigate here is Chris, and he's not your boss. Not yet. Maybe not ever. Danny said he won't start officially until next week. Maybe he's only staying until the unit is set up. He will be on a different floor. And the pitches are not happening until the end of the summer. You can avoid him completely if you want to."

"At Wolf I saw him all day every day," I say weakly.

"This is not a small production company, it's a big-ass broadcaster. You can hot desk in the basement with the editors if you have to."

"And then what?"

"You get the job, you don't get the job, you find it's not so bad, or you find it is so bad you decide to find another job. You can't plan this out like a production, Amy. You need to take baby steps and see."

Maggie takes a breath. I say nothing for a moment, allowing her advice to settle. She's right that I could avoid him. He'll be on seven, and I'll be on five. I know he likes to be in most days around 8 a.m. I know he leaves early because he eats out most nights and likes a beer after work. I know he likes a very light lunch at his desk. I know he'll join the closest gym with a pool and that he will swim twice a week and weight train the other days.

The memories wash over me.

"Maybe . . . ," I say tentatively. "But why on earth would I want to have my career in his hands again?"

"It's not just him on the panel; it's the new Stream Global team. Danny is in your corner, Amy. Think of it this way— imagine you did such a good job and everyone on the panel wants *you*. How is Chris going to stop you?"

"He did on *The Darkening Web*. He blocked it."

"Because he was responsible for presenting it. You weren't even in the room. This time it's *you*. It's all you. No one can stop you." Maggie had a point. He wasn't going to be quite as powerful in this scenario. He couldn't stop me from presenting my own work this time.

"Maggie, isn't it easier to just find another development studio? To send out my CV? I was ready to start looking. Can't I just see this as the little push I need?"

"Don't. Run," she says firmly.

"I still feel like everything is ruined," I say. "I'm not sure if I can pick myself up again, Maggie."

"Okay, you're hungover. You need sleep and you need a fresh head."

"You're right about that," I say, rubbing at my temples. "I love you. I'm going to call in sick today and just pull my shit together."

"You can really fucking do this, Amy," she says one last time.

"I wish I had your faith in me, Maggie," I say back.

"So do I, darling."

When we hang up, I pour myself a huge coffee, and I head to my laptop and send a quick email to Penny to say that I have a stomach bug. *Almost true.*

I think about googling *Amy Duffy*, just to see. But I know I'm too fragile right now, and if that damn video shows up it will crush me. I have been lucky that the clip was uploaded but not tagged with my name. Last I checked, there were a few versions: "Drunk Bridesmaid Pees on Audi" and "Bitch Totals Car with Drunk Piss." The crucial key here is that if people know there is a video of me, they can find it. Googling any combination of *bridesmaid*, *Audi*, *toilet*, *slip*, and my personal favorite, *soft-top flop*, will turn it up.

I cringe, my heart picking up as I think about Chris.

Chris.

There's a soft knock on my door.

"Amy?" says Jake, deep and low.

I move to stand by the door, but I don't open it. "I'm so sorry," I say.

"Don't think about it," he says soothingly.

"I don't want to open the door. I'm ashamed," I say, leaning forward so my forehead rests against the cool wood. "I have a sunglasses outline on my face, and I'm wearing your underwear."

"You don't have to open it. Just checking you're alive and made it home."

"Yes," I reply. "I made it the long walk home."

He laughs lightly. Then there is a long pause.

"Did you really call my agent and get a copy of my screenplay?"

"Yes," I say, my heart sinking as I do. It was an incredibly invasive thing for me to have done. "Well, not me, it was my friend at work, Maggie."

"Maggie Barnes?"

"Yes. I'm sorry. I shouldn't have."

"My agent said she was very insistent," he says.

"That's Maggie," I say, cringing as I imagine what she had to say to get the script.

"Do you *really* work in development?"

"Yes," I say, and then I close my eyes and breathe out slowly. "I used to, anyway. And maybe I will again soon. I'm not sure. I've read a lot of screenplays, like maybe hundreds, and yours was *really* good. I got this really giddy chill all over when I finished it. I could see the film. All the characters. I could see each frame. It's hard to explain it, but when you read a script and you get that feeling, you just *know*. I haven't felt like this in years. Not since the first draft of . . ." I stop myself from going into a rant about *The Darkening Web*. "Well, you get it. You can hear what I'm saying, right?"

It's hard to know how this lands without seeing him, but I *hope* he feels even a little bit proud, just for a moment.

"Huh," is all Jake says. But there is a hint of surprise in there. And maybe even a tiny hint of pleasure. Pleasant surprise.

"Don't give up," I say quickly, a knot forming in my stomach as I say it. It echoes around in my mind, wanting to settle, but I push the words away. *These* words are for Jake.

There is another long pause, and then he says, "That's what they say. But it's difficult to keep going—"

"I know," I say, jumping in. "You just have to pick yourself up and keep going."

"That's what they say," he says again. Then after another long pause he says, "Well, see you soon, Amy Duffy." And then I hear the patter of his feet as he heads down the stairs. I listen to the sound of his door opening and then closing swiftly behind him. He's gone.

I breathe slowly out. *What are you going to do, Amy? Are you going to give up?*

I look back at my reflection. *No, I'm not going to give up.*

If I can hand out that advice to Jake, I have to take it myself.

And then I get this prickling sensation on the back of my neck as something begins to form. A shadow of a plan. I head to my bedroom and open the closet, getting down onto my hands and knees, fishing around looking for a little shoebox I know is there until my hand touches it.

Inside on top is an assortment of photos of my family in

New York—I have not had the bravery to put them on display. I rummage around until I find it. A black Moleskine notebook. Each page is covered in black ink—my signature tiny writing, drawing, doodles, thoughts, sparks. My notebook of a million ideas that I used as my creative bible when I was at Wolf. Not a millimeter of it wasted; in truth it looks like the diary of a madman.

I flick through the pages, and I find the last page, my scribbled notes from just before the green-light meeting two years ago. That fateful day. The words I'd scrawled underneath a ballooned doodle: *You Got This*.

I really thought I did.

I sit back, the photos splayed out across the floor, the notebook clutched to my chest.

"No more running," I say. "No more."

Eleven

~

I feel nervous when I knock on Jake's door the following morning. I've gotten a bit more dressed up than usual, mostly to show Jake how much I am *not* the person in the red *Baywatch* swimsuit who puked on herself. I've brushed and straightened my hair to a mirror shine and I'm wearing a cute houndstooth shift with an oversized collar by A.P.C. and black ballerina flats. It's how I would have dressed in New York for a big day at work. Preppy, smart, and elegant. I adjust the dress so it sits perfectly.

He answers in a pair of salmon linen trousers and a long-sleeved Breton shirt like some sexy dark-haired yachtsman from the French Riviera. And just in time to stop me from embarrassing myself with a jauntily delivered "Hello, sailor," Jake jumps in.

"How you doing? Better?" he asks.

"Yes, here are your boxer shorts, laundered. And your T-shirt. Also laundered." I hand the pile to him, which he takes, somewhat reluctantly. I think we both are unclear if I should have returned the boxers.

"Thanks," he says, squeezing his lips together in a sympathetic smile.

"I am, once again, mortified by the state of me the other night. I had something horrible happen at work, and I handled it terribly, but I'm completely fine now."

"You are?" he says, his head cocked slightly.

"While you haven't seen me at my worst, the other night was close," I say.

He laughs at this, a throaty sound filled with merriment that just reaches the corners of his eyes. It's dazzling. I think for a moment how I'd love to see a full smile from Jake Jones.

"But yes, I *am* completely fine. And I wanted to also say sorry again for invading your privacy over your screenplay. Which, as I said, was very good." I swallow and take a deep breath. "And I have a proposition for you."

"A proposition?"

"Yes, a proposition." I nod.

"What kind of proposition?" he asks, a wry smile on his face as he glances at the floor, then slowly raises his eyes to meet mine.

"Oh, no," I say, spluttering. "Not that. Good God, *no*." I shake my head frantically, feeling the heat rising from my neck to my face. Instinctively, I lift the back of my hand to my right cheek to try to cover the scarlet blush that has surely appeared.

"I see," he says, laughing now. He's playing with me.

"Not that you're not . . ." I grimace. "*Propositional.* I mean, come on. You're . . ." I wave at his body with my free hand.

Jake fully smiles now, his eyes exuding a boyish mischief, which is so intoxicating it should be illegal in every country in Europe. *God help me.*

I cough and try to rein the conversation in. Steer it back to the serious.

"What I'm trying to propose," I begin, "is a job."

"A job?"

"Yes. You're not working right now, correct?"

"I guess so," he says, pursing his lips slightly. "Yes."

I feel nervous. Jake seems to notice with the slight raise of an eyebrow.

"In fact, do you have time for coffee? I don't think I can propose this proposition in the hallway."

"I see," he says.

"We could go up to my apartment and have one? Or, better still, have a morning coffee on the terrace?"

"I have to say, I'm intrigued," he says, narrowing his gaze. The look is intense, and I drop my eyes to the floor. I will have to find a way to look Jake in the eye if what I'm proposing here is going to work. And throw some cold water on my attraction to him.

"I'll make the coffee, because I'm *American* and you can't do coffee," I begin.

"And I'll make myself a tea," he says, "because I'm British."

"Okay, tea. *Great.* You make that and I'll meet you there in . . ." I look at my watch. It's 8:15, and if I'm going to get to work on time and face the music there, we're going to have to do this fast. "Fifteen minutes enough?"

"I can be there in five?" he says. "It's not a long journey."

I laugh once, loudly, and then feel my cheeks burn. Again. Then I curtsy for some reason, and flee.

I pace the terrace before taking a seat at Jake's little table that he brought up and concede that both that and the barbecue have made more of a positive impact here than anything I've done in the last two years. I feel shame, noting that the blow-up paddling pool has been cleaned and turned over to dry out.

Jake arrives almost right away, with his cup of tea in a bright blue mug. He walks over, his eyes flickering up to meet mine, before he slides into the seat opposite me. Our legs brush, and it takes a moment to maneuver ourselves so we're not touching. He places his tea down, spinning it once, and then, rubbing both hands on the sides of his thighs, he smiles a smile that says, *Your move, Amy.*

I take a deep breath.

"Hey. So. This . . . um . . ." I am playing with the ring on my finger and digging deep to try to find the right way to say this. "I guess, first of all, Maggie said that your agent said you were taking a break from writing."

"Yes," he says.

"Is it a fixed break? A long one? Can I ask why?"

"Is it important? The why?" he asks, furrowing his brow.

"Uh. No, I guess. I should really start with what I want," I say, nodding furiously. God, when did I get so bad at this? This is a conversation with a writer—I've had dozens such conversations. Though never like this. Always as Wolf Studios, the big, bold production house with a reputation as shiny as the trophies in its foyer. I've never had this conversation as Amy fuckin' Duffy.

"In New York, I was a development executive at Wolf Studios. Do you know them?"

He shakes his head.

Great.

"Right, well, maybe not, since you do film. But they're one of the top TV production houses in America. I mean, I'm not just saying that, you can google or just read *Deadline*'s announcements. And, Jake, I was very good at my job once upon a time." My eyes flick up to him to check his temperature—he's intrigued, if slightly amused.

"I *was* really very good, and I was directly involved with three major series being green-lighted, and several others . . ." My mind wanders to *The Darkening Web*, and I feel a pang of anger that nothing came of it. "Several others were completely my own, one of which came very close to being green-lighted."

I lock eyes with Jake. *There.* I'm proud of myself for saying it all out loud.

"Something happened with a . . . um . . . *project*, and I left New York and I left working in development. But the company I work for now, CTV, is going to launch a new development unit, with a huge financial investment from its new owners, Screen Global."

"Screen Global?" he says, his eyebrows raised slightly.

"That's right," I reply. "You can google that as well, after we've spoken."

"I don't need to google Screen Global," he says, shifting in his seat slightly. *I've got him on the hook*, I think. Now to gently reel him in.

"And so, they're hiring. They have put out some briefs. They've asked for ideas as part of that process."

"I see," he says. "And those ideas will lead to a job? For *you*?"

"Well, yes, but that isn't all of it." I clasp my hands together on the table, then, looking up from his untouched tea to him, I clear my throat. "The hope is that the idea would be picked up. And that's where *you* come in."

I smile broadly at him, biting my lip as I wait for him to join the dots. But he just narrows his eyes, waiting for me to continue.

"So, Jake Jones, how would you feel about working up some ideas with me to pitch to the new unit in the hope that if I get the job, we could get the idea—our idea—properly green-lighted? It's in just seven weeks. First week of August."

Jake says nothing but takes a sip of his tea as the question settles over us. The morning sun finally peeks out from behind the slate roof and hits me in the eyes. I won't have long until it heats up. I glance at my watch.

"I'm going to need more information," he says, his eyes skewering me. "What do you mean by '*our idea*'?"

"You know, like we brainstorm together," I say. "I have briefs, so it's not totally speculative. They're looking explicitly for particular types of shows."

"Okay," he says cautiously.

"I need a sparring partner who understands *story*," I say. "My skill is understanding the market, refining concepts so they are perfectly pitched. I can get ideas sold. Potentially *your* ideas. This is a big opportunity for both of us."

Jake nods that he understands, but I feel like I need to ram it home.

"I know what works, but I can't write a script. Like, I *could*, but it would be terrible."

Jake looks down at his hands for a moment. He isn't saying no. "So, you're asking me to work on a proposal for a TV series with you and to potentially write the script on spec?"

I take a large sip of my coffee and nod.

"I don't know exactly what's happened with *Fantasy Island*, but I have the feeling that maybe you wanted to move on from that?" I say gently.

"Yes," he says.

"And I would hate to see you not do anything with your gift. This could be something to distract you? Dip your toe back in and see if you want to keep writing? You can do as much time or as little as you want. We could start by just chatting and you could see?"

"It's intriguing," he says, and I breathe out with relief.

He leans forward, putting his hand around his mug of tea. "I'll think about it." I cannot read his tone. He could mean it, or he could be letting me down easy so he can escape this conversation. "There need to be some guarantees or something. I can't work all summer for nothing."

"Of course," I say. "You name your conditions and I'll do what I can to make them work."

He cocks his head slightly. "Because it can't just be about getting you a job."

"Absolutely not," I say, trying to remain as cool as I can. "I can't pay you cash. I'm doing this in my own time too. But we could talk about . . . maybe there is some other way I can pay you? I have a lot of contacts across the industry, for example." But, as I say it, I bite my lip. I haven't spoken to those contacts in around two years. Do they even exist as contacts anymore? Would they respond to an email from publicly shamed Amy Duffy?

Jake's face registers interest, but he remains silent.

"Do you want to see the briefs, then?" I ask a bit nervously.

"Sure, send them."

I reach down into my backpack and pull out a bright pink Post-it pad and a pen. He scrawls his number and email address on a sheet and slides it back to me.

"Thank you," I say almost breathlessly. There *is* a little hope here. "I'll think about how I can make this worth your while."

"Let's see," he says with a noncommittal smile.

I look down at his scrawled writing for a moment, and then, because I feel like it might help me understand his situation better, I ask, "Why *did* you go on *Fantasy Island*? If you don't mind speaking about it."

Jake breathes out and nods as he sits back in his chair. He fidgets, lifting a hand up to push his hair back from his face, rubbing the stubble on his cheek with his fingers for a moment.

"It's a long story," he says simply.

"I'd love to understand," I say.

"Understand?"

"Yeah, I guess, I mean. You know. You said it was a mistake," I say, stammering for the right words. *Gah.*

Jake doesn't reply, but there is an almost imperceptible nod.

It's all he gives me, and before the silence becomes awkward I jump in. "Well, Jake. I have to get to work. I'll send the briefs, and then we can talk?"

He nods and I stand, knocking the table, and his tea nearly topples. I put my backpack on and wave an anxious good-bye as I head toward the door of the terrace.

"Don't let the fucker bring you down," says Jake.

"Excuse me?"

"The guy at work who made you feel like shit?" he says. "Fuck him."

I gasp, opening the door and turning to him. "How much did I tell you?"

"Not much," he says, his jaw fixed, his eyes serious. Then he softens and smiles. "Enough to know that if I take this on, I might be complicit in some kind of revenge."

I groan.

"It's okay," he says. "That part I'm completely on board with."

Twelve

~~~~~~~~

I'm fizzing with hope. It is incredible how your spirits can lift—suddenly London feels not like a place to hide away, but rather like a place full of opportunity. The colors are brighter. I find myself walking with my head up, smiling at strangers as I head into work. Summer in London is in full swing after yesterday's record June temperatures, and there are predictions of a long heat wave to follow. This morning, I take a different route to work, heading up from the bottom of Soho's theater district, down some small cobbled alleys, round onto Carnaby Street, and up toward my office.

As I near the office, however, I can feel my nerves start to fray.

Chris. Chris is still a very real and unavoidable danger.

It takes everything in me to walk through the entrance of CTV. I have no real plan for how to avoid him, except to take a deep breath, keep my wits about me, and try to spend the day at my desk with the least amount of building wandering I can do. He's on the seventh floor, so I should be okay. Just keep to limited time in the shared areas: the kitchen, the café, the area outside the elevators.

"*Fantasy Island!*" bellows Gabby from behind the security desk as my heart slams hard in my chest and I move quickly through the lobby.

"I've stopped watching," I say, pulling a sad face as I keep walking.

"You stopped watching?" she repeats, dropping the *pain au chocolat* she's eating onto the desk in exasperation.

"*The Comeback Special* has kept me *busy,*" I say, nodding toward its paraphernalia—mirror balls, posters, cardboard cut-outs of the hosts—currently adorning the lobby. Normally I would have stopped to admire it, but not today.

"I feel abandoned!" she wails as I walk backward toward the elevators, head shaking apologetically.

The elevator doors open just as I approach, and I walk in, breathing a sigh of relief. This is what I need, a quick entrance every day. But, to my irritation, the elevator goes down instead of up. When the doors open on the basement, one of the studio runners rolls a trolly filled with sequin-covered costumes in next to me.

"Morning," she says wearily, not really looking at me.

"*The Comeback Special?*"

"*The Comeback Special,*" she replies as the doors close and we start to head up. But, to my frustration, she presses the ground floor button again. When the doors open I feel his presence before I see him.

Chris. And the CTV CEO, Jeff. Both suited and coiffed.

They enter the elevator mid–top-level secret conversation but end it swiftly as the doors shut. Jeff gives me a polite smile, his face sun-kissed and heavily lined. His smile is the kind the CEO gives to an employee they've never actually met but recognize the face of, *somehow*.

Chris, however, grins at me. My eyes briefly meet his, and he *looks* genuine. He *looks* happy to see me, even. I brush down the front of my houndstooth dress, pleased that I look so put together today. It feels like a small act of revenge when I see his eyes flicker to my legs.

"Hey again, Amy," he says, lifting his head. No hint of teasing or playfulness.

Jeff's head swings to look back at me; he's surprised, I suppose, that Chris is familiar with someone in the company already. Chris picks up on this and says to Jeff, "Amy and I worked together in New York, didn't we, Amy?"

"Yes," I say quietly, eyes to the floor again.

It's the strangest cascade of emotions. A mixture of anger and weakness. A bottled-up fury that I have never gotten to fully express because I cannot make sense of how at fault I am for all that happened. Chris may have pissed all over my show and broken my heart, but I pissed all over his Audi.

Mercifully the elevator doors open and I walk straight out, shooting a weak, "Bye," over my shoulder as I find myself disorientated on the third floor, where a dozen silent heads turn to face me.

I've walked into IT.

I back slowly toward the stairs.

. . . .

"How are you getting on?" Maggie asks, her face etched with concern, when I finally get to my desk.

"Terrible start to the day, but whatever. Fine," I grumble, opening up the email with the briefs and quickly forwarding it on to Jake. Then I turn to her and I breathe out. "I'm here. I'm alive. I'm ready to fight another day."

"I'm proud of you, Amy," she says gently, touching my arm as she does. "And I'm loving this look, by the way. You look good."

"I dusted off the old professional armor. It helps for when I see Chris. I've already seen the slippery fucker in the elevator."

"I love that you're motivated by hate," she says. "I'm here for your vengeful glossy-haired era."

"Well. Honestly, I wanted him to eat his heart out when he saw me," I say, lowering my voice and frowning. "How can I even think that when I absolutely hate the sight of him?"

"You never fully grieved—" Maggie begins.

We are interrupted by Penny, who reminds us the production meeting is starting in fifteen minutes, and that *Amy* has not submitted items for the agenda.

"I'm on it!" I say with a forced grin.

"Did you get a chance to think through it all yesterday?" Maggie asks as I open the group meeting folder and start to type in my updates.

"I sure did," I reply. "I'm taking your advice and I'm going to just fucking go for it with the job."

I am about to tell her about Jake, but I stop myself. He hasn't said yes yet.

"Thank God," says Maggie, exhaling like she's been holding her breath for the last millennium. "Oh, thank God. I was so worried you were going to pull a Duffy."

"Pull a Duffy?"

"Pull a Duffy. *Do a runner*," she replies, mimicking a comical runner with her fists, and it forces me into a laugh.

My raucous cackle startles the design team, who sit in front of us. *Sorry*, I mouth. *I'm mad.*

And I feel it. I feel giddy and excited about Jake on the one hand, and like the walls are closing in on me on the other. I'm living through a wild dream–cum–nightmare and it's slowly encircling me, like a pack of wolves. Or, no, digesting me, like a giant worm with a human face, teeth, and an acidic gut.

"Amy, you look like you're going to be sick," says Maggie.

"Sorry, I was thinking about Chris." I finish up my agenda notes, and I stand. "Shall we?"

In the meeting, Danny tells us with some enthusiasm that CTV will host a big summer party this year. "After a few quiet years, with not a lot in the way of work parties and events, Screen Global thought it would be nice to get everyone together for a proper knees-up. Celebrate the marriage. A chance to network," he says. Maggie shoots me an excited grin, and I shake my head slowly back at her. Then I flick up my computer and type out a private message on our team Slack channel.

Me: Let the schmoozing games begin.

Maggie: Hunger games more like.

Me: I'm going to have to go, aren't I?

Maggie: It's every bitch for herself in this merger.

I giggle, and Danny snaps his head to look at me, and I swallow my smile.

"The Screen Global team will be there too, and the great news is you can bring a plus-one. Though why anyone would want to bring a partner is beyond me." He pulls a face at the team and a few people titter. Danny is always so publicly bitter about his divorce.

Maggie: Partners? Jesus. What is this?
Me: It's the ultimate Job Interview by proxy. Get us drunk. See who behaves.

Penny picks up from Danny with excitement. "We're doing this in style. The Roxy off Covent Garden."

Maggie: The Roxy? Who told them it was stylish?

I laugh this time, and Penny tuts and I mouth, *Sorry*, to her.

"You'll get an invite later today and you have to RSVP by next Friday. *Now, this is essential.* So please don't ignore my email, as you usually do." I feel a pang of frustration on Penny's behalf and catch her eye to let her know that at the very least, I, Amy Duffy, take all her emails very seriously.

We are interrupted as the boardroom door flies open.

"Ahh, here he is. Everyone met Chris briefly the other day, and from today he's going to be getting a feel for all the different departments. This morning, some insight into the creative team. A glimpse at how we put our campaigns together."

I slide down in my chair behind my screen. Danny nods to Chris to please take a seat.

Me: Of course he's here. He's fucking everywhere. He's worse than the Marvel franchise.
Maggie: Breathe, Batman.
Me: DC Comics.
Maggie: ?
Me: I can't teach you this stuff. You have to want to know.
Maggie: ?

"I'll just sit in the back and watch. Pretend I'm not even here," Chris says. I spot more than one member of my department rolling their eyes, and it fills me with some satisfaction to know they might think the new guy is a bit of a dick. Of course Maggie smiles at him, and I make a quiet growling noise in her direction, like a dog about to pounce. She tuts at me to stop.

"You will get an email," Danny explains, "to let you know Chris will be getting to know his new CTV family over the coming days. He will sit in with the design team meetings. And he'll do the same with Sponsorship, Trade and Enterprise, Acquisitions, HR, and the Talent department, and even . . ." Danny pauses to look at Chris for confirmation. Chris nods. "The mail room?"

"Most important room in the building," says Chris, and I have to swallow an irritated groan. I know this tactic of his. Trying to win over the little people before squashing them. Like a cat with a mouse.

Me: CUNT. This is a cuntastrophy.

Maggie: It's a bump in the road.

Me: More like a cunt in the road.

"Anyway, team. Please let me know by email about your plus-one," Penny says in what can only be described as a business voice. Deeper, and slower than usual. It's a clear sign to the new guy that she's a serious person. It really is every bitch for herself. "As soon as you can before numbers fill up."

"Is Amy going to bring a cardboard cutout of Stanley Tucci again?"

The room explodes into laughter. In normal times, I would have laughed along at myself, but with Chris's gaze boring into the back of my head, I find myself blushing wildly. I *had* brought a cardboard cutout of Stanley Tucci as a date once, stolen from the foyer of a production company after too many pre-awards drinks.

"That was obviously a joke," I say. "I have other dates that aren't quite as stiff."

Oh, dear God. More giggles, and a playfully stern look from Danny now, but Maggie saves the day with a swift subject change.

"Wow, this new make list is light," she says, pointing to her screen.

"That's right," Danny says, the mood calming, but I'm not calm. I can feel Chris like a glowing nuclear reactor. "We've stripped things back while we go through the changes," Danny continues. "Let's start with you, Maggie. Want to let us know where you're at with everything?"

I stare at the clock on the wall, willing time to move faster so I can get out of here. It isn't going to work. I can't avoid him. Somewhere inside me, I know there will need to be a reckoning.

"Amy, do you want to do your updates?" Danny asks when it's my turn.

I can feel the heat start to creep up my neck and blossom from my cheeks to my chest as I begin. "The um . . . *Comeback Special* promo was approved and has been sent for trafficking," I say quietly. "And I'm just starting to work on concepts for *Bobby Binty Goes Swimming*, the new Scottish children's series that premieres in August. I'm not going to overcomplicate it. I'm just going to build on the *Bobby Binty Goes Horse Riding* concept we developed in the spring."

"That's terribly exciting," says Danny as I hear a cough behind me. *Chris.*

Is he mocking me? I feel my cheeks darken as I turn my head, and he holds a hand up, apologizing for interrupting.

"That's everything," I say, turning back to face Danny.

I cannot escape the room fast enough, and I decide to take an early lunch, but of course, when I emerge from the sandwich shop, two whole streets away from the office, Chris is there in line, chatting to someone from Legal. I drop my head so I can pretend not to see him, and I race back up to my desk instead of eating in the little park I usually sit in.

Then I see Chris on his phone, just outside the toilets on my floor.

Then, Chris by the editing suite.

Then, Chris guffawing over something with Penny by the fridges.

And finally, Chris chatting *Fantasy Island* with Gabby in reception as I arrive back with my afternoon coffee.

"Amy!" Gabby calls out. "I'm just explaining *Fantasy Island* to the new guy."

"This is a living, breathing nightmare," I mutter as I give Gabby an enthusiastic thumbs-up, which I'm sure comes off a little sarcastic. I can't help it at this point.

I can feel him behind me before I even know he's following me.

"Amy," Chris says, and because there is nowhere to run, I turn to him, my face completely blank.

"Yes?" I reply.

"Amy, you don't have to avoid me." He is pulling a sad face. A worried face. His hands go up, as if he's surrendering, exhausted, after a two-year siege. But it is me who is exhausted.

"I can't do this—" I begin, backing into the wall by the elevator. I frantically hit the up button.

"It's really good to see you."

"*Sure* it is," I say, rolling my eyes. *Please, elevator, please come now.*

"It is," he says softly.

The elevator *dings* and I head toward it, Chris following me in. When the doors close, we are alone together for the first time in two years. And I feel sick. And angry.

"You look great," he says, and I squeeze as close as I can to the opposite side of the elevator. But it's no use. I can smell his cologne—the same one, Chanel Bleu de Chanel. I bought him a bottle for Christmas three years ago. I wonder if it's the same bottle. Or did another woman buy it for him? Is he with a woman? I suddenly realize there is so much more to wonder about, including the huge impact his presence is having on me. Why is Chris in London? My insides seem to squeeze together, and I guess the pain on my face is obvious to him, because I feel him move slightly toward me, but he doesn't touch me. I know he would have, in the past, tugged me in by my waist, stealing a kiss before we separated and played our game in secret. I admit it—I loved the thrill of it.

"I won't tell anyone," he says quietly.

The words echo in my ears. He's said those words to me before. When our affair first started. I close my eyes and try to steady myself.

"Which part?" I reply dryly.

"Any of it. Us. *What happened*," he says, gently now. "You don't need to worry."

I glare ahead, but in my peripheral vision, I can see him smiling. I feel something painful when that strange little dimple appears just below his lip. So familiar. His smell, the intent radiating off him.

"I didn't know you were here," he explains. "I heard some rumors you'd hooked up with Maggie in London, but I didn't know you were at CTV."

"Oh, don't worry, I don't think you came here to be near me," I say as the elevator arrives at my floor and I go to step out. "It's pretty clear how you felt about me. You couldn't have distanced yourself fast enough."

I push my hair back over my shoulder and give him a single deathly serious look.

"Sorry," he says. "It was . . . difficult to think straight."

"Well, I thank you for not telling anyone. No one knows. Except Maggie, of course, but I trust her with my life."

"Let's catch up properly sometime," he says, and now he touches me on the arm. I look down at his fingers, so familiar for a moment I want to touch them. It isn't a conscious thought; it's a whole-body response. To have him comfort me, right now. But *he* is the discomfort I need to escape. His fingers start to burn like lava and I shrug him off.

"I have to go," I say, barreling out of the elevator. I don't turn back to see his face as I leave. This is going to be hard. *But I'll get used to it, right?* I'll get used to seeing my ex-boss/ex-love who ruined my life multiple times a day, while I'm in this position of arrested development and terrible underachievement. Why couldn't I have at least had a brilliant new job? Why did he have to hear me talking about making trailers for a preschool cartoon? Why couldn't I have had a new man, at least, to keep me from seeming completely pathetic?

Ugh. My phone pings, twice. I reach into my pocket and pull it out.

First message:

It's Jake here. I might be in.

Second message:

But I have some conditions.

Thirteen

~~~

I feel like today has drawn blood from me. I am emotionally drained, bone-tired, and yet singularly focused on getting Jake tied up on this project.

When I get home, I almost run into my landlady, Agnes, who is standing in the stairwell, sorting mail in a full-length fur coat and so much costume jewelry she gives the impression of a child who's been in Mommy's closet.

"Hello, Amy," she says.

"Hi, Agnes," I reply.

"You've met the new boy in flat B, I take it?"

"I have," I say, taking a step toward the stairs to indicate I'm in a hurry.

"Yes, he's a very nice boy," she says. "And he's been through so very much."

I nod slowly, wanting desperately to ask what she means. Is Agnes a *Fantasy Island* fan? But Jake is waiting for me. And so, I bow, because sometimes I'm terminally awkward. Agnes accepts it as her due.

Then I sprint up the stairs, two at a time, and straight up to his apartment. Before I knock furiously on his door, I see a little Post-it note with the words *ON THE ROOF* with an arrow pointing upward.

The first thing I notice when I burst through the terrace door is that Jake has added a large slate-colored umbrella, which will certainly make being up here in the hot sun easier. I also notice he's got his laptop out; a black Moleskine notebook, eerily similar to my own; a pen behind his ear; and three pens lined up in a row. I'm fascinated suddenly by the idea of Jake's writing rituals. Like, does he need a cup of tea? Does he roll out of bed and write immediately, with no distractions? Or is he a night owl, curled over a coffee, coming to life only when the rest of the house is fast asleep, typing away until the small hours until he's writing with one eye shut?

Chris was a night owl. In fact, on the nights I slept at his place, I would lie back in an exhausted heap after sex, rolling toward him to fall asleep with an arm over his shoulder, or a leg draped across his thighs, but then he'd gently push me away to go and work. It made the mornings frustrating, since I would have to spend a good half hour poking him and making coffee so he could get up and make it to work on time.

"There are more hours in the evening," he would tell me.

"But the early hours are more efficient," I would reply.

"Hey," Jake says enthusiastically, breaking through the weight of the memory. I hesitate for a moment, then make my way over to join him. His eyes look brighter than I've seen previously, and his thick hair is shiny. If it was possible to be more physically attractive, he's managed it.

"You're in?" I ask, getting right to it, clasping my hands together in a prayer as I slide in opposite him.

"I think so," he says, his eyes narrowing slightly. "I honestly love the sound of the dramedy. Something around working in a shop or a restaurant. I'd love that."

"Really? I liked the crime drama brief."

He locks eyes with me and smiles.

I am immediately drawn into his buzzy energy, despite my exhaustion. I know that energy so well. *Flow state*. When you're deep in the creative buzz and fizzing with ideas.

"It's just that I have a thing for grisly murders and intrigue," I say.

"And I like human stories that have heart and humor," he counters.

I pull my lips back in a wide grimace.

"This is a good start, isn't it?" he says, laughing.

I watch him roll up the sleeves of his white button-down, noticing with a lick of desire a small tattoo hidden on the underside of his arm, just below the elbow.

"So," I begin, dragging my gaze to his eyes and tapping the edges of the table with my fingers, "what are your conditions? We should get them locked in place."

"Yes," he says with a little tilt of the chin, closing his laptop halfway. "It's important."

"Essential," I reply, eager for him to know I'm okay with conditions.

"Imperative," he replies.

"Vital," I retort.

"Critical," he says. Checkmate. He's the writer. But he's not done. "On ne peut pas continuer sans contrat."

"French? That's not fair." I frown. I am not into losing. "Istis sagon gaomagon!"

"What the hell kind of language is that?" he protests.

"High Valyrian," I say. "But I'm not sure it's correct. I think I said *It must be done*, but I might have said *Can I poison you?* or *Can I fuck your dragon?*"

Jake laughs at this, and then, cocking his head to one side, he says, "Nerd?"

"I might also know Klingon, but it's getting a little rusty."

"I'll be sure to call on you if I'm backpacking through Qo'noS," he says, leaning back, folding his arms, a smile fixed on his face. He's far less intimidating when he smiles.

"Okay, in all seriousness. What do you need out of this to make it worth your time?"

It needs to be crystal clear. He's the writer, after all; it doesn't matter how good my ideas are—he will pull them together into a coherent draft script. I *need* him.

"Anything that gets pitched attaches me to it. It can't be a scenario where I do all this work just to get you a job and the project gets shelved immediately," he says. "Otherwise this is a favor and you need to repay me in kind"—here his eyebrow quirks and I can't help hoping it's suggestive—"or you need to pay me, and I don't think either of those scenarios are on the table."

Keep your cool, Amy, I tell myself. *This is business.* "I would definitely want to have your name fixed to it," I say. "Absolutely. And I've been assured these are real briefs and the successful pitches will form part of the department's slate of development projects. So yes. There are a few things that would need to come together, but I'm confident they would, and when they do you are firmly attached."

"Okay," he says. "Because finding out that we've done all this work and then CTV or Screen Global or whoever just stick it on the shelf—that would suck. It has to be a serious pitch."

"Agreed."

"And we are equal."

"Yes. I'm bringing the contacts, the experience in how to create a lasting series, and understanding the market," I say, "and you're bringing the script. Story we do together. That's the team. We'd be a team."

"Okay," he says again. "If you're sure."

"I'm sure," I reply, promising myself that I will go back and triple-check. He's right to be concerned. What if I win the pitch, get the job, and then they trash the ideas? Jake will have been royally ripped off. Or—what if we don't win at all? What then? Could we take our work somewhere else?

I need to be sure this is a serious process so Jake's work is not for nothing, though I can't completely eliminate the possibility. That's a chance we both have to be willing to take.

"And the other thing." He sits back in his chair and reaches his arms out in front of him, webbing his fingers together in a long stretch. The muscles in his arms pull taut. "You're going to be at work, right?"

"Yes?" I reply, drawing out the word in question.

"But I'll be focused on this, and only this," he says.

"Yes," I say, closing my eyes. I know where this is going.

"So, either I'm going to be shouldering a lot of the research, or you're going to need to take some holiday."

He's right. One of the key issues here is that these shows need to be set in London, which means, for me at least, *research.* I only really know Notting Hill, which is nowhere near as quaint as the movie. And Soho. How could I set a crime scene in London if I'd never been down the Thames, barely crossed the river, hardly even set foot east of Liverpool Street or west of my apartment?

"I have a *lot* of vacation days," I say.

"Good," he says, leaning back in his chair. "Because if we're going to be a team, we have to work together."

"I can't take the whole summer off."

"Obviously," he says with a laugh. "But at least a couple of weeks, soonish?"

I consider this. It's actually a really good idea. It gets me out of the office and away from Chris. I can't think of anything I need more than to put some real distance between us. I can kick-start idea planning and, like Jake says, conduct whatever research is needed alongside him.

"And just to flag, Amy," he says, "I'm going to Wales to paint my mum's living room. And maybe again to help her move. So, I won't be able to work with you on those days. Unless it made sense for you to come. You'd be welcome to."

"Sounds like it could be good," I say, wondering what Jake's mother is like.

"It's pretty remote, the house. Kind of writer's heaven."

I laugh. "If we need to." I just want to shake hands with Jake and have this deal done.

Jake nods and shrugs. "Well then."

"Is that all you want?" I say.

"Yes," he replies.

"When do you want to start?" I ask, smiling ferociously.

"Well, to be honest, I've already started," he says with a smirk, glancing down at his laptop.

"What about a proper kickoff, though? Choose the brief we're going to work on and put a plan together. Are you busy on Saturday?" I ask.

He looks me dead in the eye, a flicker of something passing through him. "Not busy, no."

"Shall we meet here, or in my flat? Or . . . I quite like working in cafés, if that's your thing?"

"Here," he says quickly. "Let's just work from the building."

"Okay. Here it is." I grin. "Deal?"

I stick my hand out, and Jake looks at my outstretched fingers. He takes my hand in his, the grip soft but firm. I feel my pulse start to quicken, momentarily thinking that I'd better nip this attraction in the bud or it's going to be a problem.

Jake, watching my face curiously, gives my hand a little squeeze, and with the most divine of smiles, he says, "*It's a deal*, Amy Duffy."

Fourteen

~~~

This has been one of the most eventful weeks of my career. Three days ago, Chris Ellis arrived back in my life, in my *new* life, in London. And somehow, among the ashes of that asteroid, I have found the sparks of my love for making television again. Just yesterday, Jake Jones agreed to work up a pitch for a new TV series with me, and tomorrow we will begin that journey.

But tonight, it's Friday, and I need a drink and a serious debrief with my best friend.

Maggie weaves her way into Explore, a little cocktail and "English" tapas place off Regent Street. The interiors are plush velvet, jungle palm prints, and faux taxidermy with several long benches and oak tables where customers come together under the light of little electric lanterns and woven-grass place mats. It's super gimmicky, but we like it for the Singapore slings and the free nuts.

"I just saw Chris," she says, sliding onto the bench opposite me and sipping hungrily on the drink I made sure was waiting for her.

"Erghhhh," I say, grimacing at the mention of him. "I've spent most of the week trying to forget he exists. Who was he with?"

"Ha," she replies. "Interesting first question, Amy."

"I'm serious," I grumble, leaning forward and resting my elbows on the table as I play with the straw of my tall, sunset-colored cocktail. "I think this would all be so much easier if I knew his romantic status."

"But *not* if he's single," she says, a finger raised. "If he's single, surely it makes it harder?"

She's right. And anyway, I think I'd know if he moved here with a girlfriend or wife. Moving from New York to London at thirty-six feels like a single person's step. But I could be wrong.

"He came into the editing suite today," I say, sitting back in a hump. "And get this—he said he was there to look around 'at the facilities.'"

"You think he knew *you* were there?" Maggie is not convinced, I can tell.

"Well," I say with a shrug. "What do you think?"

"What happened?"

"He just hovered like a buzzy fucking fly with Penny, who was given the unfortunate role of showing him around, and he says to me, in front of Moe and Penny, '*These suites need an upgrade like we did back at Wolf, don't they, Amy?*'"

Maggie grimaces. "I don't think you're going to be able to seriously avoid the fact you worked together. Anyone with a LinkedIn can figure that out."

"I know. I can cope with that, but I don't want him to be so familiar. Like, Penny said, '*Oh, do you two know each other?*'"

I mimic Penny's posh London accent. "And then Chris said, in this tone which was totally loaded, '*Oh . . . everyone knows Amy back in New York.*'"

"Oh my God, what is he playing at?" Maggie gasps, genuinely horrified for me. "He's toying with you!"

When Chris said it, I felt my insides turn over. It took everything inside me not to react by thrusting the sharp end of a pencil into his arm. But externally, I managed a fake fucking cutesy giggle as Moe turned his head in surprise and Penny gasped slightly before Chris clarified.

"Then he said, '*She had quite the reputation as a brilliant development producer.*'"

"Ah. That makes it okay, no?" asks Maggie as her phone buzzes beside her.

"The pause was too long. He made me sound infamous," I say, shaking my head solemnly.

"You kind of are," she teases, glancing at the screen of her phone.

"You wanna get that?" I ask.

"It's fine," she replies, waving her hand.

"The thing is, it's like he's got this huge power over me, Maggie. At any moment, he is in control of outing us as an ex-couple, and ultimately bringing that fucking video back into my London life."

Maggie sighs. "I wish you would just own that fucking video," she mutters. "Can't you see a future where *you* actually show it to people for laughs?"

"No," I say. "You might see a funny video, but I see total

humiliation. A girl who was cruelly betrayed and dumped by her first love."

"Was he your *first* love? At what, twenty-nine?" Maggie asks, her mouth dropping open in surprise.

"Yes," I say. "I dated a lot, I had a relationship with a hot spin instructor. But his name was Ryan Jamie. So, obviously we didn't fall in love."

Maggie laughs. "Why *obviously*?"

"Amy Jamie?" I say. "*Please*. It was a nonstarter. Plus, he had the longest and most elaborate nighttime routine I'd ever seen. Including, but not limited to, fifteen minutes of stretching, five minutes of meditation, and a face mask. Every night."

"Sounds like me."

"Yes, but you're single. No one keeps that shit up when they're in the early throes of a romance. I'd be waiting there in my best underwear, and he'd have to wake me up when he was *mentally balanced* enough to fuck. That, and he shaved his balls."

"I don't mind that, actually," says Maggie.

"Of course you don't." I chuckle, finding some brief respite in our banter.

Our waiter arrives at the table with a few sharing platters. "I hope you don't mind, I was ravenous," I explain to Maggie as they are maneuvered between us. "Another one, ladies?" the waiter asks brightly.

"Please," replies Maggie gratefully. And then she turns to me. "How do you feel about Chris now, I guess is the big question. Do you hate him for what he did, or do you still have feelings?"

I take a small, halved quail Scotch egg and pop it into my mouth as I ponder the question. Then I shrug.

"I only hate him," I say, feeling the words as they leave my lips. It isn't true.

"Do you?" she asks, her eyes narrowing slightly.

"I hate that he broke my heart and ruined my career," I say. "So, yeah, I hate him." I'm convincing myself as much as her.

"Fair," she says, sitting back. She rests her arm on the back of the chair and looks around the room. Drake is playing. There is a loud squeal coming from a party of five girls in the next booth. Maggie seems to be off in thought.

"Enough about Chris. Let's not talk about him. I want to hear about you. How are *you*?" I ask.

Maggie turns her head back toward me and smiles. "Good. I think I might be dating."

"What? Hang on! When? How?" My mouth drops open. Maggie Barnes *dating*? This is a total shock. First of all, Maggie rarely makes it past the first date. And secondly, why didn't I know?

"He's an artist," she says, playing with the edge of her glass with her finger thoughtfully. It's classic Maggie, deciding how vulnerable to be. "He's impressive, actually."

"Impressive?"

"Yeah," she says.

"Where did you meet?"

"At an art supply store on Poland Street. I was arguing with the cashier about my order, which was late, and he was next in line."

"Okay, this is a promising meet-cute," I say, settling into my seat, leaning forward.

"He told me to *relax*," she says, laughing. I watch her eyes as they sparkle at the memory. Her cheeks flush too. "I should have told him to fuck off, but instead I asked for his number. It was kind of . . . spontaneous." She says the word *spontaneous* as if it is a new word, one that she has only just learned.

"You're so brave, Maggie," I say, completely in awe.

"Well, he was hot," she says with a shrug.

"And you like him?" I ask. "You're dating now?"

"I think so," she says, nodding. "He's a ten, but . . ."

"What's the *but*?"

"There's always a *but*, isn't there?"

"Yes. But the *but* is completely subjective," I say. "If *you* were talking about Chris, for example, the *but* would be that he's your friend's ex. If *I* were talking about Chris, the *but* would be that he ruined my career."

Maggie's eyes narrow again.

"Well, he made a decision that led to the events that ruined my career," I say. "I guess I was the one who nailed the coffin shut."

"So, he's still a ten," she says playfully. Then, as if pulled out of a daze, she turns to me and grins. "And . . . you're still talking about Chris."

I slap my face with both my hands and try to be comical about it, but I can feel myself blushing. "Sorry. What I *should* be telling you about is the other non-sex-related man in my life, Jake. I'm working with him on the ideas for the pitch!"

"You are?"

"Yes. He is not doing anything at the moment. He seems to be recovering from the experience on *Fantasy Island*. Regrouping maybe? He told me he had more or less given up writing, so probably trying to figure out what's next. I've been chatting to him about working up some ideas and he's into it."

"I mean, sounds great—but shouldn't you be doing it yourself?"

"It's normal to work with people on an idea," I say. "It would be super weird not to, honestly. Development is nearly always done with other people. But the real truth, Maggie, honestly, if you had read his script, you would get it. My God. It was *so* good. I feel like I was reading something really, truly unique. I just cannot resist working with that kind of talent."

"And those eyes," she says, smirking.

"It's not like that," I lie.

"What's he like, then? Tell me about him."

I feel like the light has just turned green.

"Well, you know the Jake from *Fantasy Island*?" I say, my legs jiggling in excitement. "The moody one who jumped off the cliff and tried to swim into the distance and was a pretty odd guy?"

"Of course I do. Your neighbor," she says.

"He's *nothing* like that," I say. "He's kind of sweet, and playful. Totally at odds with his on-screen appearance. And the other night, when Chris first arrived back at CTV, I didn't tell you, but I might have drunk a whole bottle of Chardonnay on an empty stomach and then thrown up in the blow-up pool."

"The blow-up pool?" Maggie asks, confused.

"And this is the embarrassing part," I say, biting my lip. "I had locked my keys in my flat, and my landlord was out seeing *Cats* for the fourteenth time, and so I slept on Jake's sofa."

"What?" Maggie says, incredulous. It was a good moment for our new drinks to arrive. "Amy, you sly old dog."

"It wasn't my finest hour, but he was a perfect gentleman. He let me shower and loaned me his boxer shorts and he never really mentioned it again."

"Well," says Maggie, "he sounds rather dashing."

"He's really nice," I say as Maggie's phone buzzes again, and she hesitates when she looks at the screen.

"I'm sorry. It's the artist," she says. "Do you mind?"

"Take the call!" I say, waving her to answer, and she does, standing up and heading to the stairs to get better reception. I watch her go, having never seen Maggie interrupt anything to take a call from a man, and I feel a pang of guilt that I didn't ask her more about the Artist.

While I wait, I pull my phone out and see a message from Mom.

Waiting to hear from you darling. By the way—your father doesn't have prostate cancer.

And then a few moments later:

But he's still an idiot.

Moments later, Maggie returns.

"I have a plus-one," she says. "For the work thing."

"You're taking the Artist to the work function?" I say, my heart sinking. I was hoping, since I had to show my face, that I would go with Maggie.

"I am," she says, looking, for the first time since I've known her, slightly sheepish.

"Well. Holy shit. You better tell me all about him, then. Starting with his name?" I smile at her.

Maggie beams.

"Michael. Michael Weir," she says, and I see the unusual sight of Maggie Barnes looking bashful, a smile creeping up to her ears.

Later, after I kiss Maggie on the cheek and she heads off on the tube, I spot a cardboard cutout of LeBron James in the window of the Nike superstore. I walk a little closer, and I think about Chris. I have unresolved feelings. I knew it when he touched my arm in the elevator. I need to bring someone to the party, to put a stake in the ground. To prove that I've moved on. But with LeBron James and his cardboard cutout unavailable to me at such short notice, I dreamily wonder—would Jake do it?

Fifteen

~~~

"**Y**ou filled the pool *and* you're sitting in it," I say as the sun hits my face with an already fierce heat. I slide on my aviator sunglasses. It's hot already, at 10 a.m. on Saturday. Jake is wearing swim trunks, his legs raised and resting on one of his chairs. In his hand, he has his notebook, and next to him, a coffee. He should look completely ridiculous, but instead he just looks hot. And topless.

No, Amy. Rein these thoughts in, I scold myself.

"I'm extremely impressed, Jake Jones," I say with a laugh.

"Oh shit!" he says, lifting himself up when he sees me. "I was going to be out before you got here! How embarrassing."

"Stay there, it's hot!" I insist, waving my hands at him to stay seated. "It's fine."

"It *is* a bloody hot summer," he reasons.

"It is." I nod, putting my laptop on the table.

"You know what would be amazing?" he says. "A proper hot tub."

"Or even just one of those old roll-top baths," I say, pulling a chair over to sit by him.

Jake nods, and a thoughtful smile creeps across his face. "You're not going to get a bath up here," I say quickly.

"Maybe out back," he says, looking over his shoulder toward the garden.

"So, this is it," I say. "We're starting?"

"We are," he says, looking like he might get out of the pool again.

"And you're staying in the pool," I urge.

"Okay," he says.

I can feel the beads of sweat start to form on my back, and I crank the handle of the umbrella and spend some time fixing it so I'm in the shade.

"It's weird," he says, lifting himself slightly up. "I'm used to working alone. This is weird. And I'm in a blow-up swimming pool on a roof."

"It's okay," I say, laughing but also eyeing his body from behind my glasses. The thing about Jake is that he's *so* handsome that he falls into kind of unattainable territory, rendering any real attraction to him a nonstarter. Looking at his body is like looking at a very nice piece of art. I'm almost detached from it. *Almost.*

"What are you thinking?" he asks. "You want your pool back?"

"No, it's fine. You stay there," I reply, blushing slightly. Then I adjust my sundress under me as my thighs start to stick to the slats in the chair. "We have two options. You're still for the London-based comedy or dramedy?"

"I am," he says, nodding. "As I said, I love warm, human stories."

I think of *The Wild Years*. He's right. Not a worn-out, overworked detective or a headless dead body in sight. And, I mean, I *loved* it. But it wasn't commercial. It was never going to get made.

"And I'm really glued to the crime series. That's *my* wheelhouse. Dark crime," I say. "I know how to pull that kind of series together and I know how to sell it."

"Hmm," he says, his eyes narrowing. "I don't think we should try to do both."

"Well, we *could* if we wanted to do two ideas badly," I say, and then I lean forward, resting my elbows on my knees and my cheeks in my hands so I'm closer to his level. "It's just that I worry if I try to do something funny or heartwarming it will fall over. It's just not my bag."

"That surprises me," Jake says, brows descending.

"Don't get me wrong, I love me some *Schitt's Creek* or some *Abbott Elementary*," I explain, "but if you get me in front of a really well-written crime story, I'm in absolute heaven."

"Heaven?" he says, eyebrows raised.

"Crime. *Murder*. Real psychological murder and death. And if it's a suburban setting, so much the better," I say, leaning forward slightly and dropping my voice. "I was born to create stories about gruesome death. Even my dad gets that now."

Jake laughs. "Well then, Amy. Sounds like we better start with the crime idea. It's your baby, after all. And maybe if it goes well . . . we can see?"

I nod, unable to hide my glee, and Jake laughs at my little fist shake and knees jiggling in delight.

"Right. So. Where do we start?" I say, reaching across to my old notebook and opening to a fresh page. "They are looking at a London-centric crime idea, which is good because I checked out the main tropey dramas and there are a lot of *small-town detectives.*"

Jake laughs. "London crime drama is as tropey as it gets," he says. "Sherlock Holmes? Luther? Jack the Ripper?"

"Okay, okay. But just because London isn't a new setting doesn't mean it can't be mined," I persuade him.

"Just playing devil's advocate," he says, sitting forward, the water rushing down his body as he wraps his arms around his legs.

I hear my mom's voice echoing in my head. *I want to feed him. Focus, Amy.*

"A series of murders in Greenwich: the home of Time itself. An old East End cop returns to the beat after an investigation turns sour in another location," says Jake.

"A genius detective falls foul of her own hubris and allows a serial killer to go free along the South Bank, and dedicates her life to righting the wrong?" I say.

"Swimmers start going missing in Hampstead Heath," says Jake.

"I actually love the idea of something to do with water," I say. "I had something similar in my notebook about water deaths. I like them because they can easily be accidental."

"Hampstead Heath is actually a pretty cool opening setting," he says. "I haven't been in ages. Did you know there are a series of swimming ponds along the north side?"

"There are?"

"There are," he says. "Beautiful, but you know. Beauty can surprise you."

It sure can, I think, with a tremendous deal of thirst.

"Can I actually get in?" I say, throwing caution to the wind. "The picture on the box showed a family of four relaxing in there, so surely there's room?"

Jake moves over and holds out his hand toward the empty side of the pool.

When I emerge from my apartment in a pair of dignified board shorts and a not-so-dignified black halter-neck bikini, he looks at me and frowns. "Where's the *Baywatch* one-piece?"

"Stop it," I say, blushing.

"Why?" he says as I tentatively put a toe in the water. It's a lot warmer than I expect, but cool enough to relieve me of the intense heat.

"I had a thing for Carmen Electra as a kid," he says, watching me as I step both feet in beside him. It's going to be tight. "I was only eight or nine. My mum made me take the poster down."

"No fair, *Mommy*," I say, laughing.

I lower myself into the water, sitting to face him, making sure there are at least a couple of inches between our limbs. There is a moment where I feel his gaze on me, watching as the water rises above my thighs and the waterline sits just under my bikini top.

"Kind of a perfect height, really," I say brightly. *Keep it light.*

"It's as good as we can make it," he says, averting his eyes from me.

This was probably not a wise move. The proximity and the lack of clothing have created some undeniable tension between us. I fish over the side of the pool and slide my sunglasses on, and he does the same. Admittedly I do it so I don't get caught if my eyes drift to the curve of his shoulder or the ripple of muscle on his stomach that flexes when he moves. I wonder, for an indulgent moment, if he's doing the same.

"So, something to do with a series of murders, or is it just one murder-mystery?"

"I will always want to do a series of murders," I say. "There's something thrilling about the escalation; we get to ramp up the energy and the stakes are continuously raised. "Who is our detective?"

"A woman," he says.

"Yes," I reply, nodding.

"She's divorced. Lonely."

"Not lonely," I say.

"Okay. She's not lonely. She's alone."

"Yes, no family," I say, nodding. "Women *do* like to be alone."

Jake nods as if he knows this already. My mind wanders briefly to his mother in the remote house in Wales. Is she alone?

"So she's happily alone? She doesn't drink. Let's not have a drinker," he says.

"Is she into swimming?"

"What if she *can't* swim?" he says conspiratorially.

"But she likes to go to these ponds you mentioned?"

"Yeah, she jogs. A jogger? A let-off-steam jogger? And then she puts her feet in the water at one of the ponds. It's weird to people who see her. We don't know why, but then we learn she can't swim, or has become afraid of it?"

"So she would perhaps be familiar with the locals who swim

there. At least at the time of day when she jogs?" I suggest, nodding along as the idea begins to form in my mind.

"Yes. The swimmers at Hampstead are quite a community. Always the same people at certain times of day, particularly in the colder months. So the surprise is the corpse is someone vaguely familiar?" he says.

"A corpse! So, we're definitely doing serial killer?" I ask, excited.

"Well, it could be death due to fraud, money laundering, drugs, gangs . . ."

"At the risk of sounding morbid again, do remember that I love serialized murder," I say.

Jake laughs. "Getting to know you, Amy," he says, his leg brushing mine.

"So, she regularly visits these pools. The murder causes a disruption in the community," I say. Then I move my legs so I can wrap my arms around them. "I need to see these pools."

"Yeah," says Jake. "I think you do."

"Why don't we take our pens and head there and wander around? Didn't you say you like to think and walk?" I ask. "And maybe even have a swim?"

Jake looks apprehensive.

"What?" I ask, eyeing him curiously. "You don't want to go out?"

Jake looks skyward and sighs heavily. "I haven't been out much since getting off the show," he says, a slight redness blooming up his neck. He turns away, looking out toward the rooftops. I'm desperate to ask him again why he went on that show, but I stop myself.

"Ahh." The dots are connecting. He's ashamed of the show and worried about being recognized. I completely understand. After my video of shame went viral, I didn't want to see a single soul. Not my friends. Not my family. Hell, I even left the country to escape. But I wouldn't want that for Jake. He can't do what I did. He needs to get out there.

At least he's not dealing with the added heartache and family fallout.

"I reckon for every street with a hundred people, one or two might recall you enough to stare for a minute or two; not many are likely to say something," I say, trying to seriously assess the risk. "The odds go up if you're in Soho, and if you come into my work—I think you're probably looking at ninety-eight percent recall and about fifty percent physical response. Like wanting a hug. Or a selfie."

"Wow." Jake turns back to face me, raising his eyes in amusement.

"Between here and Hampstead? You'll be okay."

"Maybe you're right. Maybe I need to just get out there and face the music."

"That's the spirit. Put a cap on. Put your sunglasses on. We can take a cab, to minimize tube exposure," I say. "You'll be fine; we'll stay low-key. Just kind of cover all this up in something plain."

I wave at his impossibly perfect body, and he laughs, throwing his head back.

"All this?" he says teasingly.

"You need to be invisible," I say. "And this is not invisible. It really draws the eye."

Jake laughs again but crosses his arms around his chest protectively.

"Come on. Let's go see the ponds!"

"There's a ladies' pond, a mixed pond, and a men's pond," he says.

"Oh my God, three locations for a body to wash up. *I love it.*"

"You're coming across as kind of deranged right now," he says, pulling himself up to standing so the water cascades down his bare chest. I cough involuntarily as his swimming shorts are now level with my eyeline. They're wet and bunched up around his thighs, and it's impossible not to note the large bulge a foot from my face. There is very little left to the imagination. He holds out a hand. "Fuck it. Let's go, then."

"Really?"

"Really," he says.

I take his hand and stand too, so that we are face-to-face, his bare chest to my halter top, and for a moment, something inside me stirs. Jake looks at me, his eyes holding on mine, before he looks away again and steps quickly out.

"I'll call the taxi and we'll meet by the mailboxes downstairs," I say.

Sixteen

~~~~~~~

As the black cab arrives at the wrought iron gates of Hampstead Heath, I gaze out across the space in wonder. This is more than a park—it's a large, rambling green space in the north of London with various fields, lakes, pavilions, and natural areas. There are leisure seekers everywhere—bikes with ponytailed women and their little front-fixed baskets; families with small children racing by on scooters; strollers; dogs on leashes keen to explore the undergrowth, tugging their owners; and everywhere, young lovers hand in hand. It takes Jake—who seriously needs a lesson in blending in—a moment to steel himself to climb out.

"The white T-shirt is brand-new," I whisper to him. "It's almost reflective."

"I thought it was low-key," he mutters.

"Good grief, dude," I reply, handing the cab driver a twenty-pound note, scowling at the price as he hands me back a single two-pound coin. "I meant like something old. Something that doesn't look like it was bought at a fancy shop on Sloane Street."

"Sorry," he says. "I have all this shit that I bought for the show and never wore. I don't have my old things."

"Where are they?"

"My parents' house. I need to go and get them at some point. I need to get *all* my stuff at some point. I was staying with them before the show, and I haven't gone back yet." He mutters that last part, and I glance across at him, deciding once again not to pry, despite being completely desperate to do so.

"Don't get me wrong, I like the look. You look clean. It's like box-fresh boy band or something. But yeah, you stand out," I say, shrugging at him.

He turns to me and folds his arms. "You hardly look low-key either, you know."

I glance down at my dress; it's navy blue and cut like overalls, except with an above-the-knee skirt, and I'm wearing a white tank top underneath. It's definitely cute, but it's old, and it's not a standout look. I'm not overdressed. And then I realize he's complimenting *me*.

"Let's just go," I say quickly, deflecting.

The heath is beautiful. The trees are huge, and the leaves still bright green, as yet unblemished by the heat of the summer. Picnic blankets litter the long green lawns like patchwork. There's a soccer game with bunched-up T-shirts as makeshift goal markings, and a large brown dog that keeps pouncing on the ball, to the delight of the children watching.

It's hot in the afternoon sun, and we move slowly, walking and talking together as we make our way toward the pond.

"So where does she live, this single woman detective who used to love wild swimming?" he says.

"Nearby, I reckon. Jogging and then sitting by the pond?"

"Agreed," he says. "Why is she alone?"

"She wants to be," I remind him.

"I've been thinking about that," he says, stopping for a moment to turn to me. "I was thinking she should have some trauma from her past . . ."

"She had a terrible breakup," I say. "She doesn't trust men?"

"Okay, why?"

"She had a fling with someone who hurt her?"

"Physically?"

"No, she's physically strong. She's really tough," I say as we continue to walk.

"So, maybe her heart was broken?" he says. "By someone she loved?"

"Maybe." I feel my mind wandering, suddenly, to Chris, and I feel a knot tying in my stomach as I imagine him, instead of Jake, bouncing ideas around with me. We did it often, but never outside. Always inside. Never far from his bed, or the sofa in his office.

I feel a judder of something like desire jolt through me, but it's Jake beside me, not Chris. I gaze across at him a little longer than I should; his hair has fallen forward, and he is deep in thought. Have I tried to re-create that situation here with Jake? Is this going to be a problem? *No*, I tell myself firmly. Jake is an attractive guy. But he isn't my lover.

"What are you thinking about?" Jake asks suddenly, and I shake my head, trying to remove the intrusive thoughts.

"Her ex-boyfriend," I say. It tumbles out of my mouth involuntarily. "I don't want it to be a breakup. I want him dead."

"Dead?"

"Yes. He died," I say. "It wasn't a breakup. He died, and that somehow should relate to water."

"He drowned?"

"He drowned," I say, shaking both my balled-up fists. "*Yes, Jake!* He fucking drowned."

When I shout this with unbridled enthusiasm, a group of young girls looks across at us, and I see one of them nudge another. Then the whole party turns to us, and one tall redhead brings out her mobile phone and angles it toward us.

"Jake," I whisper, "we should move quickly. Four o'clock."

I feel Jake stiffen as he looks over, then he pulls his cap down and we pick up the pace.

"Shit," I say. "Sorry."

"It's fine. It could be worse. What has it been, like, twenty minutes?" he says, peering over his shoulder. The girls are photographing him. They're not even trying to hide it. I want to say something comforting, but Jake just wants to get away without a fuss.

"Are you worried they got a photo of you?"

"No," he says, shoving his hands deep into his shorts pockets. "But I don't want to hang around and court the attention."

"Fair enough," I say, looking back one last time.

"Just got to get through it, don't I?" he says, shrugging.

We round another corner and seem to be in the clear. There is a little pavilion on the edge of the park and Jake looks longingly at the ice-cream seller perched outside with his little vintage cart.

"I can't resist an ice cream," he says. "You?"

"Oh yes," I say.

"I'll get them. Flavor?"

"I'm a plain vanilla girl. Not very exciting," I say.

"I doubt that," Jake replies, the side of his mouth hitching. "Nothing wrong with vanilla." He turns to me while he pulls his wallet out and frees a twenty-pound note. Then he looks me dead in the eyes. "If it's done right."

Then he gives me the wickedest, most flirtatious grin.

"Jake!" I say.

"I'm just messing with you," he says. "Would you like some *really good* vanilla, then? One or two scoops?"

"I'll need two, to be satisfied," I say, and after a moment of lingering, heavy air, I slap him on the shoulder. "Quit fucking around."

The serious look on his face cracks into a smile, and he heads to the ice-cream seller to grab us a couple of cones. When he returns, with two scoops apiece, we continue our walk, slowly, under the dappled light of the oak trees that flank the path.

I decide it's time to ask. "So, I have really been wondering, Jake. Why on earth did you go on *Fantasy Island*? You're not an influencer type of guy. You're not a fledgling actor. You don't want the attention at *all*, it seems."

"A perfect storm of bad decisions," he says.

"I *knew* you made a mistake," I say, a little too triumphantly, and when he turns, looking at me to elaborate, I start to stammer my reply. "I mean . . . I just . . . you are *really* not the type. Not looks-wise, because all that is in the right place, *obviously*."

"It is?" he says, nodding in mock satisfaction.

"Shut up. You know what I'm saying. Am I wrong?"

Jake pauses his walking for a beat and looks thoughtfully at a squirrel running circles around the trunk of a tree.

"No, you're not wrong," he concedes, on the move again. "My agent called me, and because things were just not working out with the writing career, she suggested going on *Fantasy Island*. You know, I'd done some modeling and extra work, so it wasn't a massive stretch in her mind. She'd already put me forward. '*You can make a lot of money, Jake.*' That's how she put it. She's not the best agent, unfortunately."

"I see."

"I should probably say that my agent was my mum's friend from her small town in northern Wales. She's sweet. But yes, she wasn't very well connected and I didn't really understand that for years and years. I'm embarrassed to admit this, but her main specialty used to be farm recruitment. Tractor drivers and combine harvester operators and whatnot."

I cannot contain a laugh, and Jake gives me a mock-reprimanding glare.

"She was following her dream and branching out to writing and acting. Gwendolyn Griffiths: agent to the stars," he adds, running his hand across the sky. "She has three people in small recurring roles in *The Rings of Power*, and another writer who's full-time on *EastEnders*. She's doing really well."

"Good for her," I say. "Although maybe not good for you."

"We already had that talk. I said to her that I needed to sign on with a serious writing agent," he says. "But I had a lot going on at home with my family . . . I needed a paying job."

"What was going on with your family?" I ask, and then hastily add, "You don't need to say. Only if you want to share."

"Oh, it's a long, complicated story. But yeah, in short, I needed some cash," he says.

"So, it *was* about the money?"

"It was at first, and then my best friend, Callum, made it sound like a really good idea," he says. "To shake things up. Honestly, once we said yes, it was like jumping into rapids in a rubber ring. I couldn't stop the forward momentum."

"I suspect they kind of design it that way," I say. I want to know more, but Jake falls silent and I don't want to pry further. I have a million more questions now, though. What was going on with his family, and why did they need money? Isn't his mum moving to a house in Wales? Were his parents separating?

"What about you? Who *is* this Chris guy, anyway?" Jake asks before I have a chance to ask anything more of him.

"I told you his name?" I say, groaning.

"You did," he says, licking ice cream off the side of his hand. "This shit is melting faster than I can eat it."

"What did I say? Do I want to know?"

"You were more upset than drunk," he says, pulling an awkward face. "If I can say that?"

"I've just died," I say. "I'm actually dead."

"I'm not sure if I should repeat it exactly as you said it, because there are children nearby," he says, flashing me another one of his wicked grins, "but you said that someone called Chris had started at work, and that he was a—large male appendage—and also—something that rhymes with *hunt*—and he was trying to destroy your life."

"Dramatic," I say.

"You were certainly shook up," he agrees.

"He's my ex. From America. And he started at work, as the head of the department I'm trying to get a job in. Surprise, Amy!" I holler, tossing the half-eaten cone in the nearest bin. Talking about Chris continues to make my stomach turn.

"Shit," says Jake. "So, you're trying to get a job *with* him again? That doesn't make sense. That's the definition of madness, isn't it?"

"He's only the *interim* head," I say. "I wanted to go for it before I knew he would be in charge, and I feel like if I pull out, then he's won all over again."

Jake falls silent, and I'm sure he's contemplating what this means for him.

"We'll smash it," I say. "And Chris will leave when we do. He won't want to work with me either."

"We better smash it, then," he says, pointing ahead to an open field dropping away in the distance. "There's the pond."

The first swimming pond we arrive at is the men's pond. As we stand on the footpath overlooking it, we are interrupted by a woman, maybe in her fifties, who taps on Jake's shoulder.

"You're Jake Jones," she says in a thick London accent. She's round in the middle with short-cropped burgundy hair and a face that can only be described as *ruddy*. "I knew it was you. I told my husband over there, I did. I said, that's that lovely Jake Jones from *Fantasy Island*. Is it true you lost your father just before the show?"

I snap my head back to look at Jake in shock. But he's smiling gently at the lady and nods. "It's true," he says softly.

"Oh, you poor, sweet darling," she says, rubbing his shoulder. "No wonder you were so cut up on the show."

I want to tell her off, but Jake is calm and smiling. She then asks him for a photo. "Could I get one? For my daughter, Chelsea. She'll die. She fancies you something rotten."

With that she glances across at me. "You'll have to get used to it, love. He's such a looker."

Jake and the lady lean in for a photo, and then she thanks him after checking to see the result is satisfactory. She swans off toward her husband, who is waiting with a small Staffordshire bull terrier who is yanking impatiently to keep moving.

When she's out of earshot, I turn to him. "My God, Jake."

"It's fine," he says. "I said it's *complicated*. I guess it got out."

"I haven't read the *Fantasy Island* news in days," I say. I want to hug him, suddenly. I want to throw my arms around him and tell him everything is going to be okay and we can go home and he doesn't have to face anyone. "Jesus, you've hardly had any time to grieve."

"I've had time," he says, turning to indicate we should continue to walk.

"Jake," I say, touching his forearm to stop him.

"It's okay, really," he says. "I'm trying to move on. This stuff. This TV stuff. It helps keep me distracted."

I know that feeling.

"Okay," I say, walking in silence next to him, allowing the news to percolate and settle. I think of my own dad and feel a surge of sadness that I've not had one of his huge, squeezy hugs in more than two years.

The silence starts to feel heavy. I need to keep Jake's mind busy, and my own.

"So where were we?" I say after a moment. "Our detective's husband drowned?"

"Her lover drowned," he replies quickly.

"Yes, her *lover*. She would have a lover, not a husband," I say.

As we walk and talk, Jake is interrupted only one more time, by two girls who want a selfie, and I find myself enjoying the way he is starting to relax a little despite the attention. He laughs when they say he was a *right grump* on the show, and my heart squeezes, as I know the reason why. Laughing at himself, despite his grief, despite his embarrassment.

We arrive back at the apartment as the sun begins to drop, and Jake tells me he's going to write up what we've discussed today.

"Okay, but remember, it can't be all in Hampstead; that's just our 'first body' location," I remind him. "I'd like to see a body in the Thames. With an escalation in injuries. He can't just have a slit throat; we'll need something more. Like a missing limb?"

"Creepy," he jokes back. "Same time tomorrow?"

"You bet."

Then, as I put the key in the door and push it open, I ponder something I've been wanting to ask all day, but there never seemed to be a good time.

"Jake," I say, folding my arms and feeling heat in my cheeks as I anticipate how this is going to sound. "Do you want to come with me to a big TV work function? It's around four weeks away, mid-July, and then I'm on holiday for two weeks afterward, as requested." I salute him with a big grin.

Jake's mouth opens, but before he has a chance to speak I jump in. "*Just a work thing.* You would help me because I wouldn't have to be milling around like a single Nigel with no friends, and honestly, and pathetically, Chris would get a very strong signal if I turned up with a date. And I could introduce you to some TV people and maybe you could make some connections?"

Jake still doesn't say anything, but he smirks now, walking slowly up the stairs toward his door.

"No?" I say. "Quite right. A dumb-as-hell idea."

"Your fake boyfriend?" he asks, stopping outside his apartment.

"It's not like that," I reply. "It's a business deal."

"Your call guy?" he says. "Is this a reverse *Pretty Woman*? Am I getting paid?"

"Stop it," I say, feeling my cheeks burning red with the teasing.

"I'll be your date, Amy," he says, smiling.

"Really?" I know I look like a puppy who is begging for a biscuit, but I don't care. "Thank you. It will be full of TV people, so I can't promise you won't get hounded. I mean, I can kind of guarantee you will." I think of Penny and Gabby and Maggie for starters.

"It's okay," he says.

"It's also black-tie," I say. "So, you'll need a tux. I can get you one."

"Oh, I have a tux," he says teasingly.

"I mean it, a proper black-tie tuxedo," I say. "You know?"

"Amy! Relax," he says simply. "It will be fun."

Seventeen

~~~~~~~~

I've dusted off the old J Brand blazer and I'm wearing sandals this morning with a small heel, so when I enter the office to the sound of my feet *click-clacking* on the floor, I can feel myself standing a little taller. Feeling a little bit stronger.

I feel alive.

"Amy," Maggie says, nodding in approval as I swagger across the office floor to my desk. "Again with the hot business look. I'm loving it."

"I think I'm back, baby. *No*, I am fucking back," I say, flicking my hair over my shoulder in exaggerated glee.

Maggie shakes her head, grinning, and claps her hands slowly. "Well, well, well. It's very nice to get to know you again, Amy Duffy."

"Well. To be fair, I'm about sixty-six percent back. Two-thirds New York Amy, one-third *I hope I don't bump into Chris today* Amy."

"Oh, you won't," Maggie says, and I feel every cell in my body relax. "They're all out on some fucking management back-scratching, self-congratulatory brainstormy away day."

I slip off my blazer and kick off my heels in response. "He's *really* not here?"

"Nope," she says, grinning.

"Heaven," I reply. "I hope there's going to be a lot of those away days."

"Amy, there are fucking workshops starting to litter our calendars now. Creative brainstorms. Departmental off-sites. We've even got some expert flying in from Amsterdam to hold a happiness summit. What the fuck is a happiness summit?"

I chortle. "The Americans are in town, baby," I say, booting up my machine. "We'll have sleeping pods and zero maternity leave before you can say private healthcare."

"What are you two laughing at?" Penny says, sliding to my desk with a crisp white envelope between her long, beautiful fingers.

"The calm before the brainstorm," says Maggie.

"The calm before the merger," I explain.

"I won't be made redundant," Penny says. "No one in this building knows how anything works except for the network of personal assistants. Try to get a senior manager to have an invoice approved. Plus, I found a folder full of Jeff's nude photos. . . . He was clearing out his laptop and accidently dumped them into a folder he shared with me. *Oops.*" The *oops* is delivered with such wickedness, I feel almost afraid of her.

"Oh my God, *Penny!*" I say, appalled.

She shrugs. "He knows that I know. I'll never share the images, though. But, Amy, it's the power I wield," she says, tapping the side of her nose. "He can't fire me. I can't be merged out. He knows it. I know it."

Maggie looks across at me; I know she's thinking what I'm thinking. Chris has this power over me. All he would ever need to do is leak that damn video—or even threaten to leak it. In fact, it occurs to me suddenly and very clearly, just me *worrying* what Chris might or might not do with that video is keeping me small and afraid.

"A girl's gotta eat," Penny says, dusting off invisible lint from her blouse. "Are you getting your pitch ready, Amy?"

"I am," I say, raising my chin a little.

"Good. It's every bitch for herself," she says. "Here, I got these for you. Danny's playing golf that day and can't go. Consider it payment for your help booking the New York trip for Jeff last month."

"Oh, you didn't need to," I protest.

"No, really," she says.

I take the envelope off her with an intrigued smile as she swans back toward Danny's desk, grinning at me over her shoulder.

"If I'd known why I was helping with Jeff's trip to New York," I say, rolling my eyes. "It must have been the merger. Maybe even a meeting with Chris."

"She's probably known for a while," Maggie says, nodding.

"Imagine all the things she knows," I wonder aloud, staring across the office at her.

Maggie leans in. "The greatest power network in any corporation is the personal assistants."

I run my thumb under the fold of the envelope and whisper back, "They should never be underestimated."

Then I squeal as I see two tickets to Wimbledon tucked inside.

"Yes! Penny is a *goddess*."

"Ugh, I hate tennis," says Maggie.

"Aww," I moan. "You don't want to come?"

"No. Plus, I'm supposed to be coming to yours for dinner that night," she says, leaning forward and tapping on the date in the corner of the ticket. "And meeting Jake?"

"You can still come! I can do both," I say, and then I gasp. "Maybe Jake likes tennis."

Maggie turns to me and puts a hand on mine.

"What?" I say, turning to her.

She pauses, and then breaks out a smile. "Nothing. It's just great to see you fizzing with enthusiasm and beaming about everything. *Truly*. But . . ."

"But what?"

"Is history repeating?" she asks, her forehead lined with worry.

"What do you mean?"

"Well, first you're working with someone you fancy, and now you're talking about inviting him to Wimbledon," she says, extremely gently. I look at her and blink twice.

I decide not to reveal that he's *coming* to the summer work party with me just yet.

"Just be really careful about getting involved with someone you're working with? *Again*," she is saying now.

"No," I say firmly. "The work is going well. He's great to bounce ideas with."

"Are you just trying to convince me?" she asks, her face even more concerned.

"No. Nope. Uh-uh." I shake my head frantically. "Anyway, Jake is not in the right headspace for anything like that. He's grieving. His dad died just before he went on the show."

"Really?" Maggie replies, mouth open, clutching my arm. "Oh my God. Poor guy."

"I know. Right before. Can you imagine?" I sigh. "Breaks my heart."

"I'm sure he's grateful for the distraction," she says after a beat.

"Yes," I say. "We *both* need this."

Maggie nods slowly as I slip the tickets into my bag, and I turn to her. "Maggie, I am so self-involved right now, and I know you're letting me have my moment. But I wanna hear about you too."

She nods. "Wanna get a coffee?"

As we wait in line at the über-cool Soho café Flat White, I notice Maggie looking a little sheepishly at her phone.

"So, how *are* things with the Artist?" I ask playfully. "I can't wait to meet him."

"Good. Good. It's *good*," she says, eyes flickering out to the street market. "Maybe great, actually."

"Still going strong, then?" I say, eyeing her for the apprehension I was sure would come. But she surprises me.

"Yes. Oh, Amy, I don't know. He's different," she says, and I can see that hint of redness creeping up her neck to her cheeks.

"Different how?" I ask gently as a tattooed barista fixes lids onto two small coffees for us.

"Twelve pounds," she says, and Maggie shakes her head, paying.

"Daylight robbery," she mutters as we spill back out onto the sidewalk.

"Oh, but it's a gooooood coffee," I say, taking a sip.

"You know what's different about Michael?" Maggie blurts out. "He's just really fucking kind and nice and good. And he doesn't compete with me. And he doesn't speak over me. And the world is full of unkindness and horrors. And I don't need to fuck someone who isn't kind. That's where I'm at."

I startle at this from Maggie. "He really does sound great," I say, melting at the thought of someone getting underneath Maggie's skin.

"Yeah, but like, Amy. He has no business ambition. No real money," she says, looking at her cup. "It worries me, you know?"

"Maggie, I have always doubted you'd find someone who can keep up. Maybe it's better to find someone who can just keep it real."

She looks at me thoughtfully and nods. "That's exactly what he is. And it's not like he just mooches around and paints for nothing all day. He's exhibiting in Venice in autumn, can you imagine? He works for the Arts Council in Brighton. He's invested in interesting things. Honestly, Amy, it makes me think about what I *really* want."

"Pixar, right?" I say, examining her face.

"Maybe," she replies. "Maybe I'll throw all that in and have babies and wear overalls and bake cookies and stick it to capitalism."

"I mean, don't go changing completely," I say, laughing.

Maggie laughs too. "Don't worry. I actually internally recoiled at the thought of that. I might like a guy who moves in first gear, but I'm always going to be in at least third."

As we walk silently back toward work, I think on what Penny said about Jeff and the nude photos she has in the shared folder.

"That's quite a hold Penny has over the actual CEO of CTV," I say to Maggie.

"Yep, the girl's got some chutzpah," Maggie replies. "I'm kind of in awe."

"It just reminds me of Chris. I worry he feels that way about what he knows about me."

"The power balance goes the other way," says Maggie. "You also know an awful lot about Chris, honey."

But only one of us has video evidence, I think. I don't even have a single photo of us together anymore.

"Well," I say, threading an arm through Maggie's. "The only thing I'm focused on right now is knocking an amazing proposal out of the park and getting a job on that development team. Then Chris can fuck off and leave London to me. If he stays I'll make his life a living hell. That is my vengeance, Maggie."

"And I'm living for it," she says.

Eighteen

~~~~~~

*J*ake and I are standing in line at Wimbledon. He is almost in cosplay in his cream shorts and pale polo shirt, tennis socks pulled up, and clean plimsolls on his feet. Here, he blends in somehow. I'm completely, *unashamedly* in cosplay, wearing an all-white tennis dress, but with a pair of strappy flats.

"I still can't believe you were *given* Wimbledon tickets," he says.

"A gift from the PA at work," I reply, laughing. "She literally asked for a few restaurant suggestions in New York and I sent some options, ranked, reviewed, and with best table options."

"Holy shit," he says, laughing. "That's thorough."

"I'm almost always thorough," I say, folding my arms defiantly.

"And a full day at Wimbledon? What a reward!"

"We can only stay until five, remember."

"Such a waste," he says. "Just when the day gets exciting."

The last three weeks have flown. If I left work at five, I found we had a couple of hours to work every day, plus the entire weekend. Every moment I had, Jake and I would walk and talk our ideas, and then the next day, he would write those ideas up. We would pull them apart, critique them, and push forward. We even have a working title: *Black Water.*

At work, Chris was no longer wandering the floors, and when I did see him, it was easy enough to pretend I was busy. I'd had one awkward run-in during a fire drill, when the whole building milled around in the back alley and Chris wandered up to Maggie and me to chat. Maggie took the reins, polite and surface chitter-chatter. *How was he enjoying London?* And *Where was he living?* And *Did he miss that little Greek place on Fifth as much as Maggie did?* I stood slightly back, "frantically answering emails" that didn't exist.

Chris said he was finding himself *very much at home* in London, which made me stiffen. Could he stay after all? Was *interim* going to become *permanent*?

But the truth was, as long as I didn't have to be near him, Chris's presence here in London was not quite the all-consuming nightmare I had worried it would be. I was even thinking that maybe we *could* work on the same team at some point.

After Jake and I hand our tickets over, we walk past a stand selling small baskets of fresh, plump strawberries and ice-cold champagne.

"Later," says Jake, seeing my eyes light up. He playfully bumps his shoulder into mine, and I pretend to nearly fly into the side of the stadium. "You're such a dickhead," he says, laughing.

A few more paces, and we are interrupted.

"Jake Jones," says a beaming girl with long blond hair swept up in a glossy ponytail. "It's you!"

We are both now used to this. It happens once or twice every time we're out.

"It's like having a cute dog," I'd said to Jake when we were stopped by one of the canals in Camden. "People just want to say hello."

"I'm cute, am I?" he'd replied, making me eye roll hard at him. Jake is a bit of a flirt.

The girl looks apologetic as she approaches, and I step back, out of the way, examining a map of the grounds. He takes the selfie politely, and then we move on. He has let his facial hair grow a little, so he's got some stubble, and with his hair a bit more unkempt, people don't get the full, shiny Jake Jones look at first glance anymore. He's blending in a bit.

"It's becoming less, isn't it?" he says as we take our seats in the stands.

"It is," I say, "and the finale of *Fantasy Island* is coming soon, so I'd say you're in the home stretch."

"I think so too," he says, pretending to wipe his brow with relief.

"It's amazing, by the way," I say as two unseeded players emerge from the sides of the court to enthusiastic applause from the crowd. "Amazing how you just own it."

"I have no choice," he says. "What else could I do? Run? Hide behind lampposts? Become a hermit? Move to New Zealand?"

I feel a pulse of guilt jolt through me as he says this, remembering my own desire to run to New Zealand when Chris arrived in London.

He continues. "I made the decision to go on the damn show, so I have to face it. No one to blame but myself, really."

The players begin to warm up, and I take a photo and send it to my dad. The caption: *WIMBLEDON!*

"My dad is going to *die*," I say.

"My dad loved tennis too," Jake says.

"Oh yeah?" I ask.

"He had his football club, Liverpool," Jake says, "but he was more into tennis, golf, and being *the man*."

Jake says this with such disdain, I flinch.

Three weeks ago, I learned that his dad had died, and in the conversations since there have been some hints that there was even more to the story. I have begun to understand that his relationship with home is somewhat as fractured as mine.

My fracture, however, is made of love and loss. My dad is the best. He could always see when I was nervous and would pull me in for a massive squeeze and say, "I got you." At the dentist, on the first day of school, and even when I left home, he held me tight and said that if I ever needed him, to just call. And I never doubted it. I never doubted him when he said it: "I got you, kiddo."

But Jake's fractured relationship seems altogether different from mine.

"What did he do?" I ask carefully.

"Orthopedic surgeon," he replies.

"Dr. Jones," I say, raising my eyebrow.

Jake scoffs at this.

"Did you ever feel like you might want to go into medicine?"

"No," he says, the bitterness starkly apparent. "And that was the whole problem, Amy."

"Oh. Really?" I say as my phone buzzes. Dad has replied.

When are you coming home

No enthusiasm. No punctuation. Just the question. I shove my phone back in my bag quickly, an actual knotting pain inside me that makes my heart race and my breathing shallow.

"Is he jealous?" Jake says, smiling.

"Yeah," I say quickly.

We watch the match, Jake quickly choosing to root for the wild-card British player, while I root for the teenager from France. He calls me *contrary* and I tell him it makes it more fun if we're adversaries.

At this he shoots me a wicked grin. "It certainly makes it more exciting."

At one point, he puts a hand on my thigh and squeezes it when his girl wins the first set in a tiebreak. "Looks like I'm on top, Amy," he says.

I scowl at him, ignoring the inuendo.

"It's only the first set, Jake," I say.

There is undeniable chemistry of sorts between Jake and me, and as a result I make sure there is always a metaphorical and literal distance between us. Taxi rides. Elevators. Restaurants. Cafés with relaxed seating, and plug sockets. We had all but abandoned the terrace for doing anything other than hanging out and eating, since it was either too sunny to work there or it was raining.

Today, though, was perfect.

At the end of the match, Jake leads me to something called Henman Hill for champagne and strawberries. I buy both. Since Jake mentioned that the bout on *Fantasy Island* was partially because he "needed money," I felt it was the least I could do to pick up the tab from time to time. I have not minded paying for him, as somewhere in the back of my conscience I have a nagging worry that I'm going to get more out of our work arrangement than he will.

"We can't be long. Maggie will be there soon," I remind him.

"I'm looking forward to meeting her," Jake says enthusiastically.

"She's the best," I say. "I wish her new man could have come, but I'll have to wait until the work party to meet him."

"Oh yes, that's next week," he says.

"Next week," I say, looking over at him.

"Yes, I'm still coming," he says, laughing at me.

"Oh, thank goodness. I was worried I'd bullied you into it."

We lie back in the grass, looking up at the sky, under the afternoon sun, and finish our drinks. I devour the supersweet chilled strawberries. I watch Jake as he rests one playfully on his lips and then lets it drop into his mouth. I find myself admiring the edge of his profile, wanting to reach over and hold another strawberry to his lips. At times, I want to do more than that. It is a reality I'm finding increasingly hard to ignore. If Jake's feelings are growing too, he shows them by teasing me. He's always walking an edge of teasing and flirting that I cannot fully decipher.

My dad's message is weighing on me, and I sigh. I do not do *reality*. I want to stay here, at Wimbledon, with Jake, in our little bubble that does not include my family, Maggie, Chris, or my past.

"I could stay here all day," I say.

"Me too," he says.

"Can we just?"

"We can't," he says, rolling over onto his side but maintaining a good foot of distance so the move does not feel intimate. It leaves me wanting him closer.

I imagine for a moment: He leans forward and kisses me on the mouth. And with the thought, I let out a little sigh.

"I'm intrigued to meet Maggie," he says. "I already know so much about her."

"She's the best," I say again. "I think she might really be falling in love with someone. Michael. Or the Artist, as she calls him. And I've never seen her so distracted by a romance."

"We need a good nickname for our killer, you know," says Jake. "Something like the Artist."

"The Fish?"

"That's not very terrorizing," he says. "*Fish*. Who the hell could be terrorized by a fish?"

"The Shark?"

"No sharks in the Thames," he says. "At least, none that could kill."

"What other amphibious animals are there?" I wonder aloud. "The Piranha?"

"Comical B-grade slasher."

"The Eel?"

"Too slippery," he says.

"What about the Killer Whale?"

"Nah," he says. "I know orcas can kill, but they're still so damn cute. They're the pandas of the sea."

"The pandas of the sea," I agree, laughing. "Look, if a bad guy in the Batman comics can be called the Penguin, surely we can go with the Seal or something?"

"The Seal isn't bad," he says. "But all I see is a happy dude clapping his flippers, or lying about on a rock in the sun after a nice meal."

"And it's also somehow erotic?"

"Is it?" Jake says, laughing.

"Yes, it's giving slippery leather and bondage daddy."

"I feel like it's giving Navy SEAL," he says. "Maybe she's ex-army?"

The crowd around us bursts into applause as the next game on Centre Court begins, displayed all around us on huge screens.

"We really need to go," he says, standing suddenly and reaching out a hand to help me up too.

I glance at my watch.

"We should just get the tube," he says. "Taxis are so expensive and we'll get home quicker on the tube."

And that's that. The last thing that Jake was still uncomfortable with, he does. And in less than twenty minutes, and at a fraction of the cost, we disembark at Notting Hill Gate and make our way back to the house.

Nineteen

~

I'm Maggie. Sorry about the call to your agent." Maggie gives Jake an apologetic grin, but it's playful as she closes the door to the rooftop behind her.

She holds out a hand for Jake and they shake.

"It's no problem," he says. "To be honest, I think my agent and I are at the end of the road."

"Well, looks like all's well that ends well?" she says teasingly, looking between Jake and me, beaming. But I can tell Maggie is in full observation mode. She is watching me. She is watching Jake.

Her eyes move to the umbrella, the table and chairs that we've set with cutlery, plates, and wineglasses. "Well, well. Would you look at you two," Maggie says, her eyes narrowing on me. She is going to give me her unabridged opinion when this evening comes to an end.

The fish is in foil, cooking away on the barbecue, and there is a waterproof beanbag on the new rattan waterproof rug I bought to partially cover the Astroturf.

"Glad to see the old girl survived the makeover," she says, nodding at my threadbare deck chair.

I am nervous as I pour Maggie a glass of wine and she takes it in her long, manicured fingers.

"So how was Wimbledon? Everything you hoped for?" she asks.

"It was so good," I reply. "We only watched one match, and then we sat on the big grassy hill and ate strawberries and drank champagne."

"Ooh," she says. And then, as Jake fiddles with the barbecue, she whispers, "How romantic."

I shake my head furiously at her. *No*, I mouth.

"Do you want a dip in our luxurious swimming pool?" I ask by way of comedic distraction, and hear Jake snickering behind me. I wave at the rainbow blow-up, which is starting to look a bit worse for wear, one of the rings beginning to lose air, causing the whole thing to lean slightly to the side.

"Cute," she says. "If we have another heat wave, you'll be able to charge for that."

"In New York," I say to Jake, who swigs on a beer, "there are a few legendary rooftop pool bars."

"But you have to be a member," Maggie adds.

"I was a member once upon a time," I say with a tilt of the head and a smile.

"I've never been to New York," Jake says.

"Oh no." I shake my head in disbelief. "You have to go to the States. It's the home of television!"

"Isn't that London?" he says, frowning.

"HBO," I say, shaking my head in mock horror.

"The BBC," he retorts.

"*The Sopranos*," I retort with mock fury.

"*The Blue Planet*," he replies, folding his arms.

"Guys, big-ass drama and late-night live TV is New York, and David Attenborough and cheerful competitive baking is London," Maggie says, laughing, "both equally important to the content landscape."

"Agree to disagree, Amy?" says Jake.

"You can't agree to disagree when you're wrong," I shoot back, and we hold each other's gaze playfully. I feel Maggie's eyes on us and I bite my lower lip. This banter between me and Jake is absolutely, positively *flirting*. With a third person in the room, I can see it for sure.

"Do you want to grab some lemons from your bowl? And I'll grab the salad?" Jake says, as if he has had the same thought at exactly the same time.

I nod. "I have more wine in the freezer too."

"Great," he says, "I'll get the chiller."

Maggie watches this exchange. Jake walks to the roof-terrace door, and just as I'm about to follow him down, she grabs my arm.

"Okay, number one," she whispers, "he's really handsome in the flesh. And number two, you're behaving like a couple."

"No, we're not."

"You *are*," she says, letting go of me, nodding. "The play arguing. *You get the lemons and I'll grab the salad*." She says this in a deep voice, mimicking Jake. "*And I have the wine in the freezer!*" She says this in an American accent, mimicking me.

"We are so *not*. Maybe I do find him attractive as hell. But it's like fancying Ryan Gosling. Everyone is allowed to, because he's out of our league," I say.

"Jake's not out of your league," she retorts. "That's stupid."

"We're working together," I say.

"Hasn't stopped you before," she says, eyebrows raised.

"I know, but I learned my lesson," I insist. "Sure, I'm attracted to him. Jesus, look at him. He's smoking. A smoke show. It's ridiculous how handsome he is. But I'm being careful, I really am."

"Are you? Because this, this whole setup here, it isn't *working*," she says, emphasizing the word with her fingers as quotation marks. "This is hanging out."

"Oh, I don't want to overanalyze, Maggie," I say pleadingly. "Can we just enjoy ourselves?"

She shrugs and drops the subject, but the exchange unnerves me. As I knew she would, Maggie has called out the rising closeness and sexual tension that I can feel between me and Jake. I try to push it away, and I think Jake does too, sometimes, but then we both drop our guard and it's back, sniffing around like a fox who will not stop until he's got his chicken dinner. But I will not give in to it. I know that if anything happens between us, the magic of the work we're doing will be damaged.

When we sit down to eat dinner, the conversation between Maggie and Jake moves freely, but I find myself observing them rather than joining in the chatter. They talk about movies, gushing over their mutual love of magical realism and *Pan's Labyrinth*. We open more wine. Maggie smokes, and after a couple of hours, Jake asks for one and joins her. "It's a sometimes thing," he explains to me. We finish the fish and dish out a chocolate torte that Maggie brought from a supermarket on the way here. "I bloody hate cooking," she says as she liberates it from the plastic container. It's overchilled and dry, but we all give it a good go. We move on to music, and Jake suggests we head downstairs and go through his record collection.

Jake and I dance to old nineties records, and even cool-as-a-cucumber, non-dancing Maggie stands up and has a proper wiggle. We laugh. We collapse on the floor. Maggie tells Jake he needs a rug. Jake says he needs to go home soon and get his stuff, which is all in boxes at his parents' house. Stevie Wonder plays gently in the background, one of my favorite songs: "You Are the Sunshine of My Life." And then Maggie asks Jake the question I've always wanted the answer to.

"What are you doing next? Like, what are your plans?" she asks him, her arm hovering out the window, a cigarette dangling out, though the breeze blows all the smoke back into the room.

Jake shrugs. "I don't know. I'm taking the summer to regroup," he says.

"Are you serious about writing?"

"I was," he says.

"And not now?"

"It didn't really work out," he says.

"Quitter," she teases, knocking back the rest of her glass of wine. Maggie is now drunk.

"It's fucking hard," he says, eyes flickering across to me as he sits forward in the seat and folds his hands together. "My dad said it was a waste of my life, and he was probably right."

"What the fuck?" I say, jumping in. "Your screenplay was beautiful."

"Yes, but I'm thirty-two years old, and it never happened for me," he says. "Not to say it won't, but you need to have a lot of energy to keep going."

"You *have* to keep going!" I say. "I hired this amazing writer for a project once, her *first* project, and she was sixty-seven."

The needle lifts from the record player, and we all watch as the arm moves back to its cradle and the room falls silent.

"Sixty-seven?" Jake turns to me, a smile creeping across his face. "I mean, I don't want to bring you down, Amy, but that's how old my dad was when he died," he says, all matter-of-fact.

Impulsively I laugh, and so does Maggie, and then I worry I shouldn't be laughing, but Jake is laughing too.

"I get what you're saying," he says. "It isn't about age, it's about energy. Belief. Mine is waning. I'm starting to believe my dad was right, that my master's in English was a waste of paper."

"Yikes." I recoil at that. My parents never, *ever* questioned what I wanted to do. "As long as you enjoy it and have good people around you" was basically my dad's work-life motto. He was a mechanic, and he lived that motto. He loved cars and he loved his friends from the garage. They were like extended uncles in our family.

"I got really close twice," Jake says. "A film we got partial funding for that just fizzled out when the director got distracted by another, shinier, superhero project. And I was in talks with a studio in the US about a spec script I wrote. And then just as we were about to close, the studio went under. And you have no idea how many times my ideas got stuck in development and then the director or the VP left. A nightmare."

"You did all that without any connections or a top agent," I say quietly.

Jake grins sadly in my direction. "I should have been more aggressive."

"No," I say. "I just think, if you'd had better contacts, better people around you . . . maybe."

"I had to resort to some catalog modeling for a bit to keep the money trickling in," he says, lying back on his sofa now, hands behind his head. "My agent sent a three-for-the-price-of-one underwear photo to the *Fantasy Island* casting agents."

"Oh my goodness," says Maggie, laughing.

"Okay, everyone laughs, but I challenge you to an eight-hour catalog shoot with fifty-four outfit changes and a coked-up photographer called Giles Quentin-Cox who thinks you're the loser. It was infuriating. I kept wanting to shout, like, *No, dude. You're the loser. You wear an undertaker's hat, ride a motorized scooter. You embody corporate creative. You're business casual with cheap cocaine and a lover called Buffy.*"

"No wonder you hated *Fantasy Island*," I say. "That's basically the whole fun of it. Laughing at beautiful idiots."

Maggie suddenly stands. "Guys. I love you both, but I'm done, and if I don't go now I'll miss the last tube."

"Oh, staaaaaaaay," I say, not wanting this vibe, this night, this comradery, to end. Plus, Jake is relaxed and opening up like never before, and I really, really want to know more about him.

"No. Nope," she says. "I've got a lunch date with the Artist tomorrow and I really would rather not front up like I've just walked out of a basement bar."

I stand up and throw my arms around her. "Good-bye, bestie," I say.

"Good-bye, my little fool," she says, kissing me on the forehead. "He likes you," she whispers in my ear. "Be careful of your heart."

"Jake," she says now as he pulls himself up and accepts a warm, drunken hug from Maggie. "I really hope to see you again soon."

"You will," I say.

"I will," she agrees.

"No, I mean, you really will. He's coming to the work party," I say, biting my lip, knowing exactly what she will think of that. "He's my plus-one."

"He is?" she says, looking at me, and then swiftly over to Jake. "You are?"

"I am," he says. "Friday, right?"

He looks over to me and I nod.

"Of course you are," she says, shaking her head as she leaves for the door. We both move to follow her, but she waves at us to sit. "No, no, you two stay there. Open more wine. Want me to leave you a cigarette, Jake?"

"No more wine for me. . . . Probably a good idea to wrap this up," he says, sneaking a glance across at me. "I'll clear the terrace in the morning, Amy. You can just go crash and forget about it."

I feel deflated and frown, noticing Maggie has paused by the door and is holding it open so there is no way for me to try to stay. And I shouldn't. Why would I stay? It's time to go. "Right," I say. "Well. Bye, then. Thanks for an amazing day, Jake."

Twenty

〰️

Friday comes at me fast. And although part of me wants to find an excuse—stomach flu, dead aunt, Ebola—I know that I *need* to go. I need to network. And I *need* to look as fine as I can with Chris Ellis present and Jake Jones on my arm like armor.

My hairdresser's eyes turn into dollar signs when I explain I want highlights and a blow-dry of tight curls.

"You better get comfortable," he says, looking at his watch.

"Soft, shiny, and curls," I say. "Big, big, big hair."

While I wait for the magic, I text Maggie.

Me: I'm at the hairdresser . . . So nervous about the reactions from everyone at work to me bringing Jake!

Maggie: Nervous . . . or secretly excited?

Me: 😌 Maybe both?

Maggie: LOL AMY DUFFY. YOU FUCKING LOVE IT.

Me: Did you read his script?

Maggie: Not since you asked me a few hours ago.

Me: Embarrassing . . .

Maggie: Jake is. 1. Kind. 2. Funny. 3. Hot. The trifecta if you're looking for a man. Probably a disaster if you're looking for a creative partner. 😉

Me: I hear you.

Maggie: I look forward to further assessment later tonight.

Me: I can't wait to meet Michael.

Maggie: I am properly nervous.

Me: LOL. That would be a first, Maggie! Don't be.

And then I look at that last message, concerned I may have been too flippant. I add: I'm so happy you're bringing him. And I'm happy you're happy. And I bet he's perfect.

Two hours later, my hairdresser delivers. My hair is extraordinary. And very big.

"You're going to turn every head in town," he says, collecting the four million British pounds highlights and a blow-dry apparently cost in Central London. It's been some time since I've spent money on even a blow-dry. I get my nails done, deep red—classic shape. And then, when I get home, I pull a large plastic container out from under my bed and open it. Dresses. New York black-tie dresses I'd bought online secondhand and had altered. A vintage Gucci. A Michael Kors. A slinky wrap from Diane von Furstenberg. None has seen the light of day in two years, but all are still classic and immaculate.

I choose a RED by Valentino, with thick, wide straps, a soft sweetheart neckline, a side gathering, and a full skirt. I match its elegant, playful vintage style with a pair of silver pumps, and, because nothing makes you feel as daring and powerful as good underwear, I opt for seamed stockings and a vintage garter belt. I think I look pretty good. I *have* to look good. I'm going with Jake.

As I fiddle with my lipstick, also a deep red, and fuss about with my makeup, I imagine walking in with Jake just a step behind. He'll be like a lightning rod; our arrival will make an impact, but he will absorb the majority of the attention. There is no denying there is a slight thrill to having him on my arm. I picture us gliding in, laughing, and heads turning to see Jake looking dazzling. And for a moment I let myself imagine him looking at me with pure desire, and I feel a ping at the base of my spine. *No, Amy,* I whisper to myself. *Stay focused.*

I knock on his door and he opens it without looking at me as he slides on a watch and gathers his wallet and keys.

"I've been thinking about the structure around episode seven," he says, turning to face me. He stops. Looks briefly at my dress, down to my legs, my shoes, and then a little too slowly back up the curve of my body to my face. "That guy, your ex? He's going to *die*. He might already be dead with the shock wave you just sent out across London."

"Fuck off," I say, pushing him gently on the chest. "It's not all about my ex."

"Sure it is," he replies. "Fake boyfriend, remember?"

He's in a crisp white shirt and black bow tie. He slips on his dinner jacket and holds out his arm. I slide mine through his, and we take the stairs slowly down to the waiting taxi as I remind myself for the hundredth time that this is not a real date.

"What were you going to say about episode seven?" I ask as we slide in.

Jake laughs. "Oh yeah. Episode seven. Sorry, you're a bit distracting tonight, Amy."

I blush, pulling the hem of my skirt down.

"In the outline, we're saying that's when she identifies the killer; it's by a single hair. The single hair on the rotting corpse of the third victim," he says. "But the body is so wet and bloated, the coroner dismisses it as debris from the pond."

"To the Roxy in Covent Garden," I say, leaning forward to speak to the taxi driver, laughing to Jake as I realize how absolutely morbid our conversation sounds.

"Yes, the single hair," I reply.

"I think it needs to be from a type of brush, rather than human hair, because we need another revelation at the end of the episode. I did some research into some pretty interesting and totally gnarly paintbrushes with unusual hair," he says. "I think it could get us deep into the underbelly of the East London art scene. Make a great episode."

"Yes. Sounds good," I say, playing with the neckline of my dress and then resting my hands in my lap before resuming fiddling.

"You're nervous," he says, whispering this quietly into my ear.

"I'm nervous," I say. "The last date I brought to a work thing was a cardboard cutout of Stanley Tucci."

"Interesting choice," he says.

"He cooks, he knows Chanel. He's the internet's boyfriend," I say.

Jake laughs. "Well, congratulations, you've downgraded to the internet's latest meme," he says.

"I haven't seen you on PopSlut in weeks," I say. "Everyone's talking about Frannie, that Northern Irish girl who keeps flashing her boobs."

"Are you still watching?"

"No. Not since the week you moved in," I admit.

We ride in a sort of nervous silence all the way to the venue, and then, when the cab pulls up and I take a sharp breath in and out, Jake nods at me reassuringly.

"It's going to be fun," he says firmly. He takes a beat to catch my eyes and I nod in agreement. "I got you."

I melt when he says it. *I got you.* He takes my hand as we exit the cab on the curb outside the venue. He gently leads me, and I'm almost floating beside him in the heavy summer air. The sparkling fairy lights wind around the doorway of the entrance and intertwine with flowers and cascading plants, suggesting a night filled with magic and promise. I take a moment to gather myself, turning to Jake to brush clear his lapels as he puts a hand on my bare shoulder, making me jump with the electricity of his touch.

"You'll be fine," he says.

"It's *so* hot tonight," I reply, breathing slowly out, looking everywhere but into his eyes.

"It is, yes," he replies, his voice a throaty whisper. "Very hot."

The words linger in the warm air and I tell myself, sternly, that he's just commenting on the weather.

"Jake, I just want to thank you," I say.

"For what?"

"For *this*. In case I forget later. Thank you," I say, my eyes flickering to his. "I had a wonderful night."

"Come on," he says, smiling. He takes my hand again, and we're off and down the carpeted stairs into the basement area, the point of no return.

"Oh," I say as my eyes widen at the decorations. White balloons fill the ceiling with little white ribbon tails hanging down just above our heads. On the wall, 25 YEARS OF CTV AND BEYOND in silver balloons.

Waiters dart about with trays of prosecco and canapés, and I spy the Screen Global logo writ large at the far end of the hall.

"Money, money," says Jake, taking two glasses of prosecco off a tray and handing me one.

"Sort of," I say. "It feels like an exercise in team morale, but they've saved the real money for the executive memberships to Shoreditch House."

"Hey, you two," Maggie says, sidling up to us. The black one-shoulder number she's wearing oozes class and Maggie's signature clean lines. "Amy, you brought the girls," she says quietly, eyeing my cleavage.

"Time for a day out," I reply, blushing as I adjust the neckline to appear a little more modest, and I catch Jake pretending to perv, which further embarrasses me. "Can this not be a situation where my friend and my fake boyfriend tease the shit out of me all night? Great. Thank you!" I say, and Jake gives me a nudge in the ribs.

"It's my fake job," he whispers into my ear as Maggie waves to someone across the ballroom.

"Where is he?" I say, clutching Maggie's arm. "I'm dying to meet him."

"He's just over there," she says, craning her neck toward the bar as a tall, slender man with shaggy shoulder-length hair, dressed in a full black tux, including black shirt, makes his way across to us holding two gin and tonics. "Coming now," she says brightly.

He is not at all what I would have expected. But also, somehow perfect. He's almost like a mirror image of Maggie, similar kind of art-house androgynous, but shaggy-haired instead of sharp cut. When he joins us, it's clear he only has eyes for her.

Glasses are clinked and Maggie introduces him.

"Michael, it's so nice to finally meet you," I gush.

"And you too, Amy," he replies, his voice deep and gravelly. "I've heard so much about you."

"I'm Jake," Jake introduces himself, and they do a manly shake. Maggie and I catch each other's eyes and a kind of giddy amusement passes between us at this moment. It is the first time in three years of friendship that both of us have had dates at the same time and at the same event.

I watch as Michael is absorbed by Maggie, leaning in to kiss her bare shoulder, so that she giggles in a way I've never seen before.

Look at you, I mouth. He's enamored by her, and she him. It's adorable. "I've never seen you like this."

"I know," she whispers to me. "I can't honestly tell if it's a red flag. Is it a red flag?"

And it's then that I realize that Maggie is vulnerable. Probably for the first time since I've known her. She's in uncharted territory with a man who is not who she thinks she should look for, with feelings she cannot control.

"That's the dance we do with the devil," I say, trying to keep her from overthinking it.

"Amy, it's scary," she says plainly now, glancing across at Michael as he and Jake joke together. They look good. The writer. The artist.

"I know," I say. "How do you know when to trust someone?"

Michael leans in to kiss Maggie on the shoulder again, holding her arm like it's a trophy as he runs a hand down her skin.

"I feel like we're watching their foreplay," I say, turning to Jake, to which he replies, "Are you jealous? Do you need some attention, Amy? Because it comes with the job." And then he kisses me on the cheek, heat from his lips making me squirm with desire, and I push him away playfully.

"Oh, fuck off," I say.

"You're not going to be able to keep that up," he says.

"Keep what up?" I ask, but Jake just offers a delighted smile.

My eyes start to wander around the room, waiting for the moment I spy Chris. I am listening to the words Michael and Jake and Maggie are saying, but I can feel myself falling into a weird state of dissociation, where all I can think about is when I get "bumping into Chris" out of the way.

And then Penny joins us to shake me out of my trance.

"Um, oh my God?" She says this as a question, looking at me and then Jake and then back to me. She is almost annoyed.

"Hi, I'm Jake," he says, shaking her hand and offering up a spectacular smile, which makes Penny suck in both cheeks and widen her eyes in my direction. I notice the very slight hint of red on the side of his neck. He's a little embarrassed, and I find myself melting for him further. He's been so busy making me feel comfortable, I haven't really thought about him.

"Jake's my neighbor," I say apologetically.

"And your date!" he says, frowning at me.

"And my date," I repeat, elbowing him in the ribs.

"You've been keeping this quiet," says Penny, waving a hand around Jake's face but glaring at me.

A few moments later, Moe joins us, doing a clear double take as he spots Jake.

"They're dating," Penny paraphrases, and I correct her immediately.

"No, he's just my date," I say.

"Isn't he your neighbor?" Moe says, recalling the day Jake moved in and I excitedly told him all about it in the editing suite weeks ago.

"I'm both her neighbor *and* her date," Jake explains to Moe, who looks at me and offers an impressed smile.

The crowd starts to move slowly toward the dining room, where we're to have a four-course dinner, and then the tables will be moved for a "disco."

"It's like a wedding," I whisper to Jake as we look at the board containing the seating arrangements. And then he places his hand on the small of my back and gently guides me closer so we can find our names. The touch makes me jump, and so he leans forward and whispers, "Everything is going great, and you look fine as hell," into my ear.

I feel another unexpected prickle of delight down my back, moving to where his hand is and burning hot.

"Are *you* okay?" I ask, moving away from him a little. "Was Penny too much?"

"Everyone's staring," he says, "but I'm not sure it's at *me*." He looks down at my dress as he says this.

I cannot look at him but feel a giddy thrill as he says it. Jake is unbelievably good at playing boyfriend. He's sexy, he's complimentary, he's kind, and he's supportive.

"It's almost as if I *am* paying you," I say, my eyes narrowing, and Jake cocks his head.

"Take the compliment," he commands.

"*I receive the compliment*," I reply in my best Dalek voice, which makes Jake howl with laughter.

"Oh look! There's the rest of the team," I say, pointing to a round table with the names in black cursive next to each chair. "But I'm not there?"

"I put you and Maggie with the new head of content, since you worked with him before," says Penny, gliding across to join us. I stiffen. "So he doesn't feel all lonely."

"*Interim* head of content," I say quickly.

"Well, yeah," she replies, giving me a strange look. "You can schmooze a bit, Amy. You're going for the job, right?"

"Yes," I say, resigned. "Thanks, Penny."

Of course I've been seated with Chris. Brilliant.

"Well," says Jake, "let's go, then."

Jake holds his hand out and takes mine, and we head toward the table where Chris is already sitting back, looking impeccable in his sharp custom tux, with our CEO, Jeff, and presumably his wife. I'm at the power table. *Great.*

I see Chris turn his head toward me. There is no reaction

when he does, just a slight narrowing of the eyes as they flicker from me to Jake.

I have a visceral flashback to when I was in New York, with Chris, at the height of our secretive affair. Some gala or dinner out, and I arrived with a producer I'd been courting for a new project. "Come and meet the team," I'd told the guy. Chris knew, and although the entire thing was purely business, it drove him wild with desire. I think it was losing my attention to another man, even in play. And I enjoyed the way he wanted me that night. So I'd flirted a little. Played it up. Leaned a little *too close* to the producer. That night, Chris's desire for me was all-consuming.

It was a game to him, I think, rage boiling as we shake hands with Jeff and his date.

"This is Jake," I say, and I'm about to say, "my neighbor," but the woman I think is Jeff's wife beams and says, "Oh yes, someone told me about you already. You were on that television show with all the models, right? I love that show. Though I haven't been watching this year."

"What show?" Jeff dabs his mouth as he swallows some buttery dinner roll.

"*Fantasy Island*," she says, explaining to him. "It's that funny show where they bring these gorgeous young things together and make them date and walk around half-naked and do the most ridiculous challenges. All to find *love*."

She takes a moment to examine me before adding, "Caroline and the girls love it, darling." She giggles, resting her hand gently on his arm.

"Right," he says, looking at Jake and nodding, clearly disinterested.

My name is at the place right next to Chris, of course.

I take the seat, with Jake on my right, making sure to pull the skirt of my dress over my knees and scooch my chair so it's slightly farther away from Chris. But it's all so tight and my legs brush his under the table almost immediately. I hold my hand up and apologize immediately, but Chris just smiles as if it ain't no thing.

"Oh, it's a scream," Jeff's wife continues as I begin to shrink into my impossibly low neckline.

"It's a lot of fun, that's for sure," says Jake simply. I marvel at the delivery. Light, jovial. As if he's in on the joke, not the ass end of it. He's so good at creating space for himself.

"Jake is also a very good writer," I say, not able to resist a glance toward Chris as I say this.

"You are?" Jeff's wife says, I think, almost disappointed.

"What do you write, Jake?" *Chris.* So polite. So unassuming. I stiffen. "I'm Chris, by the way."

He holds out a hand, and Jake half stands because he *has to* in order to reach across and shake it. Power move from Chris. *Typical* power move.

"Features mainly. But haven't had a lot of luck," Jake says, pulling his chair back in as he sits. "Started out well, but no real bites."

"It's a tough business to break," says Chris, playing with his twenty-thousand-dollar Omega watch. I groan inwardly.

"It's why they call it the boulevard of broken dreams," Jake says.

"My husband calls it Horrorwood," Jeff's wife says, touching his arm again, "don't you, Jeff?"

"That's why you should write television," he says, waving his knife at Jake.

"Sure. I'd settle for an episode of *Teletubbies* at this point," Jake says to cackles around the table.

"Oh, you're funny," says Jeff. I just know Chris is not going to like the attention Jake is getting, and so it is no surprise when he speaks.

"Just got to keep at it," says Chris evenly. "Isn't that right, Amy? It was the worst part of the job, letting down the writers."

I want to stab my knife into his thigh.

"It's not fun waiting," Jake agrees, flashing a big smile at Chris.

A waiter arrives and pours the wine, and I bubble with nervous energy as I take a large mouthful. "Mmm," I say. "Chablis."

"I think they sell this at the local Aldi," says Jeff's wife, turning the bottle to face her. "It's not a bad table wine, actually."

"Christ, it's like three quid a bottle," Jeff replies.

"It's always been the way in TV, knock back the fancy prosecco on arrival and they follow through with bottom-shelf booze and overchilled prawn cocktails," Danny says, sitting down in a waft of lingering cigar smoke to Jeff's booming laughter.

"So much for the merging of liquid assets," says Jeff, slapping Danny on the back.

Danny offers up a big smile to Chris and a handshake around the table, including to Jake, whom he clearly doesn't recognize.

"We were just grilling this young man, James, is it?" Jeff's wife again.

"Jake," he says, tearing open his dinner roll as he sits back in his chair.

"About his time on *Fantasy Island*," she continues.

"No, we were talking about his *writing*," I say, but I'm roundly ignored.

"Oh, jolly good. That's that show on ITV?" Danny says. "How did you two meet, then, assuming you came together?"

He points between the both of us.

"We met over a delivery," Jake says quickly.

"A few deliveries," I say, smiling at Jake.

"A few *wrong* deliveries," he says, grinning at me, and I feel overwhelmingly grateful to him. But just as I mean to lean across and tell him, I feel Chris's leg brush mine and it breaks the moment, and I prickle all over with irritation.

"This sounds like a story," says Danny, knocking back almost a third of his glass in one go. "Maybe you should write about *that*."

Everyone laughs again. Danny is just drunk enough to be wildly amusing, but any more and he'll start to say things he shouldn't. Chris, I notice, has barely touched his drink. An old trick of his. Listen and learn. Don't drink. Let them drink. Then you're always in control. I push my glass slightly away from me.

"So have you written anything we might have had across our desk? I'm trying to think if I've seen your name," Chris says, and I feel myself stiffen with irritation. He tugs on the edges of his dinner jacket as he asks, and slowly, methodically, arranges the knives and forks on the table so they are perfectly straight.

"I doubt it," Jake replies slowly.

"What's your genre?" Chris presses.

"He writes *beautiful* drama," I say, jumping in, glaring at Chris.

"Who is your agent, then? Are you with one of the big four?"

"No," Jake replies, shaking his head. "My agent is actually—"

"Oh look!" I shout, desperate to deflect from Jake's bruising honesty. "Those balloons are extraordinary!"

The table turns in unison to look at the several silver and red balloons tied at the base with a large silver ribbon. "Yes, lovely bunch of balloons, Amy," Danny remarks. "Truly extraordinary. I'm so glad you pointed them out for us all."

The table breaks into laughter.

Chris turns his water glass once and then puts an elbow on the table, leaning forward so he can look across me to Jake. "You should send me something sometime," he says.

"Oh, thanks for the offer," Jake says. "I'll ask my agent. If she's still returning my calls."

This makes the table laugh again. Everyone but Chris. I frown at Jake. It's funny once to tell a joke at your own expense, but it's getting a little like he's putting himself down now.

"Amy has my contact information," says Chris.

I breathe slowly out to steady myself.

"I'm kind of fascinated that you went on a reality show, to be honest. It's not the most natural fit. Most writers I know are not . . . you know. *Extroverts*," he says, his eyes flickering slightly. Chris is walking a very strange line here, and one I've seen before. On the surface he's appearing to encourage Jake, but I know Chris, and I know he's trying to humiliate him with a million blunt jabs to the ego. It's a show of power. But why?

Chris can't be jealous. Chris dumped *me*. He thinks I'm a fool. He knows everything about me. Is he trying to humiliate *me* by humiliating my date?

"Oh, come on, you've sat in a writers' room," I reply. "Bunch of loud, attention-seeking nerds."

"True," he says, laughing, the tension easing slightly.

"Not that Jake is," I say quickly, but Jake laughs, and I feel his hand on my knee. I look down and he moves his hand up my thigh to give me a reassuring squeeze. He's telling me not to worry. He can take it. But I feel his fingers hit the elastic of my garter belt and freeze. I lift my eyes to him, feeling that dazzling thrill of sexual excitement, and he raises a single eyebrow at me.

"Amy Duffy," he says deeply into my ear. "That wasn't part of the deal."

I glance across at Chris and catch him looking at Jake's hand also. In a rising panic, I push it gently away.

"I propose a toast to the dawning of a new era," says Danny, raising his glass. Clearly reaching the point of no return. "And the arrival of our almost frozen prawn cocktails."

A chortle ripples around the table as the waiters slide the fancy tall glasses onto the table in front of each of us, and I notice the condensation begin to roll down the outside of the glass.

"To frozen cocktails!" says Danny, and we all raise our glasses.

"To frozen cocktails," we repeat before taking a sip.

"I'm not gonna complain," Jake whispers to me, plucking a tail out of the glass and biting into it.

Later, the tables have been removed and the dance floor is

in full, embarrassing swing. Jake and I have been out for a twirl to disco classic "September." Danny is dad dancing with Penny to "You're the One That I Want," his moves so excruciatingly drunk uncle I have to look away. Jake and I are surrounded by a small semicircle of people from work I barely know but who want to meet Jake.

"I'm sorry," I whisper into his ear, "we have this office sweepstakes, and everyone watches it."

"You've told me, like, a hundred times. It's fine," says Jake, who I can see is in all honesty starting to tire of absorbing the attention. I reach around him and pull him in for a side hug, and he takes this as a cue, because he reaches an arm and drapes it across my shoulders. I lean into him, thanking him with a squeeze.

Maggie and Michael are cozied up on two pushed-together chairs, almost every limb intertwined. He's sitting with his long, slim legs crossed, and I want to get over to her.

"I am going to go chat with Maggie and Michael for a bit," I whisper to Jake. "Can you give me, like, twenty minutes, and then we can go?"

"Sure. *Go*," he says.

But on the way to Maggie, I feel a hand on my arm and turn to see Chris grinning at me. "Amy," he says, the lights of the disco reflecting across him, the blue light making his teeth and the whites of his eyes glow.

"Hi, where did you come from?" I shout, looking over his shoulder toward Maggie, who is kissing Michael on the ear, and then toward a surrounded Jake. "Chris, I can't keep doing this. Can we just please drop the games?"

"What games, Amy? I'm not playing games. I just want to know how you're doing," he says, shaking his head, his sandy hair moving not an inch, as it's heavily sprayed and stiffer than plasterboard. "I like your new boyfriend."

"He's not my boyfriend," I reply. But I'm not sure why I say it. I curse myself, but Chris just smiles this little knowing grin and says nothing. And so I keep going. "He's my neighbor. We've been working up some ideas together. It's not like that."

Fucking hell, Amy, this sounds pitiful. Chris nods. He's doing that thing where he's extracting information from me by just letting me talk. It's what he does, and why he's so good at winning pitches. The less he says, the more they say, and the more he can adapt on the spot. I've seen him turn a pitch about a hospital drama into a rural love story on the spot.

"Oh, so you're working together," he says, and I can see the slightest of bites on the inside of his lip, as if this amuses him.

"Yes," I say flatly. "Sort of."

I see Jake catching my eye. He holds up a thumb and waves it up and down. I slightly raise my hand and send him a thumbs-down when I'm sure Chris is looking elsewhere.

Jake excuses himself and heads toward me, and Chris lifts his whisky up to his lips and takes a small sip as the lights dim further and a ballad comes on. He looks at me and puts down his glass, but before he makes the suggestion, I feel Jake's arm slide around my waist and pull me in. He plants the gentlest of kisses on my forehead and whispers, "Let's go," into my ear.

I feel completely enveloped by him. It's like a force field has dropped around me, and there is only Jake and me, and everything that is out there and dangerous can no longer touch me.

Chris watches, again completely poker-faced, and says, "Off already?"

"You know how it is," says Jake. "Man talk" for he wants to get me home to fuck me, but I have just played down our relationship to Chris. I basically called us colleagues. I cringe. I am dying. I turn to leave, tugging on Jake as we head for the door.

"Oh God, I'm fucking hopeless and made a total fool of myself," I say.

"What do you mean? Did I fuck up the fake boyfriend?"

I can feel eyes on us as we head through the ballroom toward the exit, and Jake, noticing the attention too, grabs my hand and squeezes it tightly.

"No," I say. "You were perfect. A flawless performance."

Twenty-One

〜〜〜

On the taxi ride home, it starts to rain, and we both stare out of our respective windows in silence. The London night swims by us in a blur of lights and noise, and I find the evening and its events have been overshadowed by an undeniable growing desire within me. For Jake. I wonder if his silence speaks the same to me.

It helped to have Jake beside me, and I reach across and squeeze his hand for the hundredth time.

"Thank you," I say.

"You don't have to keep thanking me," he replies. "I had fun."

"What did you think of him, then?"

"What did I think of Chris?" Jake ponders. "Hmm . . ."

"Yes. I'm dying to know," I say.

Jake reaches across the back seat, lifts my hand up, and kisses it on the knuckles. "I think he wasn't very pleased about me. And that he still likes you. Or wants you to like him. Unfinished business of some kind, I would say."

I laugh and pull my hand from Jake's, folding my arms.

"I don't think so," I say. "If you knew the circumstances under which we broke up. There is literally no way."

"Tell me them," he says as the car pulls up.

We climb out and I get the bill, although Jake tries to pay. "It's my night. My expense," I say, pushing his hand away.

We head into the building, and Jake suggests we sit in my apartment. "I've never seen it," he remarks. I shoo him straight into the living room, swinging by my fridge to grab a couple of glasses and a chilled bottle of prosecco I'd popped in there from the night Maggie was here.

My living room has incredible evening lighting. A dim floor lamp and several other small LED fairy lights, which give the perfect evenly lit atmosphere for TV watching. My leather sofa looks well-worn, draped with a soft wool throw and cozy down-filled cushions. I put the prosecco on the little hardwood coffee table, which is strewn with copies of *Variety*, books, bound scripts, and three—*three*—half-finished coffees.

"How embarrassing," I murmur, swiping clean the mess and shoving the coffee cups in the sink. I pop the cork and fill our glasses and take the seat across from him on the sofa, kicking off my heels. I feel the silk of my skirt slide against the top of my thighs, and the slight chill coming through my open window. But when Jake stands to close it, I tell him no. I like the fresh air and the sound of rain. He takes off his jacket, laying it across the wooden chair I use as a spare for guests, and sits next to me. We both turn inward so we're leaning back on the armrests, facing each other. I pull my legs up and curl them the best I can.

Our glasses clink.

"To a great night," he says.

"To a great night," I say, and while we hold each other's gaze for a moment, my heart flutters under his stare. There is a boyishness to Jake that is so playful. The more you get to know him, the more he comes out of his shell.

"Sorry about Chris," I say. "He was a jerk."

"He was fine. Just a dude wanting to mark his property," he says. "That being you. You were going to tell me what happened."

"Was I?"

"Yes," he says firmly.

I don't want to get into a conversation about Chris and what happened. I feel like if Jake knew, then whatever he feels about me—and it is clear, he has feelings just as I do—would change. Does he like me enough to look past it? I cannot take that risk.

Better to change the subject.

"What about you? Who was your last girlfriend?"

"She was called Ruby, and she was a nurse."

I squirm a little, eyes dropping to the skirt of my dress.

"She was cool. We were together for three years, actually," he continues, "but I was really struggling with work, and she wanted things to move forward. . . . I wasn't ready, basically."

"I see," I say, feeling a stab of jealousy as he says it.

"What?" Jake picks up on it right away.

"Nothing." I smile wryly. *He knows.* He can see it on my face. *Something else. Move on to something else.*

He eyes me, trying to read into my every movement. Then he reaches up, stretching his arms, his shirt pulling against the muscles across his shoulders as he folds them across his chest. "Come on, Amy. Enough. What happened with Chris?"

"Oh God," I murmur, shaking my head furiously.

"Tell me. What happened?"

I let out a huge exaggerated sigh and just let the words flow. "He blocked my project. The one I worked on with my whole fucking heart. For four fucking years. He just blocked it."

"He did?"

"Yes, he said it was because we were dating and about to become official and he felt the optics were bad or some shit."

Jake blows out, once. "Damn," he says.

"Damn indeed," I say. "It was so good, and so many hard-working people were let down by it. I think about the writer all the time. Her script was so amazing."

Jake is thoughtful for a moment, and then he leans forward. "But wait, he dropped your project because you were dating, and then dumped you? That's . . . that's *really* cruel. Like, that's some asshole shit. I honestly don't get it. Is he literally the devil?"

"Well, I might have kind of retaliated against the blocking of the show," I say carefully. "And he dumped me after that."

"Whoa boy, this is getting good," he says playfully, but I feel my cheeks redden and he quickly adds, "You can't stop now, Amy."

"I'd rather not tell you *everything*," I say. I grimace. "I'm still too ashamed."

Jake looks quizzical. "Did you toilet roll his garden?"

"No," I reply.

"Sex tape?"

"No!" I laugh. "Fuck off."

"Leave a turd in a paper bag on fire on his doorstep?"

"No, I'm not a ten-year-old boy," I say, laughing, but also a bit uncomfortable with how not far off this feels.

"Did you key his car?"

"Okay, this is getting weird," I say as we catch each other's eyes again, and there is a slightly lingering look from Jake behind the playful grin.

Jake laughs. "Amy Duffy, you dirty, sly, vengeful dog. I like it."

"You wouldn't like it," I say glumly.

"How do you know?"

"I just know. You'd judge me. You wouldn't see me the same," I say.

"Unless you're talking about something where you're naked, I think I've seen a fair bit of who you are, Amy."

"Not naked," I say.

"What a shame," he replies.

Jake is a little tipsy, and truthfully so am I. I offer him a smile, touching the edge of my neckline as I do. Jake looks even better at midnight than he does in the day, his eyes heavier, his smile more wicked; everything about him is loaded. I cannot resist him.

Jake watches my fingers, and I follow his eyes as they move slowly across my shoulders and then back up to my face. He considers me with a dark intent. And then he leans forward.

"Amy," he says, his voice gravelly. His desire is clear.

"Jake," I reply, wanting to close my eyes and let the moment wash over me.

"Come on, now," he says with a wry grin. Delivered like I

ought to know better. Like I ought to know what I'm doing to him. I take a moment to revel in the feeling, and then, with all the strength I can muster, I look away.

"We have to get some sleep," I say quietly.

"I don't want to fucking go," he says, determination settling in.

"I don't want you to either," I reply clumsily, the words getting caught in my throat.

"I want to kiss you," he says, and I feel my chest start to heave, the rawness of my feelings taking my breath away. *I want to kiss you too*, I think.

This is not a choice. I'm falling for him. But I cannot let it happen. I cannot have a repeat of Chris, however much I desire it. I *cannot*. Not now. It's only three weeks until the pitch. We have to put our heads down and focus.

I have to stop this before it cannot be stopped.

"Detective Caraway is waiting for us," I say, lifting my eyes back to his. I watch the desire dampen and my heart breaks just a little. Just enough to know that Jake has found his way in there and that this, whatever it is, is far from over.

Twenty-Two

~~~~

The next morning, I am sitting on the terrace, nursing my hangover with a coffee, waiting for Jake. The air is fresh from last night's rain, and the smell of concrete and greenery makes the air feel close, almost claustrophobic. I'm feeling jittery and nervous about the intenseness between Jake and me last night. I want to push it away and pretend none of it happened, but I can't.

I feel that in Jake I have found the perfect creative partner. We're both tentatively stepping back out there. A creative career demands you be vulnerable, sharing your ideas, your vision, your passion, hoping you're not met with laughter or rejection.

It's a delicate thing. One that relies on absolute trust to bring out the best you can be.

And Jake and I need that trust so we can get back into our work and thrive. Any crossing of the Rubicon into something romantic is a surefire way to endanger it. It introduces new ways to feel vulnerable, right when we need to feel at our most brave.

I think about Chris, and how our work relationship was built on his encouragement of me. I always felt I had little to offer him the other way. Chris was very good at making me feel endlessly grateful to him. And yet. In the end, what did he really do for me?

With Jake, however, we both seem to need each other. Which is why we have to, we absolutely *have* to, keep the feelings aside until this project is over.

As the terrace door flings open, an altogether different Jake comes out, freshly showered, pink-cheeked, and bright-eyed, holding a mug of coffee.

"Hey," he says, moving toward me, hesitating slightly on his approach. Perhaps he was waiting for me to stand for a hug. I'm not sure what to do, now I know that Jake feels the same way I do. *Focus, Amy. Use your head and not your . . . other parts.*

Or does he? It could have been the prosecco.

"You look fresh as a daisy," I say in a totally not weird voice.

"I went for a run," he says. "Nearly died, but the result is no hangover."

"I'd rather have a hangover," I say, though it's a lie. I used to love a hard gym session after too many cocktails. Now I just enjoy sinking into the hangover with TV, coffee, and home-delivered pizza. There are definite upsides to my quieter, less competitive London life.

"So," he says, sitting down opposite me. He looks down at his curled hands around his mug on the table and then straight back at me. "I couldn't sleep after I left you last night."

"You couldn't?" I reply. I imagine, with some degree of ego, him tossing and turning in a state of wild desire. I woke up on the floor, with a trail of crusty drool down my face, having rolled off the bed, but it feels like the wrong moment to mention this.

"No. I was thinking about this," he says. "About *us*."

I close my eyes and nod slowly. "I have thoughts too," I say. I'm not sure it's wise to let Jake speak first. I'm afraid that if we're not aligned, the willpower I'm clinging to will disappear. How would I resist if, in the sober light of day, Jake Jones told me that he wanted me? That he is also developing feelings?

"Can I speak first?" I ask.

"Please," he says.

"Jake," I say, "you're really a very fucking good person."

"Uh-oh," he says, frowning. "This is a bad start."

"I just said you were a *good* person," I protest.

"Tell me there isn't a *but* coming," he replies, a wry smile creeping across his face. "I know that line. I think I've even delivered a version of it before."

"Okay, fine, there is a *but*. But it isn't 'but I don't like you like that.' It's 'but we're working together and we should not do this.' We're going to be in each other's pocket finishing this project. And frankly, I just know where this will go if we don't listen to the *but*."

"Truth be told, there's only one butt I'm interested in here," he says, sitting back, grinning, but he's deflecting with this joke. His eyes are no longer fixed on me, instead looking out across the rooftops, darting up to the morning sky and back to the coffee in his hands.

"Jake." I can't help smiling at him. "I just wonder, in the

spirit of trying to be professional and keep things separate. My last working relationship ended up—"

"Yes, but he was your boss. You hold all the cards this time," he says, frowning. "I mean, I could do all this work and you could get the job and I could be left with nothing."

"We agreed on the terms and I won't screw you," I insist.

"Sounds like you're *definitely* not going to do that," he says teasingly.

"Jake," I say, reaching across the table and slapping him on the arm. "Take this seriously."

Jake sits back now and sighs, folding his arms and looking me square in the face. "Amy, it's fine. I get it," he says. He looks away again, at a pigeon that has landed on the neighbor's chimney and is cooing. "Just promise not to wear the *Baywatch* swimmer again." He looks back now and grins, but this time it's a resigned smile. A good-natured one. I feel the heat in my cheeks as I look away.

"Jake," I moan, covering my face with my hands to try to contain the feelings I want so desperately to share. Feelings I cannot believe he reciprocates. Feelings that I hope will still be there when this project is over.

"Amy, seriously, I understand. We need to keep things clear, separate, while we're working on this. From a practical point of view, it's foolish to get mixed up. And I have some things I need to get done. I have to help my mum move into her new house. I need to get my shit together and figure out what's next for my career, because this has been great for lighting my fire again, but I have to do things on my own. I need a plan B." He looks at

me, and he shakes his head, resigned. "Let's cool it. And then
see. I can wait. Let's not get drunk again together. And let's try
to keep this platonic. We're both mostly adult."

I let out a sigh. "Okay. Good. *Platonic*."

"I can totally keep this platonic," he insists.

"So can I," I reply, unsure if I mean it.

Things are definitely a little different as we head out to the
South Bank later that day to do a location recce for the third
body in our series. We are a bit awkward with each other. Of
course we are. We're playing this game of polite avoidance.
Trying not to touch. Trying not to linger on each other at all.

Jake doesn't catch my eyes in the same way as before. He
doesn't hold my gaze or smile playfully at me across the café
table where we compare notes and ideas. In fact, he seems to
make an effort to avoid looking directly at me at all.

I touch his arm to point out a window where our police detective could get caught by the suspect, fleeing from the scene of
murder three, and feel a stab of sadness as he steps subtly away,
so my hand falls from him. He's trying. I'm trying.

We walk down the edge of London to an area called Shad
Thames, old docks that Jake tells me were full of warehouses in
the nineteenth century.

"There was this map, made in, like, 1750 or thereabouts,
that had a lane called Shad Thames, so it's pretty old. But the
warehouses came in the nineteenth century. And here is Butler's
Wharf," he says, indicating the building beside us. "This is

where they met the shipping goods and then moved them to their various locations."

We turn, backs to the river, and look up to the large old redbrick building with its modern windows still flanked by iron pulleys that look like cranes. There is a vast network of little bridges connecting the upper windows of the warehouses above to the little lanes below.

"This is all more or less residential now. But there's some cool old features like external rigging, and the footbridges. Oh, and the names! Names like Cayenne Court, Vanilla and Sesame Court—all the spices you can think of. I have this vision of huge barrels of cardamom being loaded on pullies directly from the boats. It must have smelled wild. Well, if you could smell it above the rats and sewers and all the other delicious east-dock Victorian England delights." He grimaces.

"How does the sewage system work today?" I ask as my phone buzzes in my pocket. I glance at the time on my watch; Mom's awake and on me early. *I'll call her later.*

Jake spins around to face the north side of the river. Tower Bridge is to our left, and an assortment of hotels and residential buildings stretches east as far as you can see down the Thames.

"Well, back then this river was just an open sewer," he says.

"No," I say. "*No!*"

"It was. All the pipes just led right in there."

"Delicious," I mutter, imagining the smell and the filth.

"There was this period of hot weather called the Great Stink, and I kid you not, the smell got so bad that finally one guy in Parliament was like, 'Hey, maybe we shouldn't be pumping this much shit and cholera into the main river through our largest city.'" He says this in an exaggerated posh voice while he pretends to twirl a mustache.

"Bless that one guy," I say.

"I still wouldn't pour it on my two-minute noodles," says Jake, peering over the old stone wall to the water below. It's gray, murky, with a beer can and a medical mask caught in the back-and-forth push of waves against the stone. I watch him for a moment, leaning forward with both his forearms resting on the top of the wall, kicking the bottom with his foot.

He's just out of reach; the shutters are slightly drawn.

"So, where does this leave Detective Caraway?" I say.

"She's standing there," he says, pointing to some stone stairs that lead down the side of the walkway toward the river. "And the body is floating just here—it's caught on something. But in the dark night, she can see the curved top of a head, slightly submerged. It's creepy as hell and she's calling to her partner, 'There's somebody there, flashlight, flashlight!'" Jake starts to come alive now, his arms pointing out to the water and then the walkway, as if we're watching this unfold live. The steady stream of tourists watch on in amusement as they pass by.

"But at this point no one believes what she says anymore," I say, jumping in. "They *know* she's making little sense. She already made the terrible mistake with the second victim, claiming there was a diver in the pond when he was found. And the CCTV footage showed nothing."

"Exactly," he says. "Her partner flashes the torch around and nothing is there."

"Yes, this is *so* good," I say.

"Yep. And it's cold water, remember. She's heading down the steps; the water is getting closer. She's completely fixed on the body and stopping it from being caught in the back pull under the docks. Then something startles her, a black flipper. The diver takes off under the wall here—into the old sewer system."

I finish, "And we don't know what she's going to do but she's shouting, 'There's a person in here!' at her partner, and the partner is talking into his radio, slowly; he doesn't think so."

"'We got a body here at Butler's Wharf on the south side of the river,'" he says in a deep voice.

"He's calling for backup, but super wearily. Then we see the water, and we see bubbles, air bubbles rising to the surface. Like there's something breathing down there. And, at around forty-six minutes, we close the episode with her jumping in."

Jake turns to me, and he smiles. "Roll credits."

"That's it," I say.

"She's going to get her guy," he reminds me.

"She *is* going to get that bastard," I say. "But not until episode ten, unfortunately. Gosh, thank God we only need an outline for the later episodes."

"I have been thinking about the title," he says, turning to me, sucking on the straw of his cold brew. "It's not quite right, *Black Water*, is it?"

I look at him, my eyes narrowing slightly as I think it over.

"Probably not." I nod in agreement, staring down at the water below us, which is more of a murky blue-gray with little lines of foam collected at the seawall.

"Okay, let's describe her," says Jake. "She's, like, dryly

funny. She's *really* literal. Her clothing is very practical and a bit dated."

"Hard-core normcore," I add. "Fawn leather shoes with zips. Wool slacks."

"Yep. She eats junk food like a champion. She gives off an air of incompetence, because she's just so unslick. But she isn't. Far from it. She's haunted by the death of her lover. And, of course, she can't swim."

"Except that by the end of episode eight she can swim a little," I interject. "Don't forget the creepy private lessons she takes with the guy who approached her by the pond in episode one."

"Our third suspect," he says, nodding.

"What about just *Caraway* as a title?"

"Maybe," I say, pondering this idea. "Still, it needs to be more generic. More atmospheric. *Caraway* sounds a bit like a snobby cookbook."

"Hmm." Jake ponders this. "She's funny. She fumbles a lot. She almost acts like she doesn't know what she's doing. She draws on that incompetent charade to pull people in. That's her difference."

"*The Deceptive Detective,*" I say, laughing.

Jake does too, and for the first time today, I feel like we're somewhat back to where we were. "*The Dark Deceiver?*" he tries.

"*The Circle Line of Hell,*" I say.

Jake laughs again. "*Inspector No Remorse?*"

I elbow him now, and we both laugh, releasing some of the tension I'd been feeling this morning.

"It will come," he says. We turn to continue our walk toward London Bridge, for dinner and home. And I tell myself

I did good today. I stopped something that could have derailed me. And I pursued the *right* course. Jake looks across at me and grins, and I wonder if he's thinking the same. This—us, working together—works.

Then, in my pocket, my phone buzzes and it's my mom. *Again.* I grimace when I see her name.

"I better get this," I say, frowning. "She won't stop until I answer."

I press the green button on my screen and say, "Hey, Mom."

She launches right into it. "It's just a few short weeks. Your grandmother won't be here much longer. This craziness has to end, Amy!"

She is *so* loud that I pull the phone away from my ear and turn it down so I can listen without hearing damage.

"Mom, I'm going to look at flights, okay?" I say finally. But I know I'm just putting her off. "We have a lot going on at work right now. But I'll see what's available."

"I'll pay, for Christ's sake," she says in my ear, and then I can hear her sniffle back tears and it makes me feel like I'm breaking down inside. "Amy, please. Your father hasn't been the same since you left. It's worse than when Skipper died."

My dog. A dumb-as-hell terrier that was a fur ball of sunshine. I feel the pang of sadness I always do when I think of Skipper. I look across at Jake and slow my pace so he can't hear my reply.

"I'm not dead. But, Mom, I feel bad about what happened, and bad I'm not back," I say. "I can't move without feeling bad about everything."

"We don't care about what happened anymore, Amy. People

gave up caring when they realized you were going to punish yourself for life. *Nobody* cares. Everyone has moved on except you. And they'll all move on from you too if you don't hurry up and get home. Auntie Maria needed reminding that I had a daughter."

"Your auntie Maria thinks she's still in Galway," I remind her. Auntie Maria isn't really an auntie, but a very rich widowed Irish neighbor who, according to Mom, half the neighborhood had befriended on account of there being no living relatives. Dad always said, "But not your mom, she's there for the audience." And she was. Auntie Maria was the only person too frail to try to inject herself into a conversation. Everyone in my family shouts over one another in a half-arguing, half-laughing conversation that never really includes "listening."

"Please," she says now.

I sigh, feeling the prickle of tears in my eyes as she continues.

"Okay, Mom. I'll get back to you within the week, okay?"

I hang up and Jake looks back at me, saying nothing as he takes in my red face and wet eyes.

"My mom wants me home," I say. "I feel torn apart."

"So go home," he says.

"I can't," I say.

"Why the hell not?"

"I can't explain it to you," I say. "I can't go back."

Jake steps toward me, and the streams of tourists part around us as we stand there. I pull my hands up to my face and cover my eyes.

"Did you do something? Like, did something happen?"

"There was a whole thing. It's connected to Chris," I say. "I can't talk about it. Not to you."

Jake frowns and I worry he thinks this means that this is connected to my feelings for Chris somehow.

"I did something that hurt my family, and it was because of Chris," I splutter.

"The revenge?"

I look up at him and nod slowly. I told him a little of it last night. But he doesn't know the full story. Not the part that causes me such torment that I can't walk into the home I grew up in. Not just that fucking video. Me caught on camera, the very worst, drunkest, most wild and unhinged version of myself. Not just that; it was also because I should have been at my cousin's wedding and I let them all down.

I was definitely ashamed when Chris pulled out. I didn't know how I was going to explain it. But that was no excuse, really. In truth I was driven by pure hate that day. Blinded by anger, and the complex ache of a broken heart. All I wanted was to burn everything that was Chris Ellis down. And then, of course, the video emerged and the humiliation was complete.

"The revenge," I say.

"I'm intrigued," he says, his eyes closing in on me. He's trying to cheer me up. "I mean, no one died, did they? No one got hurt?"

"Not physically," I say, rubbing the tears from my eyes with the back of my hand. "But I just feel like such a loser. And once upon a time, they were so proud of me. I can't face it."

"You should try being me," he says, joking.

"How did you get over it?" I ask, begging for some insight.

"You humiliated yourself in front of around 1.6 million viewers, and you're still standing."

"Gee, thanks, Amy," he says, grinning.

"I mean it!"

"I don't know," he says, shrugging, kicking a paving stone with his foot. "Because I had to get over it? Come on," he says. "Why don't we get lunch and at least google flights. They won't be cheap, so it might be worth just getting them right away and then you can always cancel."

"I could do that." I think. It will at least buy me time as I figure out if it's possible to once again be the person my family loves.

Twenty-Three

A few days later, my two weeks' holiday is in full swing and Jake and I are pulling twelve-hour days as the pitch day looms. But despite our best efforts, we're struggling to keep the mutual attraction at bay.

Every time we're alone together there is a fizzing undercurrent that is intoxicating to us both. Just like with Chris, there is something so undeniably hot about the forbidden, and it's even worse with Jake, because we're not hiding our desire from co-workers; we're hiding our desire from ourselves.

And we're doing a really bad job of it. And it's getting worse.

"Borough Market," he says as we walk down a small, crowded lane toward London's hugest food market. "What I like here is that we're right on the river, so we're connected to the crime scene, and we're in a very thick tourist area."

"So, when Detective Caraway is in pursuit of the final subject, our real killer, they spill out here—" I say, my arms open wide.

"Disorientating," he says, looking all around him, as we

stand still and the crowd parts around us and a sea of faces and bodies moves around us like water.

"Oh God, it's perfect," I reply. "Can we get some breakfast before we go on to talk blood splatter and bone-sample analysis?"

"Over there," he says, pointing to a small café with a huge line snaking out the front and onto the small, pedestrianized road.

"I'm going to need to take home that baguette," I say, drooling at the bread display in the café's window. "My God, the food here."

As we sit with breakfast sandwiches of Halloumi and arugula and coffees with perfect little ferns of milk froth and cream, Jake starts telling me about his mom's new house up in Wales.

"It's like something out of a fucking storybook," he says.

"When do you have to go?" I ask, pulling up the calendar on my phone. "Next week, or . . . ?"

"This weekend," he says. "Have you given it any thought? We can work on the train—that's, like, four or five hours. And there's no reason we can't talk while I paint the lounge. We do our best work when we're walking around London."

"Um . . . ," I murmur into my sandwich, unsure whether this is wise. A night away? With Jake? Alone in a cottage in the middle of nowhere?

"Think of it like a work-away day," he says, as if sensing my concern.

"It's not a bad idea to get out of the flat," I agree. "And I've never been to Wales. Honestly, I've not really left London yet."

"Not just Wales. *Snowdonia*. It's spectacular," he says.

"Is there water I can jump into?"

"There's a beach," he says, grinning. "And a castle."

Although it sounds more like a weekend away than a work-away day, I nod.

"I'm in," I say.

"Excellent. I want to get the painting done before she moves in," he says. "I mean, the whole house is being fixed up, but I want to have contributed."

"Oh, that's sweet of you," I say, a smile creeping across my face. Jake really is so thoughtful, and so pretty. "My dad is always doing stuff like that for my mom, except he can only really fix cars, not houses. So, there's all this terrible DIY work around. He once tried to install a wood burner—and we now have a massive round hole and thick metal pipe snaking through the cladding that comes straight into the living room. Mom has covered it in tinfoil to stop the drafts. It looks like a robot."

"Shiiiit," he says.

"It even has a name," I say. "Bender."

"After the robot in *Futurama*," he says, nodding as if to say, *Obviously.*

"Marry me," I reply, laughing.

"*Arrested Development*," he shoots back, grinning.

"Oh my God, you love TV too," I say, gushing in delight. "Two excellent references and you knew them both!" I ball my hands under my chin and smile at him.

"Come on, nerd," he jokes, standing, taking my hand and pulling me up.

I stand, grab my baguette, and slide my bag over my shoulder. We walk through the crowds down toward the river, the sun forcing its way between the buildings in almost vertical shafts. I remove my black cardigan and tie it around my waist.

Jake glances sideways at me and I feel his eyes on my body, and I am again awash with desire.

"So, here," he says, guiding me back behind the cathedral toward a vast navy-black Elizabethan sailing boat sitting in a small inlet just off the Thames. Towering wooden masts shoot up between the two riverside buildings, and yellow and red decorative trimmings lead the eye to a golden deer head at the front. She's beautiful.

"That's *The Golden Hinde*," he says, pointing at the boat. "I think it would be great if the chase ended here somehow. Continuing with our water theme. So, she's climbing onto the boat, there are tourists around. And she draws her weapon. The tourists move back, someone screams that she has a gun."

I hold up the baguette in its brown paper bag like it's a gun and point it toward the stairs that lead to the lower deck.

We pause our role-play while I buy two tickets, and then we head down the little wooden stairs, my baguette still raised, and we enter the bowels of the great boat. It's quiet down here, and dark.

"It is a replica of the first boat to sail around the world," he says. "I just think this room here would be a great moment for a standoff."

"It's perfect," I say, "the dark wood bunks and furniture of the sleeping quarters mean there's plenty of places for him to hide."

"You got it. So. We're at about forty-two minutes and building up to the cliffhanger. The pace slows down now. We've been running, there's been so much noise, so many people, but suddenly . . . everything goes quiet."

"Except her breathing, and her footsteps on the floor," I say.

"And the occasional creaking of the sails above."

"The boat is stationary, though," I say.

"Shh. I'm creating atmosphere," says Jake, putting a finger up to his lips. My eyes linger on his mouth and I watch the corners turn up into a sly smile. He whispers now. "We hear the creak of the wooden boards, and she spins around."

A tourist who has followed us down to the lower deck coughs behind us, and I look at Jake and giggle.

"People must think we're nuts," I whisper.

But Jake ignores it. He takes my hand in his and pulls me toward a corner of the boat so we're behind a bunk and almost completely hidden from view. He turns me around and points toward the little stairs that lead back up onto the deck.

Then he leans in behind me, so I can feel the warmth of his body radiating into me, but we're not touching. I stay very still, feeling an almost imperceptible hint of his breath on the back of my neck. Every cell of my body seems to be reacting, a fizzing feeling blistering under my skin.

"She comes down those stairs, and we think the suspect is here," he says, almost whispering now; the little hairs on the back of my neck prickle with the intense sensation. I concentrate hard on my breathing as I try to listen to his words.

"There's a small creak," he says, leaning slightly beside me into the bunk, forcing the old wood to groan under the pressure. "And then he grabs her from behind."

"How?" I say eagerly.

"You want me to show you?"

"Yes," I say earnestly. "You can grab me."

Jake pauses for a beat. And then he puts a hand around my mouth and pulls me backward into him, twisting my arm behind me and pushing his chest into my back so I cannot escape.

"Sorry, is this weird?" he says, pausing.

"Not at all," I say through his fingers, which I am resisting the urge to nibble on.

"It is just easier to act it out," he agrees.

"It's really important," I mumble. "You can be as rough as you need to be. Do whatever you want to do. To the *detective*, I mean. For research purposes."

"For research purposes," he repeats.

"Yes," I say, not wanting this touch to end.

"In that case . . ."

I feel his body stiffen as he walks me backward, then roughly spins me around and pushes me into the side of the boat so my face is up against the cold wood.

"He squeezes her hand so hard, he forces the gun out, and it clatters to the floor. He has her trapped," Jake says as I drop the baguette gun and he leans into me, hard now, from behind, his lips at my neck, his breath hot and even.

This is hot. I'm really, inappropriately turned on. I gasp as he whispers into my ear. "The detective is scared," he says. "Her heart is racing. She's thinking about her gun, we see her eyes look downward . . . if only there was some way she could reach it."

"But she can't," I say. "And the suspect whispers into her ear again . . ."

"What does he whisper?" Jake asks.

"I don't know, just whisper something again," I say.

"Like this," he says slowly, directly into my ear, and I cannot help but let the quietest of moans escape my lips.

"Yes, just like that," I say, moving slightly so I can feel more of Jake's body pressing into mine.

"What else does he do?"

"Maybe he . . . um, runs his fingers slowly down her neck? Sort of sexy threatening?"

"Why?"

"I don't know," I say. "Because a kiss would be really inappropriate."

"Why?" he presses.

"I don't have the answer," I say, wanting to feel his lips against my neck, his tongue gently flicking at the spot behind my ear.

"He wants to kiss her," Jake says, letting go of my arm, which he's been holding behind my back, and placing it on the wooden beam next to my head. I spin around so I'm pinned now between his arms, back to the wall, looking into his eyes.

"She can't kiss him," I say, looking directly into Jake's eyes, "until the series is finished."

Jake holds my gaze for a moment and then drops his arms.

"He can wait," he says, laughing breathily.

"Also, he's a deranged psychopath, and this is a crime series, not *Fifty Shades of Grey*," I say with an equally breathy laugh. I'm breathing unreasonably hard.

"Excuse me!" says a voice. "You can't be behind there!"

Jake and I emerge from behind the bunk, and I collect my cardigan, which fell to the floor during the tussle.

"Sorry," I say to the ticket collector, who watches us move sheepishly to the stairs like a couple of naughty schoolchildren. "We're writing a TV show."

"Of course you are, love," he says, like he's heard it a hundred times.

"Don't forget your gun, Amy," says Jake, and the ticket collector bristles until he follows Jake's pointing finger to the discarded baguette lying in its brown paper bag on the floor.

Twenty-Four

A week into my holiday and I'm excited to get out of London.

Jake and I left early for our trip to Wales, computers packed, ready for an intense working session on the train. I watch him in the seat across from me, his laptop open as he chews on his bottom lip while thinking, and his lips move slightly to the beat of the dialogue he's typing out.

"I have never felt so confident something is going in the right direction," he says, lifting his head to look at me. "Normally, at this stage of a project, I'm freaking out and doubting everything."

"The worst enemy to creativity is self-doubt," I say. "Sylvia Plath."

"Ha," he says, looking back down at his screen. "Well, I've had plenty of that."

"Why did you want to be a writer?" I ask, staring out the window and not at him.

"I don't know," he says, his fingers *tap-tap-tapping* on the keyboard.

"You don't know?"

He leans back in the seat. "I remember that once I fully understood there was a job writing movies, I just never wanted to do anything else. I blame *Donnie Darko*."

"I felt the same way about making up TV shows. I blame *The Sopranos*."

I scribble titles for the series in my notebook and try to pull together a compelling logline as the countryside flies past in a blur of high summer greens, cow pastures, sheep, and small townships bleeding into the outskirts of major centers until we're ejected back on the other side to the calm of the green again.

Jake and I share the occasional look, but mostly the chatter is incidental around our work.

"Would Detective Caraway swear?" he asks, looking down at his screen.

"Occasionally, and guiltily," I reply.

Later, I look up from my job of pulling the show bible together and read him the final logline. "Harriet Caraway is an introverted low-rank police detective and behavioral investigative adviser who works in London City in the major crimes unit. When a body surfaces in Hampstead Pond, she becomes embroiled in the case of a series of brutal water-based murders, which bear an eerie resemblance to a tragedy in her past."

"Nailed it," he says, high-fiving me across the table, and we share a moment of excitement.

"Water murders?" I mutter. "Is that even a thing? I need to google if that's a thing."

"It's our thing," he says.

"Then we're there on the logline," I say triumphantly.

"Almost worth a glass of champagne," he says.

"When we're *truly* done," I reply, grinning as I tap on his computer screen to remind him the pilot script needs to be finished.

When we get off at the station, Jake is quick to arrange a rental car, and I let him do everything and just sit back, paying no attention to where we're going—just enjoying the view. Enjoying someone doing everything for me. We're pulling up to the little cottage at the end of the cul-de-sac by early afternoon.

"I can't promise we won't be sleeping on a stone floor," he says.

"You said, like a hundred times," I reply. "As if I care. I'm happy to be out of the city."

"I'm not sure you know what it's like sleeping in a stone cottage, even in July."

"I'm going with cool and refreshing," I say.

"It's a shame it's not warmer today," he says, looking up at the sky. "Still, good excuse to light the fire."

The cottage is, in fact, a mess. It is halfway through some renovations, which Jake explains are just enough to make it livable. The floor is wood, but it's rough underfoot and is in desperate need of a sand and a varnish.

Jake laughs at me as I slip my shoes off at the door.

"I wouldn't bother," he says, hauling in two sleeping bags.

The living room is set up for painting. The baseboards are taped and drop mats line the floor. The walls are patched with fresh plaster squares. There's an old sofa pushed up against the far wall, which Jake explains is going to the dump next week, along with all the timber in the hallway.

"There's no bed, so one of us can sleep on that," he says. "Or rather, you can sleep on that." He laughs. "Sorry, that wasn't very hospitable."

He slips out the back to the garden and returns with a bucket of paint, a tray, and two brushes.

"Who prepped all of this?" I ask.

"My best friend, Callum," he says. "With help from a local tradesman."

I stand there for a moment, clutching my overnight bag, unsure what to do, but Jake picks up on the hesitation immediately.

"Okay, I reckon this is going to take me the whole afternoon—six hours or something. So you can either help—but you're under zero obligation to—or you can set up your computer on the table in the kitchen and work, but we got so much done—"

"On the train," I say, nodding. "I think I'm ready to finish up now."

He cocks his head. "Okay, then you can go for a hike, or head down to the sea. Visit the castle—don't you Americans love a castle? You're on the edge of Snowdonia National Park; it's stunning. You can do what you want. You're my guest here."

"In that case," I say, reaching into my bag to pull out my swimsuit. "I haven't been swimming in the ocean in over two years."

"Knock yourself out," he says. "But word of warning: It's freezing."

· · ·

*J*ake is not kidding.

The blue sky and sandy shore look inviting, but when I dive into the water, I scream loud enough to startle a dog walker and send a crowd of gulls flocking skyward. I emerge from the water shivering and blue from head to toe. I pull the towel around me and try to dress but fall twice into the sand, as my limbs are like frozen logs. Then I run back up the road, turn down his street, and bowl through the front door.

"There's a hot bath waiting for you," Jake says, pointing down the hall, laughing at me.

"Marry me," I say, shivering, and I rush down the hallway to the waiting bath. When I step in, there is a moment of almost numbing pain as the heat seeps into my skin, and before long I'm woozy with tiredness.

I have no idea how long I'm in there, but when I emerge, Jake has been to the supermarket for provisions and is cleaning away some of the painting mess in the lounge.

"Can you put some logs on the barbecue outside? We're going to have to boil the pasta out there; the gas isn't on here yet. The wood is in a small pile at the back of the house. Also, there's wine. Red wine, because the fridge doesn't work."

"Yes, sir," I reply.

"I'm in get-shit-done mode," he says, dipping the roller into the paint tray.

"I like it," I say. "I'm in just tell me what to do so I-don't-have-to-think mode."

"Then we're a perfect match," he says, shooting me a loaded look that ignites me like a flaming flint on fuel.

I shoot him a warning look, but it's no use—the fizzing chemistry between us seeps out constantly. Even telling him off has become part of the game.

"Don't worry about anything," he says, reassuring me when he sees my concern. "I'll stop joking around."

By the time the sun is setting, the barbecue is underway. It's a hand-built stone circle barbecue with a metal grill balanced across the top. Jake jokes that it came with the house.

"It's great," I say, reaching my hands out to warm them, settling onto a small wooden bench seat with a couple of old cushions.

Ribbons of smoke are trailing into the air as we wait for the wood to burn off a little and we can add the pot for pasta. Jake delivers me a glass of wine while I read through some of his notes in the fading light.

"I'm not sure we've nailed the hook," I call out to Jake.

"Why not?" he calls back.

"I keep worrying this is just another moody crime thriller set in London."

"What?"

"I'm worried it's not original enough!"

Jake emerges in the doorway, peeling his paint-spattered shirt off to reveal a T-shirt underneath. He looks pink-cheeked and effortlessly handsome, the last of the golden sun hitting his face, catching the amber flecks in his eyes. I wish he wasn't so desirable.

"Say the quote you said to me on the train about doubt back

to yourself," he says, walking slowly toward me and the fire. "The Sylvia Plath one."

"Fine," I say, huffing.

"*You* said that the market for this kind of series is bottomless."

Jake drops onto the bench next to me. It's small and I have to scooch over to accommodate him, but still, we fit. We sit there watching the sun drop over the hills at the back of the garden while the fire warms us both. He lifts my wineglass out of my hand and takes a sip, leaving cream-colored fingerprints on the glass bowl.

"Thanks a lot," I say, taking it back, avoiding touching the mess.

"Now you can feel like you helped," he says teasingly.

I pull a guilty face, and our eyes lock, the desire building in the pit of my stomach. He smiles at me, and I can see the longing in his eyes too. Would it really hurt? Would it really count if something happened up here? Away from London and everything that is going on back there?

I have to look away from him, as I can see some of the same questions on his face too.

"I'm sorry. I did *nothing*. Don't tell your mother," I say, biting my lip.

Jake brushes the hair back from his eyes, leaving a white smear across his cheek. I reach up to clear it with my thumb, but he pulls back from my touch.

"What?"

"Sorry, protective reflex," he says, shrugging.

"What do you mean?" I reply, pulling a face.

"Amy, Amy, Amy," he says, shaking his head. Then he stands and heads toward the kitchen, pulls out a chipped mug, and pours himself a glass.

"I'm gonna cook, okay? I'm gonna put the water on to boil on the barbecue, and then we can eat."

I look back at the fire, and my stomach is in knots. My desire for Jake is becoming a consuming distraction. Every pause for thought. Every second look. Every sentence uttered, I'm starting to analyze. *Business first, Amy*, I tell myself. *Get the thing done.*

By the time we're getting ready for bed, we're both a little drunk, and Jake is laying out the sleeping bags. One for me on the sofa, and one for him on the cold floor. The room smells of paint, and I hunt through the house for a better location to sleep.

"Jake," I say, pushing open the back door. "Can anything eat us? Like in the US there are bears and coyotes and shit. Are there any northern Welsh equivalents?"

Jake laughs. "No."

"Then what about under the stars?" I say, pointing out to the garden. "By the fire?"

I watch him hesitate. "Could do?"

"Come on!" I say, tugging one of the sleeping bags out of his hand and taking it out onto the lawn. After a moment, he joins me with an armful of old, dusty cushions and blankets. We create a kind of haphazard bed on the lawn and lay out our sleeping bags next to each other.

While he clears away some things from the kitchen, I climb inside my sleeping bag and lie on my back, looking up at the stars. A few minutes later, the light inside is switched off, and

Jake comes down to join me. He's in boxer shorts and a sweater, and I try not to watch as he climbs in.

We lie there in silence for a while until I roll over and look at him.

"What was your dad like?" I ask.

"Growing up? Fine. Not around much due to his crazy work hours, but yeah. He was solid."

"But later? You seem, um, like you have some serious feelings about him," I say carefully.

"What's *your* dad like?" he asks, eyes narrowing.

"Mine? He's salt of the earth, as they say. Swears like a trooper. Everybody is his best friend, on first sight. *Come in, have a beer!* He'll say that to the fucking DHL delivery guy. Everyone loves him. Sometimes that means his family doesn't feel so special. I can live with that flaw, though. There are worse things. He probably drinks too much on occasion," I say, laughing. "I miss him a lot," I add, in case it wasn't obvious.

"You're going to see him soon, though, right?" he asks, and I squirm slightly. "Your aunt's eightieth?"

"My granny's eightieth," I say, correcting him, happy that I'm looking up at the stars and not into his eyes as I continue the pretense that I will actually catch a flight. Jake thinks I already booked it.

"Don't miss it," he says, rolling over to face me as he does.

I roll over too, so we are both on our sides, just a few inches apart—close enough so I can feel the warmth of his breath and see the firelight in his eyes. I am playing with that fire. I know it, and I'm sure he knows it.

My toes curl as I resist the urge to reach out to him. He

props himself up on his elbow; his movements are slow, contained. Restrained. It feels as though we're both acting against an invisible and unearthly pull. It's intoxicating.

Not now, Amy, I tell myself again.

"My dad hated my career," he says, finishing up the last of his wine and placing the mug out of reach on the lawn. "He wanted me to go into medicine or law or something secure and dependable like that. Said writing was a fool's game. You can imagine."

"I *can* imagine," I say, not daring to ask any more questions.

"And then I gave it up. A year ago, to come home and look after him as he died. And he never stopped letting me know how bad my decisions were," says Jake. "I sometimes think that was why I *really* went on the show."

"Revenge against your dad?" I say.

"He would have been so pissed off," he says, laughing. "But I think I just wanted to do something crazy. It was mad, that time. A year of nursing your dad, during which he goes from big and a bit intimidating to, like, so frail you're lifting him out of bed. Work was dead in the water after that. My film didn't sell and I had nothing else ready. I was burned out. And my best friend, Callum, was like, '*You gotta shake things up, Jonesy.*' And also there was the money issue—a huge debt left by Dad."

"Didn't you get . . ." I move my eyes away from his as I ask it. "Like, wasn't there a life insurance payout or something?"

"No. It turns out the big-shot surgeon wasn't so good with money," he says. Then he takes a really deep breath and lies back to look up at the stars. "We found out the house was secretly remortgaged. He'd sold the rental flat in Manchester on the quiet. One credit card was maxed out to fifty K."

"Gambling?" I say, incredulous.

"Of the white-collar kind. Bad investments," he says, shrugging. "Mum was completely in the dark, which upsets me in one sense, because, like, how the hell wasn't she more involved in her own security? In the end, *I* had more actual money in the bank than the hot-shot orthopedic surgeon did when he died."

"Shit," I say. "Jake. That's fucking terrible."

"Yep," he says. "Hell of a way to get to know the other side to your father. Going through his bank statements upon death."

I cringe at the thought of it. Of my dad, who is so capable and full of beans, and of finding out there was something critically wrong behind the scenes.

"And so, your mom?"

"There was just barely enough money for her to sell the house and buy this little cottage. But there is a mortgage, and her meager pension won't pay it, so I went halves with her."

He looks back at me with some trepidation, but my heart is going out to him.

"Callum was like, '*You can leverage this to make some cash.*' The fee was crap, but if you win, you make a lot of money. I don't know. It sounded easy. But I got in there and realized, oh *shit*. I don't like this at all. I hate it. I'm not supposed to be here. Everyone was nice, don't get me wrong. They were *really* nice people and they're on their missions to be influencers and actors and whatever, but as soon as I felt those cameras on me—like, *everywhere*—I got claustrophobic. All I could think of was Dad, and all the mixed feelings around that. I just felt sick. I wanted to get out. And I just jumped off that cliff with one single-minded idea. To be free of it."

"It all makes sense now," I say, shaking my head. "God, I feel so bad for you."

"Don't," he says. "It was my decision. But without any real money from being in the bloody show," he says, "I really need a plan B. I gotta throw myself back into writing or I have to find something else."

"You're going to keep writing!" I say emphatically. And then I reach forward for his hand and I place mine over his and I squeeze it.

Jake smiles at me. It's lingering. And some time passes as he moves his hand and our fingers intertwine. He runs his thumb across the back of my hand, and even though it's just a thumb, it's the most erotic thing I've ever experienced. There is so much want between us, I can barely take it. So, I lift his hand up to mine and I kiss him gently on the knuckles. And then I press my cheek to the back of his hand.

"What is that?" he asks.

"A promise," I say, squeezing his hand as I drop it down onto the blanket between us, still holding it tight.

Jake nods. "Good."

And then neither of us says a thing; we just stare at each other, the fire occasionally crackling, and the warm yellow flickering, until my eyes get heavy staring at the stars, and we both drift off to sleep.

Twenty-Five

$\sim\!\!\sim$

$\mathcal{W}$e take the train home the next day, and between Jake's suggestive smiles at me across the table and the way he holds my hand for just a moment too long when he helps me onto the platform at Euston station, I feel like the expectations are now set for what will come after the pitch. We're both counting down to something inevitable. But neither of us has mentioned what happens if—when—I do get the job. *One thing at a time*, I tell myself.

There is more than enough of Jake Jones and work to keep my mind completely abuzz, so that when I arrive to meet him at Portobello Road Market on the last weekend of my holiday and he mentions a brand-new idea based on the other brief, my reaction is real irritation.

"I just got inspired one evening," he says, smiling.

"But we're nearly done with the crime concept. We can't abandon Detective Sergeant Caraway now. She's literally standing outside the suspect's house with the SWAT squad about to burst in and bust him," I say, collecting my coffee from a little cart.

Jake throws his hands up. "Don't worry, I would never abandon her. I just thought that since we're wrapping that story up, and I need to really knuckle down and get the pilot script finished, *you* could take a read of this." He reaches into his messenger bag and hands me a stack of paper, stapled in the top corner. It says "THE MARKET" across it and then "By Jake Jones & Amy Duffy" underneath.

"You need to take my name off, I didn't write this," I say, more sharply than I mean to.

"Amy," he says, disappointed.

"Sorry," I reply. "Of course I'll look. But we can't do both, you know that, right? I can't pitch both ideas."

"Sure," he says, shrugging, as I take the papers, roll them up, and slide them into my own bag. I can feel him watching me sidelong as I do this.

"I'm going to read it, don't worry," I say lightly. "I can't read it *right* now."

"Can I just tell you the general idea?" he says, turning and holding out his hands. "It's, like, super British, which is what they want. Have you seen *EastEnders*?"

"The soap opera? No," I say, lip curling.

"Okay, well, they have a market just like this, and my idea would be to do a kind of *Abbott Elementary*– or *The Office*–style scripted mockumentary but set in a great London street market."

I look around at the traders, curled up in their stalls, hugging their morning teas. One guy is shouting in the thickest London accent about his flowers, which are "fresh as you like," but, I note, I do like them a little fresher than starting to droop. I watch the life, the vibrancy, and, admittedly, agree the setting is ripe for ensemble comedy. It's got a bit of *Parks and Recreation* about it.

"There would be this market coordinator who answers to the council guy, but it's the coordinator who runs the place. He's the center of it," he begins, watching my face.

"I'll read it. I promise," I insist, not wanting to spend too long on this right now. "It's better if you don't tell me anything and I come to it completely cold." I feel irritated. Jake has clearly become distracted just as we're in the home stretch.

"Okay," he says with a resigned nod. "Thanks. Just take a look, that's all I'm asking."

"When did you do this?" I press him.

"Don't worry, Amy, I prioritized Detective Caraway," he insists, his tone slightly frustrated.

"Sorry. It's just that I am back at work tomorrow, so I'm going to have way less time," I remind him. "And the pitch is this Friday," I say wearily. "And I'll be in charge of doing the weekly trailers for *The Comeback Special* now that the series has begun to air, which is going to take up so much headspace."

"You don't sound thrilled."

"I would have been a few months ago," I say, sipping my coffee as we take a bench in the middle of the market, just in front of a green space, which is filling twentysomethings and their bacon rolls and sweet teas, shaking off hangovers. "But there is no doubt I've been treading water. I've loved the last six weeks. Development is where I'm supposed to be. I feel alive again."

Across from us, a busker sets up, and I glance at Jake and give a big, exaggerated eye roll as their speaker squeals.

"I want this job so badly," I say. "I don't let myself think about how much."

"I know," says Jake.

"What?" I ask, hearing the caution in his voice.

"I wonder sometimes if you've really thought this through," he says. "Like, you know if you win this pitch and get offered the job, you're going to be working for Chris. He's the head of the department, isn't he?"

"Interim," I say weakly.

"Come on," he says, his voice oozing disbelief. "You don't think he's staying?"

"Why would he? His life is in New York," I say.

"And yours isn't?"

"No," I say. "Not all of it."

"Okay, play the game with me. Let's say, for argument's sake, he does stay and is your boss again. What then?"

I look across at the busker, willing him suddenly, in his silly deerstalker cap, to play something loudly.

"Well," I begin as I watch a dog knock over a stack of eggs and an argument start. The owner of the dog is shouting about the eggs being stacked on a rickety table as his dog tries to lick its own back clean, and the owner of the stall is on his hands and knees trying to rescue any egg that isn't broken. The absurdity of it all makes me laugh, especially when the busker begins to play a rendition of "Streets of London" in a gravelly, worn-out voice.

"Well, what?" Jake asks after a long, ponderous silence.

"I guess I work with him again. I mean, he's one of the best in the game," I say.

"Is that how you really see your big chance panning out? That you're back where you were in New York?"

"But I'm not. I'm not with Chris anymore," I say.

"I think you need to be careful," he says slowly. "Why don't we put this out more widely? CTV doesn't own the ideas yet. We could approach a dozen other production companies. You must have the contacts?"

I nod slowly. I do have a lot of contacts in the UK, many of whom are still in their posts at the BBC, Channel 4. All the majors. Plus, I know many of the streamers. But I am still too afraid to reach out to any of them, in case. I don't know where my reputation sits back in New York. When people say *Amy Duffy*, do they think of the years of work I did at Wolf? Or do they think of me in a powder-blue bridesmaid's dress, pissing on an Audi?

I frown. Jake is right. If I could get over that, we *could* just do this without Chris. But that is not the plan, and right now, I want to stick to the plan. There is no doubt that a part of the allure of preparing an amazing pitch is showing Chris what I'm made of—without his so-called help. But I also know this business, and I know what an amazing opportunity this is. And with Screen bloody Global no less. That's a big step up from Wolf.

"Jake, they're hiring from within CTV. I don't want to come off as arrogant here, but there's no one in that building that's done as much development work as me. I don't think, anyway. This is, like, as close as I'm going to get to a free throw," I say, "in basketball terms."

Jake nods. "I know you're right."

"Yeah, but part of me also agrees with you," I say. "How about we go ahead as planned, but I'll see how I get on with Chris when I'm back?"

"Okay," he says tentatively, "but remember . . ."

"Remember what?"

"Remember that he might have some feelings for you still. Just make sure you have everything straight," he says gently. It feels protective, or is it jealous? How can I get him to understand how much I *hate* Chris? I examine a crack in the pavement in front of us for a moment. Why is Jake doing this now?

"He really doesn't have feelings for me. I *promise* you," I say.

"I don't know how you can be so sure," says Jake. "I mean, I'm a guy and I can see the way he looked at you at your summer work event thing. And the way he looked at me, for that matter."

"Honestly, Jake, you just don't know the full story, and if anything, he actually hates me. I don't want to keep going over it," I say sharply. I don't want this idea to grow or be planted in my brain. I stand up. "Come on, let's go."

There is a long beat as I stand looking at Jake and he sits, examining the ground in front of him.

"*Oh*," he says, standing and swinging his messenger bag around and onto his shoulder, thrusting his hands into his pockets.

"Oh, what?" I say, shaking my head at him, irritated now.

"You still have feelings for him too," he says flatly, looking me in the eye as he says it. I feel myself rage internally. He's *wrong*.

I plaster on a smile as best I can. "Shut the fuck up," I quip, hitting him on the arm and forcing myself to laugh the comment off as ridiculous, hoping like hell he lets me, and he does. A brief playful eye roll and then he smiles too.

But the interaction lingers like a heavy cloud around us as we meander through the market.

When we get home, instead of retreating to the terrace as we've been doing each evening, he tells me he has to crack on with finishing the Caraway script and disappears into his flat. It is my first afternoon on my own without Jake in two weeks.

I spend the rest of the day preparing to get back to work and trying to mentally peel myself away from Jake and plant myself back in the real world. But it doesn't work. I stress clean my apartment from top to toe, listening to a podcast about a serial killer.

When that still doesn't work, I pull on a summery skirt and a tank, slipping on some heels and a light cardigan, and I knock on Jake's door.

He looks down at my legs and then back up at me. "Um . . . hello."

"There's a Spanish place by the station I've wanted to try," I say as I take in his casual look: soft khaki trousers and a pale pink tee, clean and undeniably delicious.

"I'm hungry," he says, his mood already softened.

"Can I buy you dinner, then?" I say quickly. "A peace of-fering of sorts? A last supper to toast the end of the holiday?"

"You don't need to make a peace offering," he says, shoving his keys in his khakis pocket and grinning at me. "Not in that skirt."

. . .

*A*s we push open the door to the tapas place and a few heads turn, I look back at Jake and grin. I will never get tired of being with him. The maître d' leads us to a small, round table by the window, and I find myself enjoying the glances from the table of women next to us as we sit.

"It's hard to know if they're staring cause you're hot or staring cause they watched the show," I say playfully, eager to encourage Jake back into our normal banter.

"I had a call from my agent today," Jake says, pulling his phone out of his back pocket and placing it facedown on the table. I slide my purse down between our feet. It's a small, poky table, and our bare knees have to slide between each other's in order to fit comfortably. The waitress takes some time lighting the candle, and when she hands us the menu I lean across the table.

"And?" I ask. "What's going on?"

"She wanted to know if I was going to the *Fantasy Island* reunion special, which is filming next Friday."

"And?"

"Hell no," he says, dismissively waving his hand. "It's taken a lot of effort to get back to being invisible."

"You'll never be invisible," I scoff, looking down at the menu, and I knock my knee against his playfully. Jake's face softens and he seems to relax a little.

After we order too many sharing plates, and two beers arrive, I raise mine. "To a really productive and amazing time working with you."

Jake frowns.

"What?"

"Feels like the end of the road," he says, shrugging.

"No, this is just the beginning," I say, knocking his knee with mine again. "For both of us."

Jake looks out the window while taking a swig of his beer. "My experience is that pitches always end in disappointment, so it's easier to prepare mentally for the worst."

A plate of hot prawns in garlic and chili and some cut sourdough is slid between us by the most subtle waitress ever. Jake tears some bread and dunks it into the garlicky oil and takes a bite, looking thoughtfully at me.

"But if you could dream?" I ask him.

"An Emmy or a BAFTA, and a membership to Soho House?" he says, laughing into the neck of his beer before he takes another swig.

"That's the spirit," I reply with a chortle.

"Maybe I'll finally sell *The Wild Years* when I've taken the award for best writing on a drama for the Detective Caraway series."

"You'll be hounded."

"In a good, no-one-knows-my-face way," he says, tipping his beer at me.

"Not exactly," I say, biting my lip in mock amusement.

"What?"

"Well, now, instead of being known as that guy from *Fantasy Island* who is a writer, you'll be known as the writer who was on *Fantasy Island*."

Jake finds this hilarious, and I also relax, feeling that the tension between us from earlier is released.

"Better update my website," he says, winking at me.

"You should *have* a website," I say. "I can't believe you don't. And you need to really think about getting signed on with a new agent," I add.

"One thing at a time, Amy," he says, putting his drink down on the table and leaning forward on his elbows. As he moves in, his knees slide farther between mine and he closes them, squeezing my leg gently. "I was thinking of our conversation earlier, and I realized I was getting ahead of myself."

I nod slowly. "Meaning?"

"One thing at a time. We agreed on this plan. And so, first things first, I want to nail this script."

Then he looks at me, mouth slightly open, and I see the hint of tongue at the back of his teeth, a wildly flirtatious look in his eyes. *And then I'm going to nail you*, he is saying.

"Jake!" I say, flushing bright red at the intensity of his stare.

"Yes, yes," he says, leaning back, laughing. "I know the rules. Just want to make sure you haven't forgotten."

The waitress interrupts us with more sharing platters, and Jake starts telling me a story about the day he and his best friend nearly careened off a cliff hiking in the Pyrenees. I tell him about summers spent on Long Island beaches with sandy knees and sticky ice-cream fingers. Jake asks me what my last supper would be, as he pulls apart the just-arrived braised pork cheek with a couple of forks. He feeds me a forkful, purposefully trying to make me embarrassed now, laughing as I try to stop him but eventually give up, fake moaning at the flavor.

"So juicy," I say to Jake's raised eyebrow.

"You're so red, Amy, you're almost purple," he says teasingly.

As we head home, Jake shoves me sideways with his shoulder gently, and I pretend to fall over in my low heels. Jake panics and pulls me up, stressing that I ought to learn how to walk in "those things."

"I can walk," I say. "In fact, I can *run* in these things." And with that, I take off, running down our street until I arrive at our front door and spin around, puffing, waiting for him to follow.

He arrives a second later, racing around the gate, and stops.

"I win," I say triumphantly. "You'll never catch me."

Jake walks toward me and puts both hands on the door, on either side of my face. He leans his body into mine, his face just inches away as his eyes drop to my lips, and I catch my breath, my entire body on high alert. Is he going to kiss me?

"You think I can't catch you?" he says, his eyes serious for a moment.

"No," I admit, suddenly weak. Weak with desire and longing and weak with something deeper that is undeniably there. Jake's eyes lift from my mouth and dart between mine. "You probably already did," I whisper.

"Good," he says, pulling back. "Good night, then."

He slips his key into the door, and with a very cheeky grin is off upstairs, leaving me panting and breathless on the doorstep.

Twenty-Six

A my, you're back," says Danny, waving me into his office before I have a chance to see Maggie, put my bag down, or even take a sweet sip of my coffee.

I swing around his doorframe and lean in, to give the impression that I'm extremely busy and have to keep one foot out the door, but he motions me toward his sofa.

"Just checking in on you," he says. "How was your holiday? Did you get away, or did you suffer this remarkable heat wave alone at home?"

"Oh, no, I was working," I say, earnestly. "On my pitch. For the job."

Danny's eyes narrow and he pinches his nose, sitting back on his chair, bouncing slightly as he does. "Right, of course. Feels like everyone is focused on that at the moment."

I nod, a wry smile creeping across my face. "Well, don't worry, I'm going to head down to cut the next *Comeback* trailer as soon as I'm settled in," I say.

"Yes, about that," he says. "I just got word from above that this will definitely be the final season."

I nod. I get it. "It's a shame. I love the camp and high energy. And I cannot believe they got Lou Bega to appear. Who doesn't love a bit of 'Mambo No. 5'?" I say.

"I felt my first pair of boobs to that song," says Danny wistfully before turning scarlet and coughing in a gallant attempt to distract me from the comment, but I'm laughing too hard to care.

"Zadie will be gutted," I say.

"Zadie will be fine," Danny says quickly. "Now, I wanted to let you know a few people in the building have been chosen to do a workshop this afternoon. On a barge, if you can imagine."

"On a boat?" I ask, incredulous.

"On a bleeding boat," he says, shrugging. "Which apparently has just been refurbished after a hole in the bow caused by years of internal rot sunk it into the mud. If you want a better metaphor for CTV, I cannot provide one."

I blink twice at Danny and then laugh nervously.

"At any rate," he continues, "you're in the group and there is a van picking you up at the top of Carnaby Street at midday. Penny can fill you in, but I wanted you to know."

"What's the workshop?" I ask.

"What do you think?"

"Is it development? Is it an ideas workshop?" I say, clutching my hands together in delight.

"Well, look at you, Amy. All fired up," he says with a wide smile.

"I'm excited, Danny," I say. "I really want to get that job."

"I'm glad you've found your spirit," he says warmly.

"So am I," I say, nodding. "I've got an amazing pitch. I will even have a pilot script to share. Can I ask, just to clarify, are we pitching as employees and therefore CTV owns the script, or are we pitching as job applicants, and therefore if we don't get the job, we can still keep the idea? I'm asking because obviously if it all turns to shit and they hire some hotshot from Netflix, I want to know I could potentially take the idea elsewhere."

Danny scratches the side of his nose and folds his arms. "It's a good question. But you can just pitch a top-line idea, Amy. You really don't need a script. Your CV will do most of the talking. And you know Chris."

"I know, I'm just *really* going for it," I say. "I've got a really cool idea and I want to see it get made. I know from experience the script makes *all* the difference."

"Ultimately it's a job interview," he says carefully. "Not a green-light commissioning meeting."

"Yes, but we're pitching ideas. Those ideas will surely go forward to form the new slate? So if they like the pitch, they will need me to develop the show."

Danny sucks air back now. "What are you worried about?"

"I suppose that I'm giving an idea to CTV for a job that might not happen, and maybe I could take it elsewhere?"

Danny offers me a wry smile. "Why don't you speak to Chris and get clarification?"

"I suppose I can," I say, sighing. "If that's the best option."

I think of Jake at home now, toiling away on the script, and I'm already itching to get back and offer notes on the latest pages tonight.

"I would have thought with Chris and you having worked together back in New York that you would be able to push that advantage," Danny says as I open his door to leave.

"Chris Ellis doesn't give away advantages out of loyalty, believe you me," I say sharply, cursing myself as the words come out. Danny gives me a strange look.

Idiot, Amy.

By midday, Maggie finally strides into the office, looking a little windswept and less polished than usual.

"Amy!" she says, throwing her arms around me with a kind of casual abandon I'm not used to from her.

"Maggie, you look . . . At the risk of sounding ridiculous, your top is *not* ironed," I say in an exaggerated whisper, covering my mouth with one hand. She floats to her chair with a satisfied smile on her face, kicking her shoes off as she slumps back into it. "You look good. But, not Maggie Barnes, extraordinarily sharp and ready for work good. More like Maggie has redis-covered weed good."

"I look wasted?"

"You look high on something," I say. "Could it be . . ."

"Stop it."

"Are you falling . . ."

"Amy!"

"You can't help falling in love with Mi-chael," I sing to the tune of the Elvis hit.

Maggie throws her head back at this and laughs a huge throaty laugh. "God help me. It's strange how it creeps up on you. He makes me feel . . ."

"Horny?"

"Relaxed," she says. "And also terrified all at once."

"God, Maggie," I say apologetically. "I feel like we need a real proper catch-up."

Maggie sits up and swings around to me. She puts her head in her hands and shakes it. "I know. I've been so busy with Michael. I'm losing all perspective. I actually suggested to him last night that I take a sabbatical from work and we travel around Spain together. Who am I? I'm not *Eat, Pray, Love.*"

"You're more like Eat Me and Leave," I say, nodding.

"I was like that," she says. "And now I *cuddle.*"

"Yikes," I reply, and then she looks at me and we both burst into laughter.

"It's been *quite* a month," I say. "I promise, once this job interview is over and done with, I'll be back."

Maggie seems to snap out of her daze and leans forward toward me. "Shit. Yes. We've *both* been busy and a bit absent. How is Jake? Have you crossed the work/romance line yet?"

"Not really," I say, a wave of longing coming over me. "I'm keeping it strictly professional. Even if it's killing me. Are you coming to this boat-workshop thing?"

"Nope," she replies. "I have so much to get done here."

Just then, Penny glides over to our desks, her long hair piled up on her head in the most extraordinarily high bun. "Can you be in reception to meet at noon on the dot?"

"Sure, will we . . . should I eat first?"

"Lunch will be provided," she says.

"Who else is going?" I ask, knowing Chris will likely be there, but also hoping there will be enough people to buffer the close proximity.

"You, Micky from design, Moe from the edits, me, two people from the children's animation team, Diego in acquisitions, and an external person called Bobby. Or Benny."

Okay, that should be enough to buffer, I think, breathing out.

"So, it's not a date, if that's what you're worried about," she says with a wink.

I know I've just gone the most delicious shade of pink, because Penny giggles and walks off, holding a finger to her lips.

"Wait, does Penny know about you and Chris?"

"I don't know," I say anxiously. "She did seat us next to each other at the summer party, if you remember."

"Penny's cool," Maggie reassures me. "She might be a vengeful personal assistant but she's also one of the girls."

The boat is a classic Thames-side barge but renovated to perfection. White wood slats, little blue-rimmed circular windows. The windows give me a flashback to Jake and me playing detective and killer on the boat near Borough Market, my breath catches in my throat, and I flush from the memory of it.

At the bow there is a curved seat for about twelve that hugs a large wooden table. The top of the barge is flat but arranged with a canopy over several deck chairs for taking in an afternoon cocktail in the sunshine, though not today. Rain is threatening from the west.

I turn my gaze down the canal at the little pathways alongside it filled with runners and walkers, dogs on leads, darting cyclists, and a child with a three-scoop ice cream that is leaning perilously. The moment I think it, the ice cream topples and there is an almighty wail.

Chris emerges from the lower deck with a coffee in hand

and welcomes us all as we board one by one. I look across to him and smile wearily, but he smiles right back at me, small crinkles appearing at the sides of his eyes, starting to show his approaching forty years. But of course, they suit him. The several gentle lines on Chris's face give him the look of someone who commands the attention he does. I remember when he was first promoted, several years back, he looked so young.

We all slide onto the seats at the back of the boat as a caterer brings up some coffee on a silver tray and places it in the center of the table with small triangular sandwiches. I'm ravenous but feel too self-conscious to reach out and grab one until Moe does.

"Welcome, everyone," Chris says as we settle in. "I'm Chris. I think I've met you all already in some way or other. We're holding these smaller breakout sessions to really dig deep into the schedule, as viewers, without all the data and ratings and online buzz to make us doubt ourselves. And we're going to talk like people who love TV."

"That's me," says Micky, raising a hand. Micky so rarely speaks in public that several of us stiffen with surprise at the sound of his voice.

"Great," says Chris. "I feel like CTV has to get back to basics again. What do we love about television? What does CTV offer that the BBC doesn't?"

"Nothing," says one of the posh girls from production management, scoffing at the idea.

"That isn't true," he says. "You have a very loyal core audience, between fifty-five and seventy-five specifically."

"You said no data," says Micky, pouring coffee into a white mug.

Chris laughs. "You're right, Micky. I did." I am fascinated, watching him work again. The easiness he presents. Micky is adding milk and sugar to his coffee, and then he lifts up the edge of one of the sandwiches with a long finger to inspect its interior. A perfect triangle of cheddar, a pale and watery tomato, and a smear of butter on thin white bread.

"All the money went to the boat," Moe whispers loudly into my ear.

Chris overhears and I prickle with secondhand embarrassment. "Sorry about those." He grimaces. "I don't want to tell tales, but the catering order did not go through, and I went to something called Tesco's, as it was the only place en route here from the hotel."

A ripple of amusement passes around the group. He couldn't have stumbled upon a less fancy sandwich shop if he'd tried, but there are Tesco's literally everywhere in this city, and how's a lonely New Yorker supposed to know where to go unless someone tells him? Chris tosses his own sandwich down on the circular wooden table, and a seagull lands on the bow almost instantly and lets out a squawk. Then I think about what he's said. He's in a hotel. *Still.* That doesn't sound very permanent. After nearly two months, I'd have assumed he would have found at least a short-term rental.

"Someone needs to take you to a Pret," Moe says with a grin.

"But seriously, you guys." Chris has everyone in the palm of his hand now. "This is not even close to a sandwich where I come from. What is with these pathetic slices of turkey with a mere gesture of salad squeezed between two slices of bread—bread that has either dried out or returned to dough and has *butter* as a sandwich condiment?" he says.

"He's right," I say, nodding to the group. "I do miss a good pastrami on rye."

"Right?" he says, nodding at me, smiling.

"You know what, fuck it. Let's get pizza. Does anyone have an app, or whatever you do here in London?"

"I can do it," Moe says, raising his hand quickly as he steps across everyone and up onto the top deck to arrange.

I smile at Chris, and he catches my eye, and for a moment there is a knowing connection.

Later, as we're comatose on pizza and deep into the perilous world of the *modern dramedy*, plus a new genre that has no legs at all, *courtroom scripted reality*, I feel full of the excitement of television once again. I picture myself as a seventeen-year-old, at Christmas, taking the bus to Rockefeller Center, staring up at the magical neon sign that says NBC STUDIOS and vowing breathlessly that one day *I* was going to work in *television*.

Moments later, I saw a near-fatal Segway collision between two tourists, who were also diverted by the magic of television.

I excuse myself to use the bathroom, and Chris suggests we all take five minutes. I head down into the boat, walking the slim hallway to the bathroom at the far end. As I'm washing my hands and looking in the little round mirror in the seaside-themed bathroom, I reflect on how much easier it is to be around Chris than I'd imagined.

So, when I emerge and he is there, waiting, my heart does not gallop as it might have a few weeks ago, but rather I smile at him and squeeze myself into the hallway, expecting him to head into the bathroom. But he doesn't. He stands still, blocking the exit so we are face-to-face in the smallest of hallways, swaying to the movement of the river.

"Amy," he says, looking back down the galley toward the others, who are still up on deck, before turning to me and raising his eyebrows. "It feels like old times."

"Ha," I reply, wanting to push past, but there is no way to do that without touching him, and touching Chris Ellis, after everything, is not something I'm prepared to do.

"You look happy," he says. My eyes move across him like a laser scanner, searching for signs of insincerity. I find none.

"I'm happy to be thinking development again," I reply, glancing over his shoulder to the escape route. "Do you need the bathroom . . . or . . . ?"

His face falls slightly as he registers my anxiety.

"I miss you," he says, leaning only just perceptibly in toward me, but the mere millimeter or so is enough to cause my sharp intake of breath. He spots it.

"I do," he says.

"Don't," I reply. "Please. Let's not go there . . ."

"Why? I didn't know where you went or what you were doing. You just left," he says. "Marie Schneider said you went to Peru."

I scoff-laugh. "Chris, we broke up," I say. "*You* broke up with *me* because I . . . broke your car."

"Amy, forget about the Audi," he says. "With a specialized cleaning service, some repairs to the frame, it was almost back to normal. If you discount the lingering smell."

I feel like my face might explode into flames. "Oh my God."

"I'm kidding," he says. "Except about the specialized cleaning service."

I drop my head. I cannot take the teasing anymore.

"Amy. Come on, you have to laugh," he says, putting a hand on each of my shoulders and giving me a little squeeze. It is such a strange feeling to have someone so familiar touch me with such gentleness, but the feeling it evokes is anger, not affection.

"Chris, I want to go back to the others," I say firmly.

"I'm sorry, I'm sorry," he says, dropping both his hands. "I just want to tell you. I *have* to tell you one thing. I regret the decision I made about your project, Amy. *The Darkening Web* was brilliant, and it should have moved forward *with* you."

My head snaps up and my mouth and eyes spring open.

"It *was* brilliant," I say carefully.

"I made a terrible mistake, and I think about it all the time," he says, leaning closer in toward me. I can smell his cologne, the spray in his hair. I close my eyes, hit by memories of him. Of *us*.

Then I think about Jake and open my eyes, staring directly into Chris's. "No," I say. "What are you doing? I thought you hated me." I wish I didn't sound so breathless. "I thought after what I did you would never speak to me again."

"To be real, I found it kind of a turn-on how angry you got," he says, smiling.

My eyes drop to the ground. "I hate you. You broke my heart," I say, unsure whether I'm talking about the TV show or him. Both things were so intertwined. "I'm not sure I can forgive any of it."

"Hmm," he says. "Are you pitching for the job?" He reaches

forward and brushes something off my shoulder. I think of Jake. What if he walked in right now? I bristle.

"Yes, I am," I say sharply, moving back to put more space between us. I don't want him to touch me.

"Then I'll make it up to you," he replies, inching forward and closing the space again.

"I don't need you to do that. My pitch is good enough without help," I say. "I've *never* needed your help."

"Well, I'll give it all the same," he says, his voice thick.

"The only thing I need to know from you is about the ownership. If I pitch a show, who owns it? Danny couldn't give me a clear answer."

"What a strange question." Chris eyes me with suspicion. "You want everyone in the room to sign an NDA?"

"I need to know," I say slowly. "Surely you understand if I have trust issues when it comes to you and my work."

"No one is stealing anyone's ideas," he declares. "So you have nothing to worry about."

"Okay. Good. Will the projects, if they're good enough, be taken seriously? Will they go on the slate?"

"Of course. If they're good enough," he says. "But there's only one job, Amy."

It's enough. I can work with that. I *have* to nail this pitch. Jake's script needs to be *Darkening Web* level. A game-changer.

"Will you stay in London?" I ask.

"I very much doubt it," he says. "I'll get the unit set up and then I'm going to move to LA and start something up myself. It's overdue."

Relief washes over me. This is all I needed to hear. My ideas are safe. And Chris is not staying.

"LA? You're not moving into . . . film?"

"Fuck no," he says, laughing. "Just moving into the sunshine."

I feel myself smiling, and Chris drops the arm that is blocking my path at the sound of footsteps coming down the hall.

"How's that actor boy you've been seeing, anyway?"

"He's not my boyfriend. Or an actor," I reply truthfully. "And don't call him a boy."

"You like him?" he asks.

"I don't want to talk about Jake with you," I say. I want to shout, *Keep Jake Jones's name out of your fucking mouth.* Chris suddenly feels like a toxic cloud about to rain acid on my terrace barbecue and make everything with Jake, which is currently pure and gentle, burn.

"Fine," he says, "relax. If the job is what you want, just bring your A game and I'll make sure it's yours."

I hold his gaze a moment longer and then I say something I shouldn't.

"Okay. You *do* owe me." This is unprofessional, possibly duplicitous, but *fuck him*, he does owe me. I deserve this job and I'm still going to do everything I can to show him just how fucking good I am.

"I'll do what I can," he replies, smiling. "And maybe we can get coffee sometime? What do you think?"

"Sure," I say, magnanimous, and then he scoots around me and heads into the toilet as Moe arrives in the hall.

"Is this the queue?" he asks cautiously.

"No, no, I'm done," I say.

Twenty-Seven

———

I've got all the comments here," I tell Jake as he finishes fixing the new bistro lights that he's strung across the railing of our roof terrace. He turns them on to test them, but it's still too light to get the full picture.

"That will be cute," I say. "Not that there's much of the summer left."

"You see, the thing you're not thinking about is how we can warm the terrace in winter," he says, tapping the side of his temple.

I hand him the printed copy of his draft with my red pen notes across it, and he glances down at the front page, with our new agreed-upon title, and smiles.

"It's perfect, Jake," I say with a contented smile. "It's come along so well. I can almost taste it."

"What, you can taste the decomposing corpse in the basement of the Tate Modern? Or the bloodstained gag Detective Inspector Caraway hides from the forensics team?"

"She had to hide it! She had to prove there was someone on

the inside!" I protest, and we both hold serious faces for a moment before laughing at the morbid ridiculousness of it all.

My phone buzzes in my pocket with a message and I dread pulling it out. I know exactly who these frenzied messages are from. My mother.

> Amy, did you book the flight?
> You've gone quiet.
> Are you busy darling? I want to know when you're coming.
> Amy Marie Duffy are you under a bus?
> You do this when you're avoiding things, but this is a new level, even for you.
> She's going to be 80 in SEVEN DAYS.
> She might die thinking you don't want to see her.

The next one is a photo of my nana with the caption *AMY WHO?*

> Uncle Ray is bringing the Proctologist.
> Your Dad has cancer.
> Please never tell him I said that. He doesn't. He's remarkably well considering his cholesterol.
> Amy please.

"Argh, Mom," I say, feeling pained.

"Is she getting excited?" says Jake.

Like a teenager ignoring their parent, I examine my phone, pretending not to hear.

"You *are* going, aren't you?" says Jake, his voice high-pitched in disbelief. "We found you the perfect flight! Leaving right after the pitch. You can celebrate a job well done on the plane with free champagne!"

I drop my eyes to the floor and slip my phone into my pocket.

"You didn't book it?" he asks, incredulous. "You didn't book it? Amy Duffy. Are you nuts?"

"I just thought the pressure of flying home, right after that presentation, would be too much," I say.

"Well, that's a load of bullshit," says Jake.

"It's not bullshit. Have you ever done a pitch like this? No," I reply sharply.

Jake sets the nail gun he's been holding on the table and puts both of his gloved hands on his hips, giving me a look of such disappointment that I hang my head in shame.

"Jake," I moan.

"I don't get it. It's fucking weird," he says. "I was lucky enough to be with my dad when he died, you know. Of all the crap that happened after, at least I can say I did the right thing and spent that time with him."

"My granny is not dying," I say, my eyes round and pleading with him to tell me I'm not doing the wrong thing. "It's different. She still boxes every day. She's strong like a tank. And drinks like a sailor."

"She boxes?" he says. "As in, in a ring?"

"My family is pretty tough," I say, feeling like I might be winning him over. "They're also big, boisterous, and never, ever forget a transgression."

Jake laughs. "What transgression? You mean they have a reason to hold a grudge?"

For one split second I imagine just telling him. Just letting the words come tumbling out of my mouth. Shrugging it off, just as Jake has been doing about his own public humiliation. But then I gaze across at him as he studies my reaction, his eyes quizzical but kind. And then the fear takes over. The fear that it might tarnish me too much.

"Maybe *grudge* is too strong a word. They tease. That's their MO. Anyway, Granny will still be there next year."

"Okay, you tell yourself whatever you need to," he says with a tone that is chastising and playful at once.

He peels off his gloves, placing them on the table next to the nail gun, and seemingly from nowhere comes across and gives me a hug. His strong arms pull me in tight, and he holds me just long enough for me to start to notice just how well we fit, with every part of me molded to him, my head tucked firmly under his chin.

"Amy," he says, pulling back but holding on to my shoulders as he does. "I know there is something you haven't told me about Chris and what happened in New York. And I know you think it is something you can never get past, but you *can*."

I sigh. "You know nothing, Jake Jones."

"Don't *Game of Thrones* me," he says, waving a finger near my nose, as my phone buzzes but I ignore it. "When I moved in here, I felt like *shit*, Amy. I felt like my life was more or less over."

"And now look at you," I say, smiling broadly. "You don't even flinch when people call your name across the street."

Jake sighs, closing his eyes and looking to the heavens.

"Allow me to elucidate, Amy. Whatever *it* is, you need to face it. The *it* is not going anywhere. I couldn't have hidden away forever, nor can you."

"I'm not hiding," I protest as my phone buzzes several more times in my pocket.

"Come on," he says, resigned. "Let's go buy some food for dinner, and then we can run through the pitch as it stands."

"Go and buy some food?" I say, eyes open wide with glee.

"Yes," he says, cocking his head to the side. "What?"

"Can we go together?" I say, gasping.

"Yes? We can?" Jake raises an eyebrow. "Why do you look so excited?"

"Can we go to the little greengrocer by the station?"

"Of course. Do you need something there specifically?" he asks, confused.

I try to remain cool as we walk into the grocer by the station, but I feel an undeniable sense of calm superiority with Jake next to me as I see Glenn. *That's right, loser. I've got a friend. A hot friend.*

I pick up a basket, and I head straight to the fresh fruit and vegetable aisle, and I grab some onions, garlic, and fresh basil. Then I pick up some imported chanterelle mushrooms, a carton of cream, eggs, a block of pancetta, and a bag of fresh tagliatelle pasta.

"We can't barbecue that," says Jake, pointing at the pasta. "Don't make a song and dance out of it, Amy. Let's just get some sausages."

"Um, sure, I just thought we could do something special."

"I'm not sure we've got the time," he says, removing half the stuff and throwing in some sausages and a loaf of bread. "We have so much to get through today. Time is ticking!"

As I move toward the checkout, making sure I align myself with the one Glenn is manning, I also toss in a full bottle of Pinot Gris, then, noting the two-for-one deal, I throw in a second.

Then Jake says, just as Glenn turns, recognizes me, and starts scanning, "Two bottles of wine? Amy Duffy, this is *work*."

Glen snort-laughs, and I turn scarlet.

"What?" says Jake loudly. "What is it?"

"Hi," Glenn says, then he looks at me, dead-eyed. "Forty-three twenty. Would you like a bag for twenty pence?"

"No," I bark.

"Do you have a loyalty card?"

"*No. I. Do. Not*," I say slowly, each word a poison dart aimed between his eyes.

"Would you like one? We do great deals on our ready meals."

"I don't really eat ready meals anymore," I say haughtily.

"I see," he says.

And then he drops his head as I hand him the card, doesn't even look at Jake, and then we're back out into the evening air.

"What the hell was that all about?" Jake says. "Why were you so rude to that guy? He's basically a kid."

"I'm far too embarrassed to explain it," I say, my cheeks burning red. "But let me just say, he's given me silent and judgmental hell for months."

Jake looks over at Glenn, who is staring out of the shop

window at me, his head snapping back to his next customer when we lock eyes.

"Is he another ex-boyfriend?" Jake says teasingly.

"Let's just go," I say, pushing him from behind toward our house.

Back on the roof, Jake is grilling sausages while I'm running through the pitch aloud, stopping to cross things out on my notes. Jake interjects, waving around his large barbecue tongs with suggestions for how to tighten up and streamline everything.

After the fourth run-through, I collapse into the chair and hungrily devour three sausages and plenty of bread and butter. Jake draws a smiley face with ketchup on his plate. I pull on a cardigan as the sun begins to set and the new lights cast a golden glow across the terrace.

"Okay, they were the best introduction yet," I say, nodding at the lights and putting my feet up on the edge of an upturned crate, sipping on another glass of wine.

"I'm going to miss this," he says, waving a fork with a whole half a sausage skewered on it at me and then back at himself. "The *working* with you over the summer."

I roll my eyes at the little suggestive emphasis he's placed on *working*.

"Miss it? This could be the beginning of a beautiful thing! Next up, we pitch. I win the pitch. Then we introduce you as a lead writer on the series. I don't know if they pay Writers Guild rates here, but if they do, you're going to get a great fee for this script. Then we'll bring in an EP to work with you, and I'll have to find a way to be a bit distant. And then you and I live happily ever after with a brand-new blow-up pool next summer, and a lifetime of amazing television to collect endless Emmy Awards for. Or BAFTAs. We're going to get you your dream. Can you imagine? And me. *And the award goes to AMY DUFFY.* God, I hate my name."

Jake laughs, swallowing his sausage; he leans forward across the table and says, "I've got a bloody job interview next week."

My head snaps around to face him. "What?"

"*You* don't need a backup plan, Amy," he says, laughing. "If this doesn't work, you're going to keep your job at least. For *me,* if it doesn't work, I'm going to need to find a job. I should have been looking for one all summer, really." He frowns as if chastising himself. "But I couldn't face it when I moved in. I'm ready now."

"But you won't need that—" I begin.

"Amy," he says, "be reasonable. There is a chance that someone else might pitch something better."

"Where is the job interview?"

"Apex Insurance. They need a copywriter," he says, shrugging.

I open my mouth to speak and then close it again. Should I tell him what Chris has promised me? Should I let him know that he won't need that other job? It is a gift of reassurance, but also an admission that I may have leveraged my relationship with Chris to get ahead. He doesn't know the full story, and he's already shown himself to be concerned—even jealous of Chris. If he knew how deep the entire saga went, maybe he would understand why Chris owes me and I'm ready to collect. *No.* I can't risk his disapproval getting into my head before the pitch.

Besides, he's only interviewing for a job, for God's sake.

That's not a bad thing, all interests considered. The script deal will likely take months to tie up.

I feel a distinct sense of unease, suddenly. This whole thing better come off. It just has to.

A sparrow dive-bombs in and looks for crumbs under our seats, and I chastise it. "You should be asleep, buddy," I say, and then, as if the mere mention is enough, Jake yawns.

"So should I," he says, standing. "I need to make these changes tomorrow and then, what? Another run-through to-morrow evening?"

"*Definitely*," I say.

"That wine has gone to my head a bit," he says, reaching up to touch his face before leaning over toward the barbecue to close all the grates and let it burn out.

I stand and help stack the plates, but I am distracted by Chris's promise and the dilemma of whether to tell Jake. I feel like I need to reassure him that the summer will have been worth it. I put a hand on his shoulder and he turns to face me.

"Yes, Amy Duffy?" he says. "What is it?"

"I want you to succeed as a writer. You're so good at it."

He flushes a little. "Well. Thanks."

"I would do anything to help you," I stress.

"Not *anything*, I hope," he replies teasingly.

"You know what I mean," I say.

He nods thoughtfully, and then he says, like a bolt out of the blue, "How are things back at work? You've not mentioned Chris in a while."

I catch my breath in my throat and pause long enough to hear a car with hip-hop blaring drive the length of the street.

"Oh, we seem to have found a respectable working distance," I reply, feeling my eyes flutter through the mistruth. I can feel Jake watching my reaction closely and I know I must give him something to explain my discomfort at the question. "You were right about one thing. I think he does have feelings for me still."

Jake puts down the plates he's about to carry downstairs. "And you?"

I am frozen in the spot. "It's complicated. It's hard to say I don't have any at all. Though most are different degrees of rage," I try to joke.

"I see," he says, frowning.

"It's just some unresolved feelings, which was fine when he was a thousand miles away. Well, I looked it up, and it's three thousand four hundred and fifty-nine, actually."

Jake lets out a small laugh.

"At any rate, if you're asking me *do you still love him?* The answer is no. If you're asking me if there are still *feelings*, then the answer is yes, there are *feelings*, but they are not love. They are something closer to bitterness."

I look at Jake, who is watching me closely, but I cannot be more honest with him on that at least.

"I understand," he says finally. And I think he does. However, I also think he will be pleased when Chris finally leaves the UK.

But then there is the final, big, unasked and unanswered question that I feel passing between us. *When? When can I have you?* I look at him, my breath slowing.

Jake's eyes round slightly, his pupils so dilated in the low light his eyes look black. I wish it could be now.

"Let's get through the pitch," I say. "Chris is leaving as soon as they find a full-time head of development. He told me he isn't staying. He wants to move to California, which is . . ." I look up at the sky and try to take a guess at how much farther away this would put Chris.

"Five thousand four hundred and forty-two miles," says Jake, looking up from his phone, having already checked on Google Maps.

"That's a lot of distance," I say.

"Only if you both want it," he replies lightly.

I jab him playfully, but the cool evening air is heavy with things unsaid. I let him leave, picking up the bottle of ketchup and the tea towel and the rest of the wine, and I head to my apartment.

Twenty-Eight

~~~

"This one?" I hold up a pin-striped blazer with upturned sleeves and a silky cream lining.

"They're all good, Amy," says Maggie, lying back on my bed while I try to put together the *perfect* pitch outfit. "But I'd go for the black blazer, those wide sand-colored pants, and the T-shirt. Accessorize with the red belt for a pop of color and wear some flats."

"Not that you've been thinking about it," I say teasingly.

"I'm so fucking excited for you," she says. "I wish I could be a fly on the fucking wall when you deliver this pitch."

"You don't even know what I'm pitching," I say, shaking my head at her.

"Yes, I do. It's a crime thingy. Something about water. Grisly murders. Something about spice? Cumin or caraway?" Maggie says, rolling over on the bed, yawning. "I don't know. I just do the pictures."

"Okay, you listened a bit," I say, laughing. "Enough to do the design. Which is just so good, thank you, Maggie."

"It's fine. It's *you*, so it's fine," she says, grinning at me. "I also came here at fucking seven a.m. and brought you bagels, for fuck's sake. It isn't easy to find bagels either."

"And I love you for it."

There's a knock on the door and I wave at Maggie to go and get it. "It's Jake," I say.

"Is he coming to help dress you? I'm impressed," she says, pulling herself up off the bed.

"Come in, Jakey boy," I hear Maggie say, followed by the sound of a kiss. "I hear you're good with fashion."

"Am I good with fashion?" he says, raising both eyebrows at me as the two of them flop down on the bed, and Jake helps himself to my leftover bagel.

"You are," I reply.

"Well, I am an only child, and so unfortunately I spent a lot of time shopping with Mother," he says in a posh accent.

"With *Mother*," I parrot, chortling.

"Is your mum into fashion, then?" Maggie says, impressed.

"She *was*. She studied design at St. Martins College, in fact. But Dad's work took them to Liverpool, so she didn't really do anything with it in the end. She definitely resents that decision now. She wants to write cozy crime novels, if you can believe it."

"I'd like to meet her," I say, tossing the black blazer on the foot of my bed and meeting his eyes.

"She would like to meet you too, I think," he says, blushing slightly.

Maggie coughs and then pretends to play with a string necklace from my dresser, eyeing me sidelong.

"I'm going to go and help her move next week," Jake says,

shooting Maggie a grin first. "The cottage should be almost ready now."

"Oh cool," I reply, beaming at him.

"Yeah," he says. "You could come if you want."

I look at him, surprised. I can't read the expression in his eyes. "We can get the train up again," he says. "Or we could even drive? I'll let you off moving duty?"

"Sounds cozy," says Maggie. "Meeting the mum? I can't remember when I last met a *colleague's* parents."

I roll my eyes at Maggie, but Jake laughs in his breezy way. And then I look to Maggie. There is so much to catch her up on. I realize she doesn't even know I've been to the cottage, let alone lain by the fire under the stars, looking into Jake's eyes, making a promise. I glance over at Jake as I think of it, suddenly desperate to go back there.

"I met your parents and *we're* colleagues," I say, knowing the excuse isn't washing even a little bit with Maggie.

"You two are ridiculous," Maggie confirms, looking at her watch. She stands up, making a bit of a show that it's time to go. "I'm sorry I won't be around after you come out. I'm going to take the day off. Hang with the man." She adds this last bit with a contented shrug.

"It's okay," I say, throwing my arms around her. "You came all the way here with bagels, remember? And you picked my outfit; I'll have you with me in there. Kicking ass."

Maggie fist-bumps Jake and then, after a pause, pulls him in for a bear hug before she slips out the door. Then Jake and I are alone with my jittery nerves.

"What do you think about coming?"

"I'd love to," I say. "I can't think about it right now. But let's talk when I'm done, okay?"

"Right," he says, slipping his phone away again.

"Okay," I say, relieved. I fix my makeup. After, Jake stands and hands me the black blazer and I slide it on. "There's a thin red belt in that tote hanging on the back of the door. Can you grab it? For God's sake, don't look in there—it's probably full of crap."

Jake walks to the door and he fishes around for a moment.

"Hurry up!" I say as he stills slightly.

"Yeah, got it," he replies, and I turn back to the mirror and hold my hand out. After a moment, I feel the wound-up leather in my hand, and I thread it through my trousers.

"It feels weird doing this without you," I say.

"You need me to put the belt on for you?" he says wryly.

"I mean the pitch, silly," I say, turning to face him again.

"It's how it goes," he says, shrugging. "You look like a power-hungry TV shark."

"Perfect," I say, pulling a nervous grin.

Jake follows me to my door and hands me my keys, and then as we emerge out into the hallway he closes the door and says, "Did you read the other idea, by the way?"

"Oh." My heart stops in my chest for a moment, and I feel the pink in my cheeks. "Oh, sorry, Jake, I haven't yet. I was so busy with Detective Caraway, I thought I'd save that for after this is over."

He nods slowly. "Well, that's kind of disappointing," he says. "It maybe could have been good, you know. Something to have in your back pocket during the pitch."

"I'm sorry," I reply, and I mean it. That was shitty of me.

"*Please* let's not do this now. I'll get to it straightaway. When I get the job, we'll be able to bring that idea into the mix too."

He studies me for a moment and then nods. "Go knock 'em dead, then," he says, and I throw my arms around him and squeeze him tight, breathing in the smell of fresh-out-of-the-shower Jake, which always smells like spring rain.

"It's as good as won," I say, grinning.

I arrive at work and head straight up to the seventh floor. I don't often have meetings in the seventh-floor boardroom; it's usually reserved for the very senior people. As soon as the elevator doors open I feel that familiar giddy thrill, like I'm perched at the top of the roller coaster, or on the edge of a high diving board, about to go.

Penny is sitting outside the boardroom and waves me over to a sofa to wait. As I sit down, I see another message from my mother.

> There's still time to do the right thing, honey. Everyone
> will be waiting with open arms.

And then, a huge red love heart. I breathe out. She's not giving up, even though the birthday is tomorrow.

"They're running a bit behind. You've been pushed to nine forty-five," Penny says unapologetically. "And you need to sign this."

"What is this?"

"It's just a standard NDA," Penny says.

"Right," I say, standing up and scrawling my name across the bottom of the page. "Who's in there?"

"A wall of men," she replies, shrugging.

"How many, um, pitches are there?" I ask casually.

Penny opens her notebook, begins counting in a whisper, and, after a beat, looks at me wearily, turns the page, looks back down at her notebook, and continues counting.

"It's fine," I say. "Maybe better if I don't know."

"Thirty-four," she says.

"Thirty-four?"

"And more yesterday," she says, shrugging.

"What the hell?" I say, glancing down at the paper handouts I'd had printed and bound, and then across at the NDA I signed.

Just then the door swings open and out strides Zadie, the executive producer from *The Comeback Special*.

"Hi," I say meekly to Zadie as the door swings shut, and I just catch Chris's eye before it closes. He smiles, and I smile back, waving discreetly so that Penny and Zadie do not see.

"Oh, hi. It's Amy, right?" she replies, not looking for an answer as she unbuttons her blazer and leans in toward Penny, a hand on her waist and another on the edge of her desk.

"Danny asked if you could book dinner for seven tonight at the Ivy."

"Sure," Penny replies, with none of the sass she would give me if I'd requested such a thing.

"And, Penny? Make sure they put us away from the bar this time. It's a working meeting," she says.

As Zadie leaves, I feel a tightening in my stomach.

"I didn't expect Zadie to be applying," I say weakly.

Penny pats my hand and looks back down at her notebook.

"You'll do great, Amy," she says.

Twenty-Nine

~~~~~~

The pitch was an absolute triumph. NAILED IT. Can't wait to see you! I text Jake about thirty seconds after I exit the boardroom and rush out of the building to get home. There was no point hanging around; senior management were completely absorbed in the pitches, so everyone else was leaving early, or, like Maggie, didn't even go in. But when I arrive at home, eager to see Jake, he isn't there, and a message on my phone simply reads:

> I knew you could do it! Back later tonight. Let's celebrate.
> Jx

I go into the house and pace the floor, calling Maggie when I can no longer bear to sit with the excitement on my own.

"Maggie, the pitch went really, *really* well!" I say down the phone.

"Amy!" she says, and I hear the muffled sheet crumpling of someone extracting themselves from another person. Probably, likely, in bed. "That's great. I'm so fucking proud of you."

"I know." I pause. "It was great. It felt great."

"Talk me through it. I want to hear it all!" Maggie says, with more rustling in the background.

"Maggie," I say, "I can hear you're otherwise disposed."

"No, no, it's okay, really," says Maggie. "Come on!"

"It's fine. I'm just in that jittery fucking place where I need to speak to someone. I'm sure Jake will be back soon. Call me later, okay?"

"Sorry. I want to know everything, though, okay?" she says, and then she giggles at, presumably, Michael in the background. "I'll call you! And well done!"

When I hang up, I sit on the edge of my sofa for a moment, looking around the room, buzzing with adrenaline and nowhere to put all the fizzing energy, and before I know it, I'm throwing clothes in a carry-on and hightailing it to Heathrow to make the midafternoon flight out of London to New York. There are only premium economy scats lcft, and one costs a huge chunk of my meager savings, but I'm going home.

Just as the plane pulls back from the gate, I message my mom a screenshot of my boarding pass, which has me arriving in NYC at 6 p.m.

SEE YOU SOON MOMMA.

And then, because I want Jake to be proud of me too, I send him the same screenshot:

I'M GOING TO NYC!! I did it. Back Sunday very late. Then we celebrate. I can't wait to give you a hug!

I'm somewhere over the Atlantic, three shots of tequila in and now drinking champagne, reliving every moment in the boardroom over and over again.

When I walked in, I was faced with a semicircle of suits at the far end of the conference table, and they were all men, including Danny. I'd shamelessly opened with a quote from Shakespeare:

"A little water clears us of the dead."

Then, with as much drama as one can muster in a stale, white boardroom, I brought up the title slide: *Dry Bones*. The slides were simple and clean, thanks to Maggie. The title intriguing, mysterious, and offering a strong promise of murder-mystery.

"It's Monday morning, around five thirty a.m., when a call comes in, rousing Detective Inspector Caraway from her sleep in a dingy top-floor flat in North London. A body has been found by the edge of Hampstead Heath men's pond," I begin. "Caraway closes her eyes in terror as she hears the young man has been garroted and is partially submerged, perhaps weighted down. 'Call the divers,' she says, her hands shaking as she hangs up her phone."

I said this as solemnly as I could, Jake's suggestion that I try to not look so excited when I mention the grisly murders ringing in my head.

I looked at Chris, leaning back in his chair, his arms folded like a proud father, as I moved through the beats of episode one. Then, rather than hand out my series bible as planned, I talked them through it. And as I talked, I felt myself getting more and more confident. I knew. *I knew* that I had nailed it. Chris was going to give me the job.

And then I finished the pitch by handing across the series bible and the script. "If you want to know more about Detective Caraway and the case of the Hampstead drowning, I have mapped out the entire ten-part series in that bible, and I have a pilot script attached as well."

One of the men laughed, and Danny nodded as they handed around the materials.

"Such hubris," said Jeff, looking pleased with me.

Oh, it feels so good to be back.

"You did all of that?" Danny asks. "A pilot. A script? Everything?"

I look at Danny, and then at Chris, and I don't mention Jake.

"Yes," I say, my eyes flicking to Chris, who looks somewhere between impressed and jealous as hell. "I've been working on it all summer." Now is not the time to complicate things by mentioning Jake and risk putting Chris off, even though I'm ninety-nine percent certain I have the job in the bag.

"Nice work, Amy," says Chris. "I think I speak for everyone when I say we definitely want to hear more."

"Well, there won't be any more until I get the green light," I say. And then, high on myself, I add, "My people will be in touch."

Everyone in the room laughs, and I know I have them on my hook. I've done it. Jake and I have done it, of course, but I pitched it perfectly.

I do not expect the adrenaline to wear off and for the reality of where I am and what I'm doing to slowly dawn on me, midair, during a viewing of *Maid in Manhattan*. But suddenly, I find myself sobbing into a gray polyester in-flight sock, trails of snot cascading out of my nose, giving my elderly neighbor cause to take an extended trip to the bathroom.

In a few hours, I'm going to come bounding through arrivals and I'm going to see my family for the first time in years, and I am so very, *very* nervous.

"One more?" I ask the air hostess, who sympathetically tuts and then brings me a white wine filled up to the rim.

"So you don't have to keep pushing the call button," she says, smiling.

I could just turn around when I get to JFK and head straight back—tell Mom the flight went back to London because of a bomb threat or someone having a heart attack. And she would see that I had *tried*, at least. She could share my boarding pass, hand her phone around in Granny's front room so everyone could see the proof.

That's what I'll do, I think, wiping away my tears and downing the full glass of wine.

"You look better, dear," says the elderly lady when she lowers herself back into her seat next to me. "I thought someone had died."

"No," I say, hearing myself slurring, and struggling to keep both eyes open. "No one is going to die. I think we will find the bomb *just* in time."

"Oh," she trills, "what lovely news." Then she stands up to head back to the bathroom again.

As I disembark, mildly hungover, and head toward passport control, I finally connect my phone to the wi-fi and am hit by a cascade of messages, most of which are from my mom. I can't read them. I'll message her as soon as I have a flight back to London.

I whiz through the much shorter US-passports-only aisle, and head out through the NOTHING TO DECLARE gates, wanting desperately to declare that *I've made a terrible mistake* to the maternal-looking customs inspector, who says, "Welcome to New York."

When I step through the sliding doors into the arrivals area, I stop dead in my tracks. My brother, my father, my mother, and my two young nieces are standing there with pale pink balloons. Balloons that for some inexplicable reason look like blown-up boobs. But the centerpiece is a huge close-up image of me, crudely fixed to the end of a piece of scrap wood. It's a particularly ridiculous still of my face, one eye half-closed, a look of bliss on my face, taken from the exact moment I peed in the video. *The* video.

And underneath, scrawled in thick black marker:

WELCOME HOME AMY— YOU WERE PISSED!!

And then, something entirely unexpected.
I laugh.

Thirty

〰️

"Look at you!" Dad says, throwing his arms around me as I fall into his big embrace. "You got a bit bigger, darling." He grabs on to a chunk of flesh on my hips. "It suits you."

"For God's sake," says my mom, pushing him out of the way and pulling me close, kissing me all over my face. "You stink of alcohol. Do you have a problem? You know I worry about your father."

"I might have a temporary one," I say, grumbling as my brother slaps me on the back and the twins cuddle my legs awkwardly. "My God, you both got so big. I love your long hair!" I crouch down and hug both their little bodies into me and feel the prickle of tears, which I shake away. "Thank you for coming to meet me."

"We're seven next month," they say in unison.

"No one is working on stopping this?" Then I whisper to my brother, Floyd. "The matching clothes, you think it's cute still?"

"It's Sally, she thinks it's *adorable*," he says.

Floyd pulls me in for a side squeeze and tells me I look rough as hell. And before I can argue with anyone, I'm bundled into the back seat of Dad's truck, with my suitcase and the new golden retriever, Maddie, who covers me in slobbery kisses, and we're heading home. *Home.* I wave to Floyd and the girls, who are following us in his truck.

"I'm so glad you came," says my mom, looking over her shoulder and gasping at the sight of me every few minutes between frantic phone calls to everyone in my family, which all go the same way:

"She came!" and then silence, and then screaming, "*I know!*"

I feel sniffly and want to cry, but instead I stare out the window and watch New York roll by and listen to my dad telling me about the trouble he's been having with the fence on the south side. Mom explains that the new neighbors are Canadian and really great. Dad tells me that my cousin Marty made ribs for tomorrow, and they've been cooking since noon. Mom adds that he used applesauce, and then an argument breaks out about the perfect way to barbecue ribs. And then, before I have a chance to think, the car pulls up outside my house.

Home.

I want to drop to my knees and kiss the ground, but I'm swept up in the frenzy of slobbery dog kisses and doors being opened and rooms being prepared with fresh sheets.

By 8 p.m., I'm so tired I can barely keep my eyes open.

"It's like one a.m. in London," I say to Mom.

"You've just got to get through dinner," she says gently.

To help, coffee is brewed while I shower. The porch table

out back is set for dinner and Mom is using the *good* china with the little feathers on the rim.

"Is that for me?" I say, grinning.

"Well, Amy, it's been over two years," she says, heading off to get some kind of casserole out of the oven.

"I never get the good fucking china, Mom. Why don't I get the good fucking china?" shouts my brother after her.

"You tried to sell it on eBay when you were fifteen, that's why!" Mom shouts from the kitchen.

Two hours later everyone is tipsy, except me. Dad is shouting at the dog, and Mom is shouting at Dad, and my brother is shouting at the kids. Then Sally comes home after her shift at the hospital and there's yet more excitement and more hugging.

"London, my God," Sally says, looking as gorgeous and high-maintenance as ever, her dark hair glossy and rich, her nails perfect. "Did you see the new king?"

"Of course she didn't see the king," says my brother. "You think the king is just walking around getting takeout?"

"I don't think the king is having takeout, but he might have been around, waving and whatever from a gilded carriage," Sally says, coming to kiss the girls, who are valiantly trying to stay awake. "Anyway, Amy, how you been, honey? You dating anyone?"

"No," I say, thinking immediately of Jake. "Well, maybe. I did meet someone."

"I hope he's better than that piece of shit with the German car," says my dad.

"Dad," I say, grumbling.

"We all need to stop swearing in front of the girls," says Floyd, sending them into the living room to watch TV. "They should be in bed anyway!"

"I hope that man knows what he did to you," calls my mom from the kitchen.

"Exactly, I mean, we *all know* what you did to him. The whole of fucking New York knows," says my brother, and then everyone roars with laughter. And I'm surprised, once again, that I laugh. Has enough time finally passed that I can just blush and laugh it off?

"You know he's in London now," I say, and the porch falls silent, except for the chirping of crickets and the occasional *thwack* of moths on the electric blue light.

"What?" Sally says, dropping her fork in shock.

"Get the hell out!" my brother says. "Did he follow you?"

"No, he didn't follow me," I reply. "He took a temporary contract at my company. *Brought in to turn the ship around*," I say in a mock-English accent. "He got as big a shock as I did when we saw each other."

My mom returns with more coffee and slides into her seat. "I hope you're keeping your distance, Amy Marie Duffy."

"It's okay. We kind of talked about it. He's going to make it up to me," I say. "But we'll see."

"That sounds like a loaded promise to me," says my dad, and then he wipes his face with his napkin and settles back into his chair. "Do you know the expression 'Fool me once,' Amy?"

"Yes, it's 'Fool me once, shame on you; fool me twice, shame on me,'" I say. My mother has the expression in a little frame in the hall. "I know it well."

"I suggest you think on it before you believe anything that man says to you," he says, pouring himself a black coffee.

I swallow hard. "Look, I've applied for this new job, and Chris is one of the people doing the selecting. Promise or no promise, I'm easily the best one in that building. It should be mine, with or *without* his help."

"Fool me twice," says Dad again, burping.

There is an unease that follows and I want to reiterate that I know what I'm doing, but I can just imagine Dad asking me if I know the expression "The lady doth protest too much." And so, I fall silent.

"You look good, li'l sis," my brother says. "Really. London suits you. *For now.*"

I glance down at the grass, thinking there would be nothing better than lying down on it with my brother, looking at the stars, drinking a beer. But not tonight. I'm already too tired.

After dinner, I head to the living room, where my dad is watching a rerun of a football game, and I curl up beside him on the sofa. Mom brings me cocoa with whipped cream and marshmallows, a literal heart attack in a mug. Dad gets a version with Sweet'N Low and nonfat whip, which he grumbles at.

Later, Sally and Floyd leave with the twins, and a stern warning from me to stop making them dress the same. "It's time," I say.

Floyd shrugs. "You try to stop Sally. She's fucking terrifying. We should send her to negotiate with North Korea, I swear to God."

Later, Mom takes me upstairs and puts me in the spare room with the sofa bed, apologizing for the state of my old bedroom, which now houses a huge Ping-Pong table, big enough for the table but not for anyone to swing a paddle. "You know how he never measures things," she complains, nodding at the primary bedroom door, which Dad replaced and which has been an inch too wide for the doorway ever since. To this day it does not close but is pulled mostly shut using a small length of rope hooked around a nail.

"I'm going to church on Sunday. Will you be here?"

"Mom, I never go to church," I say, "and neither do you."

"She does since you left," my father calls from the toilet down the hall. A moment later we hear him pissing.

"Close the door," shouts my mom.

"You go to church now?" I ask as I sit on the sofa bed, the full force of my exhaustion suddenly hitting me.

"We missed you," my mom says. "You didn't talk. I needed to talk to someone."

She gives me a kiss on my forehead and says, "You need to sleep. We can talk tomorrow."

I wake up to the smell of bacon and eggs and coffee floating through the house, and I pull myself out of bed, grab the NY Jets hoodie hanging on the back of the door, and head downstairs. When I get to the table, Mom and Dad are already fighting over how much bacon Dad has eaten.

"Amy, come and eat," says Mom, handing me a mug of coffee. "Before your dad eats it all and dies of a myocardial infarction, right here at the table."

"Can I have some milk?" I ask, and she slides the huge carton of half-and-half across the table.

"Okay, here's the schedule," Mom says. "I'm going to

Cynthia's to get my nails done; there's an appointment for you too. Then we're picking up the cake from the Kellys' new bakery on Jerusalem Avenue. The parking there is a nightmare but for heaven's sake don't complain in front of them. We have to pick up flowers from the Jackson florist, which, by the way, has been taken over by that son of theirs. Then, if you like, we can have coffee with Cousin Ruth before the party at two."

Mom looks across at me, her eyes darting back to the eggs she's dishing out.

"Cousin Ruth?"

"Yes. I called her this morning and thought maybe you'd want to see her before we see the whole family?"

I feel the first hitch of my breath since I walked out of the arrivals hall.

"You don't have to worry," Mom says, putting down the wooden spoon with a clatter. "You know she's got a baby now; she's got no energy to hold a damn grudge."

I nod, taking a sip of my coffee.

"It's the right thing to do, Amy," she says now.

"It is," I agree.

Ruth opens the door with a burp cloth over her left shoulder, little baby Elizabeth in her arms, and two small corgis barking at her feet.

"Keep the noise down," she says to her dogs. "Come in, Amy. It's good to see you again."

She waves us in with her free hand, holding open the screen

door and pushing the dogs back with her feet. "Can I help with something?" I ask.

"Unless you want to clean up another shitty diaper, no," she says. "You know their shit is yellow? It looks like someone threw up split pea soup."

I try to stop my nose from curling up, but Ruth laughs.

"We won't stay long," says my mom. "I'm going to make tea."

When my mom is out of earshot, my cousin puts Elizabeth on the play gym on the floor and smooths her own hair back into a clasp. I see she's removed two of the three small silver hoop earrings that she used to have at the top of her ear. "I look like shit. All day, every day," she says when she sees me watching her.

"I think you look good. You look like a real mom. Just like you wanted," I say.

There is a brief pause, where Ruth looks fed up, and then she sighs heavily. Wearily.

"Amy, you really upset me," she says, looking over toward her kitchen, where my mom is hovering but pretending not to listen.

"I know. I'm really sorry," I say, biting my lower lip. "I think about it all the time. I should have been there. I fucked up."

"You're dumb as hell, you know that?" she says, folding her arms.

"I know," I say, readying myself to absorb as much anger as I deserve. "I should have called an Uber. I should have come without him. I shouldn't have lied."

"No, Amy," she says, "I can get over the wedding, seriously. But you should have picked up the phone, like a damn grown-up, and called me. You should have come here the second I was back from my honeymoon and apologized and explained what happened. *Instead,* you jumped on a plane and disappeared like D.B. fucking Cooper."

I laugh. Ruth doesn't hate me. She is letting off steam, sure, but she doesn't hate me.

"You're right," I say. "I ran away."

"Like a baby," she says.

"Like a baby," I agree. This one is harder to take from my eight-years-younger cousin, but I do.

"Okay. I'm done," she says, breathing out. "Auntie Katie? It's over."

My mom's head appears from around the side of the kitchen like a Whac-A-Mole and she grins at me. "You girls all caught up?"

As we leave, I hug Ruth, who says, "It's good to see you. I'm always so proud of you, with your fancy jobs."

"I'm proud of you," I say truthfully. "You always knew what you wanted."

My cousin looks around at the chaotic mess that is a universal sign of new motherhood, and she grins.

By the time it's 2 p.m. and we're pulling up outside Granny's house, I feel lighter than I have in years. I put my hand on Mom's arm before she gets out, and I lean forward between my parents.

"I'm sorry to both of you, for running away," I say.

"Forget about it, kid. You're back. That's all that matters," says Dad, looking in the rearview mirror at me.

"Your father is right, one time in his life," Mom says while he gets out of the car, lifts the huge cake out of the trunk, and carries it up to the house.

"Dad?" I call out, and he turns around to look back at me. "Can you come back so I can go in with you?"

"*I got you*," he says.

I got you. I think of Jake, outside the summer work party, taking my hand and telling me not to be nervous. *I got you.* I know why it made me melt: because it's what my dad has always said to me. Whenever things got scary, he told me that. *I got you, Amy.*

The crying lasts for nearly twenty minutes, a deep cathartic wail contained by the doors and windows of the car. My mom never stops rubbing my back. An oddly silent spectacle to the lady passing on her motor scooter, but loud and dramatic in the interior of my parents' Ford Ranger.

After I stop, gasping to catch my breath, Mom starts fixing my makeup.

"There's a boy in London, Mom," I say as she wets the end of a tissue with her tongue and runs it under my eyes.

"There is?" she says, sounding disappointed.

"Yes," I say. "And I'm worried I didn't treat him right."

"You better fix that," she says, sitting back to assess her cleanup job.

I look out at Granny's house, with the front door decorated with more of those balloons that look like boobs. My dad is standing patiently by the driveway, popping the hood of my granny's '89 Dodge to check the oil while he waits.

"They were supposed to be pink love hearts," my mother says, her eyes falling on the same balloons. "Pink hearts, but if you don't blow them up properly, they look like boobs, with little pink nipples and everything."

"They really do," I say.

"This family never gets it right, but we will die trying," she says wistfully.

"I just felt so ashamed," I say for the hundredth time.

My mom points to the house. "You think there isn't a man in that house who hasn't peed on a car?"

The comparison is ridiculous, but still I laugh a little.

"Peed on a hubcap or the back of a truck? The only difference here is that you got filmed," she says, the first hint of regret I hear in Mom's voice.

"It's not the only difference," I say weakly.

"The Lord our savior got a lot right, but the way women have to practically disrobe just to go to the toilet is a real design error," she says.

"Mom," I say, laughing at her.

"I'm still so angry at those men who shared it. What did you ever do to them?"

"I think it was an editor I fired," I say.

"Your brother still thinks we should sue them."

"No, thank you," I almost shout, picturing the scene in the court where they play the video to an unwitting jury.

"Are you ready?" she says now.

"Oh my goodness! I can see Granny at the door," I squeal, and before she can reply, I am out of the car, running across the lawn, and throwing my arms around my granny, squeezing her tiny frame tight.

"Amy Duffy, as I live and breathe!" she says, her voice croaky and sharp. "Where the hell have you been?"

And then I hear a loud cheer go up inside the house.

"Go on, they got ribs and beer," she says wearily, as if the party were for everyone but her.

I look back at Mom, who motions to me encouragingly. When I take a step inside I look straight down the corridor and spot my brother and Sally, and behind them, cousins, aunts, uncles.

Here goes, I think, taking a tentative step forward.

And then I hear it. The stereo is turned up and the opening riff of "I Ran" by A Flock of Seagulls plays to the already semi-drunken cheers of my family.

Thirty-One

On the flight home on Sunday morning, I sleep. Somehow, in that upright, uncomfortable seat, with a snoring man next to me, I sleep better than I've slept in ages. I feel a weight lifted off me.

As the black cab pulls up outside my building, the sun is setting, and I feel like the shaken snow globe that was the last forty-eight hours has started to settle. I breathe out slowly, pay my driver, and get out of the car, pulling up the zipper on my NY Jets hoodie. It's cooler this morning, and a sharp contrast to New York's stifling heat.

After I drop my suitcase off, I knock on Jake's door, but there's no answer. It's been a long time since he's messaged me, and I'm starting to worry. I was distracted with family but had sent Jake a few texts, which I scroll through.

Did you get my message? I'm in NYC! I saw my family. I went to the party! It was very busy, but really great.
I can't wait to tell you all about it. Xx Thinking of you!
Hey! Everything okay? Where are you?

I make a cup of coffee and dream of calling in sick tomorrow, the emotional exhaustion of the last hours is so overwhelming, but a quick shower refreshes me to some degree. I lie back on my bed, hair wet, and press play on my memories of the last few days.

After a short nap, I get up and pace the apartment, checking my phone regularly to see if Jake has replied. As the evening hours stretch into the night, I start to really worry. I call and leave him a voice mail.

"Jake, it's Amy. I don't know if you've gotten my messages, or what's happening, but I really want to see you! Where are you? Are you okay? I'm starting to worry."

I wonder if I should call Maggie and tell her about my unexpected trip, but it's Jake I want to speak to. I'm restless waiting to hear his voice.

Wired from jet lag, I decide to unpack my suitcase, turning on the TV and finding *Schitt's Creek* to run in the background as I potter.

The sound keeps me company, as it has done for the last couple of years, filling the space in my head where thoughts could get heavy and grim.

As I'm hanging my purse on the back of my door, I spot the rolled-up pages of Jake's other proposal poking out from inside my tote. I feel a pang of guilt when I see them, remembering the day I was getting ready for the pitch and Jake went to retrieve my belt. He would have seen it there too, unread.

I'd not really even thought about it.

I unroll it and see "By Jake Jones & Amy Duffy" in anticipation of my involvement, and I feel yet more guilt.

"The Market (Working Title)," I read out loud. And I laugh. Jake might be a wonderful writer, but he is *dreadful* at coming up with titles. I want to text him straightaway and tease him, but I don't.

I take the pages into the living room, turn the television off, and curl up on the sofa. I pull a throw over my legs and open to the first page, a hastily written proposal that explains the overview of the series. I stop reading after the first couple of sentences. This is where I can bring so much to Jake's work, in the selling of an idea, the creation of a story world that we're going to draw hours of entertainment from. I bring that. Jake *needs* that.

I flick through until I get to the beginning of the sample draft, and I dive right in, devouring page after page.

An hour later, "*Jake*," is all I can say as I clutch the script to my heart.

It is hilarious, firstly. Uplifting, secondly. And somehow he's managed that magical thing that is so hard to do in comedy: He touched my heart.

And it is *all* Jake. Warmhearted and open, with a lead character who is just so endearingly *good* that I want to unleash his joy on the world. I grimace for a moment at forcing him to write *Dry Bones*—this is his wheelhouse. *This* is Jake at his best.

I have the same giddy feeling I had after reading his screenplay. The same after reading the first draft of *The Darkening Web*. It's good. It's better, dare I say it out loud, than *Dry Bones*. Certainly more original.

I pick up the phone and I look at the messages to Jake, and I groan. Where the hell is he?

Even though it's nearly midnight, I head down to his front door again and knock, though it is useless.

"Have you lost something, dear?" says a voice behind me, and I jump. *Agnes.*

"Hi, Agnes," I say. "How are you? Gosh, what are you doing up?"

"Couldn't sleep. You?"

"Me neither," I say, stepping back from Jake's door and turning to face her, my cheeks scarlet. "Jet lag. I went to New York and saw my family. It was over two years since I last saw them."

"Oh, that's wonderful," she says. "I thought you might have been away."

"You did?"

"Yes, dear. You had a gentleman caller on Friday, and although I buzzed him in, I saw him leaving again about fifteen minutes later. So, I concluded, like a detective might, that you were not here."

She looks proud of herself. Does she mean Jake? I worry she's gotten confused, and I don't want to upset her, so I smile.

"Thanks, Agnes," I say, retreating upstairs, and to my bed.

"Where are you, Jake?" I say into the darkness of my room. "What's happened?"

And then, as my heart squeezes at the thought of him:

"I miss you."

Thirty-Two

~~~~~

Of course, I'm up half the night with some kind of overtired, slept-in-the-day jet lag, and then I'm late for work. It's after nine when I sit up in bed, filled with the terror of some dream I can't recall.

I pull my clothes on and rush out of the house. Barely stopping to look in the mirror, I shout, "You, Amy Duffy, are not one bad day in July anymore. At least, not to your family!"

I grin to myself, a momentary happiness that is followed by a wave of worrying about Jake. *Where is he?*

At work, I make it just in time for the production meeting, huffing and puffing as I enter, my face pink, sweat beading across my forehead. Moe gives me a warm smile and wave across the table. I feel a sense of love, suddenly, in a different way for my team. It's like a romantic breakup where both sides know that it's time to move on, but with care. A conscious un-coupling, if you will. A feeling that it's *time*. This lovely soft team that kept me feeling safe when I arrived here so broken.

"Amy," says Danny, looking concerned. "Is everything okay? Has something happened?"

"New York happened!" I say triumphantly, sitting back in the chair next to Maggie, beaming around the room.

"You went?" Maggie says, clasping her hands together. "Fucking finally."

"You went for . . . forty-eight hours?" Penny says, doing the math from when I saw her on Friday. "You flew eight hours to New York, for two days?"

"I did," I say, and then quickly lie, "It's not that bad. There wasn't enough time to undo the jet lag in NYC, so I still feel quite normal."

"So, you weren't home all weekend?" Penny presses me.

"Nope. I was not," I say. "I went home to New York, and saw my family and chugged beers, and ate way too much cake at my nana's eightieth. It was brilliant." I say this last part to Maggie, the only person in the room who understands the complexities of this exciting news and hugs me right in front of everyone.

"You did it," she says into my ear. "That's the first step to moving on."

"The last step, you mean?" I whisper triumphantly, as Danny does a little impatient whistle to indicate he's waiting and it's time to begin the meeting.

"First," Danny begins, "a big thank-you and well done to everyone who pitched ideas last week. The content team tell us they have the beginnings of a slate to start to build on."

I feel slightly smug as everyone looks at one another, smiling, a collective pride sweeping the room. Moe gives me a wink; he's rooting for me.

"Incredibly, and I really shouldn't share this, but there was one pitch so unique and original the team are going to pull the trigger on it right away," says Danny, folding his arms on the table and leaning in. "Chris, who knows this gig a lot better than me, is convinced of its potential. This is an exciting day for CTV, that's for sure."

"Oh wow, that is exciting," I say.

I feel a few eyes glance in my direction, and I wonder if the news that my project was chosen has leaked somehow. *Penny*, I think. Penny heard and has told people. That's why Moe winked at me. I feel my stomach flip with excitement.

"I'd love to hear more about this amazing pitch," I say, eyes wide with expectation. There are a few knowing laughs from my friends.

Danny looks at me, his brows descending slightly.

"Oh right, you can't say yet," I say, unable to hide a smile.

Danny gives me a strange look, purses his lips together. It makes me feel a bit . . . unsure. I try to laugh away the comment, and Danny moves forward to our other business.

But later in the day, as the exhaustion, travel sweat, and jet lag I brazenly claimed to have escaped descend over me, I notice an altogether different vibe begin to sweep through the floor like ominous fog.

Penny is first. All smiles this morning, but after lunch she avoids eye contact, holding a calendar up unnaturally high when I pass her desk.

Maggie is next. She mouths, *We need to talk*, as she is hunched over another designer's computer, directing their work.

And then later still, as I head down to the *Comeback Special* studio to pull together the materials I need for this week's trailer, I spot Chris, who is spread out on the stage, his laptop perched on his lap, going through paperwork as the crew sets up for rehearsal around him.

I wave, slightly awkwardly, and he looks across at me. There is no *knowing* smile, however. There is no warmhearted look in his eyes, as before. There is only his mouth fixed firm in a line that resembles a grimace, and one mere finger raised in salutation, his eyes dropping back to his laptop quickly. I bristle. How *dare* he?

Later still, I pop into the kitchen to make a peppermint tea, and as I'm pouring the water, Moe pops his head in. I see him hesitate just slightly as he sees me. "Amy. Hi," he says, his voice more muted than usual.

"Hey, Moe," I say, pulling out my tea bag and tossing it into the trash.

Moe nods once. I frown.

"Is everything okay?" I ask.

"Sure. Is everything okay with *you*?" he says carefully, but I can see his cheeks turn a little pink as he turns away from me and focuses on the contents of the communal fridge before fishing out a carton of almond milk.

"Fine," I say wearily. *What is going on?* "Has something happened, Moe? Why has everyone gone weird? Have Screen Global realized their terrible mistake and rescinded their offer to merge?" I laugh nervously.

Moe looks at me for a moment with a pitying smile and then shrugs. "I don't know, Amy," he says, meek and withdrawn.

I make my way back to my desk, passing Penny, lifting my tea toward her in a hello gesture. She squeezes her lips together and then drops her head.

When Maggie gets back to her desk, she looks a little apprehensive as she takes in my concerned face. "We have to talk. *Now*."

"Yes. What the hell is going on around here? Has someone died?" I ask, following her to the elevators, where she bashes the down button with such force she has to shake out her hand. "Chris was just so rude to me as well, by the way. I saw him down in the basement again—what is he doing there? Are they going to keep *The Comeback Special* going after all?"

"Come," says Maggie, pulling me into the elevator. "Let's get out of the building." She takes a look at her watch. "Though it's too early for the pub. Let's go to the café in Liberty. It's quiet, and we can talk."

My heart rate picks up as I race through all the possibilities of what Maggie wants to speak to me about, especially since she seems so focused on getting me out of the building. She tugs on my shirt as I follow her out onto the street. Then I shrug my arm free.

"What's going on?" I say frantically. "What is it?"

She turns around and squeezes her lips together. "Come on," she says, tugging me again.

"No," I say, my heart beginning to pound in my chest.

Maggie is elbowed by a man pushing past us on the narrow sidewalk. "Please. Let's go to the café," she says, rubbing her ribs.

"Is this something to do with him? With Chris?" I ask, not moving, just standing in place, breathing out slowly, trying to calm myself.

Was it out? Had it come out? It *was* going to come out. It was. I *knew* this. I couldn't keep a lid on it forever. But it doesn't mean they need to hear the full story. *So, Chris and I dated.* Was that such a big deal?

Except it was if Chris were to hire me, I think.

"It's not that," she says carefully. "But I do think people are starting to guess there is more to you and Chris than old colleagues."

"But not the video," I say quickly.

"Not the video," she says, sighing.

"What, then?" I am momentarily relieved.

"You didn't win the pitch, Amy," she says, squeezing my hand as she tries to pull me away from the building. "You didn't get the job. They gave it to someone else. *Chris* gave it to someone else. Everyone knows."

"No," I say, "that can't be true."

"Apparently it is," she says with a sigh. "Micky said that the pitch went to someone on the production team. He knows because he's been asked to help work on a sizzle reel."

"*Shit*," I say, stammering. "No, it's . . . that's not possible. I'm supposed to get that job."

Had he done it again? I feel my stomach turn over, and I catch my breath.

Maggie frowns. "Micky says—"

"Maggie!" I say, incredulous. "Micky doesn't know anything. I was promised. Chris promised me."

"*Chris* promised you?"

"Yes," I say, "he said he was going to make it up to me."

"Oh God. Amy," she says sternly. She looks over my shoulder at something and then pulls on my arm again. "The café, *now*."

But I look back to see whatever it is that Maggie is trying to drag me away from.

"Don't look—"

I see Chris and Zadie—executive producer and most talented person in the building—climbing into a waiting black cab.

"What?" I say, looking back at Maggie, and then it falls into place. "Oh my God. He hired Zadie?"

"You know it makes sense," says Maggie slowly. "I saw them working late a couple of times last week. Apparently, it's some new Saturday night entertainment show."

"But that wasn't on the brief!" I say, almost shouting now. No. *No.*

"No," she says. "Shit, Amy. Why did you trust him?"

I watch as the black cab pulls away from the curb and heads down Great Marlborough Street toward the West End. And then I rest my butt on the black iron post that marks the top of Carnaby Street and I sigh into my hands.

"So, I didn't get my pitch through again," I say. "Again. It's happened *again*. And fuck. Oh my God. If Chris lied, then they might own the fucking idea too."

"Of course they do," Maggie says. "You work for CTV."

"But Chris said . . ."

"What did that fucking asshole say?" she replies, folding her arms.

"He told me not to worry. . . . He said . . ." I put my hands to my face and I feel tears start to fill my eyes.

And then I look at Maggie, and the words that Agnes spoke yesterday ring in my ears again. *The gentleman caller.*

Chris. Chris came over on Friday to tell me.

Only I wasn't there and now Jake isn't answering my messages.

What the fuck did Chris say to him?

I call Jake and I call him and I call him until he answers as I am already on my way back to the apartment.

"Jake!"

"Amy. Is everything okay? Are you okay?" he says, panting. "Are you hurt?"

"No, I'm okay," I say breathlessly. "Thank God you answered. *Finally.* Are *you* hurt?"

"No. I'm just busy," he says. "Has something happened, Amy?"

"No. No, sorry, I don't want to worry you," I say quickly.

"I'm literally carrying a sofa, so you got about sixty seconds," he says. I can hear the shortness in his tone. My heart sinks.

"Where are you?" I ask. "Are you with your mom?"

"Yes, North Wales," he says.

"Oh," I reply. He went without me. "You went already?"

"You're calling to tell me you didn't get the job," he says, his tone making it clear that he already knows. It isn't a question. My heart sinks further. He *has* spoken to Chris.

"Yes. But I think that—"

"Amy. Can we do this when I'm back? I'm carrying about three hundred pounds of sofa," he says.

"I know Chris came to see you, Jake," I say quickly. "I don't know what he said to you, but I can assure you—"

"Of *what* can you assure me?" he asks sharply. "Of a job? Of your feelings? Because I'm not sure anything you're doing is to assure *me*."

"I deserve that," I say.

"I have stuff to do," he says. "Let's talk when I'm back." And then I hear some grunting and then fumbling with the phone, and he hangs up.

I sit on the edge of my bed and drop my head into my hands. But I don't cry. I just sit there, trying to piece everything together. What happened? How could it all have gone so damn wrong? He's in Wales, on the trip I was supposed to go on with him. I was supposed to meet his mom, and walk along the coastline and eat fish and chips, and open my heart up to him.

Against my own better judgment, I try to call him back, but he doesn't answer. So I send him a message.

Dear Jake, What did Chris tell you? Please tell me so I
can explain. Amy. x

The WhatsApp message is read, not replied to, and my agony deepens. Should I just lay out my whole side right now, over text? I know that I shouldn't.

I lie back on my bed, desperate to see Jake. I pull up my photo album and see that my phone's app has created a movie called **Jake, Summer, London**. Fucking smartphones. Turning my trauma into a cute video with wistful music.

But I hit play anyway and watch the ninety-second film of

our short time together. Jake at dusk, manning the barbecue. Jake pulling something fabric out of Hampstead pond with a long stick. Jake lying topless on the grass in the sunshine (he didn't know I took that one). Jake smiling at me. Jake signing autographs for some teenage girls on South Bank, his eyes on me as his pen is poised, pulling an embarrassed face. Jake pretending to jump off the pier outside the Prospect of Whitby. Jake in a tux outside the Roxy.

In any TV series, this would be the moment I jumped onto a train and hauled my ass up to Wales and shouted, "I love you!" from the rainy lawn outside his mother's house.

I sit up suddenly. Of course.

Thirty-Three

~~~

I'm sitting opposite an old couple at a four-seater table on the way north, the train jolting us left and right as we traverse the English countryside. I called Danny and told him I needed to take a little time off. He wasn't pleased, as I'd just taken two weeks' vacation, but I pressed, and in the end I think he felt bad for me.

The lady opposite me has a tea and an open packet of chocolate biscuits and is rationing them out to her partner, who looks like he could down the entire packet if he was given half a chance. I am jiggling my leg under the table, biting off all my nails, and desperately trying not to open the bottle of wine I picked up at the station, which is currently poking out of the top of my tote, winking at me.

I run through everything in my mind to try to figure out where it all went wrong. Jake and I worked on the pitch together on the understanding that I would bring him in. Fifty-fifty.

Then Chris comes to the apartment and bumps into Jake.

He tells him, *I'm here to speak to Amy.*

Maybe he explains he has some bad news.

Maybe Jake asks what that bad news is.

Chis explains that I pitched something at work today but it didn't go through.

What else could he have said?

I think back to what Jake said on the phone. "*Of* what *can you assure me? Of a job? Of your feelings?*"

Did Chris insinuate, somehow, that he still had feelings for me? Or worse, that I had feelings for him?

Did he say something about the script? That I let them all believe I had written it? Because that is what I did. There is no doubt I did wrong by Jake in that moment. I just . . . I thought it might matter to Chris.

It wasn't a big deal when I thought I was going to get the job, and that the script would be made, because then I would have brought in Jake. I would have been running the project.

But now I don't have the job, and CTV owns the script, and Jake thinks I screwed him.

I feel sick at the thought of it. I'm so *stupid*.

I feel the anger in the pit of my stomach like hot lava ready to blow. I will fucking finish Chris Ellis. I will finish him. But first, I need to make things right with Jake.

I don't try to call Jake from the train; I am fixated on one thing.

I found the digital copy of his script for *The Market* in my email, and for the rest of this train ride I am going to pull his pitch into shape. I'm rewriting the bible and the main proposal, but I won't touch the script—that's all him—except of course to give it a decent new title.

I want to finish before we stop, when I'll have to get my rental car in a place called Llandudno Junction. I remember the road to the little cottage, and the name of the town. And I know it is at the end of a cul-de-sac.

I have about an hour to go. I drop my head and focus, trying to push out worries that Jake won't be there. That I'll get lost. That I won't find his mother's cottage. And the worst concern, that it is a great intrusion to head all this way without his blessing. But he did ask me, once. He did.

It takes a lot more faffing around to get my rental car started than when Jake did this a month ago. But eventually I do, and plug the little town into Google Maps. The car is tiny. And yellow like a lemon. It was the cheapest and smallest they had. It barely has a back seat, but it is plenty big enough for the tiny roads I have to navigate with GPS that continuously drops out.

"Jake, I know Chris came to see you," I say into the rearview mirror, "but he's a massive cunt, and you're amazing."

"Jake," I begin again, "I miss you. I want you back on our terrace so I can perv at you with your shirt off.

"Jake Jones," I try one last time, "I miss you. I want you. It feels like hunger. It feels like I've spent my life in some fucking purgatory of longing, wanting to come back to life. To come back to *you*."

I tip my head. "That wasn't bad, Amy."

I have never wanted to be in someone's arms more than I want to be in Jake's, right now.

A huge, heady flush comes over me just outside the village. And then I start to have a massive breakdown and need to pull over and catch my breath.

I look in the rearview mirror at myself, fixing the mascara smudge under my left eye. "Come on, Amy. You can do this," I say to myself. "Don't be a dickhead. Be brave! You're a Duffy, you dumb motherfucker."

I hear Floyd and my dad in my head as I start the car back up and pull off the shoulder, forgetting which way to look for traffic and only just missing a woman on a horse. I roll down the window.

"I'm sorry! I was on the wrong side of the road!" I shout at the lady on the horse as she scowls at me. "I'm so sorry!" I shout as she turns and gallops down a path and off into the craggy hills.

I drive forward slowly, creeping toward the town center, paying more attention to what I'm doing, and after a few moments and another several wrong turns I pull down the small cul-de-sac and spot the stone cottage perched right smack at the end. There it is.

I park a little way up the street, so I can approach on foot. I don't know why it feels less invasive, but as I near the house, a man—not Jake—emerges from the little blue front door.

I freeze on the spot, but he looks over at me. He's got ginger hair, long sideburns, and a carefree smile that he turns in my direction. "Can I help you?" he asks with an accent almost identical to Jake's. "Are you lost? The main tourist information building is thataway." He points back down the road.

"I'm looking for someone," I say quickly. "Um, I don't know if you know him. Jake Jones?"

"American?" he says, his eyes narrowing.

"For my sins," I reply, feeling my cheeks flare with heat.

And then he startles slightly and looks back at the cottage, closing the front door behind him.

"You're *Amy*," he says, and my heart jumps a little. "Are you? Am I right?"

I nod. "How did you—"

"You don't think best friends talk?" he says with a knowing smile, tilting his head to the side. He pulls a set of keys out of his back pocket and presses a button. I startle as I hear a *beep* behind me, and turn to see a blue Jeep, its lights flashing as the doors unlock. I'm so jittery.

"Are you . . . Callum?" I ask, and he nods.

"It's nice to meet you," he replies, holding out his hand and offering a firm, if formal, shake. "But . . . ah . . . Jake isn't here."

"He isn't?" I reply, my heart sinking, as I look over Callum's shoulder toward the cottage.

"He isn't," he confirms. "I'm about to pick him up from the shop. We were going to fire up the old lady's new grill. You want to come with me?"

I hesitate, looking shamefully at the ground. "Uhh . . . I'm not sure. Maybe this was a mistake." I look back at my car and weigh up the situation as quickly as I can. Callum has clearly come to help with the move, and now I feel like I've intruded.

He scratches the back of his head. "You know, Jonesy's a good dude."

"I know," I say quickly.

"I mean, the best of dudes," he says, trying to catch my eyes.

"I know," I say, finally looking at Callum as meaningfully as I can, though I feel everything inside me wobbling.

"I'm going to take a guess that if you've come all the way here, it isn't to break his heart," he says.

My breath catches when he says the words *break his heart*.

"So, let's go get him, hey?" he says, holding out a hand and pointing toward his Jeep. I nod nervously and slide into the truck next to him.

"Are you helping his mom move?"

"Yep," says Callum.

"I thought it was happening later."

"Jake wanted to bring it forward," Callum says coolly.

It is the only question I have time to ask, because the town is tiny, and Callum explains that Jake is only two minutes away but called to say he got carried away with barbecue food and can't carry it home.

"That sounds like Jake," I say, and Callum smiles at me and nods.

"Sure does," he says.

As we pull into the parking lot of the supermarket, I realize this is *not* how I want to be seeing him, with the awkwardness of his best friend beside me. There are so many things I need to say. To explain. The first of which is why I have spent more than six hours coming to find him, without warning.

I feel a jolt inside me as I spot him leaning back on a pole outside the grocer with a crate of beer and four shopping bags. He's drinking water, and he wipes his mouth with the back of his hand, then waves lazily at Callum as we pull up. He has the swagger of someone who's been working all day. Moving boxes, lifting furniture. He's fatigued.

Jake doesn't notice me in the passenger seat and begins loading the food and beer into the back. I suddenly get another strong sense of being home in this moment; it feels like a memory of my brother and my dad, but it's also otherworldly in this town of slate cottages and green rolling hills.

I open the door and get out.

"Jake," I say, and his head moves so fast in my direction that I jump.

"Amy?" he replies, his mouth dropping open. "What are you doing here?"

After his initial surprise, and warmth in his eyes, his face drops and he looks annoyed.

"Callum drove me," I say. "Oh, you mean in North Wales? Right. Um, I came to see you. I wanted to talk. I thought it would be better to do it face-to-face."

Jake hits the side of the van twice, and Callum turns on the engine, seeming to get the message, and drives off, leaving us in the parking lot alone.

"You came here to talk?" he asks.

"Yes," I say.

"You couldn't wait," he remarks.

"I couldn't. Jake, I really fucked up," I say. "With you."

Jake looks down at the ground and groans. "Jesus," he mutters. "I don't think I can do this."

"Okay, okay," I say. "Will you listen to me for the ten minutes it's going to take to walk back to your mom's? My rental car is there. It's, like, bright yellow. Like a massive lemon. If you want me to leave by the end of the walk, I'll go. I have an emergency booking at a hotel in another town that I cannot pronounce."

"Llandudno Junction," he says.

"That's probably correct," I reply.

"It *is* correct," he says, the corner of his mouth turning up. "Ten minutes."

Jake looks at his watch, then in the direction of the cottage, and then he shrugs. "Ten minutes," he says, and he begins to walk. "You've come all this bloody way," he adds, sighing.

"Chris came around, didn't he?" I say.

"Yes," he replies. "Agnes let him in. We spoke."

And then he looks across at me, and I can feel the weight of his stare.

"He told me he'd come to discuss some bad news with you," he says. "He looked stressed. I said you were in New York, which he was *very* surprised to hear. But he was cool to me. Nice even. I nearly asked him in for a fucking beer, actually." Jake scoffs as he says this. "Anyway, he was pretty frustrated you weren't home."

"If he'd have called he would have—"

"Apparently, he did call, when you were in the air? It went straight to voice mail."

"Oh," I say, remembering the flurry of messages and missed-call alerts I'd skim-read at JFK Airport, hungover and frazzled.

"Yeah, so he tells me that you didn't get the job and he wanted to talk to you before you found out from everyone else," he says. "Said you'd put in tons of work. *You* even wrote a whole script, apparently."

"I can explain," I say, gasping at the complete horror of the misunderstanding.

"Oh, there's more," he says. "Then he goes on to say that the idea might go ahead without you, and he wanted to let you know that so you weren't too disappointed."

"Oh my God," I gasp. "Did he really say that? Are they going to do that?"

"Oh yes, apparently you signed a piece of paper before you went in," he says. "They own the whole idea and you don't have a job."

"That fucking asshole," I shout, and Jake flinches.

"You didn't know?"

"I didn't think they would do that," I say. "He said they wouldn't do that."

"Well," Jake says, "there *is* more. He asked me outright if we were dating. And I didn't know what to say to him, so I said no. Because it is the truth, *obviously*. And he replied that it was just as well, because you'd agreed to go out with him. And he was looking forward to it. '*She's fucking wild in bed*.'" Jake mimics Chris's voice and I cringe.

"Oh God," I say, closing my eyes at the horror of it.

Jake stops and turns to look at me, a single car driving slowly past, and I drop my eyes to the ground. "I nearly fucking punched him."

"I'm so sorry. It sounds so bad. How he's put it all. It sounds terrible."

"Just tell me everything he said is wrong," he says, trying to catch my eyes. They flicker up to meet his, and although his expression is meant to give very little away, I can see the hurt there. "Just say it, Amy," he says, challenging me.

I want to say it's all wrong. I want to so badly, but everything he said happened. I squeeze my eyelids together, trying to figure out where to start.

"You can't, can you? Because it's all true."

"It's not how Chris made it sound," I say, my voice thin, cracking slightly as I fight back the tears.

"Seems pretty simple from where I'm standing," he says, continuing the walk back to his house. "I didn't think you would be so ambitious that you'd . . . use me like that. I mean, I get the work event. I get playing the fake boyfriend. But you went pretty deep."

"Wait. *No*," I say, stopping him now, grabbing his arm, the touch electric. "The script. I did let them believe I'd written it. In the moment it felt too convoluted to explain I'd been working with a writer. I only had, like, twenty minutes in there. Also, I didn't want Chris to know you'd written it, and worked on the show with me, in case it would be a point against us. I didn't think that ultimately it would matter, because the pitch went so well. And I thought Chris had promised me the job, so then I could bring you in later—"

"He promised you the job?"

"Yes, I mean, yes. So I thought when I got in the door I'd be able to just bring you in."

Jake chews on the inside of his cheek, waiting for me to continue.

"I had every intention of protecting you. Of lifting you up," I say. "I want that for you so badly. You *deserve* it."

"You didn't even read my other script," he protests, throwing his hands in the air now, in frustration at me. His cheeks flush red.

"I did. I promise you I did. I *eventually* did," I say, wanting to elaborate on that too. "And it was brilliant. And yes, I should have read it sooner, I just really had my eyes on that job. I wanted to fucking show Chris that I could do it."

"*We* could do it," he says, incredulous.

"Yes, I lost sight of everything," I say. "And, Jake, I lost sight of you. Chris told me one afternoon—we were on this dumb boat thing for work, and he basically cornered me and said that he would help get me the job."

"He did, did he?"

"He did," I say. "He owed me a favor for what happened—"

"I don't know the full story of that, either," he mutters, seemingly exhausted now at the drama of it all. "So many fucking half-truths going on here."

"He killed my project and all I could picture—" Jake tries to keep walking, but I know I need more time and I grab hold of his arm to stop him. "All I could picture was you getting what you deserved, and me getting what I deserved. *Us.* Together. That's *all* I saw. So, I agreed. And he asked me for a coffee sometime and I didn't commit either way. I just let him believe what he wanted to help us."

Jake shrugs his arm free and continues down the road, but he's not moving as quickly now.

"I miss you," I say. "Jake, please. I miss you. Please."

This stops him momentarily, but we are now right by the rental car and almost out of time. Jake glances at the bright yellow car, with the slogan emblazoned on the side in hot pink, and for a moment, he seems to break into a half smile.

"What?"

"I'm surprised we didn't see that thing coming," he says.

"It's not as visible as you think. I nearly knocked over a horse," I say, trying to keep his smile alive. But as fast as it came, it's gone again.

"I just need to know I can trust you," he says after a long pause. "I've had enough of people I care about not being real. I need people I can count on."

I look over toward the tiny stone cottage and imagine his mother in there, and everything Jake has been through this year. How fragile he was when we met. How fragile I was. Maybe we're too fragile for each other.

"You *can* trust me," I say, pleading. Begging. "I got stuff wrong here, but my heart was in the right place. My heart was always with you. Always. You can count on me."

"Can I?" he asks, but I can see he has softened. Slightly.

"I'm going to make it right, Jake," I say.

We are interrupted by the sound of a woman's voice from the kitchen window, calling Jake's name.

"Jake?" the voice trills. "Bring Amy in, for the love of God."

Thirty-Four

~~~

Whereas my family is enormous, loud, and borderline aggressive, Jake's is just him and his mom, but there's still plenty of banter. I learn, over the course of a gin and tonic made with rosemary spears and grapefruit rind, that Chloe Jones has no siblings, both her parents have passed, and Jake's paternal grandparents live in South Africa.

"We don't really know them. They didn't have a relationship with David," she says, waving a hand away at the mention of her deceased husband.

"They didn't?"

"No, I mean, we should have seen it as a red flag, shouldn't we, Jake?" she calls out to him. "There were so many red flags. I think you get so used to them all, you think it's normal."

Jake is grilling the salmon as Callum talks to him, but all his attention, every atom in his body, is directed toward us. His mother is—frankly—beautiful. She has dark brown hair, just like Jake, with a pronounced gray streak that she has parted in the middle so it frames her face in a bouncy, glossy bob. Her clothes are what my mother would describe as *rich witch*—floating knits in soft mauve and gray, a little hint of eccentric in the pin she has fixed to her cashmere wrap: fingers raised in the universal sign for rock and roll.

"Don't you think, Jake, that your father's non-relationship with his parents should have been a red flag?"

"Yes, Mum," he says wearily.

"I'm sorry for your loss, Mrs. Jones," I say.

"Which one? My husband? Or my goddamn assets?" she says, letting out a hollow laugh. "Because I'm grieving one more than the other."

"Shit," I mutter.

"Oh, don't worry, Amy. I have found that laughing is the only thing I have left. Quite literally." She laughs again.

"But this house is so great. I mean, every storm cloud has . . . you know, a silver lining," I say, trying to encourage her to see the best in things, cringing as I hear myself sounding just like my own mother.

"You know what I miss?" she says. Then she leans forward. "My *actual* silver. We used to have a whole collection. It was my grandmother's. From 1912, if you can imagine. All gone. Taken by the creditors."

"Oh, I'm so sorry," I say. It is hard to keep laughing at the tragedy of it all, but it seems to be her only method of coping.

Callum emerges from the house with two more beers for him and Jake and another gin and tonic for me. I look nervously at Callum and Jake, wondering if they've spoken. I've been here, drinking with Chloe Jones, for more than an hour, and Jake doesn't want me to be here.

"I'd better not," I say to Callum, raising my hand. "I have to drive."

"Nonsense, you're staying," says Jake's mom in her very bossy voice.

"No, really," I say, putting my hand on top of the drink. "I need to use the bathroom." I use my other hand to shield my eyes from the low sun.

"I need to grab a sweater," says Callum, falling in step beside me.

When Jake's mom had waved us in earlier, she'd pointed us toward the garden. "Sit out back, it's nothing but boxes in here!" she'd shouted. And so we'd followed the little path down the side of the stone cottage to the backyard. I didn't expect the flush of memories from my night here with Jake to nearly bowl me over. I saw the barbecue, and the little area where we'd made up our beds. I remembered the promise I'd made to him by the light of the fire, under the stars.

I want to fulfill that promise.

It looks different today, the afternoon sun shining down on this lively scene out back, new outdoor furniture perched on the lawn, a grassy oasis on the edge of a slowly rising craggy rock hill. It's a breathtaking, almost prehistoric-looking landscape, begging you to hike from their back door straight into the national park.

Inside the house everything is completely changed from the last time I was here. The low ceilings are freshly painted. The small windows too. There's a brand-new kitchen, and the wooden floors look freshly sanded and polished.

"Big miss not to put in underfloor heating," says Callum with a chagrined smile. "This place is an icebox in winter."

After I use the bathroom, maneuvering myself there through a maze of boxes titled things like *Books, Photographs, & Memories* and *Keepsakes* and *Kitchen Misc*, I join Callum in the kitchen.

"I wonder what's in Kitchen Misc," I say, pointing at the sign scribbled in thick black marker on the brown cardboard box. "In my house it would be fourteen novelty bottle openers and some kind of handheld appliance Mom bought off the tele-shopping channel that broke after three uses."

Callum laughs, turning the kitchen tap on to pour himself a water. "Jake said you were funny," he says. The low sunlight streams through the little window onto the wooden floor, catching the dust in the air like tiny snowflakes.

"Chloe . . . I mean, her feelings are about more than the money, right?" I ask bravely.

"What? The banter about Dr. Dave?" Callum replies, raising an eyebrow. "Yep. He was a difficult man, to be honest."

"How?" I ask, peering out to make sure Jake and his mother can't hear us.

"I don't know all of it. I do know when Jake went to college to study English instead of medicine, his dad cut him off," he says. "And growing up. Well, he was this big guy, you know. Big voice, big in stature. The man around the house. An imposing dude."

"Jake said he was a big character . . ." I look at Callum and then out toward Jake.

"I don't want to talk ill of the dead, and I think that's

probably why Chloe jokes all the time. Losing something can be awful. But it can also be a huge relief. You get me?"

He turns to me and shrugs grimly. "They're okay, Amy. Don't look so worried. Jake's dad was not a great person. I can't imagine how much easier it would have been for Jake if he'd had some support from the guy. And Chloe wanted to live near Snowdonia her whole life. He wouldn't come. Took her holidaying to the Canary Islands instead."

My heart squeezes, and I raise my hand to my chest. Callum sees my reaction.

"I told Jonesy to go on that show," he says quietly.

"He said you encouraged him."

Callum flinches.

"I wanted him to do something different, but it was dumb. He was still so raw, and his dad hung on for so long . . . like, months longer than his prognosis. Jake didn't expect he would have to fly out to the set a few days after the funeral. I tried to talk him out of it at that stage, but there was the chance to earn money, and they'd just heard from the lawyer about the will . . . and I think he just thought . . . *fuck it*."

"God, no wonder he was so . . . *down* on the show," I say. "He must have been sideswiped by grief."

Callum nods. "You can imagine the rage with which I've read the gossip columns and social media posts about him."

I nod.

"Especially because Jake is one of the funniest and happiest guys I've ever known."

"He's a good writer," I say. "He's funny and so observant."

"You haven't seen him when he's on full form. Fully Jake,"

says Callum, grinning. "It's coming back, though. When I spoke to him as you were working together, I could tell he was coming back."

I cannot speak. I feel overwhelmed for a moment with the weight of it. I met him when he was at his most vulnerable, and I took advantage of that in ways I didn't realize. I could *never* have realized.

"He spent a decade, Amy, since university trying to prove his dad wrong, that he *could* make it as a writer. And when his dad was diagnosed, and it became clear that writing wasn't going to happen, that he would never have that moment to say, *look what I did*. It was like he just . . . gave up."

"Oh my God, that's so heartbreaking," I say.

"Yeah," says Callum, looking at me intensely. "So, you can see why whatever happened with you two working together was such a blow . . ."

"Yes," I mutter, grim with regret. "I can see."

Callum motions toward the door, but just before we head out into the garden, I feel the sadness of the situation over-whelming me. I want to pull Jake aside and hold him. I want to be his friend and his confidant and help grow him as a writer. I want him to have all the things his father believed he couldn't.

Dinner in the fading sun is salmon and wild herbs, sourdough bread, butter, and long strands of beans pulled from an overgrown allotment in a town nearby. It's rough and rustic, with Jake's mom calling out loaded things like "Fuck the fish knives. Throw them in the damn bin" to Jake as they navigate together what must be a brand-new family dynamic free of the person who held the loudest opinions.

Jake continues to watch me in silent contemplation, but there is not a moment we are alone to continue our conversation. And as much as I want to give in to Chloe's constant invitations to stay, I know I need to leave them tonight.

"What will you do here?" I ask Chloe. "I saw the sewing machine in the corridor. Jake said you studied fashion?"

"You know what I have always wanted to do, Amy?" she says, looking across at Jake with a wink. "Sit in a stone cottage for a year and write a bloody novel. Keep the weekends free for my son and his friends to visit, and cook for me and drink all my wine. Then, we'll see."

Thirty-Five

On the porch, Chloe and Callum tactfully retreat into the house after saying good-bye so that I have a moment alone with Jake.

"I'm sorry I intruded," I say, my eyes on the floor.

"It's okay. I did invite you . . . ," he says, with the first genuine smile directed at me, just for me, that I've had all night. But it's a sad smile. A smile full of loss.

And then I say to him, "Jake. I know how much you want this. And I know I really fucking fucked up by trusting Chris. I just wanted some kind of moment of triumph against someone who wronged me, and I thought, I really thought, that he was going to make amends for what he'd done. Fool me twice. That's what my dad says. I'm a fucking fool."

"You're a fool with a big heart," he says, shaking his head at me.

"I have your best interests at heart. I have *you* in my heart."

Jake forces his lips together and folds his arms. "I think, somewhere deep down, I do believe that."

"And Chris—"

"I don't give a shit about him," he snaps.

"No. And neither do I," I reply. And I mean it. I really do.

"I'm going to send you something when I'm on my way home tomorrow and I want you to please take a look. It's something I should have done a while ago, and I didn't."

"Okay," he replies, intrigued.

"Do you promise?"

"Yes, I promise."

I don't want to go any further. I don't want to explain any more. The time for talking is over, and now it's time for action. I want so desperately to talk about his proposal for *The Market*, and I want to tell him what I've done, right there on the doorstep, but it's better to wait.

"You look so good," I say. It tumbles out of me. "It's *so* good to see you. I meant it when I said I missed you."

"It was only a few days." That's all he says. But I see something in his eyes that gives me hope. A glint. A hint that he might feel something similar.

I drive away from the cottage in the fading light. I take it slowly, breathing in the beauty all around me before it slips out of view, into the darkness, and it's just me and the snaking blue line of my GPS leading me to the little bed-and-breakfast by the train station.

In the morning, I sit on the train home, my finger hovering over the send button, knowing this is the point of no return, but that if Jake and I are to continue, to build on what we've started, I owe him this much.

. . .

*W*hen the train pulls into Euston, I take a black cab straight into work. I feel calmer than I have in days, and clear on what I'm going to do.

I'm surprised to see Maggie outside, her hair thrown back into a small, messy bun.

"Amy," she says. "Did you go? Did you see Jake?"

"I did," I say, feeling the prickles of sweat on my forehead. "But I'm here to speak to Chris. Time to have it out."

I pretend to crack my knuckles, but there is no denying the shaking. I'm nervous.

"I thought you might need to do that," she says.

"Chris saw Jake, and he totally insinuated that he and I might date," I say, grimacing as I retell the entire conversation to her, in fast-forward, as she nods and gasps in quick succession.

"Just go and do the thing, Amy. Just go shout at him and get it all off your chest."

I nod furiously, fixing my shirt and straightening my trousers. I stride inside with purpose, hitting the button for the elevators, and as I await the opening, I take a deep breath.

All I can think about is how much I want to piss on his car again.

I step into the elevator and hit the seventh-floor button. When I emerge, I walk straight to the corner office Chris is rumored to be in, and I see him there on the phone, staring out the window, stroking his chin.

I knock on the door, and he startles. Looking across at me

with an apprehensive wave, he motions for me to come in. As I enter, he stands, finishing his phone call and gesturing for me to sit and join him. The room smells thickly of his aftershave.

"Amy," he says. "How are you? You went back to New York?"

"I did," I reply, looking at him coolly. "I won't need a seat."

"I guess you heard, then," he says, leaning back in his chair. He eyes me with a hint of . . . what? Boredom? Irritation? I have to suck back in some air to remain steady. "That's what the visit is about?"

"I loved you, Chris," I say. "It was a dumb power imbalance, the whole thing, but nonetheless I did."

Chris sits up, surprise etched across his face. He folds his hands on the table. "I'm sorry, Amy, it's just that Zadie is a brilliant EP, and I became concerned that . . . well. I didn't want a repeat of what happened at Wolf."

"I'm happy for Zadie. She deserves it," I say. "Actually, she deserves *better*."

"Well, that's very magnanimous of you," he says, smiling cautiously.

"I hear you are going to stay in London. Is that right?"

"Yes," he says, sighing. "I think so. In the end, they made me a very good offer. Very good indeed."

"Well, that must be a big relief for you," I say, "because I was wondering, you know, why on earth you left Wolf in the first place."

"Wolf?" he says, startling a little. *Good.*

"Yes. I wondered when you arrived, actually. Who on earth would leave the biggest studio in New York to come and be part of this massive gamble?" I nod toward the framed poster of CTV's *Christmas Season*, starring several actors, none of whom Chris would know. "And then two days ago I sent some long-overdue emails to some old friends after dusting off the old LinkedIn profile," I say with a grin.

Chris shifts uneasily in his chair now, and I feel an incredible pleasure watching him squirm.

"I knew you denied we dated, to distance yourself from that video. I knew I was framed as the crazy-girl employee who got all obsessed with you. But I was very surprised to hear that you *left* after losing half a million dollars in investment in the development of several new shows."

I look out the window toward Liberty department store and sigh.

"And one of them was my show, in fact. *The Darkening Web*."

"You didn't own that idea," he spits. "Wolf did."

"Apparently the writer refused to work with you," I say. "In fact, I have the email here. Shall I read it?"

Chris hesitates, his cheeks reddening, and so I continue.

"It reads, '*Hi Amy bloody Duffy. I'm so glad to hear from you. Yeah, about* The Darkening Web . . . *I pulled out of that shit show when you left. The guy who took the lead on the series was dumb as hell, sorry. The whole thing was a mess. I'm sorry the idea collapsed, but better sooner rather than if we'd moved properly into pilot.*'"

"When you left, I revived it. Why shouldn't I? The reason I didn't want to move it forward was our relationship. When the relationship was over, there was no more issue moving it forward."

"You are a piece of shit, you know that?" I say, losing my temper momentarily.

"It's just business, Amy. Your problem is that you make everything so emotional. So personal."

"Television *is* personal," I say.

He sighs heavily. "So, I lost some money. That's development, honey. It happens all the time."

"Don't *honey* me. You lost money because the team I'd pulled together were people I'd found and nurtured. *Not you*." I say this with such venom, I even shock myself.

"Ideas fall down all the time," he says, a show at being weary, but I can see that I've rattled him.

"I just wish that Jeff knew who you really were," I say. "You'd never have this corner office. This job. You can be a brilliant development executive, but if you fuck over all the creative people you work with to get there, you're just a cunt."

"You forget, Amy," he says, standing and walking around his desk to face me. To intimidate me. He's angry. "That I can ruin you with the click of a button."

"Yeah? *No*. Once upon a time that idea would have terrified me."

"Tread lightly," he warns, taking a step closer. I want to comment on the *Breaking Bad* reference but will not be sidetracked.

"You're counting on me to be ashamed so you can keep me small," I say.

"You're the one who pissed on my fucking car, Amy," he says, sighing. "There's a whole video online to prove it."

"Yes, there is. But you know, Chris, over the summer, I learned that it is my choice to be afraid. I met someone who humiliated himself on a much bigger stage than I did. And I watched him recover, own his shame, and move forward."

"The fucking reality TV dude," he spits. "The *writer*?"

"And I realized," I continue, ignoring his jibe, "I realized that the bravest, most radical thing I could do was to own it. Maggie has been telling me all along that's the way out of shame, but I couldn't believe it until I saw him do it. If I decide to not be ashamed, your power over me, it *disintegrates*." I bring all my fingers together and release them, like a magician casting a spell. "*Poof*," I say. "It's gone."

Chris's phone starts to ring and I smile.

"What did you . . . ?"

"I think, maybe, you might not want to stay in London," I say. "But I don't know. Maybe you're braver than I was."

Chris picks up the phone. "Chris Ellis," he says. "Yes, of course. I can be right there, Jeff."

"Jeff wants to see you?" I say, folding my arms.

"What did you do, Amy?" he says, a vein starting to throb in his forehead.

"Chris, I decided that the best way for both of us to be free from our past was to own it. And so, about an hour ago, I sent the video of me to all my friends, and the senior managers in the building. Anonymously, of course."

"Amy!" he shouts, his cheeks reddening with anger. "You fucking idiot. You'll be ruined too!"

"Will I?" I say, jutting out my bottom lip. "Maybe? Or

maybe *not*. Either way. It's time to forgive ourselves and move forward, don't you think?"

And with that, I turn and I walk out of the office, slightly tripping as I shut the door behind me. The last thing I hear as I walk across the floor toward the elevator doors is the sound of the phone hitting the wall, and Chris Ellis's career imploding.

Thirty-Six

~~~~~~~

A week later, I am sitting on Brighton Beach as the sun begins to set, eating salty fish and chips as Maggie sips a canned wine.

"It was a good summer," she muses, looking out to the clouds starting to form on the horizon. "I don't want it to end."

"I can't believe you're going to move here. It all seems so fast," I say. "What about Pixar? What about going to LA?"

"Who needs that much sunshine?" she says, pulling her cardigan up over her shoulders. "Besides, a girl can be fully remote these days."

I nod. "True."

With the sound of seagulls and terrible dance music in the background, I lie back on the pebbled beach and stare up at the sky, feeling lighter than I have in so long.

"Moe messaged me, by the way," I say. "He thought the video was *hilarious*."

"It *is*," says Maggie.

"And Penny said I looked nice in that color blue, and that

she would have taken a full-on shit on the car, if a guy had done that to her."

"That was *always* my sentiment," says Maggie.

"I handed it in, by the way. My resignation," I say, turning to Maggie, propping myself up on my arm. "I emailed Danny this morning."

"You did?" she says, unsurprised. "What did he say?"

"Two words: *well done*," I say, laughing.

A shadow falls across my face, and I look up to see Michael standing above us, holding three cans of beer. "It's six o'clock," he says, and Maggie and I sit up while he lowers himself to join us on the edge of the blanket.

"Maggie says that congratulations are in order," he says before peeling back the lid of the can, which makes a satisfying fizz.

"For which bit?"

"Well, the skewering of a toxic suit sounds like a good start?" he says cheerfully.

"Quite," I say in my best British accent.

"What happened to him?" he asks, and I look across at Maggie and we exchange a grimace.

"No one really knows. Danny thinks he went back to New York," Maggie says. "Whatever happened, I guess he didn't take the full-time job."

"He ran away," I add. "Ironic."

"But he didn't run away because of the video, did he?" Michael asks. "I mean, hasn't half of New York already seen it?"

"No, I spoke to an old friend, a writer who is now an exec, and she was more than happy to write to Jeff and give an alternative reference," I explain. "Between that and the video, I think he became a liability."

"How did he get the job in the first place, then? With everything falling apart at Wolf for him?"

"He was approached in private in New York, before all the mess became fully known, and he was already in London as the house of cards came crumbling down. When they poach people, you know, you can't ask for a reference from the current employer. I didn't realize how much his career was thanks to me. People like me. His whole team."

"I can't believe he tried to revive your project after you left. That's the thing that makes me want to fucking stab him in the eye. The sheer audacity of it!" Maggie exclaims.

"I know," I say. "When I left Jake's house, I was going to sort things out kind of amicably. But when I got that email on the train home, I was like, nope. This is *war*."

"And you haven't heard from Jake yet?" Maggie remarks.

"Only a message to say he was thinking about everything and taking a bit of time to get his mom settled in. I've been giving him the space he needs; I want to get this right," I say.

"Look at you," says Maggie, pulling Michael close and kissing him on the cheek. "All in love."

"I'm not in *love*," I say, feeling my cheeks flame at the thought.

"Sure you're not," she says. "You should have seen yourself at that fucking summer party. You were in deep already."

"Shut the fuck up," I say. But the bloom of pink in my cheeks gives me away, and I grin, giddy. "I'm high on hopium," I say.

And then I check my watch. "I should head back to the

train station. Agnes needs me to look after her tortoise this week."

"Your landlord has a tortoise?"

"Elfie," I say, nodding. "Not sure how much babysitting it will need."

"The price we pay for decent digs in Central London," Michael says, laughing.

I nod. "She just offered me another one-year lease."

"You gonna sign it?" Maggie says.

"I think so. I need to speak with Jake first." I stand, brushing some of the pebbles off. I look down at Maggie, who has entwined herself with Michael already. I smile at her.

"Suits you," I say, grinning. "I'll call you soon?"

"Bye, Amy, go get your guy," she says, winking.

On the way home, I stop by the grocer to collect a ready meal and a half bottle of wine for dinner. This time, I barely think of Glenn and his cool, teenage opinions as I slide both things onto the conveyor belt and check my phone for the hundredth time to see if Jake has messaged.

As Glenn scans the meal, I look him in the eye, and I smile.

I watch with surprise as his cheeks start to color and his eyes flicker from the conveyor belt to me. Then he nearly knocks the wine over with his arm.

"Meal for *one*, again?" he says.

"Yes," I say confidently, winking at him. "Back to my good old meals for *one*."

He nods, and his eyes drop down to the register. "Eighteen fifty-two," he says.

I fish out a twenty-pound note and he passes me the change, but as his hand touches mine, he leans forward. "Are you . . . like . . . hitting on me?" he says.

"Oh my God, no," I yelp. "Hell no."

"Oh," he says, looking disappointed for a fraction of a second before pivoting to rude in a heartbeat. "*Whatever.*"

As I arrive home it starts to rain. And I mean really rain. I shower and wash my hair; pull on my beloved *F.R.I.E.N.D.S* nightgown, which fit me at thirteen but is now threadbare and far too short to be considered anything but a long T-shirt; and curl up on the sofa to FaceTime Mom while I let my vegetarian lasagna for one cook slowly in the oven and opt for a cup of peppermint tea instead of wine.

"When are you coming back?" is the first thing she says.

"I'm not sure," I say. "Mom. I finally quit my job this week."

"You did? Oh, Amy, you *are* coming home," she says, her voice quivering with delight. "I'm going to have to get that Ping-Pong table out of your bedroom."

"Chill, Mom. *Chill.*" I laugh so hard at her trying to straighten the phone while she slices onions. "What are you making?"

"Your dad's whisky beef," she says, rolling her eyes. "I'm under orders."

"I'm not coming home, at least not at the moment," I say. "But I do have some plans that I hope will bring me home more often."

"Well," she says, putting the knife down and sighing. "That's a start. But you'll come for Christmas?"

"I'll come for Christmas for sure," I say.

It is the first conversation with my mother in two years that is not strained, and I sit back and let her go on and on about home, the Canadians next door who have a really loud terrier, Floyd's new job.

After half an hour, the sun sets, the dark closes in, and the tiredness starts to creep. I want to eat, and I want to put on the television and fall asleep watching something comforting.

"I have to go, Mom, it's getting late," I say, though when I look at the time, I realize it's only seven.

"Sure, honey," she says lightly.

I eat my dinner and eventually have a large glass of red wine, flicking through all my streamers before the tiredness is too much, and I decide to just curl up right here under my cozy throw, with the sound of the rain and my heart full of hope.

I fall asleep in a state of suspension, waiting, hoping, praying, for Jake to come home.

Thirty-Seven

~~~

I am woken an hour later by a knock on my door, and I crawl off the sofa, in my nightie, my hair in a long plait down my back.

"Hello?" I say through the door.

"It's me," Jake replies, and I gulp.

"Just a minute!" I shout, checking myself in the hall mirror. I undo my hair and brush it with my fingers, pulling on a plaid shirt to cover my nightie—the first thing I can grab.

"Everything okay back there?" Jake says from behind the door.

I fling the door open and he's standing there. "Jake," I say. "You're back!" Looking impossibly gorgeous in an emerald-green hoodie, his hair damp from the rain, his face flushed. He smiles at me, and it's that dazzling, full-faced smile again. The one where his whole face brightens. He's back. He's come back *to me*.

I rush forward and throw my arms around him and squeeze him tight. "I'm so sorry about everything," I say.

There is a pause before he relaxes into my embrace, but then he puts his arms around me and squeezes back.

"I can't believe you came all the way up north," he says as he pulls back and looks me in the eye.

"I would go farther than that," I say. "Cheesy. I know."

Jake laughs, shaking his head at me. "Sorry I've been so quiet," he says. "I got the email, but honestly, I decided to totally unplug for a week and take some time out with my mum. It was important. We didn't do it after the funeral because I just left."

"Yes," I say, nodding. "I totally understand. I would have given you as long as you needed, but I'm so glad you're back."

"Can I come in?" he says quietly.

"Yes, yes," I say, "of course you can."

I wave him in and through to the living room, cringing as I spot the half-eaten dinner and the wine on the coffee table.

"Vintage Amy Duffy," I say, shoving blankets and pillows aside to make room for him to sit.

"All right," he says, pushing his hair back as he settles against the armrest to face me. I have flashbacks to the night of the summer work party. Him in his loosened black tie, looking impossibly handsome, wanting me. It was all *I* had wanted too, but I was afraid to let it happen.

"Mum thought you were cute," he says.

"Cute?" I reply.

"Yes. She said you were a nervous creature who needed a good hug," he says, laughing. "I had to spend half the week convincing her that you're actually quite a gobby and opinionated woman who knows exactly what she wants."

"Oh, Jake," I say, cringing.

"It's okay. I like it," he says. "Gobby and opinionated is my favorite flavor."

He grins wickedly and then scratches the back of his head, momentarily lost in deep thought. I let him go at his pace.

"So, you never had feelings for Chris? At least, I mean, this summer. You weren't going to date him?"

"No. It was like I told you. I had residual unresolved feelings that were not love and are now pretty much disdain," I say. "I confronted him at work and he smashed a phone against the glass door of his office, and now he's left London. We *think*."

"Okay," says Jake, eyes wide. "Things have progressed quickly, then. What the hell led to that?"

"I heard he revived my project in New York," I begin, outlining as succinctly as I can all I've learned since I left Jake in Wales.

"What an asshole," says Jake, his hand balling into a fist as he says it. "I mean seriously. These people who just suck on other creative people's hard work and then use it to—"

He stops himself abruptly from ranting and frowns at me.

"I nearly did that to you," I say. "I got sucked into this obsession with claiming back what was stolen from me, and in the process, I nearly stole from you."

"Nearly?"

"We can keep *Dry Bones* going. I begged Danny. He said given everything that has happened, he will speak with the new directors at Screen Global about the series and see if they will revert the idea back. And regardless, we can totally repitch to the new head of development."

"That's great," he says.

"I'm pretty sure we will get it back. Nothing has been sent digitally. It's just a few paper copies."

"Okay," he says slowly. "But what would *you* do with it . . ."

I take a deep breath, tucking my hair behind my ears as I do.

"I'm going to set up on my own. My own company. Duffy Productions. Or something more elegant, that doesn't sound like a couple of stoners in a basement making porn."

Jake laughs. "Are you able to . . ."

"Do I have the connections? Yes, I have some. I'm going to start developing and pitching ideas independently, and then, you know, when I get my first bite, a development deal—money—I'll be able to bring some people in. Like you? I was really surprised when I reached out to my New York contacts how many people, um, you know . . . liked working with me, and would like to, you know, talk. There are some doors, Jake. I can open them."

"You're welcome to have a brag," he says, reaching over to squeeze my calf. I shudder a bit under his touch. "It's supercool."

"Maggie is going to do my logo," I say, grinning.

Jake smiles again, his eyes rounded and soft.

"I wanted to apologize to you too," he says, taking in a deep breath. "There are a few things I really struggled with."

I shuffle closer to him on the sofa, nervously. He reaches his hand across and wiggles his fingers, an invitation. I reach forward and our fingers connect, intertwining, and it feels so good. So *right*.

"At the moment, I'm finding it hard to put into words. Which is a bit devastating for a writer."

My heart aches again, and this time I feel it like a wave through my whole body, and I squeeze his hand tightly. He tugs slightly on me, and I inch even closer to him. We are angled toward each other on the sofa, facing each other.

"This was just the summer I desperately needed. You picked me up when I was at my absolute lowest and kicked me out of the house and forced me to face everything. And before I knew it, I was writing again. After a year where I'd almost completely lost faith. My dad died believing I'd failed; that was probably the hardest part to take."

"Oh, Jake," I say.

"Enough of all of that." He jumps in quickly. "There's time to talk about that. What I'm trying to say is thank you. All the misunderstandings and crappy ex-bosses and nonsense aside. Thank you for believing in me."

I hold my free hand up to my chest and I bite my lip.

"Oh, Jake," I say again. "You did the same for me. I was only able to face Chris because you showed me how to be brave, by being so brave yourself." I feel the prickle of tears, but I breathe them away and look back at him. He tugs me closer still. I only move a little.

"Closer," he says, and now he is close enough to touch my shoulder, and he runs his hand up the back of my neck, trailing a finger down my spine. I can feel the electricity fizzing.

"I wasn't *that* brave," he says. "Going to your work function was an exercise in pure masochism. I hated it."

"You did it for me," I say as he strokes my neck with his hand, brushing my hair away.

"I did it all for you. Until I was doing it for myself too."

It's enough. I crawl onto his lap, straddling him, and wrap my arms around his neck. Then I pull him into me, squeezing every part of him as close to me as I can. As if he might get away if I let him go. Then I kiss his forehead. I leave my lips there for a beat, feeling his warmth, listening to his steady breath.

I rest my head on his shoulder. It is more than holding someone; it is a release. It is letting go and holding on at the same time. It is the very beginnings of love.

We sit there still and calm, until I become acutely aware of how little I'm wearing and begin to feel Jake pressing into me. He remains completely still, aware of the same. As if one small move and he would move into me.

"I could kill you," I say into his ear. "Do you know that?"

Jake laughs and moves me back gently, so he can see my face. Our eyes lock and he reaches a hand up to my cheek.

For a moment, I think we might finally kiss, but then something niggles at me, and I remember, pushing back from him in a panic.

"I've just realized, you *still* haven't read the email," I say, gasping. I jump off the couch and start to pace.

"No," he says, pulling out his phone. "Should I read it now?"

My heart picks up into a gallop, and I feel the cold sweat on my palms.

"Okay, I'm going to go to the kitchen, and you're going to read the email and I'm going to wait for you, and if you never want to speak to me again, you can just slip out the door—"

Jake waves me away. "Begone!" he jokes. "How bad can it be?"

"Oh, it's pretty bad, Jake. It's definitely pretty bad."

I head into the kitchen and I hold my breath as I wait for the crackling audio. It is only a moment later when I hear it begin, and then after seventeen awful seconds, I brace myself for his response.

But I don't hear anything.

"Jake?" I say after a moment.

"Yes, Amy?" he says, his voice completely neutral.

"Well?" I say, taking a tentative step out of the kitchen, peering around the door.

He's sitting in the same position, a neutral face to match his neutral tone.

"Well? What do you think? Do you hate me? Am I a terrible embarrassment? Do I look like an extra from *Shameless*? Say something."

"Who here hasn't pissed on a car?" he says plainly.

"That's what my mom said!"

"I mean, I would have gone for the boot, or maybe the driver's door? But I get it."

I drop my eyes to the floor, a reaction I can't control. I can take some of the teasing some of the time, but I'm not free of the shame. Not completely.

"You sent that to your whole office?" he says now, standing to walk toward me, tossing his phone on the couch as he moves.

"Yes," I say. "I felt like it was the only way to take back control from Chris. And of course, I realize now, a lot of people think he deserved that and more. I'm something of a hero among the girls at work."

He laughs, and, putting a hand on either side of my arms, he rubs them up and down.

Then he leans in for a kiss. Just one, on my cheek. It's tender, but it isn't enough. I want more. I look at him, trying to calm my hunger.

"We said when we finished the project, we might try . . . something," he says.

"Yes," I reply quietly, although inside I'm shouting: *FUCK YES LET'S GOOOOO!*

"Okay. Tomorrow night. Eight p.m. The rain will be gone. Let's meet on the terrace."

"Okay," I say. "Like a date? I have to wait for a date?"

Unable to restrain myself, I lean in and I kiss him right on the lips. They meet, soft and full and warm, and I immediately let out a soft moan. But Jake, still holding my arms, pushes me back slightly.

"A date," he says. "Let's do it properly."

Thirty-Eight

I'm not sure what to wear and I've been fussing all day.

Jake has been busy too. I've heard the sound of sets of feet moving things up and down the stairs and am starting to tingle with anticipation for what I'll find on that rooftop.

I stand in front of the mirror, trying on several different things, but cannot decide. Eight p.m. is only ten minutes away. I finally opt for a little black slip dress and hot-pink pumps. At eight on the dot, I emerge from my apartment and take a few tentative steps up toward the terrace.

At the door at the top of the stairs, I take a huge deep breath and push it open.

I gasp at the sight.

The lights, twinkling in the low evening light. The little table, covered in a tablecloth, set with candles in jars. There is music playing from portable speakers. But the thing that is most astounding, the thing I'm not expecting, is the bath.

Jake has somehow brought a huge clawfoot look-alike tub up the stairs and onto the terrace.

"Oh my God," I say, my mouth slackening at the sight of it.

"I know," he says. "I just thought . . . why the fuck not? It was from the old place in Wales, because Mum got the new bathroom done, and it's been sitting out the front bound for the dumpster."

"But when did you get it down?"

"Callum drove it down yesterday with a bunch of my stuff," he says. "I was fucking praying you didn't come upstairs and see it."

I trail my hand through the warm water in the tub and grin at Jake.

"For later?"

He shrugs cheekily.

The top of the barbecue is closed, but I can smell something delicious and my stomach rumbles. Jake is wearing a black button-down shirt and chinos rolled at the bottom with brown loafers. He looks sharp. Gorgeous.

"Beer or wine?" he says, nodding toward a bucket filled with ice and drinks.

"You know what? Have you got anything that sparkles?" I say.

Jake pushes the hair back from his forehead. "In fact I do. I have champagne," he says, sliding out a bottle and expertly popping the cork. He pours two glasses for us.

"You even have champagne flutes," I reply.

"I tried to think of everything," he says.

I breathe slowly, trying to ease my nerves. He reaches his hand out and guides me toward the chair opposite him. The charge from our touch makes me weak at the knees and I have to hold the back of the chair to steady myself.

"When I look at you, like this, Amy . . . you kind of take my breath away."

He blinks slowly, tearing his eyes away from me and smiling to himself. I resist the urge to joke, to shy away from the compliment. Instead I let it soak in.

"Does this feel weird?" I ask him.

"Yes," he says, "but also weirdly natural."

We touch the tops of our glasses together. Jake's eyes are sparkling under the warmth of the lights, just like they were that night by the fire in Wales. He is divine. Edible. And he's all mine.

"I don't know how I'm going to get through dinner," I say, running my fingernails down the back of his hand. "When all I want is you."

He puts his glass down on the table, reaching across to hold my hand, and I give it to him. And then he stands, leaving his drink behind, and he pulls me up and into his arms.

"I don't want to come over too romantic here," he says, running his hands down my back, across the curves of me. "I mean, I'm doing all of this because I want to get into your pants."

I laugh at his mischievous grin. "Oh, now that's romantic."

He looks down at my lips and I bite the bottom one playfully.

"I want to make good on my promise," I say, taking his hand in mine and then kissing his knuckles as I did under the stars in Wales, looking up into his eyes and watching them darken.

And then he leans forward, and I follow, our eyes not

leaving each other as he kisses me gently. A soft kiss, his mouth open slightly, the smallest hint of his tongue along my lips.

Then his hands move across my body, nothing hidden by this dress, and yet, he wants it off. I feel his finger at the zipper, which runs from the neck to the curve of the small of my back. But I stop him.

"Wait," I say, reaching up and unbuttoning his shirt, one at a time, making my way from his neck to his chest with my mouth, savoring his taut skin and the spray of dark hair that leads in a trail, lower. I run my fingers across his nipples.

"Amy," he says, tilting my chin up to him and kissing me again.

I take my time, slowly undressing in front of him, first one strap, then the other, then unzipping the dress and allowing it to fall to the floor. He stands back and I reach around and unhook my bra, letting it drop, watching his face as he takes my body in. "Fuck me," he says, stilling himself. "Sensational."

"What about a bath?" I say.

"Amy, you're so sexy . . . ," he says.

I walk, naked, to the bath, which is still warm, a little steam rising from the surface, and I step in. "Come on, then," I say.

Jake follows and, after removing his clothes in record time, steps in behind me, sliding down so I'm lying skin to skin across his naked body. It isn't long before I feel his hardness against me.

"I don't think we're eating, are we?" I ask.

"Maybe not," he says into my ear, kissing the spot just behind it.

Thirty-Nine

Six Months Later

I wake Jake as soon as the plane touches down on the tarmac.

"We've landed," I say into his ear, and he stirs in the seat beside me.

"God, I slept all the way," he says, pulling out his phone.

"You did," I reply, kissing him lightly on the cheek as he rubs his eyes and stretches out his long legs.

"First time in New York," he says. "I have a lot of expectations."

"You said," I reply. "Don't worry, you're going to have an amazing time."

This week I'm going to see two digital streaming services and NBCUniversal. After a lot of dithering about, I decided to own my name, and so Duffy Studio was launched at the end of September, with a logo and website designed, with glee, by Maggie.

It has been a serious amount of work, but I'm excited about what the future will bring, now I'm in charge of my own destiny.

"BBC want the meeting next week," Jake says as he reads through an email.

"Oh, that's great," I say. "That's three different networks. You're going to really be able to play them off against each other."

"But it's the BEEEEEEEB," he says, moaning. "I don't want to go anywhere else."

"Jake, as your lover and your friend, I'm telling you. Don't take the first agent your mom recommends, and don't take the first offer on your series."

Jake laughs and juts his lip out. "Fine. I'll shop around."

Jake's screenplay for the new version of *Trader Town*, formerly *The Market*, was shipped out, by me, when I was on the train home from visiting him in Wales all that time ago. I'd called on all my contacts, and two weeks ago, the head of comedy at the BBC got in touch with Jake asking him for a meeting.

He was surprised to hear from them, but I wasn't. *I knew.* I just knew he had something there.

And so, while I begin a journey to build a production company, Jake is starting his own very real adventure writing for a series he created. We decided that while we could always work together, it was better if we embarked on our adventures separately and got to enjoy supporting each other.

"Now, as I was saying about my family," I begin as we cruise through passport control.

"They're loud and I might be given a bit of a hard time," he says, repeating what I've told him at least a hundred times on the flight here.

"To say the least," I reply. "Whatever you do, just be yourself.

They can smell any kind of pretention. They can smell fear too. So try not to be terrified or you'll be crucified."

"You sell them so well," he says, laughing.

And then the doors open into arrivals, where my mom is waiting with Dad.

"Amy!" my mom yells and throws her arms around me. "You must be Jake?" she says when she releases me. "Turn around, let me look at you."

Jake does an awkward spin, holding his hands out, and then my mom looks across at me. "He needs to eat. You don't feed him?"

"He's not a dog, Mom," I say, rolling my eyes.

"What the hell are you doing, kid, give me a hug." My dad beams at Jake, pulling him in for a massive squeeze. "When are you two moving to New York, then?"

"Jake's mom lives in Wales, I told you, Dad," I say as he and Jake tussle over who will get the bags, my dad finally acquiescing and giving Jake an approving thump on the back. We start walking to the car.

"What's Wales got that we can't offer on Long Island?" he says.

"I'm sure my mom would love New York," says Jake.

"You bet your ass she would," he replies, and Mom and I fall back as they walk together toward the car.

"He's handsome, Amy," she says, turning to me and stopping.

Then she squeezes both of my cheeks and kisses me right on the mouth.

"And he seems good. Good and kind," she says. "Like your father."

"He is, Mom," I reply.

"And I pray for him, I really do. He's about to be drawn into the lions' goddamn den. The whole family are at the house."

"The whole family?" I say, groaning.

Later that evening, when everyone has left, and Jake and I are both crippled with jet lag and exhaustion but too wired to sleep just yet, we curl up on the sofa together. Jake is flicking through the *TV Guide* to try to find something to watch, when he gets a beep on his phone.

"What is it?" I say, as I hear him laughing.

"It's Callum," he replies. "He just bumped into Agnes, naked, in the rooftop bathtub."

"Oh my God," I say. "What a house-sitting present."

"Yes, and apparently she's talked him into running to the shop to get her some sherry."

"Close your eyes and think of the low rent," I say. "One more delicious year of it."

Jake and I have both signed our new leases, retaining our own spaces . . . for now.

"What are you two giggling about?" says Floyd, dropping into the armchair opposite us.

"Just our bossy landlady," I say. "Jake's best friend just saw her naked."

"Sounds hot," says Floyd nonchalantly, and we both laugh uproariously. Ignoring us, Floyd continues, "Amy says you saw the film of her pissing all over that prick's Audi?"

"I did," Jake says, catching his breath and giving me a reassuring squeeze.

"Because I got a bunch of videos digitized for our granny's eightieth birthday to make a little montage thing—is that what you call them, Amy?"

"A montage, yes. Floyd, what the hell is coming?" I ask as he fiddles with the remote control and points it at the television. "Floyd?"

"Well, I found a bunch of videos of Amy, and one of them is the first time she took a dump in a potty. I also have her first nudie dash on a beach. And her first day of school. And the time she sang the national anthem at Little League—but completely out of tune. She sounded like someone put Mariah Carey in a blender. You want to watch? It's gold."

"Oh my God," I say wearily, looking over at Floyd. "And you wonder why I moved to London?"

Jake laughs and stands. "I think I'll need another beer for this."

I watch him go, then, turning to Floyd, I have to ask, "What do you think of Jake?"

"What do I think of Jake? It doesn't matter what I think of him, Amy," he says. "The only thing that matters here is, what do *you* think of him?"

I smile at my big brother just as Jake returns. And with that, Floyd stands and pretends to yawn. "Leave you lovebirds to it, save that gold for tomorrow," he says, shooting me a grin.

"What were you two talking about?" Jake says. "Me, I hope." He grins.

I pull him down onto the sofa and lean against him, my head on his chest, as he places his arm around my shoulders. "Oh, nothing," I say, smiling up at him.

"Unlikely," he insists, his lips meeting the top of my head.

"I wanted to know what Floyd thought of you," I say.

"What did he say?"

"He *wouldn't* say," I reply, turning my head to look up at Jake. "But I think, on balance, he probably likes you."

Jake looks down at me.

"Well, that's good news," Jake says as he strokes my hair. "I like him too. But I'm afraid I rather like his sister a lot more."

I look up at him, blinking a little as I feel the sting of happy tears. "In fact," he says, "I love her."

"You do?" I ask, my heart swelling in my chest.

"I do, Amy," he says, kissing me on the lips. "What's not to love?"

"Well . . . ," I begin, about to explain all the ways he should reconsider; then I stop myself, and instead, I kiss him gently on the lips. Because I am not a hashtag, I am not one bad day in July, I'm not even thirty-two years of awesomeness. I'm in love.

Acknowledgments

As always, thanks to my agent, Hattie; my editor, Tara; and all the team at Putnam / Penguin Random House. Thanks for continuing to believe in me, you fools.

Thank you to my long-suffering partner, Bernie, for his ongoing support and encouragement. You feel every step of this writing journey with me; now it's time to finally read one of my books. ☺

Thank you to AJ West, one of the nicest guys in the game, for briefing me on the ins and outs of reality TV.

I dedicated this book to my dearest friend, Nicki Sunderland. Last Christmas we met halfway between our two towns for eighteen hours (half of which I was passed out with jet lag). It was all we could manage between family commitments and travel. By the end of the second bottle of wine we had talked about everything, but it is never enough. I miss you every day. I wish you were here to fold the washing with me while I complain about boring shit that doesn't matter. I hope, hope, hope you have a peaceful 2023.

I'd also like to thank my Red Bull family for giving me a family away from home during the pandemic. And a love of F1. And beer.

And of course, much love to all the people I worked with in the promotions department of Cartoon Network between 2003 and 2010. What an amazing time we had in Soho during those years. I will forever remember the Shaston Arms and the White Horse and that French wine bar with the Piquepoul (looking at you, Vicky Shields). Still have some of the best friends of my life from that time.

The Sweetest Revenge

LIZZY DENT

A Conversation with Lizzy Dent

Discussion Questions

BOOK
ENDS

PUTNAM
— EST. 1838 —

A Conversation with Lizzy Dent

What inspired you to write *The Sweetest Revenge*?

Since I've worked in television for most of my life, I was desperate to set a book in that world. I had so much fun working there. There were a lot of interoffice scandals and affairs. In fact, I met my partner there!

This is your third adult novel. Was the writing process different than for *The Summer Job* and *The Setup*? Was anything harder for you? Easier?

Much easier. After a shaky first draft, my editor and I outlined this book together, and so the writing process was far more fun and less fraught. Also, I'm leaning a bit more into the rom-com genre with this one, so the story itself was super fun!

**The Sweetest Revenge* takes place in the world of television, an industry you are very familiar with after working for MTV, Cartoon Network, and the BBC, among other media companies. How much of Amy's story is based on your experiences in television? Were there any details you included about the industry that felt close to home?

I set the book in a fictional TV studio in Soho, London, but that was exactly where I worked at Turner Broadcasting. We were right at the top of Carnaby Street, and the whole of Soho was geared toward making TV and film, so there was a big community of media people in a very concentrated area. It was *so* much fun. I used to work in a promos department just like Amy (the best times of my working life), but I yearned to work in the development of big TV dramas. I always felt too insecure to put myself out there properly, so it remained a quiet dream. My weird parallel is that I *am* now working in TV development—of *The Summer Job* TV series. So, I got where I wanted to go . . . eventually!

If *The Sweetest Revenge* was picked up for the big screen or a TV series, who would you choose to play Amy? What about Chris, Jake, and Maggie?

Okay, Chris is definitely Cameron (Theo James) from *The White Lotus*. A perfect casting. Jake is someone ridiculously good-looking, like Henry Cavill (Superman) or Ben Barnes or Regé-Jean Page. Maggie could be Emily Blunt, and Amy I always imagined as a young Jennifer Aniston.

Although fictional, the script Amy and Jake create together, *Dry Bones*, involves great detail about London and the crime

genre. What was the inspiration for this fictional script, and did you perform any research while essentially writing it?

A bit of research, yes! I have always wanted to write a thriller/horror, and so this was my way of dipping my toe in a little, I think.

What were some of the core characteristics you wanted Amy's character to embody? How did you craft Jake's character? What do you think lies at the heart of Amy and Jake's relationship?

I wanted her to be talented, hardworking, and a deeply good person, but capable of doing some crazy things when pushed. And in Jake I wanted someone who was quite shy and introverted, to do something that challenged those traits hard. I think they are both intrinsically very gentle souls, and I'm so glad they found each other.

Amy loves shows centered on the macabre, while Jake enjoys heartfelt stories. Which do you prefer to watch? Do you have a favorite TV show that Amy and Jake reference in *The Sweetest Revenge*?

I am somewhere in between these days. I used to love crime and the macabre, but now I love high drama that has a lot of comedy: *Succession*, *The White Lotus*, *The Bear*.

Without giving anything away, did you always know how the story would end?

Yes. I knew who needed to come together and who needed to pay for being a bastard, and I enjoyed writing those points immensely.

What do you want readers to take away from *The Sweetest Revenge*?

To not give up on your dream, of course!

What's next for you?

I'm writing another foodie rom-com, this time set in Italy. Italy is my favorite country on EARTH, and there is so much more to the food in each region.

Discussion Questions

1. If you were Amy, how would you have reacted after learning your show was blocked by your boss/boyfriend? Have you ever acted irrationally or purely on emotion when faced with a heightened situation? If so, how, and do you regret it?

2. If Amy's stunt hadn't gone viral on social media, do you think her life would have gone in a different direction? Why or why not?

3. Amy has a mantra that she repeats throughout the novel to psych herself up. Do you have a motivational saying you reflect on when anxious? If so, what inspired it?

4. Discuss how embarrassment and humiliation played a part in both Amy's and Jake's lives. How did those feelings dictate their choices? Do you think they would have connected had they not had those similar experiences?

5. What was your favorite scene in the novel, and why?

6. Why do you think Amy and Jake are drawn to each other? What is special about their connection, and what do you think they ultimately learn from each other?

7. Amy has anxiety about returning home after her embarrassing incident. What do you think ultimately pushed Amy to overcome her fears? Have you ever had reservations about seeing your family or loved ones after a long period of time? Why or why not?

8. What is your favorite TV show, and why? If you could write a TV show, what would it be about? What would the title and genre be?

9. How do you think Amy ultimately gets revenge in *The Sweetest Revenge*? What do you think was her defining moment at the end of the novel?

10. What were your thoughts about the ending?

About the Author

Kerstin Weidinger

Lizzy Dent is the author of *The Summer Job* and *The Setup*. She (mis)spent her early twenties working in Scotland in hospitality, and after years traveling the world making music TV for MTV and Channel 4, and creating digital content for Cartoon Network, the BBC, and ITV, she turned to writing. She now lives in Austria with her family.